HIDDEN MILES

A SMALL-TOWN ROMANCE

MILES FAMILY
BOOK 4

CLAIRE KINGSLEY

Always Have LLC

Published by Always Have, LLC

Edited by Elayne Morgan of Serenity Editing Services

Cover by Lori Jackson

ISBN: 978-1-959809-20-3

www.clairekingsleybooks.com

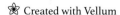 Created with Vellum

To all those who have come home bearing wounds and scars-seen and unseen-after serving our country. Thank you to you and your families for your many sacrifices.

ABOUT THIS BOOK

"I wasn't ready for this. Hannah deserved a man who was whole, not a broken shell. But I couldn't resist her. Couldn't resist this. It felt too good.

And would that be so bad? To have something that felt good for once?"

Leo Miles came home broken—wounded and scarred. It's been five years, and he hasn't left his family's land. Not once. It's not much of a life, but the way he looks now, he prefers to stay hidden.

His only reprieve is her voice. He puts on his headset, logs in to his game, and she's there. They talk while they play, sharing everything but personal details. She's his best friend—his happy place—even though he doesn't know her real name.

Until one day, he hears a voice he recognizes.

Meeting Hannah Tate in person rocks the reclusive Leo's world. And discovering she's in trouble—serious trouble—changes everything.

Hannah is Leo's every fantasy come true. And the badass gamer girl is determined to break through his defenses. But between the mess that is his life, and the threats to his family's safety, he can't be anyone's hero. Least of all hers.

But maybe they both need saving.

Author's note: A wounded hero who'll squeeze your heart. A girl in trouble. And the family who won't let either of them down.

1

LEO

$\mathcal{T}$he terrain rose and fell in a series of hills, each one higher than the next. None of it looked familiar. Ankle high brown grass blew in the breeze. Every so often, a copse of trees popped up in the distance. I kept a steady pace, making sure to stay on the path. Veer too far in any direction and we were sure to encounter trouble.

Of course, we were out there looking for trouble. We just didn't want to walk into any surprises.

"What do you think?" I asked.

"This is boring as shit," Gigz said. "Why are we out here again?"

"Quit your whining," I said. "It'll get better up ahead."

"I swear to god, if you lured me out here just to mess with me, I'm going to kick your ass."

I laughed. "Right. I'd like to see you try."

She stopped long enough to make a rude gesture, then kept running.

"You're such an ass," I said.

"Nice manners, dick," she said. "You talk to all the ladies like that?"

"Just you, baby."

"Lucky me."

I laughed again. God, that felt good. I didn't laugh very often, but Gigz had a way of bringing it out in me. Even when we were running through the most lackluster terrain I'd ever seen.

She was right. It was boring as shit.

"Okay, maybe we should—"

The arrow came out of nowhere. I flinched as it whizzed by.

"Down," Gigz yelled.

"Not so loud," I said as I hit the dirt. "I can hear you just fine."

"Sorry. What was that?"

I looked around from my terrible hiding place in the six-inch grass. "An arrow from up ahead."

"Oh, you think?" she asked. "I saw the arrow, too, dork. I know where it came from. Who was it, and why just one?"

"Single archer?"

"A lone archer is a sitting duck out here."

"He's probably behind those trees over there." I pointed ahead of us and to the left. "Ready for this? Cover me on three."

"Got it."

"One. Two. Three."

I jumped up, drawing my weapon, and ran. The archer revealed himself, stepping around the trunk of a tree to shoot at me. Gigz was faster. Her arrow shot past, sinking into the trunk. The archer disappeared just as another arrow flew by.

"There might be more of them up there," Gigz said.

"I'm counting on it."

I rounded the trunk and came face to face with a drawn bow, the arrow aimed at my chest. Archers were fast, but I was faster. My sword came down, knocking the weapon out of his hands before he could get off his shot.

It was then that I noticed the rest of them.

"Gigz, get your ass up here." I ducked around the tree.

"How many?"

"Ten."

"Awesome."

Knowing Gigz was just behind me, I jumped out, sword ready. I charged into the group, swinging for all I was worth. One went down on my right. A giant hammer raced toward my head but an arrow to the warrior's neck stopped him short. I hacked and sliced, killing with abandon. Another foe went down. Then a third.

"Shit," Gigz said. "That one almost hit me."

"Careful back there."

"You do your job, Badger, and let me do mine."

I laughed again, slicing through a chest that already had two arrows sticking out of it. The warrior went down at my feet, but I was already on to the next one.

Adrenaline surged through me. My heart beat furiously as we cut through the group of outlaws. I watched them go down, feeling a rush of energy. Almost euphoria.

"Yeah, baby," Gigz said. "You got the last one?"

"I got him."

Three swings and he was down. I let out a long breath.

"Nice work," she said. "You made that look easy."

"That was just the beginning," I said. "There's a ton of random shit out here and it gets harder the closer you get to those mountains."

"Good loot, though," she said.

"Exactly."

"Okay, I take it back. This isn't boring as shit." She paused, her end suddenly silent. "Damn it. Badger, I gotta go."

"Now?"

"Yeah, now. Sorry."

Gigz disappeared, winking out of existence as if she'd never been there at all.

A wave of emptiness washed over me so hard it almost knocked the breath from my lungs. I took off my headset and tossed it on my desk. I needed to log off—I'd get killed if I left my character standing there out in the open—but suddenly, it was very hard to care.

After all, it was just a game.

I scrubbed my hand through my hair and stretched my neck, wincing at the pull of scar tissue. It still hurt. Probably always would. I was twenty-nine, but sometimes I felt like I was ninety.

The loss of Gigz's voice in my ear left me feeling hollow—almost numb. It happened every time she logged off, but it was worse when it was abrupt. Usually she'd let me know how long she'd be on and I could keep one eye on the clock. Be prepared for the sense of loss when she was gone.

I leaned back in my chair, wondering what the hell was wrong with me. That was a long list, but this struggle seemed particularly stupid. Gigz was just a gamer friend. I had lots of those, male and female. When I played with anyone else, it was just a game. When it was over, I logged off, took off my headset, went about my business.

But Gigz was different. When we were online together, I tended to forget. The weight I carried lifted, and it was just us. Just her voice in my ear, making me smile. Making me laugh.

I lived for those hours we spent online. And when they were over, it was hard to recover. Hard to bear the weight that once again sat so heavily on my shoulders.

Gigz—my cat, not my elusive online friend—jumped up onto my desk. I ran my hand down her white fur while she purred. "Hey, kitty."

My cat wasn't bad, as cats went. My mom had adopted her

for me a few years ago. She liked to knock shit off my desk, but she was nice to have around.

Before I logged out, I checked to make sure Gigz was still offline, just in case. Of course, it was three in the morning. I should get some sleep, not spend another few hours gaming. Not that I slept a lot in general. But I needed some. I'd wind up as nuts as my brother Cooper if I didn't fall into bed for at least a few hours every night.

Although all-nighters with Gigz were always worth it.

For now, I left the mess on my desk and shuffled into my bedroom to get some rest.

2

HANNAH

I tore off my headset and slammed my laptop closed. My heart raced and my hands shook as I lay down on the couch and drew the quilt up to my shoulder. I tried to slow my breathing, hoping it would look like I'd fallen asleep while working. There'd be no reason for him to get mad about that.

Not that Jace needed a reason to get mad.

His shoes clicked against the stairs as he walked up to our apartment. I'd lost track of time. Again. I did that all too often when I played with Badger. Iron Badger was kind of a silly gamertag. I'd started using it as a joke, and he'd eventually adopted it. But the guy was a badass. Hard like iron, and like a badger, he didn't give a fuck. I loved that about him.

Jace's keys jingled as he opened the door. *Deep breaths, Hannah.* I forced my face to relax in case I looked tense. I didn't want to give him any reason to think I was awake. Best case scenario, he'd assume I'd fallen asleep working again and go to bed. By himself.

Worst case? He'd wake up the neighbors yelling at me. Again.

The door shut and his feet moved across the floor. A few

tense seconds later, I heard the bump of his holster hitting the dining table.

I swore, he did that on purpose. Just to see if I'd jump. Or to remind me he carried a gun. I was all too aware of that fact. His profession was never far from my mind.

Jace was a cop. And that made my life infinitely more complicated.

My back tightened as he walked slowly through the apartment. What was he doing? Was he going to leave me alone? Wake me up? Was he testing me? For all I knew he was staring right at me, waiting to see if I'd crack an eyelid open.

Stay calm, Hannah. He'll go to bed. It'll be fine.

Jace moved around the apartment for another minute—I still didn't know what he was doing—then the bathroom door shut.

I breathed out a long breath. My back ached from the tension knotting my muscles. I tried to relax. It was late; I needed sleep.

Several minutes later, the bathroom door opened. Through my closed eyes, I could see the light go out. Jace's footsteps faded. He'd gone into the bedroom.

Thank god.

I turned over, adjusting the quilt, and my thoughts strayed to Badger. Had he gone on toward those mountains in the game? Maybe teamed up with someone else? It was silly how much I hated the thought of him playing with someone other than me. I had no claim on him. He was just a guy I gamed with sometimes.

Of course, that wasn't true. Badger was much more than some guy I gamed with. He was my friend. Maybe my best friend—which was a little sad, considering I didn't even know his real name.

There was a lot I didn't know. How old he was. Where he

lived. I suspected he lived in Washington, like me, based on a few things he'd said. He certainly seemed to be in my time zone. Once in a while, I indulged in the fantasy that he lived in my apartment complex. We'd meet and realize we knew each other. And of course, in my dreams he was devastatingly handsome. Tall, muscular, maybe with a sexy beard and piercing blue eyes. Naturally, he was single, and found me as attractive as I found him.

Those were nice fantasies.

The reality was, I didn't know his name, but I did know a lot about him. I knew what his voice sounded like when he was tired. Or frustrated. Or happy. I knew he liked to charge into battle first. He liked to tank so he'd be the one taking the big risks. I knew he had strong protective instincts—which had a tendency to piss me off. All too often, he tried to keep me out of melees because he didn't want me to get hurt.

Virtual me, of course. Gigz. He'd started calling me that a few years ago. Short for *giggles*. He'd said he liked the way I laughed. Called me Gigz, and the name had stuck.

I had a little bit of a crush on Badger, which was ridiculous and stupid. We'd never met. We probably never would. The few times I'd tried to get him to open up about who he was in the real world, he'd shut me out so fast it had felt like whiplash. He'd made it abundantly clear he didn't want to connect with me outside the games we played.

He was probably married. The thought made me sick to my stomach, but it was a real possibility. It could explain why he was so intent on anonymity. And a man like him... it was hard to believe he was single.

Of course, technically neither was I. Although I'd been sleeping on the couch for months.

I turned over and stared at the ceiling, still too hopped up on adrenaline to sleep. I needed to get out of here. I'd known it for a long time. But knowing Jace was bad for me and leaving him were two very different things.

What I needed was a plan. But every time I tried to map out an exit strategy, I came up short. My parents lived in Phoenix, and I hadn't spoken to them in months. My friends had all drifted away. My only friends now were gamers, and they all might as well have lived in Narnia. They were either like Badger —totally anonymous, so I didn't know where they lived—or scattered around the world.

No one close. Nowhere I could go in a pinch.

I even worked from home. I was a graphic designer, and Jace had encouraged me to go freelance. Being my own boss had its advantages, and at the time, I'd preened at the thought that Jace believed in me. But it also meant I had clients, but no coworkers. And I didn't have a lot of reasons to leave the apartment. Jace preferred it that way.

Twenty-seven years old, and my life was a mess.

Turning over again, I closed my eyes. It might be a while before I could sleep, but I needed to try. I had a lot of work to do tomorrow.

I WOKE WITH A START, gasping as I sat up. My eyes were gritty and my neck hurt from the way I'd slept.

"Morning, sleepyhead," Jace said, glancing over his shoulder. He stood in the kitchen, dressed in a t-shirt and pajama pants. "Work late again last night?"

"Yeah." I brushed my tangled hair back from my face.

He came over with a steaming cup of coffee and set it on the table next to my laptop. "I made coffee."

"Thanks."

I swung my legs around and stretched before getting up to

use the bathroom. My hair was a mess, but I didn't care. I went back out and sat on the couch to drink my coffee.

Jace was sitting in the armchair next to the couch, his ankle crossed over his knee. He had his phone in one hand, his coffee in the other. His eyes flicked up to me as I took my mug from the table, then went back to his phone.

"We have that wedding this weekend," he said. "Do you have something to wear?"

It took some effort not to groan like a kid who'd just been told to do their chores. His cousin was getting married and I had no interest in being there. But I didn't want to start an argument. It was easier to just go along with it.

"Yeah, I can wear my black dress."

He glanced at me again. "The one with sleeves?"

I took a sip of coffee before answering so I wouldn't say something snarky. He wanted me to wear sleeves so my tattoos wouldn't show. "Yes, the one with sleeves."

"Okay."

"What time do you have to work?"

He narrowed his eyes at me. "You know my schedule."

"I've just been busy with clients lately. I lost track."

"Jesus, Hannah, you're a smart girl. You should be able to remember my schedule. I'm on at two."

"All right, got it."

"Why don't you go shopping and get a new dress," he said, his voice suddenly softer. "You've been working really hard. You deserve it."

I blinked at him a few times. "I don't really have any extra—"

"Don't worry about it, babe," he said, pulling out his wallet. "It's my cousin getting married. The least I can do is make sure you have something nice to wear."

He took out some cash and held it out.

Confusion and fear swirled through me. I didn't want to take it, but if I refused, he'd get mad. Probably yell at me for being ungrateful. But why was he suddenly being nice to me? He'd yelled at me yesterday because his uniform was wrinkled and he couldn't find the socks he wanted. He'd come home to me sleeping on the couch—again—and now he wanted to buy me clothes?

"Thanks," I said, taking the cash. Maybe if I did what he wanted, we'd have one day—just one—where we didn't fight.

He nodded, then went back to whatever YouTube video he'd been watching on his phone.

I put the cash next to my laptop, then settled back on the couch, cradling my hot coffee. Moments like this were almost as tense as when we argued—for me, at least. Jace seemed perfectly content. But the calm and quiet left me on edge. We sat in the living room, drinking coffee as if the silence between us was comfortable. As if we hadn't been in a yelling match last week that had the neighbors coming to see if I was okay.

I'd lied and said I was fine. I'd fallen all over myself apologizing. Taking the blame.

I hated that I'd done that. It made me feel weak. Maybe that was why I liked gaming so much. When I was gaming, I could be the badass warrior I wished I was in real life. My gaming friends probably thought I was. They probably figured I was confident and successful. Gigz was. Gigz was amazing. She was self-assured and strong. A sassy killing machine.

But I wasn't Gigz. Not really. I was Hannah Tate, and I didn't like her nearly as much.

3

LEO

I stared at the text from Cooper. The shortness of it was enough to tell me he wasn't kidding. No jokes, no rambling. Just two words. *It's today.*

He didn't need to explain. We all knew it was coming. But the lack of surprise didn't stop the sick feeling from spreading through my gut. Glancing at the time—it was just after seven in the morning—I groaned and rolled out of bed.

The DEA was moving in on the opium poppy-growing operation my dad was trying to run on our land.

Dad had roped Cooper into helping him, claiming he was growing cannabis. He'd said that he'd sell the crop and, once he cashed in, drop his demands on the property and grant Mom her divorce. Cooper hadn't liked it, but he'd thought it was the only way to get Dad to cooperate and save the land for our family.

Only Dad hadn't been growing cannabis. His crop was a strain of poppy used for making high-potency heroin.

At first, I'd been baffled by his plan. He couldn't possibly make enough money to set himself up with one crop.

But I'd done some digging, and the opioid crisis in this

country was fueling demand for more potent strains of heroin. And changes in border protection had made it more difficult for drug operations to import their product. They were increasingly looking to domestic growers to get what they needed. With the demand for these drugs at an all-time high, they were willing to pay good money.

It still surprised me that he'd gone this far. His decades of unfaithfulness to my mom certainly highlighted his low moral code. But drug trafficking was serious shit.

His life had gone on a downward spiral in the last couple of years, and I wondered what was behind the fall. Had it started when my mom had kicked him out? Or before? What else did we not know?

The rest of my family wasn't interested in finding those answers. It was easier for them to see it as black and white. Dad was a cheating bastard—which was true—and a criminal—also true. He deserved everything he had coming to him.

And yeah, he did. I wasn't going to dispute that. I was furious for what he'd done to my mom. For how he'd threatened our land and put our home in jeopardy. I didn't know if I could ever forgive him for the long list of ways he'd been a shit human being.

So why did I have mixed feelings today? Why did I have pangs of sympathy for the father who'd rejected our entire family? I was sure my siblings didn't feel the same.

It was easier for my brothers. Dad had always been hard on them. He and Roland had butted heads for as long as I could remember. They were too much alike, but instead of Dad recognizing their similarities and using that to connect with his oldest son, he'd been harsh and demanding. Setting expectations Roland could never meet.

I'd been pissed at Roland for moving away—for not being here, especially when I was deployed. But when he'd come back last year and I'd seen him dealing with Dad, it had hit me how shitty Dad had always been to him. I felt like an ass for not seeing it before. Roland hadn't distanced himself because he didn't care about his family. He'd done it because Dad had driven him away.

Cooper, on the other hand, was as tied to this land as a person could be. He loved his vineyards too much to leave, so he'd dealt with Dad by avoiding him. That, and partying his ass off with Chase. Dad hadn't set the same high expectations for Cooper. He hadn't set *any*. It was like he'd given up on Coop. Written him off as a screw-up.

I wasn't sure what was worse. A demanding father you could never please, or a father who thought you were too far gone to matter.

I checked the security cameras I'd set up where Dad was growing his crop. They were well-hidden—I knew what I was doing—and they'd been recording for the last several weeks. I'd provided the footage to Agent Rawlins with the DEA—an old friend of Ben's who'd been working the case. Between the footage and the other shit they had on my dad, they had enough to move in on him. And put him away for a very long time.

He was out here, now. Standing in the field, giving directions to the crew he'd brought to harvest the poppies. With no idea he was about to be arrested.

My relationship with Dad was... complicated. My brothers had mostly bad memories of him. Brynn probably didn't have many memories of him at all. With her, he'd been distant. Gone too much to be a big presence in her life.

But he and I had gotten along. Maybe it was a personality thing, or the fact that I was a middle child. He hadn't subjected me to the same pressure he had Roland, or blown me off like Cooper. He hadn't exactly been a nurturing father, but my memories of him were different. Better.

And it was hard to put aside everything he'd done for me when I'd come home after my medical discharge from the Army. I'd been a disaster. I still was, but at least now I was a semi-functional disaster. In those days, I'd barely been sane.

He and Mom had given me a safe place to land. Helped me through those first horrible months when I'd still been in so much pain I'd wanted to die. He'd calmly talked me through panic attacks and found me a therapist who would see me remotely.

It didn't excuse the things he'd done. I was not only angry with him, I was hurt and betrayed. But I was still having a hard time reconciling the Lawrence Miles who was about to be arrested for drug trafficking with the father I'd thought I'd known.

Apparently I hadn't known him very well after all.

I took a quick shower and threw on some clothes, then walked the short distance to my mom's house. Mom's car was gone. She must have gone to Roland and Zoe's already. She'd protested our plan to get her off-property when we heard shit was about to go down, until Zoe had brought out the big guns: Hudson. Mom couldn't say no to time with her grandson.

The kid was pretty damn cute. He was almost three months old, and he already had the entire family wrapped around his tiny finger. Someone else in this family needed to get busy having babies, or Huddy was going to end up spoiled from all the attention.

The rest of my family—and Ben—were all here. Roland, Brynn, and Chase sat at the dining table. Roland's sleeves were rolled up, his brow furrowed with tension. Chase had a protective arm around Brynn.

Ben leaned against the doorway to the kitchen, a mug of coffee in his hand. He frowned through his salt-and-pepper beard. Although he looked calm—like he was just here quietly observing—I could see the tension in his stance. In the set of his feet and the tightness in his forehead. I couldn't remember a time when Ben hadn't been at Salishan. He was as deeply ingrained in this place as any of us.

I was also pretty sure he was in love with my mother.

If I'd realized that a few years ago, I would have been uncomfortable with it. Ben was a good guy, but thinking he'd stuck around all these years to ogle a married woman would have pissed me off.

But that wasn't Ben, and I knew it. He might have had feelings for my mom for a long time, but he'd never acted on them. In fact, I didn't understand why Ben had stayed. None of us had known my dad was a cheating asshole. Why had Ben tortured himself by staying here, watching her raise a family with another man?

I'd probably never know. It wasn't the kind of thing you could just ask a guy.

Regardless of his reasons, he was here, and I was damn grateful.

I expected to see Cooper pacing around the room, but instead, he was on the couch with his girlfriend, Amelia. She was nestled against him, rubbing his ear between her thumb and forefinger. I had no idea how she did it, but Amelia was the one person in the world who could keep Cooper calm. He still looked stressed—no surprise there; we all were—but he wasn't bouncing off the walls, talking a mile a minute.

I really liked Amelia.

"Any word yet?" I asked.

"Nothing new," Cooper said. "Dad's crew should have started arriving about an hour ago to start the harvest. I convinced him to be there in person."

"Yeah, he's out there," I said. "Nice work."

Cooper just shrugged. He looked tired.

"Leo's right, Coop," Roland said. "You've handled this whole thing really well. Thank you."

He twined his fingers with Amelia's and nodded. "Thanks, bro. I'll just be glad when this shit is over."

"How's Mom?" I asked.

"You know her," Brynn said. "She's basically the queen of making the best of things. She tried to cook us breakfast when we got here."

Roland cracked a smile. "I bet she'll spend half the day baking cookies at our house."

"Cookies?" Cooper asked. "I know where we're going later."

"So what's the plan today?" I asked.

"The DEA are using the back entrance, so I'm hopeful this won't impact guests," Roland said. "If we're lucky, most of it will be over before we open. But I still think some of us should be over at the Big House in case we get police activity when guests are here."

"We'll be there," Chase said, and Brynn nodded.

"Thanks," Roland said. "Ben, if you could make the rounds on this end of the property, that would be great. And when we get the all clear, can you go check on Zoe and Mom?"

"Will do," Ben said.

"Can I drive out there and watch?" Cooper asked. "I want to see this go down."

"No," Roland and I said at the same time.

"Come on, Coop, you don't really want to see that, do you?" Chase asked.

Cooper leaned forward, resting his elbows on his knees. "Hell yes, I do. And I want that fucker to know it was me who helped set him up."

"We're supposed to stay back," Roland said. "And it's best if we cooperate. Leo, the cameras are still running, aren't they?"

"Yeah. You can't see everything, but I have pretty decent coverage."

Cooper sat back, crossing his arms.

"It's okay," Amelia said softly to Cooper, reaching up to rub his ear again. He visibly relaxed, melting into the couch next to her. She whispered something I couldn't hear, then shushed him again.

"Look, this is almost over," Roland said. "They'll make their arrests and we'll go from there. Mom's lawyer has everything ready to take the next step with the divorce. Even if he still decides to be a prick about it, he won't have a leg to stand on anymore."

"What about Grace?" Cooper asked.

"I texted her," Brynn said. "She's with her mom and Elijah today. I'll let them know when it's over."

Grace was our half-sister, the product of my dad's affair with her mother, Naomi. We hadn't known that Grace, or my dad's youngest son, Elijah, even existed until last summer. Since then, they'd become part of the family. Given what my dad had done, it was a testament to my mother's character that she'd embraced them.

But Brynn was right. Mom was the queen of making the best of things. Even Dad's affair.

I glanced at Cooper. I understood his desire to see Dad get what was coming to him.

"Hey, Coop. Why don't you come back to my place with me. We'll probably be able to see most of it on the security feed."

Cooper's eyes were uncharacteristically hard. "Good."

We left, and Cooper and Amelia followed me back to my place. I grabbed a couple of folding chairs I had in a closet and set them up in front of my desk. Amelia took one and Cooper scooted her over so she'd be right next to him.

I sat and brought up the surveillance cameras I'd set up out on that end of the property. One didn't show anything—just plants fluttering in the breeze. The next one winked to life on another monitor. Still nothing. The third showed some workers busy harvesting the poppies. In the fourth, you could see Dad.

Cooper growled and Amelia rubbed her hand up and down his back.

We didn't have long to wait. About ten minutes later, unmarked cars pulled into view and the DEA agents poured out, pointing guns at the workers. And at Dad. There was no sound, so we couldn't hear what anyone was saying. But he froze in place, putting his arms up.

The resolution was just clear enough to see his expression. I'd expected him to get angry, for his face to redden and that vein in his neck to stick out. But he didn't. His shoulders slumped and his head dropped. He didn't look mad. He looked defeated.

One of the agents came toward him, gun still pointed at his chest. Dad dropped to the ground with his hands behind his head. More agents swarmed in and, one by one, everyone was put in handcuffs. Including my father.

I watched with an odd sense of detachment as a DEA agent led him to a waiting car and shoved him in the back seat. It was over. Lawrence Miles arrested. He'd go to prison for this. Between Cooper's testimony and the footage I'd gathered from my surveillance cameras, it would be an open and shut case.

Would he survive prison? I honestly had no idea.

"Fuck," Cooper muttered. He rose from his seat and paced across the room, toward the front window. "Where are we allowed to go? Can I go out to the south vineyard? I need to get the fuck out of here."

"Yeah, you should be fine in the south vineyard," I said.

"I'll go with him." Amelia rose from her chair and adjusted her sweater. "He'll be okay."

"Thanks," I said.

Cooper grabbed Amelia's hand and led her outside, shutting the door behind them.

I leaned back in my chair and let out a long breath. Before Amelia, I would have followed Cooper. Tracked him without him knowing, just to make sure he didn't do something crazy. Most likely, he just needed to get outside. He always walked in his vineyards when he was stressed. But knowing Amelia was with him took some of the weight off my shoulders.

Knowing none of my siblings were alone made this whole thing easier. Roland would go home to his wife and son. Brynn had Chase, and there wasn't a more loyal guy than him. Grace and her mom had each other to lean on. Elijah didn't know what was happening with his father; his mom had shielded him from the worst of it. No doubt he'd have some shit to work through when he got older, but at least he had a family to help him sort it out.

I rewound the video and watched the last few minutes again. My father with his hands up in the air. Getting down on the ground so they could cuff him. The DEA agent leading him to the car.

He deserved it. Justice would be done. But I still felt like shit.

Clicking away from the security footage, I logged into the game Gigz and I had been playing last night. She rarely played in the morning, but I thought I'd check to see if she was logged in, just in case.

No luck. She was offline.

I clicked the window closed, the hollow space in my chest threatening to swallow me whole.

4

LEO

The weights clinked as Cooper set the bar down. He helped Zoe take the forty-fives off so she could do her set of squats. I wasn't sure when my place had become a goddamn L.A. Fitness. First Cooper had started coming over to work out. Then Zoe had asked if she could work out with us. And what was I going to do? Tell them no?

Cooper was exhausting, but threatening to kick him out if he talked too much seemed to have worked. That and he tended to shut up if he was doing something physical. He'd always been that way. Zoe wanted to get back in shape after having Hudson, and Cooper had volunteered my home gym.

Truthfully, having them here a few times a week broke up my otherwise monotonous days. And it forced me to clean up my house, which probably wasn't a bad thing.

"You're up, bro," Cooper said.

I put the forty-five back on one side while Coop got the other, then did my set. Squats hurt. They hurt everyone, but they strained the scarred tissue on my left side. But I had to move and stretch, otherwise it would only get worse.

After my set, I cracked open a window. My place might have

turned into the Miles family gym, but I didn't want it to smell like one.

Zoe grabbed a towel and wiped her forehead. "God, I hate leg day. Leo, can I shower here? We have a wedding this afternoon. Jamie's handling it, but I want to pop over and make sure everything is running smoothly."

"Sure," I said. "Clean towels are in the closet."

"Thanks."

"I'm out, dude," Cooper said. "Thanks for the workout."

"You too, Coop," I said. He started to leave but I turned back to the door. "Hey, Coop. You doing okay? After Dad and everything."

"Yeah, man," he said. "I feel pretty good, actually. Closure and all that shit. Plus I have my hot woman to go home to. Life is awesome."

My brother was tiring, but his enthusiasm for life was kind of infectious. "Okay, good."

"Thanks for asking," he said with a smile. "How are you, though?"

"I'm okay." I didn't really want to take the conversation in this direction. I wasn't exactly *okay*, but this was probably as good as I was going to get.

"You sure, bro?" He opened his arms. "Do you need a jump?"

"A jump? I don't know what that means."

He widened his arms. "Emotional jumper cables."

"Do you mean a hug?"

"Yep," he said with a grin. "Bro hug, buddy."

"No thanks."

"You sure?" He raised his eyebrows. "It totally works. Everyone's battery gets low sometimes. Emotional jumper cables, man. It's a thing."

"No, I'm good."

He dropped his arms and shrugged. "Let me know when you change your mind. I'll see you later."

I shook my head. My brother was so weird. "Bye, Coop."

Zoe left a little while later, dressed for work with her hair up. She was on a video call with Roland and Hudson as she walked out the door—cooing to her baby that she'd see him in about an hour.

And then, all was quiet again.

I showered and changed, then got myself some food. It was a Saturday, so technically I wasn't working. I managed the winery's security, as well as all the technology—computers, phone system, internet access. But I sat at my desk anyway and checked the cameras.

I did that a lot. Browsed through the feeds. I wasn't sure what I was looking for, but it calmed my nerves to do it.

My phone buzzed with a call.

"Hey, Mom."

"Hi Leo. Are you busy?"

"Not really. Do you need something?"

"Lindsey's having trouble over in the Big House. Something about our scheduling app being down? I'm not sure. Can you run over there and check?"

"Sure."

"Thanks, honey."

"No problem."

I ended the call and pocketed my phone. I didn't particularly want to go over to the Big House on a Saturday when there was a wedding. I hated being around the guests. I didn't like being around people in general. My family was fine—they were used to looking at me. But other people weren't. Every stare was a silent reminder of what had happened to me. What I looked like now.

But it was part of my job. I tugged my sleeves down and left.

It was a short walk to the main grounds. I took the back way, circling behind the Big House so I could go in the side entrance, through the kitchen.

A wedding reception was in full swing. Muffled music drifted through the wall and the caterers buzzed around the kitchen. I caught sight of Zoe in the hallway, but she disappeared.

I ducked out of the kitchen and down the short hallway to the lobby. It was quieter up front. Most of the guests were in the back event room, or in the tasting rooms.

Lindsey smiled when I went around behind the front desk.

"Having issues?" I asked.

"Yeah, it won't let me enter any new reservations," she said, gesturing to the computer. "I tried restarting already."

"I'll take a look."

"Thanks."

A handful of people wandered in and out of the lobby while I worked. I kept my face down. It only took me a few minutes to fix the problem, but I was already itching to get out of there.

"You should be all set," I said.

"Thanks so much, Leo," Lindsey said.

"No problem."

I went back through the kitchen, dodging the bustling caterers. The wedding guests were spilling out into the back garden, not far from the kitchen entrance. They stood in small groups, chatting with wine glasses perched in their hands.

A man in a suit glanced in my direction. His eyes widened and he looked away quickly. I was used to that. Most people tried to pretend my appearance didn't shock them, but it did. It had to. I could cover most of my scarring with clothes, but there was nothing I could do about my face.

I turned away. It didn't matter.

"Thanks." A woman's voice behind me. "Yeah, it's new. I got it yesterday."

I stopped in my tracks. That voice. She was somewhere behind me, among the wedding guests. Electricity raced up my spine and I held my breath, waiting for her to speak again. I recognized that voice, but it couldn't be...

"I love it," someone else said. "Any chance you and Jace are next?"

A nervous laugh.

"I'm just saying, this is a great place for a wedding," the second person said.

"It's very beautiful." That voice again. Her voice. Gigz.

What were the chances that she was here? A lot of people came through the winery, for tastings or tours. Thousands came for weddings every year. Could Gigz be one of them?

I looked over my right shoulder, still keeping my back to the growing crowd of wedding guests. Two women stood close to the path I was on, apart from the rest of the guests. One had bright red hair, dark-rimmed glasses, and a short blue dress that showed a number of tattoos on her arms and legs.

The other woman—the one whose voice had caught my attention—wore a black dress with sleeves that went to her forearms and a skirt that flared at the waist, ending at her calves. Her light brown hair looked naturally wavy, hanging down past her shoulders, and she clutched a glass of white wine.

The redhead took a drink of her wine. "God, I'm so glad the weather is nice. At least we can escape out here."

"Me too."

"I know we're at a winery and everything, but I don't think there's enough wine in the entire world for a full day with my family."

The woman in the black dress laughed—a genuine laugh—

and that sweet voice almost knocked me off my feet. Oh my god. It had to be her. I'd know that laugh anywhere.

"I'm just glad you're here," Gigz said. "I don't know who else I'd talk to, otherwise."

Redhead took another drink, emptying the last of her wine. "Yeah, my mom was ready to disown me if I didn't show. I figured, it's my brother. I can be here when he gets married. Again. It's not like this one's going to last. They're only going through with it because she got knocked up."

"Oh my god, are you serious?"

I didn't care what they were talking about—whether the bride was pregnant or what sort of family drama they had going on. I just wanted to keep hearing her voice. Every second she wasn't speaking, waves of doubt washed over me. It had to be wishful thinking. There was no way Gigz was here, at Salishan.

And then she spoke again. With every word, I was more certain.

I backed up toward the kitchen door, where I could still hear them, but I wouldn't be standing in the open like a creeper. Of course, I *was* being a creeper, eavesdropping on their conversation like this. But I couldn't help myself. I wanted to drink in her voice while I could.

"Our mom still doesn't know about the baby," the redhead said. "She's going to freak."

"She'll be happy to have a grandchild, won't she?" Gigz asked.

"Once she's done with her judgmental ranting, probably."

"I guess I can't blame them for not telling her yet," she said.

"They just wanted to get through this wedding."

"Hannah. There you are."

I whipped my head around at the male voice. A guy in a suit sidled up next to Gigz and slipped an arm around her waist.

"I wondered where you'd gone," he said.

A hit of anger flashed through me, potent and intoxicating. Who the fuck was this?

"I was just out here chatting with Meredith." Gigz crossed her arms. Nothing about her facial expression or body language indicated she wanted that guy touching her.

He didn't seem to notice, or maybe he didn't give a shit. He rubbed his hand up and down her back while she kept her eyes on the ground.

I was a heartbeat away from charging in when I stopped myself. It was definitely Gigz. I couldn't deny that voice. But I had no right to burst in on a wedding just because I didn't like seeing her with another man.

And if I did, she'd see me.

That thought had me walking away quickly. I absolutely could not let that happen. Gigz was my happy place. Her voice was one of the few things that still felt good. I didn't want to ruin it.

I went back to my house and shut the door behind me. Except for the one window I'd opened earlier, the blinds were all drawn, the light dim. I sat heavily in my chair and pinched the bridge of my nose. What the hell was wrong with me? My heart hammered and I was breathing too hard. I felt edgy, like my fight or flight response was about to kick into overdrive.

I took some calming breaths, trying to center myself. Gigz was here. She was a short walk away. And she wasn't alone.

Leaning back, I swiveled around. Hannah. Was that her name? I'd never asked, and she'd never told me. We'd always stayed hidden behind our online identities. I'd been tempted to find out who she was, but it had always seemed better if I didn't know.

But now I'd seen her. And of course she had to be fucking beautiful. A badass little sassy gamer girl, and in real life she was every guy's fantasy. Or mine, at least. Petite with soft curves. Long hair. Pretty brown eyes. Pink lips.

Jesus, what was I doing?

Had it really been her, though? Maybe I was finally losing it. I could have hallucinated the whole thing. Imagined her voice.

I needed to know for sure.

Before I thought about what I was doing, I was heading down the path to the Big House again. I'd take a quick look, just to see if I'd imagined her. That was all. It wasn't because I was suddenly desperate to look at her again. To be near her. To breathe the same air, share the same space.

That would have been crazy.

But maybe I was.

5

HANNAH

*M*y back tightened at the feel of Jace's hand. It was suddenly difficult to make eye contact with Meredith. She was the one person in Jace's family I enjoyed talking to, but with him standing here, I felt silenced—strangely tongue-tied.

"Come back inside," Jace said, gripping my elbow. "I'll get you more wine."

I held up my almost-full glass. "I'm fine with this."

He didn't reply, just pulled on my arm so I was forced to follow.

The dress I'd bought yesterday swished around my calves. It was a pretty dress. Perfect for an afternoon wedding in the fall. But the fabric scratched against my skin, making me fidgety. I resisted the urge to tug at the collar or push the sleeves up.

Jace led me back inside where the buzz of conversation and soft music filled the air. The wedding had been nice enough. Fairly standard. The bride and groom now stood by the appetizer table, chatting with an older couple, and the rest of the guests milled around the large room, or outside.

I took a sip of my wine while Jace got another glass for

himself at the bar. The one bright spot about today was this venue. I'd never been to central Washington before and I'd loved it from the moment we'd driven in. We were surrounded by mountains, and the highway was lined with pine forests, pear orchards, and vineyards. The winery itself was idyllic, nestled among the mountain peaks. The main building was spacious and airy, with dark wood beams, old wine barrels, and cabinets with rows of sparkling wine glasses.

Jace went back to ignoring me in favor of chatting with various wedding guests, so I wandered out toward the lobby. I noticed a few old black and white photographs on the wall. One showed a couple standing in the middle of an empty field. They had their arms around each other, and the woman was smiling up at the man. The caption said *Madeline and Luc Rousseau, Founders Salishan Cellars*.

My heart ached a little. They looked so happy. I wondered what their life had been like out here, all those years ago. I imagined them deciding to buy this land and start a winery. Had it been scary? Had they struggled? I wanted to believe that this place had been their dream, and they'd given each other the courage to pursue it.

I moved down the line to a wedding photo. It was a bit faded with age, but looked newer than the first picture. Based on the names in the caption beneath—Thomas and Dorothy Rousseau —I guessed this was the next generation. Perhaps the founders' son and wife.

The next photo showed Thomas and Dorothy Rousseau holding a little girl—by the caption, it was their daughter, Shannon. Based on the dates, she must be an adult now—probably in her fifties.

Next to that was another wedding photo. This one was much newer—maybe even recent. The caption just said, *The Miles Family*. It had been taken here, outside in one of the gardens. I recognized the setting. The bride was pretty with dark hair and a bright smile. The groom was attractive, but I noticed his tie was crooked. In fact, a few of the men in the picture looked a little disheveled. I wondered if there was a good story behind that.

I didn't want Jace to come looking for me again, so I went back to the reception. I found a spot near the wall, standing by myself with my wine. I usually talked to Meredith when I came to one of Jace's family gatherings. She was the self-proclaimed black sheep of the family with her bright hair and tattoos, and the one person who didn't seem like she was hiding behind a façade. I'd found the rest of his family to be either stuffy, or acting stuffy to fit in.

Jace was still talking. I wondered how long we'd have to stay. I leaned against the wall and took a sip. I'd heard from some of the guests that people were spending the night at the hotel next door, but we didn't have a room. Jace had to work tomorrow, so he'd wanted to get back to Seattle. That was fine with me. A night in a hotel with him sounded like torture.

That thought made me sigh. He was supposed to be my boyfriend, but our life was a sham. How had I let things come to this? I gazed at the man I'd been dating for the last couple of years. I hadn't shared a bed with him in at least six months. We'd never talked about it. Sometimes he yelled at me because I'd slept on the couch again, but otherwise, he seemed to be ignoring the shift in our relationship.

Was he in denial? Could he not feel me pulling away? He was enough of a narcissist, maybe he didn't see it.

Once again, my thoughts strayed to the truth I'd been struggling with for months. I needed to leave Jace. He wasn't good for me. He wasn't good *to* me, either. I needed to start taking my life back. I just wasn't sure how.

The reality was, Jace scared me. When he was in a good mood—or in front of an audience—he was charming and sweet.

He'd swept me off my feet when we'd met. He was strong and stable, with a good career in law enforcement. At first, his controlling tendencies had felt like love. He had opinions about my life because he cared about me. He wanted what was best for me.

But he didn't love me. I certainly didn't love him. Maybe I had, in the beginning. Or maybe it had been simple infatuation. But the real Jace wasn't the charismatic, likable man I saw chatting with wedding guests on the other side of the room. He was moody and unpredictable. Controlling and manipulative. He'd never hit me, but I couldn't ignore the times he'd pushed or shoved me. Nor the way he lorded his physical strength and size over me when we were alone.

The fact that he was a cop made everything harder. There were plenty of good cops on the force. But Jace used his position to intimidate me. It was subtle, like the way he'd drop his holster on the table when he got home. Reminders that he carried a gun. That if I called the police for help, it would be his fellow officers who would answer the call.

The whole thing made me sick to my stomach. I glanced at my half-empty wine glass, suddenly wondering if I should down this one and get another. A wine buzz might make the ride home bearable.

I needed a plan. A way out. I just didn't know where to begin.

Jace glanced my direction and held me for a few seconds with his gaze. I understood the look. Approval. He was pleased he could see me—that he didn't have to come find me again.

I hated myself in that moment. For staying put. For not walking away right then and there. This man had my life in a stranglehold, and it didn't matter how much I wanted out if I wasn't willing to take the risk and walk away.

But if I did, what would he do?

He looked again. Those dark eyes bored into me in the half-a-heartbeat they were fixed on my face. And I knew exactly what he'd do if I tried to leave him. He'd hurt me. Maybe worse. He hadn't forced me to go back to sleeping in his bed. But he did insist we act like a happy couple when we were in public. I had to be the good little girlfriend, always at his beck and call. The appearance meant everything to him. And he'd lose his mind if I tried to get away.

I glanced down, wishing I could be more like Gigz. She'd never allow a man to manipulate and control her this way. She'd kick his ass and take his loot.

I set my wine glass on a side table made from a wooden barrel. When I looked up, Jace had wandered toward the open doors. I decided if he went outside, I'd stay here. A tiny act of rebellion, to not follow. Hollow and meaningless, to be sure, but it made me feel a little better. I'd worn a dress he'd approve of. Came as his date when I didn't want to be here. It was like sleeping on the couch. It wouldn't accomplish anything, but it made me feel like I still had a shred of control over my life.

Movement in the corner of my eye drew my attention. A man stood near the entrance to the room. He had a thick beard and long brown hair that obscured part of his face. He wasn't dressed for the wedding—he wore a long-sleeved shirt and jeans—and I thought I might recognize him from the picture in the hallway.

My body lit up at the sight of him, a rush of heat scorching me from the inside. He was stunning. His hair and beard made him look rough, but his eyes were clear. Their piercing blue-gray held mine, like I was momentarily hypnotized.

He blinked once and I didn't look away. Every cell in my body felt his magnetic pull. There was something wrong with his face—scarring on one side. But it didn't diminish his appeal. If anything, it made him more intriguing. He looked warm and strong, like he could wrap me in his arms and keep me safe.

God, what was wrong with me? I sucked in a quick breath

and looked down at the floor. Why was I standing here, staring at some strange man?

When I looked up a second later, he was disappearing through the door that led to the lobby.

My heart thumped wildly and I shifted my feet, trying to make the tension in my core dissipate. My damn panties were wet. I hadn't had sex in a long time, but this was ridiculous. A few seconds of eye contact and I felt like I'd turned to liquid.

Who was he?

Against my better judgment, I shot a glance at Jace—he was still talking to someone—and followed the mystery man.

The hallway was empty. I glanced into the tasting room on one side, but I didn't see him. Just some couples sitting at the bar and a young woman pouring wine. Wedding guests had meandered out to the main lobby, and there was a winery employee behind the front desk. But no sign of the man I'd seen.

I took a quick breath and glanced behind me. Jace wasn't following. What if I just poked my head out the front doors? If he'd left, I might catch sight of him.

And then what? Stare at his back while he walked away? I had a tiny two-second fantasy of running after him and launching myself into his arms. That was silly enough to stop me. I was being ridiculous. I had no idea who he was. What was I going to do? Tell him he'd lit a fire inside me I'd thought long since quenched?

Still, I couldn't get his face out of my mind. How had he made me feel that way? My entire body had reacted to him. Why? There were men all over—both wedding guests and otherwise. Dressed in nice suits and ties. None of them affected me this way.

But him? I'd been mesmerized. Transfixed by his gaze. I'd never felt anything like it.

I stopped on the way back to the reception and looked at the wedding photo again. Sure enough, there he was, standing in the back. His face was angled slightly so his scars weren't visible, but there was no doubt it was him.

I wondered who he was. His name. How he'd gotten those scars. And why his eyes had held me captive. There was a universe behind those blue-gray eyes, and I was oddly heart-broken that I'd never get the chance to explore it.

6

LEO

I'd never been nervous to log on to a game before.

I felt out of control and anxious in the real world a lot. I'd been diagnosed with PTSD—no surprise there; a lot of soldiers dealt with it—but gaming was my safe place.

That was why I did it so much. I could let go. When I was in a game, I wasn't Leo Miles anymore. I wasn't the guy with burn scars over half his body. With a disfigured face and grotesque stiff tissue. I was Iron Badger, badass warrior.

And Gigz was there.

From the first time we'd played together, we'd gotten along. We gave each other shit a lot, but that was part of what made her fun. Gigz could make me smile, even on my worst days. When everything felt hopeless, like I was drowning in emptiness, I'd log on and if I was lucky, she'd be playing. I'd hear her voice, and things weren't quite so bad. That empty space in my chest not quite so hollow.

But now that I'd seen her—the real her—everything had changed.

My heart was beating too fast, the way it did when I got close to the edge of our property. Palms sweaty. The jittery feeling made me want to get up and pace, like Cooper was always doing.

This was ridiculous.

I leaned back in my chair and took a four-count breath. Held it for four. Then released it, same count of four. Hold. Then I repeated the pattern. Combat breathing. Soldiers could be in some intense situations, and the ability to stay calm was a life or death skill. Back when I'd still been on active duty, I'd been amazing at it. Two rounds of combat breaths, and I'd be completely focused. Ready for anything.

I wasn't as good at it anymore, but it still helped. Although I felt like an idiot for needing a breathing technique just to log in to a game.

Fucking pathetic.

My heart rate slowed, and my muscles relaxed. I did another round of breaths to steady myself, then clicked on the icon to log in. Typed in my password.

I quickly scanned my friends list, looking for Gigz. She wasn't online.

Fuck.

Part of me was afraid to talk to her. But the other part—much bigger than the first—was craving her like a fucking drug. I needed her voice in my ears like I needed to breathe tonight.

Please log on, Gigz. Please.

I ran through a few dungeons by myself, ignoring the group requests I got from a few gamer friends. It was hard to stay focused, and I died twice doing stupid crap. I was about to log off in frustration and just go to bed, when her name popped up on the side of my screen.

Gigz is online.

I jammed my headset on, holding my breath, waiting for her to join the voice app we used when we gamed together.

My headphones crackled, the distinct buzz of another person logging in tickling my ears. Then, her voice.

"Hey, Badge."

I closed my eyes, her voice pouring over me like warm water. So soothing. My heart rate slowed and the knotting in my muscles eased.

God, this woman. Why could she do this to me? It wasn't normal.

I swallowed, hoping she wouldn't hear the strain in my voice. "Hey, Gigz."

"Sorry I'm on later than usual. I was at a wedding today."

I froze. I'd known it was her. It had to have been her. But hearing her say it left me practically speechless.

"You there?" she asked.

"Yeah, sorry. So, a wedding?"

"Mm hmm. I didn't want to go, but it wasn't bad. It was at a winery, and that was the highlight. It was freaking gorgeous out there."

I couldn't help but smile. She'd liked it here? "That's good, at least."

"Yeah."

I needed to tell her. Now. She'd just given me the opportunity to bring it up. To tell her I'd seen her today. But I hesitated.

"Something weird happened, though," she said.

"What?"

She took a deep breath. "This is still a judgment-free zone, right?"

"I thought after the sexy blue aliens dream, we'd established that."

"Dude, don't make fun of me," she said. "It was so real. And disturbingly hot."

"I said I wasn't one to judge. I've had crazy sex dreams too." I wasn't about to tell her the woman in my dreams had her voice.

"True. You did have that dream about the vampire stripper."

"I'm never going to live that down, am I?"

She giggled. "Nope. This wasn't a dream, though. At least, I don't think it was. When I was at the wedding, I saw this guy..."

My heart dropped straight through the floor. Fuck, I didn't want to hear this. Not from her. I closed my eyes and leaned back in my seat, clutching the armrests, bracing for impact. To hear her say she'd seen a deformed freak in the otherwise perfect setting.

I almost couldn't get the words out. "A guy?"

"Yes, and I had such an intense reaction to him. It was insane. Like a physical response. Has that ever happened to you?"

Had she been *that* repulsed by me? "I'm not sure. What do you mean?"

"It's hard to describe. I've never felt that way about a stranger before. I was so drawn to him. And, don't make fun of me, okay, but I was... really attracted to him."

Well, she wasn't talking about me then. "Wow, sounds like it made your day more interesting."

"Right? Seriously, this guy was so hot. Not in the traditional sense, though. He wasn't clean cut with a suit or whatever. He was really rough-looking. Long hair, thick beard. I guess it makes sense—I was always into the Beast. Totally does it for me."

If I hadn't been stunned into silence before, I was now. Long hair and thick beard? But there was no way she was talking about me. A lot of guys grew out their hair these days. And men with beards were all over the place.

I forced out a laugh. "Sounds like a scruffy bastard."

"Aw, Badger, are you jealous of my fantasy beast-man?"

"Yeah, so jealous," I said, keeping my voice flat. I wasn't jealous, I was confused. "I'm sure you two will be very happy together."

She sighed. "I wish. Isn't that weird, though? I saw him for a minute at most, and I can't stop thinking about him."

"Who knows, maybe he can't stop thinking about you."

"I doubt that. Although... our eyes met for a couple of seconds and it was kind of amazing. Like something in a story. But before I knew what had happened, he was gone. I don't know, maybe I'm crazy and I imagined the whole thing, including the scars on his face."

It felt like I'd just been stabbed. The sensation was so acute, I put my hand to my chest, expecting to find hot, sticky blood.

"Um, what?" I choked out.

"I'm sorry, you don't want to hear me go on and on about how I was basically hypnotized by some guy at a wedding. But Badge, I'm telling you, he had some kind of magic over my lady parts."

Blood rushed south so fast it almost made me dizzy. Holy shit. I shifted in my seat so I could adjust my pants.

"Wow."

"I know. God, I'm fanning myself over here just thinking about him."

Kill me. Kill me right now. I cleared my throat, not sure what to say. The thought of her turned on had me so hard it hurt. I needed to change the subject. "Are we doing this, or what?"

She giggled, her sweet laugh reverberating through me. "Yeah, sorry. I'll stop talking about my lady parts."

"Jesus," I muttered. This was an absolute clusterfuck. She'd been turned on by *me*? That wasn't possible.

Maybe she was the one who was crazy.

"So I'm thinking we run through the haunted city tonight," she said. "The boss fight is brutal, but I'm in the mood for a challenge. You up for it?"

"Yeah, let's do it."

Her character took off running, so I scooted my chair toward my desk and grabbed my mouse so I could follow.

We got to the haunted city and I died no less than six times before we even made it to the boss fight. I was a fucking disaster tonight, and Gigz teased me mercilessly for it.

But I couldn't stop thinking about her. About how close we'd been. What she'd looked like in that dress, her long hair flowing down her back. I wondered what she smelled like. How soft her skin must be.

And she'd been attracted to me?

I couldn't reconcile that with reality. I wasn't a man that women found attractive. Not anymore. I was disfigured and scarred. I tried to minimize it as best I could, but there was only so much I could do. How could she have looked at me and felt anything but revulsion? Or fear? That was what I saw in most people's eyes when they looked at me.

That, or pity. Frankly, I preferred fear.

By the time I went to bed a few hours later, I wasn't any closer to sorting this out. Should I have told her it was me? What could I have said? And what had happened when our eyes had met? I'd felt something so acute, the aftereffects still reverberated through my body. For the first time, someone had stared at me and I hadn't immediately turned away.

Granted, I'd been mesmerized by the sight of her.

Still, something had passed between us. Had she really felt it? Was that what she'd meant?

I didn't know what to think.

7

LEO

*T*he first light of dawn had been peeking through the blinds before I'd finally fallen asleep last night. I'd woken a few hours later to hazy memories of a dream. Something about Hannah, running through a field with a bow on her back.

Not Gigz. Not a computer-rendered animation in a game. Hannah, the real woman. She'd been dressed like her character —armor, weapons, and all. But she'd been a real person. I'd been running after her, a sense of urgency spurring me on. Like something terrible would happen if I didn't reach her, yet she was always ahead of me. Always just beyond my grasp.

Reluctantly, I got out of bed. I could already tell I wasn't going back to sleep. It was a Sunday, so technically I didn't have to work, but I still went through my morning routine, checking the security footage around the winery.

I'd installed the system after we'd had some trouble with theft. Two years ago, we'd had a break-in, and later, an employee had been stealing wine from the cellars in the Big House. I'd wanted to have more coverage, but Mom had insisted I keep it to the Big House lobby and outside areas.

So far, that seemed to be working well enough. We hadn't had any more theft problems, at least.

After sucking down some coffee, and checking to see if Gigz was online—she wasn't—I decided to get outside. During my first year home, Cooper had forced me outdoors a lot—made me walk with him in the vineyards. I'd resisted at first, but eventually realized those walks were probably good for me.

As long as Cooper didn't talk too much.

Now I tried to remember to get outside at least once a day. It seemed like the healthy thing to do. I wasn't anywhere near *healthy*, and despite my therapist's encouragement, I didn't think I ever would be. It wasn't like I could bring myself to go anywhere. Not past the boundaries of our land, at least. But I could do better than hiding in my house all the time, my face in a screen.

We'd just come out of harvest season—the busiest time of year at Salishan—and now the vineyards were quiet. I took the utility vehicle—the closest thing I had to a car—and drove out to the south vineyard. Our other utility vehicle was parked out here, not far from the main grounds. Cooper. Harvest was over, but there was always work to be done.

I thought about driving by. Cooper wouldn't be out here on a Sunday if he wasn't busy with something. Not now that he had Amelia. But something made me pull over and park behind him.

The truth was, I was feeling particularly out of control. Seeing Hannah had left me reeling, and after talking to her last night, I was confused as hell. I had no idea if Cooper could help me sort this out, but at least I wouldn't be alone.

I found him not far from where we'd parked. He didn't seem to be doing much of anything, just wandering down the row, fingering some of the leaves, murmuring. He had this weird habit of talking to the grapes. I guess it made sense.

Cooper talked to everyone, so why should his grapes be an exception?

He must have heard me coming, because he turned, a wide smile crossing his face.

"Hey, bro. What's up?"

"Hi, Coop. Not much. Just... needed to get out and walk."

"Yeah, dude, me too," he said.

"Is everything okay?" I asked. "Did you get in a fight with Amelia or something?"

"Nah, we're good. She had to be at the ranch early this morning for an all-day riding workshop. I woke up when she did and now I'm bored."

"Fair enough."

"What about you? You okay?"

I put my hands on my hips and looked down at the ground. There was a time when I wouldn't have considered talking to my brother about this. But he was successfully navigating a serious relationship—a relationship that was still new. He was in the shit, so to speak. So maybe...

I took a deep breath. "So, there's this girl."

He made a strangled noise in his throat and his eyes widened.

Great. Here it comes.

But instead of spewing a mass of word vomit all over the vineyard, he cleared his throat. "Awesome. How'd you meet?"

"Online. Playing games."

"Is that what you're always doing in your cave?" he asked, then waved his hand. "Never mind. The girl. What's going on with her?"

I eyed Cooper with suspicion. He didn't usually display this kind of tact. Must be more of the Amelia effect. "We've been friends for a long time, but only online. I didn't even know her real name until yesterday."

"Did she give you the personal deets, or did you ask?"

"Neither." I blew out a breath and rubbed the back of my neck. "She was here at a wedding yesterday."

"No shit?"

"Yeah. I had to go over to the Big House to help Lindsey with something. When I left she was standing outside."

"How'd you know it was her? Pics?"

"No, I'd never seen her before. I heard her voice."

"Holy shit, Leo. You knew her by her voice? That's romantic as fuck."

I laughed, shaking my head. "I guess."

"I'm serious, dude, that's amazing."

It *was* amazing. Not that I'd recognized her voice. I'd been listening to her for years. But I still couldn't believe she'd been here.

"Yeah, so... it gets weird, though," I said.

"Okay."

"I saw her, but I left before she saw me. I went home and I thought maybe I was going crazy. Not like that would surprise anyone; I'm probably halfway there already. But I wondered if I'd imagined the whole thing. So I went back."

"Jesus, if I was sitting down, I'd be on the edge of my seat right now. Please tell me you talked to her."

"No," I said, looking at him like he'd just suggested I shoot someone. "Hell no, of course I didn't talk to her."

He let out a frustrated growl. "Okay, what did happen?"

"She caught me staring at her. I freaked and bolted."

"Where does it get weird? Because that's not exactly weird. It's more like... I kind of want to punch some sense into you. Not slap some sense, by the way, I mean punch. You didn't talk to her? Come on, man."

"No, I didn't talk to her."

"Why not?"

"Look at me," I snapped.

A rare expression of anger crossed Cooper's face. "I am looking at you. So?"

I turned away. "That's not the point. It got weird later. We were online last night and she told me about... seeing me."

"Holy balls, this just got good again."

How was I supposed to say this out loud? It was too ridiculous to be true. He wasn't going to believe me anyway. "She told me this story about seeing a guy across the room at the wedding reception, and how she was... attracted to him."

"And the guy was you."

"Yeah, the guy was me. I guess."

"You guess?" he asked. "Was it you or not? What did she say?"

"Just... you know." Why was this so hard to get out? "She said he had long hair and a beard."

"Fuck yes, bro," he said. "Did you tell her it was you?"

"No."

"Well, shit. Leo..." He trailed off. "You should tell her, man. It's dishonest if you don't."

"I know—that's the problem. She caught me off guard, and I didn't know what to say. And then she changed the subject. Now what am I supposed to do? Tell her hey, I know your name is Hannah, and by the way, I'm the long-haired bearded guy you saw at Salishan Cellars?"

"Basically, yes."

"I can't do that."

"Why not?" he asked. "You've been friends with her for a long time, right?"

"Yeah."

"And you obviously like her. And by like her, I mean you want to bang the shit out of her."

"Jesus, Cooper."

"I'm right though," he said, pointing at me. "Don't try to tell me I'm not."

"It doesn't matter. She was at the wedding with her boyfriend."

He snorted. "Soon-to-be-ex-boyfriend."

"How would you know?"

"It's common sense. If she was with the right guy, you wouldn't be making her panties wet just by looking at her from across the room. Well, that's not true. You're a Miles, and we have that effect on women. But still. She's already halfway to breaking up with that douchebag. Trust me."

Never in my life had I wanted Cooper to be right more than in that moment.

"Why'd she have to be fucking beautiful?" I asked, changing the subject. "She's fun, and smart, and a total badass. She has to be gorgeous, too? She couldn't be a four, she had to be a ten. And then there's me—"

"Don't do that, dude."

"Leave it, Coop. I know." I didn't need him telling me my scars *weren't that bad*. I'd heard it before. I knew it was a lie. "So, you think I should tell her it was me?"

"Yeah, you have to," he said. "But this is awesome."

"How is this awesome?"

He held out his hand and ticked off the reasons on his fingers. "One, this means she probably lives close enough to come visit you. Two, you said yourself she liked you on sight. Three, you guys are already friends, so it won't be awkward when you hang out. Four—"

"Okay, okay, enough," I said. "Four, she's not coming out here to visit me. And five, she has a boyfriend."

"We already went over the boyfriend thing," Cooper said. "I don't think we need to revisit that. By the way, when the time comes, I have a bunch of duplicate boyfriend t-shirts. I'll give you a few. I actually don't need twenty or whatever. Who knew."

"What?"

"It's cool. You'll know when the time is right. For now, tell her the truth."

I took a deep breath. "Yeah, you're probably right."

"Of course I am. Okay, tell me truthfully, bro," he said, his voice suddenly serious. "Did I help you out with this?"

God, my brother was so ridiculous. He always had been. But no one cared like he did. "Yeah, Coop. This helped a lot."

He did a fist pump. "Yes. Bring it in, buddy."

I stepped away from his attempt at a hug. I didn't do hugs. "That's okay, we're good."

"You sure this time?" He held his arms out.

"Positive."

"Okay, but you're missing out. I give the best hugs. Bro hugs, and sexy hugs. But obviously only my Cookie gets the sexy hugs."

"Good for her."

"It *is* good for her. She's the best. I fucking love that girl. Anyway, good talk, man. I'm glad you came to me. I think we made good progress here."

I shook my head, smiling a little. "Yeah... thanks."

Instead of going back to the utility vehicle, I kept walking. I needed to think.

Cooper was right. I needed to tell her it had been me. I should have last night. It was a dick move for me to let her tell me that whole story, like I didn't know what she was talking about. I'd just been so surprised—so off-balance. I'd have to fess up and hope she wasn't too mad.

And hope she didn't want to meet in person. I didn't care if she'd said she found me attractive. She hadn't seen me up close. Once she got a good look at me, that would change quick.

Although the thought of being close to her again was almost more than I could bear. I wanted that. I wanted to see her. Be near her. Hear her talk in person, not through a headset.

This was fucking torture.

I couldn't decide how I felt. I desperately wanted to see her again. But I didn't want the sight of me to ruin what we had together. Our friendship meant everything, and I couldn't let my goddamn face screw it up.

8

HANNAH

I was supposed to be working. But Jace was home—it was his day off—and I couldn't relax.

The second room in our two-bedroom apartment was ostensibly my office. In reality, it had my desk, plus a bunch of Jace's crap that wouldn't fit anywhere else, leaving it cramped and cluttered. I'd pushed a few boxes into a corner not long after we'd moved in—a year ago—and they were still there. Random stuff was piled on the bookshelf. There was an extra lamp, a chair that didn't fit anywhere else, and some sports equipment Jace didn't use anymore.

Once in a while he'd rant at me about how messy it was in here, as if it were my fault. I glanced around at the clutter, wondering if I should just get rid of some stuff. Those boxes were still taped shut. I bet he had no idea what was even in them.

But I wouldn't. It wasn't worth the risk of provoking him.

Although, since his cousin's wedding, we'd been getting along. Not a single argument all week. Maybe it was because he was back on days. The change in shift—and more predictable sleep schedule—seemed to have improved his mood.

Instead of giving me a reprieve from the stress of living with him, Jace's good mood left me on edge. Waiting for the crash—for him to blow up at me.

I leaned back in my chair. Maybe I was being too hard on him. His job was intensely stressful, and his changing shifts made it difficult for him to get enough rest. Sleep deprivation was a real thing. He'd been better this week. Calmer. Nicer to me.

That tiny ember of hope I held onto glowed, just a little. Was it possible for things to get better? Maybe this week hadn't been a fluke.

"Hey," Jace said, peeking his head through the half-open door. "Are you going to break for lunch? I thought I'd go grab takeout."

I tucked my hair behind my ear. "Yeah, I can take a break."

"I'll be back in a few."

"Okay. Thanks."

Jace's keys clinked, then the front door opened and closed. I took a deep breath, trying to calm my frayed nerves. Why was I such a mess? Jace hadn't bitched at me for not cooking. He wasn't stomping off to get takeout because he was angry at me. He was just getting us lunch.

This was fine.

After saving my work, I got up and stretched, reaching my arms over my head. I'd hardly been out of my office all morning. My stomach rumbled and I hoped Jace was picking up something good. He hadn't said where he was going, but my guess was either gyros from the Greek place up the street, or tacos from the food truck around the block. Either one worked for me, especially since I'd skipped breakfast.

A shower was probably a good idea, since I hadn't taken one yet. That, and real clothes. I was still in pajamas. There were perks to working from home, but I was tired of feeling sloppy.

I took a quick shower and put my wet hair in a bun. Threw on a t-shirt and jeans. Jace was still gone, so I grabbed my laptop and took it to the couch.

The downside to Jace working days was that he was home at night—which meant I couldn't get online to game with Badger very much. Jace hated video games, so I didn't play when he was around. I felt bad for ditching Badger all week, but there wasn't much I could do. It wasn't worth the argument with Jace.

But Jace wasn't here now. I didn't have long, but I could at least log on and see if Badger was online. Let him know I was still alive.

I missed him. I didn't often go more than a couple of days without talking to him. I missed the sound of his deep voice in my ear—especially the way it got husky late at night when he was tired.

The load screen took a few seconds after I put in my password. A nervous tingle fluttered in my tummy. I'd checked to see if Badger was online several times over the last week—during the day, when Jace was at work—but he hadn't been. We didn't have each other's contact information outside of the games we played. No email addresses or phone numbers. No real names, so no social media profiles.

Maybe I'd finally ask him for another means of contact. Just so we could keep in touch while Jace was on day shift. I didn't know how long this was going to last. It could be months before he was back on nights.

I held my breath, waiting for his name to pop up as active. Several of our friends were online, their names scrolling past. One sent me a join request, but I ignored it. I wasn't here to go on a side quest. I just wanted to see—

His name seemed to jump off the screen, like it glowed brighter than the others. I bit my bottom lip, feeling silly for smiling so big. It was just a game, and he was just some guy I didn't really know.

But I kept right on smiling as I slid on my headset and sent him a message request.

"Where the hell have you been?" he asked as soon as we connected.

I laughed, the tension melting from my shoulders at hearing his voice. "Ugh, I know. I've been busy."

"Shit," he said under his breath. "It's been almost a week, Gigz. I was worried about you."

I sat back against the couch cushion, leaving the laptop on the coffee table. He'd been worried about me? "I'm sorry, Badge. I logged in a few times, but you were never on."

"So you're okay?"

"Yeah, fine." I almost couldn't choke out the word. *Of course you're fine. Jace has been fine. Everything is fine.*

"Good," he said, but his voice was hesitant.

"What about you? Anything interesting happen this week?"

"Um..." He cleared his throat. "Actually, there's something I wanted to tell you."

"Oh yeah?"

A car parked out front and I sat up straight, my eyes darting to the door. It could have been one of our neighbors. The car door shut, and I almost jumped out of my seat. I pulled off one side of my headset so I could listen for the sound of Jace's shoes on the stairs. Nothing.

"Yeah, so remember when you told me about that guy you saw?" Badger asked.

The blinds on the front window were open, but there wasn't a view of the parking lot from our apartment. I didn't want to be online when Jace got home—especially not online with Badger. The last thing I needed was him finding out I talked to people online when he wasn't around.

Badger had asked me a question, and I hadn't answered. "What?"

"The, um... the guy you saw. At the wedding."

Still no footsteps. I opened my mouth to answer when I noticed a pair of black shoes by the door. Jace's work shoes. The ones that made that telltale click on the stairs.

He wasn't wearing them.

I heard the metallic scrape of Jace's key fitting in the lock.

"Badger, I'm so sorry, but I have to go. Everything's fine. I'll try to get on later."

Without waiting for his reply, I ripped my headset off and slammed my laptop closed.

"I hope you're hungry." Jace held up a takeout bag as he walked in, then closed the door behind him. "Gyros."

I blew out a breath, my shoulders slumping with relief. "Starving."

He smiled and took the food into the kitchen.

My heart raced and I shook out my hands, feeling tingly from the adrenaline. That had been close. I couldn't imagine what Jace would do if he came home to find me not only talking to someone online, but talking to another man.

Maybe it was shitty of me to keep it from him. Sometimes I felt like I had a second life—one he knew nothing about. But gaming was my sanctuary. The only place I felt safe. And I wasn't doing anything wrong. I didn't even flirt with Badger—or any of the guys I gamed with—let alone anything that could be construed as *cheating*. We were truly just friends—friends who'd probably never meet in person. But Jace wouldn't understand.

He brought our food out and handed me a plate before taking a seat on the couch.

"Thanks."

"Sure," he said.

The tension was back, knotting my shoulders. Was he being

nice because things were getting better? Was it really just a matter of a change in his schedule? He hadn't always been angry and unpredictable. When we'd first started dating, he'd been charming and sweet. Maybe the Jace of the last year was the fluke, and the guy I remembered from the beginning of our relationship was the real deal.

Or maybe this was all wishful thinking, and the peace wouldn't last.

I picked at my food, but hungry as I was, it was difficult to eat. It was exhausting to bounce back and forth between waiting for him to snap at me, and wondering if this calm could possibly be the new normal.

And what if it was? Would I want to stay?

I knew the answer to that question. No. I didn't want to stay, even if he never yelled at me again. I glanced at him from the corner of my eye, feeling anxious and guilty.

"What's wrong?" he asked.

I flinched. "Nothing."

"Are you sure? You're not eating."

I pinched a bit of pita bread between my thumb and forefinger and ripped it off. "I'm eating."

His gaze was on my mouth and I recognized the heat in his eyes. *Oh no.*

"You're done sleeping on the couch."

I froze with the bread halfway to my mouth. He'd said that so suddenly, and without any preamble, it took me a second to process. "That's... out of the blue."

"Yeah, well, it's been long enough, don't you think? Maybe you can quit punishing me?"

Straightening my spine, I met his eyes. "Punishing you?"

"I realize being with me isn't always easy," he said. "But things are good now."

My mouth opened, but it took me a few tries to respond.

Things were *good now*? As if a week of him being halfway decent made up for everything?

"This week has been fine, but Jace... it's a week. You really expect me to climb back in bed with you?"

He abruptly stood and walked into the kitchen. Slammed his plate on the counter so hard, I was surprised it didn't shatter.

"Yes, I do," he said through gritted teeth. "What the fuck is this about, Hannah?"

"Well... you're such a loose cannon, I never know what I'm going to get. One minute you're fine, and the next you're calling me a stupid bitch for leaving dirty dishes in the sink."

"You're fucking home all day," he said. "You can do the fucking dishes."

I held my fists against my forehead. "I don't want to fight about the dishes, Jace."

He pointed a finger at me. "You're done sleeping on the couch. Do you hear me?"

"No."

His eyes widened and he gaped at me for a long moment. "No?"

I stood, trying to bury my fear. "That's what I said. No. I'm not sharing a bed with you."

A few quick strides and he was in my face, lording his height over me. "It wasn't a request. I'm telling you, you're not sleeping on the fucking couch anymore."

I tried to step back, but my legs bumped the couch. "I'll sleep wherever I want."

The way his face flushed was terrifying, the red creeping up his neck to his cheeks. "The fuck you will. I don't deserve this shit."

"You can't—" I gasped as he grabbed my wrist, his grip painfully tight. "Jace, you're hurting me."

"How long did you think I'd let you play this game?" he

asked, his voice growing louder with every word. "I work my ass off, and for what? To come home and find my fucking girlfriend on the couch every night? That's bullshit, Hannah, and you know it."

"Jace, stop."

"Everything I do for you isn't enough?" He was yelling now. "What the fuck does it take to make you happy?"

I twisted my wrist, trying to get out of his grasp, but he only held tighter. How was he so strong? "Let go."

"No, really. Answer my goddamn question. What the fuck does it take to make you happy?"

My wrist burned with pain and tears leaked from the corners of my eyes. "You're hurting me."

He shoved me backward, finally letting go. I fell onto the couch and tucked my arm against my chest.

"This is bullshit," he shouted. "It's not too much to ask for my fucking girlfriend to sleep with me."

He was terrifying when he got like this. But I was sick of it. Sick of tiptoeing around my own home. Sick of fighting. Sick of being afraid of him.

"It's too much to ask when you treat me like shit."

He grabbed my still-full plate off the table and threw it against the wall. It broke with a loud crack.

"You're spoiled rotten, you dumb bitch," he yelled. "I'm out there, risking my life, working my ass off every day. And what the fuck are you doing? Sitting on that fucking couch with your fucking laptop."

"I work. I have a job."

"You sit around on your lazy ass all day. You can't even do the fucking dishes."

"Are you really standing there yelling at me and wondering why I sleep out here? This is why, Jace. What makes you think you can treat me like this?"

"Because you piss me off." He shouted so loud, it hurt my ears. He grabbed both my wrists and hauled me to my feet. "This shit is your fault, Hannah. Why do you have to make me so fucking angry?"

He pulled me forward, yanking on my arms so hard it felt like he might dislocate my shoulders. I twisted my wrists, but his grip was like iron.

"Stop it," I sobbed. "Let go."

I stumbled as he dragged me toward the bedroom, his hands tightening painfully around my wrists.

"Get your ass in there."

"Jace, stop."

He was so much stronger than me. I dug my heels into the carpet and leaned my weight back, but he dragged me into the bedroom.

"This is your room." He kept his grip on one wrist and grabbed my jaw with his other hand. "Do you hear me? This is where you belong."

His fingers pressed the insides of my cheeks against my teeth and tears streamed from my eyes. His face contorted in an angry snarl and a vein stuck out on his forehead.

"Let go," I said, the words coming out garbled from his grip on my face.

"I let you get away with this shit for too long," he said, his face mere inches from mine. "Too fucking long. This ends now. You need to be reminded of who you belong to."

Fear and sickness poured through me. I'd never felt so powerless. I knew exactly what he was about to do. What would he do to me if I fought back? He'd never hit me before, but seeing the rage in his eyes, I had no doubt he would.

Pulling my arm back, I tried to break free from his grasp. He squeezed my face harder and I tasted blood.

"On the bed." He pushed me backward.

I stumbled, but kept my feet, the backs of my legs hitting the edge of the bed. Jace was on me in an instant. He spun me around and shoved me face-first onto the mattress.

"Jace, no."

He rammed his hands beneath the waistband of my pants and tore them down.

A heavy knock sounded from the front door, three loud bangs in quick succession.

Jace paused with my pants down to my knees.

Another three knocks. Bang, bang, bang.

"Armstrong." The male voice was muffled through the door. "Come on, man. Open up."

"Fuck," Jace muttered under his breath. He let go and went to answer the door.

I stood and pulled up my pants with shaky hands, then quickly fixed my bun.

"What's going on, guys?" Jace asked.

Cops. Oh my god, there were cops at the door.

"We were just around the corner, and we've had two calls from neighbors," the first guy said, sounding apologetic. I'd met him before. Matt Perez. His partner stood just behind him, a guy named Colton Caulfield.

I stepped into the living room, resisting the urge to rub my sore wrists.

"Hannah." Matt nodded to me. "What's going on in here? Everything okay?"

Jace cleared his throat. "Yeah, man, everything's fine. We got in a bit of an argument, but it's over. The walls in his place are paper-thin, you know?"

"Right." Matt's eyes traveled around the room, pausing for a moment on the food splattered across the wall, the broken plate below.

"Sorry you guys had to come out here," Jace said. I could tell he was trying to sound calm, but there was no mistaking the anger in his voice. "Neighbors are fucking nosy."

"Yeah," Matt said, his gaze still moving around the apartment. They came to rest on me.

If I spoke up now, they'd have to arrest him. It wouldn't matter that he was a cop. But he'd be out in a day or two. A restraining order wouldn't stop him. Not if I got him arrested.

I looked down at the floor.

"Listen, Armstrong, we had two separate calls," Matt said.

"I told you, the neighbors are fucking nosy," Jace said. "It's none of their goddamn business."

"Yeah, I know," Matt said. "Why don't you come with us, though. Cool down a little."

"I don't need to cool down," Jace said.

Matt stepped closer and lowered his voice. "Work with me, here, man. Grab some stuff. You can crash at my place tonight. Give you two some space. Otherwise…"

Jace's jaw hitched. He glanced at me, his eyes narrowing, then he swept past me into the bedroom.

I couldn't look at Matt and Colton. Couldn't meet their eyes and pretend I wasn't about to fall apart. I was terrified Jace was going to lose his temper in front of them. Terrified they'd have to arrest him. He could lose his job. And he'd blame me.

Jace came out with a duffel bag. Without a word, he walked out. Colton followed, but Matt hung back.

"Hannah, are you sure you're okay?" he asked.

I nodded, flicking my eyes up to his for a second. "Yeah. I'll be okay. Some space will be good."

He took a deep breath. "I'll talk to him tonight. Maybe he'll agree to counseling or something. Anger management."

"Sure, yeah."

I could see the conflict raging inside Matt. Loyalty among cops was strong. But he wasn't an idiot. He knew this had been more than an argument, and he was a good guy. He wouldn't look the other way on this if I said I needed help.

"Call if you need anything," he said. "I mean it."

"Thanks."

With another nod, he left, closing the door behind him.

9

HANNAH

I had to get out of here.

The walls of my apartment closed in, threatening to suffocate me. I could still taste the metallic tang of blood in my mouth, still feel the tightness of Jace's grip on my wrists. The way he'd manhandled me. Pushed me onto the bed. He'd been about to...

I didn't bother cleaning up the mess on the wall and floor where my lunch had splattered. Just tossed some things in a bag, grabbed my laptop, and left.

Not that I had anywhere to go. My parents were a two-day drive away, maybe three. And I wasn't exactly on good terms with them. The only people I knew in Seattle anymore were Jace's family. It wasn't like I could show up on his parents' doorstep, asking for a place to spend the night. His cousin Meredith was always nice to me, but I barely knew her. I didn't have her number, or know where she lived.

So I tossed some things in my silver Honda Civic, and just drove.

I headed north, then east, toward the mountains. I didn't have a plan. And the destination I had in mind made no sense.

Why go back to Echo Creek, the little town where Jace's cousin had gotten married?

Mostly because I didn't have anywhere else to go. And I didn't want to stay in Seattle. I needed to get away from the city. Away from Jace. Echo Creek sounded like as good an option as any. It was two hours from home—enough distance that maybe I'd be able to sleep tonight.

The more miles I put between myself and Jace, the more I relaxed. Even if he didn't stay at Matt's tonight, he wouldn't be able to find me. Granted, he'd be livid to come home to an empty apartment. But that was future-Hannah's problem. For now, I zoned out to music and watched the scenery change.

Seattle gave way to suburbs, which turned rural the farther I drove. I passed empty fields and evergreen forests. The land started to rise and the highway wound up and around the foothills. My ears popped as I gained altitude.

I crossed the pass—there wasn't any snow this time of year. Pine trees replaced the thicker firs and the mountain peaks rose up around me. The highway ran alongside a wide river, the water sparkling in the sunlight. Some of the leaves were changing, adding a splash of fall color to the forests around me.

Echo Creek was just off the highway. It was a cute little town, surrounded on all sides by mountain peaks.

Before I'd given my final destination much thought—I still needed to get a hotel room for the night—I found myself turning into Salishan Cellars Winery.

I couldn't explain why, but as soon as my tires crunched on the gravel drive, I felt safer. Like I'd passed an invisible force field that would protect me from Jace. I shook my head and rolled my eyes as I parked.

A force field? Nice fantasy, dork.

I got out and glanced around. It was just as beautiful as I remembered. The main building was warm and welcoming, with dark wood beams and wide double doors. A sign with the winery logo hung from curved iron brackets. The building was surrounded by well-tended gardens, the scent of lavender floating on the breeze.

The memory of the man I'd seen here came back to me. He'd gone through those doors. Heading where, I didn't know. But I was almost positive it was his family that owned this place. Was he here, somewhere? Did he work here? Or was it a coincidence that he'd been here that day?

I tucked my keys and phone in the pocket of my hoodie and told myself I had not driven all the way out here—right after my boyfriend was almost arrested for assaulting me—on the off chance I'd get a glimpse of some guy I'd seen for thirty seconds at a wedding. That was crazy.

I'd come out here for some space. That was all.

The fresh air felt good after the long drive. I didn't want to trespass, so I stopped inside and asked the woman at the desk if it was okay to walk through the gardens. She assured me it was fine. Guests were always welcome to wander through the open areas of the property.

I found a path that went around the back side of the main building and passed the garden where the wedding reception had been. I kept going, following it through a grove of what might have been pear or maybe apple trees.

The silence was soft and comforting. Just the rustle of the breeze through leaves. The distant sound of tires on gravel. I hugged my arms around myself as I wandered along the path. What was I going to do? Go home? What would Jace do to me if I did?

But what would he do to me if I didn't?

"Hey, Gigz," a male voice said behind me. "What are you doing over here?"

My back stiffened and I drew in a quick breath. No one

called me Gigz in the real world. I glanced over my shoulder just as a white cat rubbed up against my leg.

A guy in a gray Salishan Cellars t-shirt, jeans, and work boots crouched down. "Come here, kitty."

The cat sauntered over to him, her tail in the air.

"She's friendly," he said, looking up at me. He had tousled dark hair and bright blue eyes. The cat paused so he could pet her head.

"She's pretty," I said. "What did you say her name was?"

He stood and brushed his hands on his jeans. "Gigz. She's my brother Leo's cat."

That was... weird.

"Go home, kitty," he said. "Sorry if she was bugging you. Some people don't like cats."

"No, she's fine."

The cat darted off through the grass.

"Cool. Well, have a nice afternoon." He smiled and walked in the direction of the main building.

His brother's cat was named Gigz? Where had he gotten her name?

Badger had a cat. I thought back, trying to remember if I'd ever heard his cat's name. Nothing came to mind. Once in a while he'd get distracted and shoo a cat away, but he always said things like *dumb cat* or *little asshole*. Never a name.

What were the chances that he was *here*? That this guy's brother Leo was Badger? There was no way. But... what if?

Maybe I could find out.

I went back to my car and got out my laptop bag, then went inside the main building. The tasting room was mostly empty, just a pair of women at a table.

The woman behind the bar was pretty, with long brown hair and a friendly smile. I ordered a cheese plate along with a glass of Riesling, then sat at one of the smaller tables.

She brought my wine and cheese, setting it down on the table. "Can I get you anything else?"

"Do you have a wifi password?" I asked. "The public wifi isn't working for me."

"Oh, sure," she said. "Do you mind if I type it in for you?"

I turned my laptop. "That would be great. Thank you so much."

"No problem," she said as she typed. "I'll let Leo know there's a problem. I'm sure he'll be able to fix it. Anything else?"

"This looks great," I said. "Thank you."

A mention of Leo again. Was he their IT guy? A lot of IT guys were gamers. Maybe he was Badger.

The woman walked away, and I got to work. This was risky. I'd been in trouble for hacking before, back when I was in high school. But I wasn't going to do anything bad—not really. Just trace the network traffic.

I ran a program against their firewall to hack into it. This gave me access to the network traffic—the data packets moving to and from the computers here.

It was tedious to skim through all the outgoing traffic. Most was typical—the sort of thing you'd expect to see. Google, news sites, Netflix, that sort of thing.

But then I found what I was looking for. Outgoing traffic connecting to the game servers we used.

Bingo.

This wasn't exactly proof that it was Badger, but someone here was definitely a gamer. Between this and the cat, I wondered if I'd found him.

I leaned back and took a sip of wine. That had been remarkably easy. Badger was a smart guy, and he'd always been protective of his identity. He could have taken more steps to stay hidden—made it harder.

Did he want to be found? Or maybe he'd never thought

someone on his wifi would hack into his firewall and trace the data packets on his network.

I nibbled on a piece of cheese, debating what to do. Badger wasn't online. I'd checked twice since I'd been here. I was dying to know if it was him. How could I be this close and not find out for sure? But randomly showing up unannounced and telling him I'd hacked into his firewall to find him would be a jerk thing to do.

The temptation was strong, but I didn't want to invade his privacy. I'd go to the hotel next door and get a room. Keep trying to reach him online. Hopefully he'd be on tonight. Then I could feel him out. Maybe see if I was right and take it from there.

I packed up my laptop and went back outside. I was just about to get in my car when the man I'd seen earlier—the one who'd told me about the cat—walked by. And like a cat, curiosity got the better of me.

"Hi there," I called. "Excuse me."

He turned. "Oh, hey. Can I help you with something?"

"Yeah." I tucked my hair behind my ear. "So, this might be weird, but can I ask you a question?"

"Sure. What's up?"

"That cat that I saw earlier. You said her name is Gigz?"

"Yeah."

"And she belongs to your brother?"

"Leo, yeah."

"Is Leo by any chance into playing online games?"

His eyebrows lifted and one corner of his mouth turned up in a slight smile. "Why yes. Yes, he is."

"So... this could turn out to be very embarrassing if I'm wrong, but I think I might know him."

His smile grew. "You might know Leo? Like from gaming with him?"

"Yes, exactly. I have this friend who goes by Iron Badger, or just Badger. And I think maybe he's your brother. I'm Hannah, by the way."

He smiled so big it looked like he was about to laugh at me. But he didn't. Instead, he stepped forward and held out his hand. "Nice to meet you, Hannah. I'm Cooper Miles."

I shook his hand. "Nice to meet you, too."

"This way," Cooper said, nodding toward a path that led past the gardens.

"That way to what?"

His brow furrowed, like I'd just asked a stupid question. "To Leo's place."

"Wait, I can't just show up. He has no idea I'm here. And it might not even be him."

"It's him."

"How do you know?"

He turned to face me, a cocky half-grin on his face. "Trust me. This is going to be awesome."

Cooper kept walking. I jogged a few steps to catch up to him.

"I don't know if this is a good idea. This is a pretty big invasion of privacy. I should message him first."

He waved a hand, like it didn't matter. "Why wait? You're here. He's here. Let's do this."

We approached a small cottage with some kind of utility vehicle parked outside. The landscaping was tidy and the paint looked fresh. It had a large window in front, but the blinds were closed.

"Leo lives here," Cooper said.

"Are you sure he's home?" I asked. "It looks dark."

"Oh yeah, he's home," he said. "He's almost always home."

A wave of anxiety poured through me. "I think this is a mistake."

"Sweetheart, trust me," he said. "It's going to be fine."

"No, Cooper—"

He rapped on the door, looking back over his shoulder with that big grin plastered on his face.

Oh god.

"Oh, Leo," Cooper called through the door. "Open up, bro."

The door opened and I gasped.

It was *him*. Not him, as in Badger—I didn't know what Badger looked like. It was the guy from the wedding. The guy who'd practically made my heart stop with just a glance.

Holy shit.

He stood in the open doorway, dressed in a t-shirt and sweats, staring at me, wide-eyed.

Cooper stepped back. "Leo, this is Hannah. Hannah, Leo. But I think you guys already know each other. Have fun." He smiled again and walked off, back the way we'd come.

Leo shifted his body, angling his face to one side.

"Badger?" I asked.

He nodded.

"I'm so sorry," I said, my words coming out in a rush. "It's me, Gigz. I saw your cat, and your brother called her Gigz and I thought wow, what are the chances? And then I kind of hacked into your firewall and traced the data packets so I saw that someone here was gaming. I figured it had to be you. And then I talked to him, and he said I should come with him and now I'm standing here and this is crazy."

"You hacked into my firewall?" he asked.

I paused, because I couldn't tell if he was angry, or impressed.

"I did, and I'm really sorry." I pressed my lips together so I'd stop the rambling apologies. "Look, I'll go. I shouldn't have bothered you."

"No," he said, reaching a hand out. "No, don't."

"Are you sure?"

"Yeah. Don't leave." He gripped the door frame so tight his knuckles were white. "Hannah."

Oh god, hearing that voice I knew so well say my real name gave me swirly feelings in my belly. "Yeah, Hannah Tate."

"Leo Miles," he said. "Do you want to come in?"

"Sure, if you don't mind."

"I don't mind," he said. "I wasn't expecting company, though."

"No, of course you weren't. I won't be any trouble."

"I know."

He met my eyes and there was that sensation again. Heat pooled between my legs and I felt my cheeks flush.

His thick beard obscured the lower part of his face and long dark hair hung loose past his shoulders. Scars were partially hidden by his facial hair, but I caught a glimpse of more trailing down his neck. He had tattoos on his left hand that disappeared beneath his sleeve, but the skin looked scarred there, too. I wondered how he'd been injured, and how bad the scars were under his clothes.

Crap, I was staring. I tore my gaze away and he moved aside so I could go in.

He closed the door behind me, and I got close enough to catch a whiff of him. He smelled fresh and clean, like soap, with a hint of something warm and woodsy. It was deeply masculine —almost irresistible. For a second, I imagined burying my face in his neck. Running my fingers through his beard and hair.

God, what was I doing? I was glad the lights were dim because my face was on fire.

"Can I take your bag or something?" Leo asked.

"Sure." I handed him my laptop bag and he set it near the door.

Part of the space was taken up by a home gym—a squat rack, bench, weights. There was a couch pushed up against the wall, almost like an afterthought. The other half was his gaming setup.

"Holy shit, this is where you game?" I asked, gazing at the desk with multiple monitors and sleek red and black office chair. "I'm insanely jealous right now."

"Oh, yeah, it's pretty cool."

I walked to his desk to get a closer look. "Pretty cool? Are you kidding? This is amazing. I have a couch and a laptop."

"Thanks. I, um... sorry, I'm not great at this. I don't really have people over. Ever. Except my family, but they just sort of show up. Do you want anything?"

"No, it's fine," I said. "I'm sorry, I shouldn't have done this to you. I was going to message you first, but then I ran into your brother."

"It's okay. Cooper... he does that. It's hard to say no to him."

"I bet."

I gazed at him. Badger. No, this was Leo. The mystery man with the universe behind his eyes.

And I was standing in his house? Maybe I'd get to see who he was after all.

10

LEO

*G*igz was in my house, and I had no idea what to do with that.

Hannah. I turned her name over in my mind, reconciling it with the woman I'd been listening to for the last several years. The name fit. Knowing it now, it made perfect sense. Hannah Tate. This was her.

When I'd seen her the other day, she'd been dressed up. This woman, dressed in a black t-shirt and ripped jeans, seemed more like the Gigz I knew. Petite, with thick light brown hair. She had it up in a ponytail, showing a tattoo on the back of her neck, right on her hairline. More tattoos snaked down her left arm, a pattern of vines and flowers. My gaze strayed to her ripped jeans, and I wondered where else she had ink.

She was even more beautiful than I remembered. I wasn't sure what to do with that, either. I looked away. A woman like this wasn't for a guy like me.

"I guess we should stop standing here awkwardly," I said, gesturing toward the couch. "You sure you aren't hungry or anything?"

"No, I'm fine." She took a seat.

I thought about sitting on the couch next to her, but she'd taken the left. I wasn't about to sit with my left side facing her, so I turned my office chair around and scooted it closer.

Keeping the left side of my face angled away from people was habit. But right now, I was keenly aware of my position as I lowered myself into my chair. She watched me without any sign of revulsion. But it was dim in here.

"So, um, I guess I should probably just bring up the elephant in the room," she said.

"What elephant is that?" I asked. My face. She was going to ask about my face.

"We've seen each other before. I was here last weekend for a wedding. We, um, saw each other. And then I told you all about it when we were gaming, but at the time, I didn't know it was you."

"Oh, that." I cleared my throat. "Right, yeah, I was trying to tell you earlier, but..."

"What?"

I met her eyes. "I knew it was you, when you were here last weekend. I saw you, and... yeah, I knew."

"How? You'd never seen me before. Had you?"

"No. I walked by and heard you talking. I knew your voice."

She stared at me for a few seconds before replying. "You heard my voice? And you knew it was me?"

"We've been talking to each other for what, three years? Four?" I tapped my ear. "I'd know your voice anywhere."

"Wait, that night when I was telling you about seeing the mystery Beast man, you knew I was talking about you?"

"Yeah. I wasn't sure at first, but then you said long hair and beard, and I thought it was probably me."

She covered her face with her hands. "Oh my god, I'm so embarrassed."

"No, don't be."

"You ass." She dropped her hands back in her lap. "You knew and you let me tell you about it, like you had no idea?"

"I didn't know what to say. I thought maybe I was finally going off the deep end completely, and I'd imagined you. What were the chances we'd run into each other in real life? The whole thing took me by surprise."

Her expression softened. "You were trying to tell me last time we talked. But I had to go."

I rubbed the back of my neck. "Yeah. I felt bad about it, but I didn't want to make it weird."

"Is it weird now?"

I gazed at her for a few seconds, letting it sink in that she was here. In the real world. "No, not weird."

She tucked her legs up beneath her. "It's not, is it?"

I liked the way she looked, curled up in the corner of my couch. Little wisps of hair framed her face and she picked at her fingernails.

"Is everything okay?" I asked. "You logged off so fast earlier today, I wondered if your stove was on fire."

She kept her eyes on her hands and opened and closed her mouth a few times, like she wasn't sure what to say. "It was, um... I kind of got in a fight with my... with my boyfriend."

Hearing her say *my boyfriend* made my back clench and I ground my teeth together. At least she hadn't said *husband*.

"That sucks. Is everything all right?" *Say no.*

"No. No, everything isn't all right."

The hitch in her voice caught my attention. As did the red marks around her wrists. I'd been so shocked at seeing her here, I'd missed details. She had light bruising on her wrists. The finger-shaped marks on her cheeks were so subtle, they were hardly noticeable. But now that I was looking, I could see them. I couldn't see any other signs of violence, but I didn't know what she was hiding beneath her clothes.

"Did he do that to you?" I asked, gesturing to her wrists, trying to keep my voice calm.

"Yes," she whispered.

I swallowed hard, keeping the white-hot rage under strict control. "What happened?"

A tear streaked down her cheek. "We were arguing and... he, um... he grabbed me and shoved me. He held my face and I cut the inside of my cheek. But mostly he was just yelling."

"Does this happen a lot?"

"He yells a lot when he's angry. And he's grabbed or pushed me a few times. But today was worse than usual. He—"

Her voice broke and suddenly I was next to her, pulling her hands into mine, heedless of the way my scars looked against her fair skin.

"You can tell me."

"I've been sleeping on the couch for months," she said, her voice so soft. "I don't know why he brought it up today. We'd been getting along so well all week. Anyway, he told me I had to start sleeping in the bedroom again and I said no. We were arguing—yelling at each other. He hauled me into the bedroom and... he was going to force me."

I wanted to kill this fucker so bad, it was all I could do to stay still. I kept my grip on her hands gentle, burying my rage. Waiting for her to continue.

"Neighbors called the cops," she said. "We were loud, and he'd thrown a plate against a wall."

"So they arrested him?"

She shook her head. "No. Jace is a cop, too. I think they kind of gave him an out. Kept it unofficial to protect his job if he agreed to leave with them. He's staying with one of them tonight to cool off."

"Is that why you came out here?"

"Yeah. I don't even know why, really. I didn't know you were here. I just needed to get out of my apartment. Put some distance between me and Jace. It's pretty out here, and I knew there was that big hotel, so I just drove."

The feel of her hands in mine was oddly comfortable. I didn't normally like being touched. It felt like being shocked— harsh and jarring. I hugged my mom sometimes because I knew she wanted me to. But other than that, I avoided touching people. Even shaking hands made me uncomfortable.

But Hannah's skin didn't feel like needles. It was soft and warm. I slid my thumbs along the insides of her wrists, wishing I could take the red marks away.

I wanted to tell her to leave him. Now. That I'd drive out to her apartment with her and help her pack. Help her get somewhere safe.

But just the thought of leaving Salishan made the crippling panic threaten to overtake me. It felt like a weight had been dropped on my chest. I could barely breathe.

"Are you okay?" she asked.

"Yeah, I'm fine." Deep breath. "Do you know what you're going to do?"

"I was hoping a night away would give me some clarity."

My phone buzzed and Hannah pulled her hands away. Damn it, I shouldn't have touched her. I probably made her feel awkward. I got up and grabbed my phone off my desk. I had a text from Cooper.

Cooper: how's it going?

Me: fine

Cooper: need anything?

Me: like what?

Cooper: condoms, food, cookies... condoms

Me: no

Cooper: u sure?

Cooper: I'll make a store run

Cooper: it's no problem

Me: yes, I'm sure

Cooper: how's Hannah?

Me: she's fine

Cooper: we really need to work on your communication skills

Cooper: "fine" is something women say when they're not fine

Cooper: so do you mean actually fine, or not fine but you want me to keep digging for the truth?

Me: actually fine

Cooper: not sure if I believe you, but I'll let you get back to your hot gamer girl

Cooper: I can say she's hot because it's just a statement of fact, not a reflection of my sexual attraction to her. I'm super monogamous now.

Me: good for you

Cooper: it IS good for me

Cooper: I've never been happier

Cooper: it's good for my Cookie too

Cooper: are you SURE you don't need condoms?

Cooper: you should really be safe, no matter how well you know her

Me: I'm sure. Stop texting.

"Everything okay?" Hannah asked.

I put my phone back on the desk. It buzzed again, but I ignored it. "Yeah, it's just my brother being... himself."

"Are you close to your family?"

"Yeah, you could say that."

"It's funny, I feel like I know you so well, but there's so much I don't know about you."

I lowered myself into my office chair. "I was thinking the same thing."

"Okay, so... you have a brother..."

"Yeah, I have a bunch of siblings. Roland is older. He runs

the winery. Cooper is the head grower and he's... crazy. My younger sister is Brynn; she's finishing school and she works in the tasting room. And then there's my half-sister, Grace, and half-brother, Elijah. That's... a long story." I really didn't want to get into details about my dad.

"Wow. Big family."

"Yeah. What about you?"

"Only child."

"Did you grow up in Seattle?"

"Nope. Army brat. I was born in Japan, but I don't remember anything about it. We also lived in Germany and a bunch of places in the States. I moved to Seattle in college and just... never left."

I wondered if her piece-of-shit boyfriend was the reason she'd stayed. I couldn't stop thinking about him. Of how he'd hurt her. And how little there was that I could do about it.

We talked until well after the sun went down. I ordered a pizza, and we kept talking as we ate. Our conversation turned to gaming. The games we'd played—the ones we loved, and hated. The old ones we missed. Dungeons, boss fights, loot. We spoke the same language, and even though we weren't talking on headsets anymore, it felt the same.

Only better.

Eventually she pulled out her phone. "It's getting late. I should get going. I still need to get a hotel room and—"

"You can stay here." The words left my mouth before I thought them through.

"That's really nice of you to offer, but I don't want to impose."

"You're not."

"I really am. I showed up here unannounced and took up your whole evening. I'll get a hotel. It's fine."

"No." I couldn't do much for her, but I could give her a safe place to sleep tonight. And I desperately didn't want her to leave. "It's really fine. You can take my room, I'll sleep out here."

"Now I really can't."

God, what was I doing? She probably thought I was a serial killer planning to murder her in her sleep. She didn't even know me.

"Hannah, I swear, you're safe here."

She stared at me for a few seconds, her lips parted. When she spoke, her voice was soft, almost breathy. "Okay."

Relief washed over me. I had a few more hours with her, at least.

I stood. "I'll go put clean sheets on the bed."

"No, don't, I can sleep on the couch. I'm used to it."

"Not a chance, Gigz," I said, already on my way to the bedroom.

I got her set up in my room. She thanked me a few more times until I told her to shut her face. We said a slightly awkward goodnight, and I went out to the other room.

My couch wasn't bad, as far as couches went. It was comfortable enough. But I knew there was no way I was going to sleep. For the first time ever, there was a woman in my house. Not just a woman. My friend. Probably my best friend, although I doubted she knew that.

I lay there, wide awake, thinking about her. About those bruises on her wrists. The fear in her eyes when she'd talked about her boyfriend. And I wished there was something else I could do.

But I was too fucking broken to help her.

11

HANNAH

$\mathcal{I}$ stared at the ceiling, stuck somewhere between exhausted and wide awake. I'd been in bed—in Leo's bed—for over an hour, and I wasn't anywhere near falling asleep. My mind spun in circles—a never-ending whirl of thoughts and feelings. I couldn't get my brain to turn off.

Normally when I had trouble sleeping, I'd get up and game for a while. Running a few quests with Badger always calmed me down—helped me relax. Now he was one room away—the real guy, in the flesh. And it was messing with my head.

I could feel him out there, as if his warmth radiated throughout his little house. It brushed against my skin, making the hairs on my arms stand on end.

Leo Miles. The man I'd known for the last few years as Iron Badger was everything and nothing like I'd pictured. He'd always had an air of mystery to him. An invisible wall he'd maintained around himself. No personal details. No real names, no pictures. No links to his social media accounts. Just a made-up name and his deep husky voice.

Now I was lying in his bed, in the softest sheets I'd ever felt, and I couldn't stop thinking about him.

It was his eyes. Blue-gray and soulful, they were so sad. Like they held a million dark secrets. I recognized something in them —something I knew all too well. Shame.

What burden did he carry? I could see the weight of it. It wasn't in his bearing, or his body. Even through his clothes, I could see he had an amazing physique. That home gym he had didn't go to waste. He was fit and strong. But his spirit bowed, like a shelf with too many things stacked on top.

Could the people in his life see it? Did they know? They had to. I'd only just met him, and I could see it clear as day.

But I knew him. I hadn't known his name or seen his face. But years of late-night talks had taught me a lot about him. And somewhere, deep down, I'd always known there was something wrong. Something he was hiding. Now that I'd seen him in person, it was glaringly obvious. Leo was hurting.

Of course, so was I. Maybe that was why I could see his pain so clearly.

What was I going to do when the sun came up? When Jace started blowing up my phone, demanding I come home? Demanding I share a bed with him? Now that he'd insisted, he wouldn't back down. He'd get what he wanted, one way or another. He always did.

I sat up, letting the sheets fall. I didn't want to wake Leo, but I was thirsty. I'd get a quick drink and go back to bed.

The lights were off, but one of his monitors glowed. He sat in his office chair, dressed in the same long-sleeved shirt and sweats. I paused, gazing at him. At his face.

The left side was marred with scar tissue from his hairline down his neck. His hair hung down, but I could see the remnants of his ear between the strands. It was nothing but a stub. The corner of his mouth was misshapen, like the flesh had been torn—or maybe burned—showing a flash of white teeth, even with his lips closed.

I'd noticed the tattoos on his hand, but now his sleeve was pulled up to his elbow. The ink continued all the way up his arm —and so did the mottled skin. Unless they were confined to his face and arm, he could have scars over a huge portion of his body.

What had happened to him?

He looked up and blinked in surprise, then quickly shoved his sleeve down.

"Sorry," I said. "I was going to get a drink."

"That's fine." He got up and his chair rolled away behind him.

I followed him into the small kitchen. It was clean, with almost nothing on the counter tops. "You're up late."

"I'm always up late." He filled a glass with water and handed it to me. "You know that."

"True. Were you gaming?"

"No, just watching pointless YouTube videos."

"Do you want your room back?" I asked. "Because I can totally sleep out here."

"No, it's fine."

I didn't particularly want to go back to his room and stare at the ceiling. And since he was up anyway...

"If you can't sleep either, maybe we should run a quest or something. I have my laptop."

The corner of his mouth turned up. "Yeah. Let's do it."

I grabbed my laptop. I sat on the couch and logged in, but left my headset in my bag. Badger was here, so it wasn't like I needed it.

He brought up the game on the large center monitor. "What do you want to run? Just something quick?"

"Sure. I'm down for whatever."

We paired up in the game and got started. It was a quest we'd done before, but the loot varied, so it was worth doing again.

Plus, it was fun to play through something relatively easy. The quest went fast, and it was fun to game with him in person. Even more fun than it had been online.

We chatted as we played, like we always did. And he glanced at me over his shoulder now and then, that half-smile on his face. It made me feel a little melty inside.

By the time we finished, my eyelids were heavy. I stretched my arms overhead. "I should probably go to bed."

"Yeah, me too."

"Thanks," I said. "That was fun."

"It was." He turned his chair around and when he spoke, his voice was soft. "Are you going to be okay?"

I knew he didn't mean tonight. I wanted to say yes—brush off the concern I could hear in his voice and assure him I'd be fine. It was what I always did.

But I couldn't. I couldn't lie to him.

"I don't know." I tucked my legs beneath me. "I feel so stupid."

The glow of his monitor lit him from behind, leaving his face shrouded in shadow. "Why?"

"Because things have been crappy for a long time. And I haven't left him."

"Why?" he asked again.

I hesitated, turning his question over in my mind. Why had I stayed? "He wasn't always like this. Or he didn't act this way with me. Not at first. When we started dating, he was so charming. He was a real take-charge kind of guy, you know? Back then, his behavior didn't seem controlling."

"But things changed?"

"Gradually, yeah. He convinced me to start working free-lance, and said he'd support me while I built my client base. So I quit my job and moved in with him. And he gave me a hard time when I saw my friends, so I stopped seeing them as much. Little by little, I lost touch with people—friends and coworkers. Even my family."

"He was isolating you."

"Yeah, I guess he was. And after I moved in, we started arguing more. I don't even know why. It just seemed like any little thing could start a fight. He'd get so mad."

"He always made it seem like your fault, right?"

"Exactly. I don't know how he did it, but somehow he'd turn every argument around. I started feeling like if I could just do the right thing to keep him happy, things would get better. Like we could go back to the way things were in the beginning."

"But nothing worked."

"No, nothing worked." I looked down at my hands. "You seem to know a lot about this kind of thing."

He took a deep breath. "He sounds like my father. The details were different, but he always blamed my mom when they had problems. He made her feel like she was the one failing, when it was all on him."

"I'm sorry."

"It's okay. It's over now."

It wasn't over for me. I had some hard decisions to make, and I'd have to make them soon. A couple more hours, and the sun would be up.

"I guess at first, I stayed because I was in denial about how bad it was. It was hard to admit, even to myself, that I'd chosen to be with a man who could treat me this way. But now…"

"Now?"

"I'm afraid of him." I rubbed my hands up and down my face. "I hate feeling like I'm weak, but I am."

"You're not weak," he said.

"Yes, I am. I've known I need to leave him for months and I keep… not leaving."

"That doesn't make you weak. It makes you a victim in a shitty, abusive relationship."

"Still..."

"You're not weak, Hannah. Trust me. I know weakness."

His screen went black—he must have had it set to go to sleep after a period of inactivity—plunging us into darkness.

When he spoke again, his voice was quiet. "I was in the Army. Overseas, doing intelligence operations. Things went bad. I got injured. I came home to recover, but it wasn't just my body that got fucked up."

He paused, but I didn't fill the silence. I waited to see if he'd continue.

"I haven't left since. That's weakness."

"What do you mean?"

"I mean I haven't left my family's land since the day I got back. I can't. I can't set foot off our property. That's weak, Hannah. You stood up to that fucker, even though you knew he could hurt you. That took courage and strength. Me? I'm stuck here because I'm too messed up to even go into town."

I stared at his silhouette. Was he serious? "I'm sorry. That must be really hard."

He cleared his throat. "Yeah, well. It is what it is. You, on the other hand, have a choice."

"I know." I looked down at my hands. "If I don't leave, it's going to get worse."

"Then leave," he said.

"I don't have anywhere to go."

"Come here."

I looked up. My eyes had adjusted to the darkness just enough that I could see his eyes. They were intent on me.

"I'm serious, Gigz. If all you need is a place to go, I can do that. We have an empty guest house. It looks a lot like this one, except it has normal furniture and stuff. No one's using it. You can stay there as long as you want."

"Really?"

"Yes," he said, his voice full of conviction. "Go home in the morning. Pack whatever you need. I can get my brothers to help you move big stuff later. But get your stuff and come back. You'll be safe here."

Safe. I took a shaky breath, trying not to cry. The thought of feeling safe—the way I felt right now—was almost intoxicating. I wanted it so badly. And I knew he was right. I would be safe here.

Maybe that force field fantasy hadn't been far off.

"Okay. I'll do it."

"Yeah?"

"Yes." I took a deep breath. It felt good to say it aloud. "I'll leave first thing and be back by afternoon."

"Good." He leaned back in his chair.

A sense of calmness settled over me. I was tired, but that wasn't it. I had a plan. A way out. I'd go back to my apartment, pack some things, and come here. I'd have a place to stay while I got my shit together. And most importantly, it would be away from Jace.

"Thank you," I said, my voice quiet, although that wasn't enough. I didn't know how I'd ever thank Leo for what he'd just done for me. He'd given me a safe place to land, and that was priceless.

12
————

LEO

 *M*y house felt empty without Hannah. She'd been here less than twenty-four hours, but now that she was gone, nothing seemed right. It was too quiet.

Or maybe I was just that fucking lonely.

It said something about my mental state that I was so bereft, even knowing she was coming back. It wasn't as if she'd walked out of my life and I'd never see her again. She'd be here tonight, staying in the other cottage.

That would put her right next door to Cooper and Amelia. Coop had moved out of the apartment that had once been the bachelor pad of sin. Brynn and Chase lived there now, and for a while, Cooper had roomed with them. But he'd decided to move back to Salishan, into the cottage Amelia had been living in. I wondered if he'd even asked Amelia if she wanted him to move in. Knowing Coop, he'd just moved his shit over when she was at work, and then congratulated himself on doing her a favor by being there.

Then again, Amelia was almost as weird as my brother. She was just quieter about it.

With the mood I was in, I didn't really feel like dealing with people. But I did need to give my mom a heads-up about Hannah staying in the guest cottage. I doubted she'd promised it to someone else, but I still needed to let her know.

Besides, seeing my mom regularly was one of the things I made an effort to do. Especially since everything had gone to shit with my dad.

I changed into a clean pair of jeans and a long-sleeve shirt before walking over to my mom's house. I knocked as I opened the unlocked door.

"Hey Mom? Are you home?"

She was on the couch with a book in her lap. "Hi, honey."

"You should keep that door locked." I gestured over my shoulder to the front door.

"Sure, but then I'd have to get up to answer the door when you come over," she said with a smile.

I walked in and sat down on the other side of the couch. "You need to be more careful. Dad was into some shady stuff, and that's putting it mildly."

"You think there are drug dealers wandering around Salishan?" she asked, doubt in her voice.

"Maybe."

She picked up her mug of tea off the table and cradled it in her hands. "You worry too much."

"Security is literally my job."

"Fair enough. But you still worry too much. Do you want some tea?"

"No, I'm fine. But thanks."

"So, to what do I owe the pleasure of a visit from my son?" she asked, smiling at me again.

I leaned back, relaxing a little. "I was wondering if anyone's staying in the Hummingbird Cottage."

"No. Why?"

"My friend Gi—I mean, Hannah—needs a place to stay for a while."

"Oh?"

My mom's question was only one word, but I knew what she meant. She wanted to know everything. She probably didn't realize I had friends, let alone one who was also female.

"We've been playing online games together for the last few years. She's trying to get out of a bad situation. She needs a place to crash."

"Bad situation? Do you mean bad relationship?"

I nodded, trying hard to keep my face neutral. I didn't want her to see how angry I was—both at that motherfucker of a boyfriend, and at myself for not being able to do more to help her. "She's afraid he's going to hurt her. I told her to get her stuff and come here."

"Poor girl," Mom said. "Of course she can stay."

"Thanks, Mom."

"Oh, everyone's coming over for dinner tonight," she said. "Can you make it?"

I rubbed the back of my neck. "Can I be a maybe?"

"That's fine. Come over if you want. But if you don't, you better get over here early for leftovers tomorrow. You know Cooper and Chase will raid the place by noon."

"Yeah. Thanks."

I chatted with my mom for a few more minutes, then left. Instead of going home, I decided to take a walk through the south vineyard. I was restless, my limbs jittery—like I was going to crawl out of my skin.

I'd feel better when Hannah was back. When I could be sure she was okay. I pulled my phone out of my back pocket, knowing she was still on her way to Seattle, so she wouldn't have called or texted yet. But I didn't think I'd be able to breathe until she was on her way here.

I should have gone with her.

My heart rate sped up and my chest felt heavy. Amid the panic threatening the edges of my sanity, I was hit with a rush of self-loathing. I was such a mess, I could hardly even *think* about leaving Salishan.

A good friend would have gone. Stood outside her door and made sure that piece of shit didn't get anywhere near her. Cooper and Chase would have gone with me. Hell, even Roland would have. We could have waited outside her apartment while she packed. Kept her safe.

Except I was broken and I couldn't leave.

If anything happened to her today, I'd never fucking forgive myself.

I needed a distraction, so I went back home to get some work done. After lunch, I took a trip out to the east vineyard with Ben. He didn't need me for anything, but he didn't protest—or ask too many questions—when I said I'd go out there with him.

The afternoon wore on, and she didn't call. Didn't text. She was probably still packing—that could take a while—but with every minute that passed, my anxiety grew.

When the sun went down and I still hadn't heard from her, I thought I might lose my mind. I texted her to check in, but she didn't reply.

I paced around my house, dread growing in the pit of my stomach. Something was wrong. She was supposed to call when she left her apartment. That was the plan.

Where was she?

I'd never felt so helpless. And that was saying something, considering what I'd been through when I was overseas. At least then I'd felt like I had some degree of control. Or I had until I'd passed out from the pain of half my body being burned.

Raking my fingers through my long hair, I walked back and forth, passing the front door over and over. Willing her to come through it every time. Desperately hoping she'd dropped her phone or the battery had died.

My family must have been sitting down to dinner. I thought about going over there—maybe being with them would help me calm down—but what if I missed her? What if her phone was dead—or lost—and she came here looking for me?

I'd wait it out. Mom would understand.

All this pacing wasn't doing me any good, so I slumped down in my office chair. Checked my phone again. It was plugged in, battery at one hundred percent, the sound turned all the way up. There was no way I'd miss her call.

It rang and I shot bolt upright out of my chair. My heart stuck in my throat as I looked at the screen. Hannah.

"Hello?"

"Leo?"

"Yeah. Are you on your way?"

Her voice was shaky. "No."

There was definitely something wrong. "Are you okay?"

"No," she said, her voice breaking. "No, I'm not. He, um... he came home."

I sucked in a quick breath and balled my hand into a fist so hard my fingernails bit into my palm. "Where are you?"

"Hospital."

"Fuck," I whispered. That piece of shit bastard fuck. "How bad?"

"It's pretty bad," she said. It was like she could barely get the words out. "They're not keeping me overnight, but, um... I'm hurt."

"Which hospital?"

"Swedish on Cherry Hill. I'm in the ER."

"I'll be there in two hours."

"What?"

"I'll be there."

"Leo..." She trailed off, but I knew what she was about to say. *You can't.*

I couldn't. My entire body screamed at me, threatening to panic. My heart beat so fast I wondered if I could give myself an anxiety-induced heart attack. My vision blurred at the edges, my fingers and toes went numb, and my chest burned.

"Hannah, I'm coming."

"Okay," she breathed.

I ended the call, feeling like my skin was on fire again, melting off my body. Setting my hands on my desk, I leaned forward and closed my eyes. Took a few deep breaths.

This was my fault. But I was going to fix it. Even if it killed me.

Before I could talk myself out of it, I was out the door. My body was so full of adrenaline, I ran down the path to my mom's house and burst through the door.

My family was all seated at the big farmhouse table, in the middle of dinner. Mom, Cooper, Amelia, Zoe, and Roland holding baby Hudson. Brynn and Chase. Everyone looked up at me as I rushed in, leaving the front door wide open behind me.

"I need someone's car keys."

No one moved for a beat, silence hanging in the air.

"Car keys," I said. "Please."

"Why do you—" Mom started to ask, but Cooper stood. His keys jingled as he fished them out of his pocket and threw them to me.

I caught them with a clink.

"What's the emergency, bro?" Cooper asked.

"My friend Hannah's boyfriend put her in the hospital. I'm going to Seattle to get her."

Instantly, Chase and Roland stood, their chairs scraping against the hardwood floor. Cooper was already halfway to me when Roland handed Hudson over to Zoe. A second later, all three of them were heading for the front door.

"I'll drive," Roland said. "My car fits more people. Let's go."

My mom gaped at me from her spot at the table. I couldn't stop to explain any further. If I did, I'd freeze. I'd panic. I had to keep moving, or I'd never be able to do this.

Failing her wasn't an option. Not again.

Zoe said something, and maybe I heard Brynn and Amelia. I wasn't sure. The next thing I knew, I was in the passenger seat of Roland and Zoe's Toyota Highlander. Chase was complaining about being stuck in the third-row seat—Hudson's carseat was in the middle—and Cooper was teasing Roland about driving a daddy-wagon.

It barely registered, just noise in the background. Roland backed his car up, then drove to the winery entrance. To the line I hadn't crossed in almost five years.

My blood felt like it was boiling, searing me from the inside. I took a deep breath, remembering Hannah's voice. How small and scared she'd sounded. That wasn't my Gigz, badass warrior. This was real life, and my friend was in trouble. She needed me. I'd failed her once. I wasn't going to fail her again.

"Go," I said.

Roland didn't hesitate. He pulled out onto the street.

And just like that, I was no longer safe.

As much as I wanted to keep calm on the outside—not show what a fucking mess I was as we drove toward the highway—it was impossible. I clutched my hands into tight fists and a cold sweat broke out on my forehead. I was breathing too hard, my heart beating too fast. A voice in my head shrieked in panic, demanding I turn around. Go back. Get to safety. Take cover.

Get down.

Take cover.

The street lights blurred as we drove. I blinked against their glare, forcing my breath to slow. Combat breathing. In for four. Hold for four. Out for four. Hold for four.

In.

Hold.

Out.

Hold.

In for four. Hold for four. Out for four. Hold for four.

I didn't let my brain do anything but count. Breathe. Count to four. Hold. Count to four. Breathe. Count again.

Gradually, my heart rate slowed and I unclenched my fists. Cooper handed me a bottle of water and I took a few drinks, wetting my dry throat. Roland glanced at me from the corner of his eye but didn't ask if I was okay. None of them did. Which was good. I wasn't okay, and we all knew it. I was holding myself together by the thinnest of threads and talking about it was the last thing I needed right now.

As the miles went by and we came down the west side of the mountains, my relative calm held. I still felt like I was liable to fall apart at any second. But more and more, a sense of resolve settled over me.

Hannah. Her voice on the phone. Her fear and pain were like a beacon in the chaos. She was an anchor for the swirling madness that threatened to consume me.

By the time we reached the city, I was a man with a singular purpose. Nothing existed in the world except for Hannah Tate. Reaching her was the only thing that mattered. I was in a tunnel of midnight black and she was the light at the end of it.

I'd get to her and keep her safe. Keep us both safe.

"Leo." Roland's voice startled me. "We're here."

I blinked, realizing we were in a parking lot, a bright red emergency room sign casting a ruddy glow over the wet pavement. Rain beat down in a steady rhythm outside, pattering against the windshield.

"Right," I said. "Let's go."

The short walk to the entrance left us all drenched from the downpour. I didn't pay attention to the droplets running down my hair and glistening in my beard. That didn't matter.

The woman at the front desk looked up and opened her mouth—probably to ask if we had an emergency—but I didn't wait for her to speak.

"I'm here for Hannah Tate. My name's Leo Miles."

"Hmm," she said as she clicked her mouse and looked at her computer screen.

It took an enormous amount of willpower to keep my body still. My brothers stood behind me, a solid wall of support. Now that I was here, I was no longer on the edge of panic because I'd left home. My only thought was Hannah. I had to make sure she was okay.

"She's expecting me to pick her up," I said. "I got here as fast as I could."

The woman eyed me and my brothers. "I'll be right back."

I twitched, ready to bark at her, but felt a hand on my shoulder.

"Easy, Leo," Roland said, his voice quiet. "They just want to keep her safe, same as you."

Roland's steady presence behind me kept me from shouting all the obscenities going through my head. She was here, so close. I had to see her.

An automatic door opened and a nurse in blue scrubs stepped out. She glanced at my brothers before her eyes settled on me. "Leo? I can take you back."

She led us to a small curtained-off room. "She's in here."

Roland, Cooper, and Chase stayed back while I stepped around the curtain.

My heart cracked wide open at the sight of her. She sat up in bed, a beige hospital blanket spread out over her lap. One eye was blackened, and her bottom lip was split and swollen. Her arm was held tight to her body in a sling and she had a bandage on her forehead.

A tear trailed down her cheek, and when she spoke, her voice cracked. "Leo?"

"Yes." I rushed to her bedside. "I'm here."

13

HANNAH

I couldn't believe what I was seeing. Leo, standing next to the hospital bed. He'd really come. And it felt like suddenly, the nightmare was over.

"You're here."

"I'm sorry," he said, his voice rough. "God, Hannah, I'm so sorry."

"It's not your fault."

A flash of anger crossed his features, so fast I almost missed it. "Where is he?"

"Jail."

He nodded once, his eyes like cold steel.

"He came home while I was packing," I said, my voice starting to shake. "Obviously he lost it. Did all this. Neighbors called the cops again. They stopped him. Ambulance brought me here, and then I had to talk to the police, and—"

"Shh." He touched a finger gently to my lips. "You don't have to talk about it yet."

"Thank you."

Leo's brother, Cooper, poked his head around the curtain.

"Hey, how's it going in here?" His eyes landed on me, and his expression fell. "Oh shit."

"What?" another voice said behind him. Next thing I knew, there were three other men standing inside the tiny room.

"My brothers came too," Leo said with an apologetic shrug. "You met Cooper, and that's Roland and Chase."

Grinning, Cooper stuffed his hands in his pockets and rocked up onto his tip-toes, then down again. "It's how we roll, sister."

"When you're ready, we'll take you to get your stuff out of your apartment," Roland said. He was tall with dark hair and neatly-trimmed stubble. The family resemblance between the Miles men was clear.

"Dickmonkey's in jail, right?" Cooper asked.

"Dickmonkey?" I asked.

"The guy who, you know." Cooper pointed at my face.

"Oh, yeah. For now, at least."

"That kinda sucks, actually," Chase said.

"Why does it suck?" Cooper asked. "That's a very weird thing to say, Chase. I think we can all agree that Dickmonkey belongs in jail."

"Yeah, but if he was out, we could get a piece of him."

Cooper grinned at Chase, but it wasn't humor in his expression. Roland's eyes narrowed and he crossed his arms. There was danger in these men's eyes. But it was the fire in Leo's expression that sent a shiver up my spine. He was violence. Pent-up and controlled, but violence nonetheless.

Jace would never know how lucky he was to be in jail tonight.

"Can I have your address?" Roland asked. "That way we can get as much of your stuff as we can fit in my car. I don't have room for furniture or anything, but you can at least pack some things."

"Thank you." I gave him my address and he plugged it into his phone.

"Of course," he said. His eyes flicked to Leo, then back to me.

In fact, all three of them kept looking at Leo like he was a bomb about to go off.

Then again, maybe he was.

I didn't have the head-space to reconcile the fact that Leo hadn't left his family's winery in years, and now he was standing here, in an emergency room two hours away. The side of my head hurt from my hairline down to my jaw. My arm wasn't broken, but I had deep contusions from where Jace had hit me. My lip was split so badly I could barely speak, and my eye was almost swollen shut. I was a disaster wrapped in bandages, and I couldn't stop staring at this man who'd done the impossible for me.

Why had he come?

When I'd called him, I hadn't thought he would. But he'd been expecting me back at the winery tonight, and I'd wanted him to know where I was. And that it would probably be another day or two before I made it out there. I'd figured I'd need an Uber to get back to my apartment when they finally discharged me.

And yet, here he was.

The nurse came around the corner, holding a stack of paperwork. "I have your discharge instructions."

Cooper reached out to take the stack, but Leo nudged him out of the way. "I'll hang onto those for her."

"She needs to be careful of that head injury," the nurse said. "She doesn't have a concussion, but if she starts experiencing dizziness, vision problems, or nausea and vomiting, bring her back. Understood?"

"Yes, ma'am," Leo said.

"All right, sweetie." The nurse stepped closer and lowered her voice. "These are your friends?"

"Yes," I said. "I called him. Well, them, I guess."

She nodded. "Okay, I just have to be sure. You're free to go."

"Thank you."

She squeezed my hand and gave me a sympathetic smile before she turned and left. I simultaneously wanted to hug her and crawl under the covers in shame. How had I become this? A domestic violence victim sitting in a hospital bed.

I needed to get out of here.

"I'm ready to go." I pulled off the blanket and shifted my legs to the side of the bed.

"Whoa."

I wasn't sure which one of them had said it—or maybe all of them had. Leo stepped forward and took my hand to help me down. The others stepped closer, as if they were all about to pick me up and set me on the ground.

"I'm okay," I said. "My legs still work."

Leo didn't let go, nor did the intensity of his gaze leave my face. I slid down off the bed, my good hand clutching his. It didn't escape my notice that he didn't use the hand on his scarred side.

"Do you need to grab anything?" Chase asked.

I didn't have anything else with me. I wasn't even wearing shoes. I'd taken them off while I packed, and the paramedics hadn't grabbed any for me.

"I don't have shoes."

"Don't worry," Cooper said. "We've got ya, sister."

"I'll pull the car up to the entrance," Roland said.

"Let's just get her out of here," Leo said.

Roland led the way out to the front lobby. I tried to ignore the stares of the people in the waiting area, but I knew I looked a mess. I wondered what people thought of the battered woman walking out of the ER surrounded by four men.

Because surround me they did. Leo stuck by my side, close enough that our arms touched. Cooper walked on my right, while Roland took the front and Chase brought up the rear. I wasn't sure what they thought I needed to be shielded from here —Jace was in jail at least overnight—but I appreciated the feeling of security nonetheless.

Roland went outside to get the car while the rest of us waited. The blast of cold air through the automatic doors made me shiver. I was wearing a thin t-shirt and jeans, a pair of blue hospital socks on my feet.

"Sorry," Leo said. "I didn't grab a coat before I left, or I'd give you mine."

"That's okay. I'll be fine once we're in the car."

"Do you want my shirt?" Cooper asked. He wasn't wearing a coat either—none of them were—but he pulled up on the bottom of his shirt, like he was about to strip it off right here.

"Cooper," Leo said. "Keep your clothes on."

He paused with his shirt halfway to his chest. "Why? She's cold."

I held my hand up. "You don't have to give me your shirt."

"I don't mind," he said.

"Coop, we all know how much you love to get naked, but maybe tone it down a notch," Chase said.

Cooper sighed, dropping the hem of his shirt. "Fine. I was just trying to help."

Chase patted him on the back. "It was a nice gesture, though."

"Thanks, man."

"Sorry," Leo said low in my ear. "They're... I don't know."

A car pulled up just outside.

"That's our ride," Cooper said. "Last call for the shirt. I won't blame you if you think I look awesome without a shirt on, but I'm totally in a committed relationship, so I'm perfectly harmless."

I opened my mouth to reply, but I didn't know what to say to that.

"Let's just go," Leo said.

The entrance was covered by a large overhang, so the ground was dry. But the cold pavement bit at my skin, even through the socks. I tip-toed to the car so less of my feet would touch and Leo hurried in front of me to open the passenger-side door.

I eased into the seat, and the next thing I knew, we were headed to my apartment.

Correction: Jace's apartment. I didn't live there anymore.

We parked in a guest spot in front of the apartment building. I knew Jace wasn't up there, but I tasted bile on the back of my tongue.

Leo came around and opened the door for me. "Come on. Let's just get this over with."

I met his eyes and found strength there. I could do this. "Okay."

Leo kept his hand on my arm as we walked up the stairs. The men checked around corners, as if we were about to be jumped by bad guys, and Leo insisted on going into the apartment first.

I took hesitant steps inside. Evidence of our altercation was everywhere. My clothes were strewn around the apartment; Jace had grabbed the things I was packing and thrown them. He'd left a dent in the drywall near the bedroom door and tipped over the coffee table. The mess from where Jace had thrown my lunch was still on the wall, the broken plate in pieces on the floor.

Chase went into the kitchen and grabbed garbage bags from under the sink, then handed them out to the others. They started walking through the apartment and bagging things up.

Cooper opened a closet and pulled out a large plastic bin with a lid. "This yours?"

"No, that's his stuff."

Without a word, Cooper opened the bin and dumped the contents on the floor. "We can put stuff in here, guys."

I took a deep breath to pull myself together and went into my office to finish packing what I needed. Cooper and Chase found more boxes and bins to empty so I could use them. While I went through drawers and closets, they asked about items, packing what was mine and dropping the rest like it was hot.

After getting everything I needed from my office, I went into the bedroom. Leo took a bag of clothes and he and Chase left with a load for the car.

Cooper came in and cast a glance over his shoulder. "Hey, sister. I gotta make this quick, which isn't really my style, and I know we haven't been BFFs for very long, but I need you to do me a solid tonight."

I blinked at him. "What?"

"If Leo tries to get you to stay in the guest cottage, tell him you don't want to be alone. Stay at his place."

"Why?"

He looked over his shoulder again, then leaned closer, lowering his voice. "I don't know if you know this, and I probably shouldn't be the one to tell you, but it's really fucking relevant right now, so I will. This is the first time Leo's been off our family's land in almost five years."

The gravity of that was only just starting to sink in. "Yeah, he told me."

Cooper's shoulders relaxed and he smiled. "That makes it so much easier and now I'm not an asshole for spilling his secret. Not that it's exactly a secret, but you know how it is with a big thing in your life. You want to be the one to tell the people who are important to you. Feel me? And this is a really big thing in

Leo's life and I'm worried he's going to lose his shit sometime in the very near future. Can I have your phone?"

"Um, what?"

Somehow Cooper already had my phone in his hand. "I'm just adding everyone. If he flips out tonight, start with... I was going to say me, because I'm an awesome brother, but I think Mom first—her name is Shannon—and then me. Call us both. If you can't get one of us, just start going down the list. We're all Miles, except Chase and Brynn, they're Reillys. And Ben is Gaines, and actually Ben is a really good choice too. He's third. In fact, just consider my mom, me, and Ben to all share the number one spot. Roland is great in a crisis too, maybe because he's the oldest, but he has a baby now. So yeah, let's go with Shannon, Cooper, and Ben. If Leo needs help, call us."

"Um..."

"Look, I know you're the one in crisis here, and I don't think you should be alone tonight either. You've been through some shit and trust me when I say, if we ever have the opportunity to get back at the motherfucker who did this to you, we will. But the shit could get shittier if Leo loses it, and Ben taught me to always be prepared. So this is me being prepared."

"Okay."

He handed my phone back and gave me a crooked grin. "Welcome to the family."

I stared at him as he walked away.

"Are you okay?"

Leo's soft voice broke me from my daze. "Yeah. I'm good. I just don't want to be here anymore."

"Let's get you to the car," he said. "We can finish up in here."

"Are you sure?"

"Yeah. Is there anything else in here that's important for us to get?"

I glanced around the bedroom. At the furniture and disheveled bedding. "No. I don't want any of this stuff."

"Come on," he said, his voice soft. "Let's get out of here."

I nodded and let Leo lead me out of the apartment, and away from the nightmare of my old life.

14

LEO

*I*t was well after midnight when we got back to town. Hannah was asleep in the passenger seat in front of me, her head cradled against a throw blanket we'd taken from her apartment. Cooper had passed out partway through the drive. Hannah's stuff crowded around us, but he'd made a pillow out of a bag of her clothes. Chase followed in Hannah's car.

I needed to thank them for coming with me. They hadn't hesitated, even for a second, when I'd told them my friend was in trouble. My brothers were good men.

We turned into the winery entrance and the tension in my back and shoulders eased. I almost hated how good it felt to be back. That wasn't normal. I'd been filled with blinding panic anytime I'd tried to leave before. Now that I'd done it once, would I be able to do it again? Or was it a one-time deal? A moment of adrenaline-fueled purpose brought on by a friend in crisis?

I didn't know.

Roland parked in front of my house and turned to look at me. His voice was quiet. "You going to be okay?"

I looked out the window, torn between gratitude that he cared enough to ask, and shame that he had to. "Yeah. I'm good."

"It's all right if you're not," he said.

He was wrong about that, but I appreciated the sentiment nonetheless. "Thanks. But I'm okay, at least for now. And she's safe with me."

"I know she is. There's probably nowhere safer."

I met Roland's eyes and nodded. He and I had had our share of differences over the years. I'd resented him for moving away. But since he'd been back, our relationship had changed. I trusted Roland, and there was a very short list of people I could say that about.

Hannah stirred and looked around the car. "Are we here?"

"Yeah," Roland said. "How are you feeling?"

"Sore," she said, and a spark of rage shot through my veins. "But mostly just tired."

"We'll take care of unloading," he said. "You can just go inside and get settled for the night."

"Thank you," she said. "Really, I don't know how to thank you enough. You don't even know me, and you did all this, and..."

"It's no problem," he said. His eyes flicked back to me again.

He kept doing that. Cooper and Chase too. They'd all been eying me like they were expecting me to burst into flames or freak out or something. Obviously, I knew why. At this point, I was just glad I hadn't lost it.

"Where's my pants?" Cooper mumbled in his sleep.

I reached back and nudged him. "Coop. Wake up."

"Hmm?" He rubbed his eyes and stretched—as much as he could in the packed car. "Shit, I was having the weirdest dream."

"Yeah, we know," Roland said. "But what about you losing your pants is weird?"

"Was I talking in my sleep?" Cooper asked. "That's weird. I

don't think I've ever talked in my sleep before. I'll have to ask Amelia if I do that regularly."

I ignored my brother's rambling about sleep-talking and got out of the car. I opened the passenger's side door for Hannah and offered her my hand—my good hand—to help her out.

She moved slowly, wincing as she stood. A renewed surge of adrenaline poured through me. God, I wanted to kill the fucker who'd done this to her. I wanted to give him a copy of every injury he'd inflicted on Hannah. And then I wanted to give him more. Break his arms. Crush his knees. Bash in his nose so it would never look the same. I wanted him to hurt like she was hurting. Leave him a ruined mass of bruises and blood so he'd never touch a woman again.

I took a deep breath to stay calm and led Hannah inside. Roland, Cooper, Chase, and I made quick work of unloading her stuff. We piled it next to my weights for the time being.

My brothers all said goodnight to Hannah, giving her gentle hugs. She teared up as she thanked them for their help.

I closed the door behind them after they left, so exhausted I was ready to drop.

"You can have my room again," I said.

"Thank you," she said, her eyes shining with tears. "I don't even know what to say."

I shrugged. "This is what friends do."

"Are you okay?"

"Don't worry about me," I said. "You're the one who's hurt."

"I know, but..." She stepped closer. "You left."

Her concern for me burned, as if it were cauterizing a wound. A necessary pain. "Yeah, I did. I'm not sure what to think about it right now."

"Right, I'm sorry. It's late, and you must be tired."

"I am, but you don't have anything to be sorry for," I said. "Let's just get some sleep. We can talk tomorrow."

She nodded, but her eyes didn't leave mine. She was looking straight at me, but I didn't shift away. I didn't turn my face to the side or angle my body so she couldn't see.

A few seconds of that was all I could take. It left me feeling intensely vulnerable. Exposed. I was about to move—get out of her line of vision—when she came closer. A heartbeat later, she crossed into my personal space and put her arm around my waist, leaning her head against my chest.

I braced myself for the impact. For the unpleasant stinging sensation I felt when anyone touched me.

But it didn't come.

Her body pressed against mine, warm and soft. Her head tucked beneath my chin, her hair silky against my throat. After a second's hesitation, I put my arms around her and squeezed gently.

And I almost fell apart.

My legs weakened, nearly buckling beneath me. Something burst inside my chest, making me tingle all over. Hannah's embrace didn't hurt. It didn't make me desperate to pull away. To maintain a bubble of space around me. It made me want to melt in her arms. To hold her tighter. Drown in the scent of her hair. My eyes rolled back and before I could stop myself, I let out a low groan, deep in my throat.

Holy shit, this felt good.

I held her gently, careful of her hurt arm tucked between us, and just breathed. I was as bruised and battered on the inside as she was on the outside. But for one brief moment, I felt whole.

She pulled away, and I reluctantly let her go. The feel of her body next to mine echoed through me, like the afterimage of the sun.

"Thank you again," she said. "I'll see you in the morning."

"Good night, Hannah."

"Night, Leo."

I watched her walk down the hall toward my bedroom, then took off my shoes and settled on the couch. Surprisingly, I felt sleep come for me quickly. Maybe exhaustion was catching up with me. But with the memory of Hannah in my arms still fresh, I drifted off.

I JERKED AWAKE, my heart racing. Morning light filtered in between the cracks in the blinds. I checked the time. It was almost eight. The house was silent—no sign of Hannah. She must have still been asleep.

Images and sensations flashed through my mind. The lights along the highway as we drove. Mile markers. Automatic hospital doors and the harsh scent of sanitizer. I started to breathe faster, panic trying to edge its way in.

I wondered if I was having a delayed reaction to leaving last night. I'd held it together out of necessity, but now I felt like I was halfway to rocking in a corner.

If I was on the verge of a breakdown, I didn't want to do it in front of Hannah. I sent her a text to tell her I'd be back, hoping that wouldn't wake her, and headed outside into the crisp morning. Going to the one place I knew I could in the state of mind I was in.

My mom's.

She was up, but still dressed in an old Salishan t-shirt and pajama pants, her hair in a bun. She took one look at me and grabbed my hand to drag me inside.

Next thing I knew, I was sitting on her couch, not quite sure how I got there. My chest hurt, like a heavy weight sat on it, making it hard to breathe.

"Slow breaths," she said. My good hand was in hers and she

rubbed the back of it in time with her counts. "In, two, three, four. Hold, two, three, four."

I let the sound of her voice anchor me. Followed her commands to breathe in, then hold. Out, then hold. She knew exactly what to do. It had been a while since she'd had to talk me through a panic attack, but it certainly wasn't the first time.

"Thank you," I said when I thought I could speak clearly. The pressure in my chest still felt suffocating, and I couldn't escape the sense of impending disaster looming in the background of my thoughts. When I got like this, it felt like the world was ending. Like I was about to die, and there was nothing I could do to stop it from happening.

"Take your time," Mom said.

I nodded and took more slow breaths. I wasn't sure how much time passed before I stopped feeling like I was going to crack. Gradually, the agitation eased. My heart slowed. Breathing returned to normal.

There was a knock on the front door. Mom squeezed my hand. "It's probably Benjamin. I have a leak under the kitchen sink and I think I made it worse last night when I tried to fix it. I'll be right back."

I nodded again. I wasn't ready to say much yet. Mom got up and answered the door.

Ben came in, carrying his battered red toolbox. He was dressed in a plaid flannel shirt and jeans. It might have been my imagination, but it seemed like his beard was more neatly trimmed than usual.

"Morning. I hope I'm not here too early, but you said to come by first—" He paused, his eyes landing on me. "Leo."

By his expression—his brow furrowed with concern—he clearly knew something about last night. It shouldn't have surprised me. Nothing stayed quiet for long around here.

"Ben."

"You all right?"

"I don't know."

Ben nodded, then glanced between me and my mom. He put the toolbox down and came over to sit in an armchair beside the couch. "I was going to stop by later. See if you were okay."

"News travels fast," I said.

Mom sat down next to me. "Your brothers were group-texting us the play-by-play last night."

"Were they?"

She laughed softly. "Did you expect anything less? Cooper sent a lot of selfies."

"Sorry if I freaked you out last night," I said. "I know you must have been wondering what was going on."

"It's okay," she said. "How's your friend—Hannah?"

"Hannah Tate. She's okay, I think. She was asleep when I left."

"Roland said the man who hurt her is in jail."

I nodded.

"Good." There was no mistaking the heat in her tone. My mom was a gentle soul, but the past couple of years had brought out the fight in her. "I hope he stays there."

"Believe me, so do I." I didn't want to scare her with all the things I wanted to do to that piece of shit. "And even if he's released, she'll be safe here."

"She will," Mom said. "I'm glad you brought her here."

"Where are you at, Leo?" Ben asked. "Scale of one to ten."

I took a deep breath. "One being totally chill, and ten being losing my mind... about a six, I guess. I was worse when I woke up, but I'm feeling better."

"Sounds like you're headed in the right direction." He gave me a small smile. "I'm proud of you."

"Thanks."

I didn't want to get into what this meant. Whether I'd be able to leave again. I was still too raw. But somehow, Ben seemed to realize that. He met my mom's eyes again—something passed between them, but I wasn't sure what—and stood.

"I'll see about that sink." He grabbed his toolbox and went into the kitchen.

It wasn't surprising to see the look he gave my mom when he thought she wasn't looking. A glance of longing I recognized all too well. It was what I felt every time I looked at Hannah.

What was surprising was the look my mom gave him, after his back was to her. That wasn't just longing in her eyes. I could see pain and gratitude, and something else. Something deeper. I knew my mom and Ben had become good friends, especially since my dad had left. And although he'd never admitted it to me, I knew Ben had feelings for her.

But watching her watch him convinced me of something I hadn't realized before. My mom had feelings for Ben, too.

That was interesting.

I was never one to pry. I knew what it felt like to have secrets you'd rather not share. So I didn't say anything.

"I think I'm okay now," I said. "I should get back and see if Hannah's awake."

"Okay, honey," Mom said. "Let me know if either of you need anything."

"Thanks, Mom."

I called a goodbye to Ben, then left. My heart rate felt mostly normal, and although the aftereffects of all that adrenaline would stay with me for a while, I felt better. Calm, at least. I didn't think I'd lose my shit in front of Hannah, so that was good.

When I got home, I opened the door to find her curled up in the corner of my couch, eating a bowl of cereal. Her black eye and swollen lip looked painful. Dark purple bruises discolored her cheek and jaw. She held the cereal bowl propped on one knee, balanced by her injured arm, and she had a blanket draped over her lap.

She looked up, meeting my eyes, and smiled. "Morning."

It squeezed my heart to see her like that. Broken, and so fucking beautiful.

"Hey." I shut the door behind me. "How are you feeling?"

"Not bad, all things considered. I slept like a baby."

"Glad to hear that." It was remarkable how much her voice soothed my raw edges. Already I felt so calm. Almost normal.

"I helped myself to breakfast." She gestured to her bowl with her spoon. "I hope you don't mind."

"Not at all. Make yourself at home."

"Thanks."

There was something about seeing her relaxing on my couch first thing in the morning. No makeup. Messy hair. The bruises didn't matter; she still looked amazing. Her black tank top showed the ink on her arm and her toes peeked out from beneath the blanket.

I liked it. She looked like she belonged.

But she didn't. Not like that. There was no way I was dragging her into my dumpster fire of a life. One trip into the outside world didn't mean I was fixed.

I'd help Hannah pick up the pieces of her life, but only so she could go out and live it again.

15

HANNAH

*L*eo took a seat in the other corner of the couch, and I felt a little glimmer of satisfaction. When I'd sat here before, he'd kept more distance—sitting in his office chair instead of next to me. I had a feeling I knew why, and this seemed to confirm my suspicions.

He was trying to keep his scarred side away from me.

There was a practiced flow to his movements. In the way he always turned slightly, keeping his left side back. In the way he let his hair fall around his face. He was constantly trying to hide his scars. Present his right side to the world.

The other night, I'd been sitting on the left side of his couch. If he had sat next to me, it would have put his scarred side facing me. I wasn't sure if he'd made a conscious decision to sit elsewhere, or if it was simply habit. But I'd hoped he might sit closer if I left him an opening by sitting on the other side.

He had, and it made me smile.

I was also worried about him. I had no idea what he must be feeling now, in the aftermath of what he'd done last night. Judging by the tense furrow of his brow and the stormy look in his eyes, he was struggling.

"Are you sure you're okay?" he asked. "Do you need ice or anything?"

So much tension in his expression—in his body—and he was still concerned about me. I brushed my face with the tips of my fingers. "It hurts, but I think it just needs time to heal."

Leo's eyes flicked up and down and his fingers twitched. I wished I could read him. Was he thinking about touching me? Was that what had prompted that little movement? Or was he anxious to get rid of me and get his space back? It was so hard to tell.

And why was I thinking about Leo touching me? I was fresh out of a terrible relationship. The last thing I needed was to get wrapped up with another guy.

Granted, my body was telling me a different story. Whispering soft suggestions that lit up places I'd shut down months ago. Imagining those hands on my skin. That mouth—

God, what was I doing? Leo was just a friend.

Besides, the guy clearly had issues. I couldn't pretend that wouldn't be a problem. We were both a mess. And when did two messes ever make anything but a bigger one?

"Listen, I really appreciate you letting me crash here last night," I said. Leo's cat, Gigz, jumped up on the couch and curled up next to me. "But I don't want to intrude on your space."

"You can stay as long as you need."

Temptation murmured in my ear. *Stay.*

Well, no one was saying I had to make permanent decisions today. "Thank you." I set my empty cereal bowl down and pulled the blanket up higher. "It's so cozy in here. Like a secret hiding place. Is that weird?"

He smiled, a subtle turning of his lips. "No, that's... pretty accurate, actually."

"It's so nice to feel safe. I can't remember the last time I felt that way."

His hand twitched again. Was he thinking about reaching out to touch me? Was it wrong that I wanted him to so badly?

Probably.

"You're very safe here," he said. "I have video surveillance set up around the grounds and I can run it through facial recognition software. I can even set up alerts if there's a match. If he shows up here, I'll know about it."

"That's some high-tech stuff. Why do you have that kind of security at a winery?"

"We had some issues with theft a while back. Security cameras helped. And I guess…"

I waited for him to finish, but he didn't. "You guess what?"

"My therapist thinks I'm trying to feel in control. That I go overboard on security in an attempt to create the illusion of safety."

"Do you?"

"Probably."

"Does it help?"

He looked down and rubbed his hands on his pants. "Some. But not enough."

"Well, I don't think we need to worry about Jace. For now, at least. I talked to the victim's advocate assigned to my case at the hospital. She said he'll be held without bail until there's a hearing, which usually takes a day or two. If he's released on bail, a protection order will be put in place. Even if he does find out where I am, he won't be allowed near me."

"He won't find you," Leo said, his voice suddenly hard. "If he comes anywhere near you, I'll end him."

I probably should have felt alarm at that statement. Leo had basically just said he'd kill my ex, and I could see in his eyes that he meant it literally. But all I felt was a warm sense of security and gratitude.

"I'm done with him," I said. "I just need you to know that. I'm not going back. Ever."

"I know."

That crackling tension was back, charging the air between us. I'd thought that spark I'd felt when I'd seen him at the wedding—before I'd known who he was—had been a fluke. But I felt it now, and if anything, it was stronger than before.

Gigz stood and stretched, arching her back. Leo absently scratched between her ears. With a quick jerk of her head, she tried to bite his hand.

"Hey." He shooed her off the couch. "Why do you have to be an asshole, Gigz? I was being nice."

I laughed. "Cats generally are."

"Yeah. She wasn't my idea. My mom adopted her for me a few years ago. I guess she thought I needed company."

I nibbled on my bottom lip. "Did you name her Gigz after me?"

He opened his mouth to reply, but his phone buzzed. Scowling, he pulled it out of his pocket and swiped to answer. "Yeah?"

I could hear the voice on the other end.

"Leo! Morning, bro."

"Hi, Coop. What do you need?"

"Nothing, man. I'm just calling to check up on you two. How's Hannah-banana? Wait, that's a shitty nickname. I bet everyone calls her Hannah-banana. That's shockingly unoriginal of me."

Sorry, Leo mouthed.

I shrugged. "He's not wrong."

"Hannah's fine."

"I'm so disappointed in myself," Cooper said. "I'll do better next time. So what time should we come over?"

"What?" Leo asked.

"What time?" Cooper asked again. "Amelia's making cookies. Cute, right? My Cookie baking cookies?"

"Sure, cute. But you don't need to come over."

"We totally can. It's no problem."

Leo took a deep breath. "Maybe later, okay?"

"Later? But—wait, hold on a second." His voice got quieter, but I could still hear him. "That's true. You're so good. Why are you so amazing? Leo, Amelia said Hannah probably needs a little space today, so we'll just drop off our cookies this afternoon. Because you still need cookies, am I right?"

"I guess so. Thanks."

"I'll run interference for you today, too, buddy. Keep everyone away. Because you realize the entire family is kind of freaking out. But that way you can spend time with your girl."

"She's not my..." Leo closed his eyes and let out a breath.

"Right, I get it. Not yet. Cool. How are you, though?" Cooper asked.

"I'm okay. I saw Mom this morning and..." He met my eyes. "Yeah, I'm all right."

"Good to hear it, bro."

"Thanks for checking up on us," he said. "But I have to go."

"Yeah, you do. Hannah needs you, man. Take care of that girl. She's a sweetheart. She has awesome tattoos, too. I forgot to tell her that. Did you tell her about mine?"

"No."

"I'll show her next time we hang out. Later, brother."

"Bye, Coop." He ended the call and put his phone down. "Sorry about that. Cooper's basically a puppy on crack. But he means well."

I thought about what Cooper had said last night. How he'd given me everyone's phone number in case Leo needed help. "He obviously cares about you a lot."

"He does. I shouldn't let him annoy me so much. He's just a lot to handle sometimes. Don't worry about my family, though. They're nosy as fuck, but they won't bother you." His phone buzzed again, and he picked it up. "See? Nosy. My sister, Brynn. At least she just texted. She wants to know if we need anything from the store."

"That's sweet."

"She's just looking for an excuse to come over. Joke's on her, though," he said with a little grin. "I'm an expert at ordering what I need without leaving the house."

"You must be." It was nice to hear some levity in his voice when he talked about this. "Can I ask you a question?"

"Sure."

"Can you leave again?"

Swallowing hard, he looked away. "I don't know."

"Do you want to try?"

"Now?"

"Sure." I could see the anxiety in his expression, but I had a gut feeling about this. If he waited too long to go out again, he might never do it. He needed a little push.

He rubbed his hand over his beard a few times. "Okay. Where?"

I thought about it for a second. He was clearly self-conscious about his appearance. A restaurant was probably too much. He might feel like people were staring. But maybe a store. We'd be moving, walking around, so less likely to garner looks. And if he started to freak out, it would be easy to leave quickly.

"Let's go to a store. We don't even need to buy anything. Just a quick trip."

"A store?"

"I'll be right there with you the whole time." I stretched out my leg and nudged his thigh with my toes. "Come on. I'll go looking like this."

"You look fine."

"I do not." I nudged his thigh again, mostly for the excuse to touch him. "I saw myself in the mirror. I look like hell. But I still think we should go out."

"One store."

"Yep."

"Then come back."

"Right back here. Then we can stay in for the rest of the day."

He laughed softly, reaching out to squeeze my foot. I felt a little zing at the contact. "All right. Let's do this."

I got up—somewhat reluctantly, because he was still touching my foot—and went back to his bedroom to change. As much as I wanted to hunker down in his house and lick my wounds, I knew he needed this. He'd been such a good friend to me. The least I could do was return the favor.

There wasn't much I could do about my face. Makeup wouldn't cover the bruises, let alone the swelling. Sunglasses would help, but I'd just have to accept that I looked like I'd had the shit beat out of me. Which I had, so what did I expect?

Looking at my face made me think of Jace. I was still worried about what was going to happen with him. He was in jail for now, but what if he decided to come after me when he got out?

I couldn't worry about that today. And being here made that feel like less of a present threat. Leo had said he'd keep me safe, and I believed him.

Pushing Jace from my mind, I fished a sweater out of my bag. The leggings I had on would have to do; putting on jeans would be too difficult with only one arm. I wasn't sure how I was going to get the sweater on by myself, so I brought it out to the other room.

"Can I get a hand with this?" I asked.

Leo stood. "Sure."

With gentle hands, he helped me out of my sling, pulling it

over my head. I stretched out my arm and opened and closed my fist a few times. He bunched up the bottom of the sweater and held it open while I put my arms through, then helped me get it over my head. I leaned closer as he pulled it down—close enough to smell him.

We both paused, as if we were frozen, hesitating just inches apart. His arms were around me without touching, his hands still holding the hem of my sweater. Both hands. His body was so close. That broad chest and wide shoulders. That beard, beckoning me to run my fingers through it.

He cleared his throat, letting go of my sweater, and stepped away.

"Thanks," I said. God, I'd probably made him uncomfortable. He kept more distance between us as he helped me put my arm back in my sling. "Ready?"

"Yeah."

We went outside but I paused next to my car. "Sorry if this is a dumb question, but can you drive?"

"It's been a while, but I can, yeah."

"Good." I tossed him my keys. "It's an automatic, but driving one-handed isn't easy."

We got in the car and drove to the winery entrance. Leo only hesitated a few seconds before pulling out onto the road, although he gripped the steering wheel hard enough to turn his knuckles white.

There was a corner store not far from Salishan. Leo pulled into the parking lot and took some slow breaths.

I reached over to gently touch his shoulder. "You okay?"

"I know this is fine," he said. "It's just a store. People come here every day. But my body feels like it's a war zone and if I don't get to safety, I'm going to die."

His confession startled me. I wondered—again—what had happened to him. But now didn't seem like the time to ask.

"Is this enough?" I asked. "Should we go back?"

"No," he said, his voice full of conviction. "No, let's go in. I'll feel like a failure if I don't."

My heart ached for him. Such a simple thing, and yet it was so difficult.

"You can do this. You're safe with me."

He turned, meeting my gaze, and nodded.

We got out of the car. Without thinking about it, I slipped my left hand into his right, giving it a squeeze. As soon as I'd done it, I wondered if I should have. It was clear he was protective of his space.

But he squeezed back as we walked to the store's entrance.

I kept my hand in his as we walked up and down a few aisles, and tried to judge whether he'd be up for standing in line to buy a few things. I felt strongly that he needed this push, but I didn't want to take it too far.

We paused in front of a display of chips and crackers. Leo hesitated and the hand gripping mine twitched. Finally, he reached out with his left hand and took a bag of pretzels.

"Do you need anything else?" he asked. His voice was quiet and controlled, but I could hear the strain.

"No, I think this is good for now."

He nodded, squeezing my hand again.

The cashier was finishing up with another customer when we approached. Leo put the pretzels on the short conveyor belt. Reluctantly, I let go of his hand so he could get out his wallet.

"Find everything you need?" the cashier asked. She was young—probably late teens or early twenties—with a blond ponytail and perfectly groomed eyebrows.

"We did, thanks," I said.

She looked up, her gaze landing on Leo. Her expression fell, her eyes widening, and her lips parted in surprise.

For a split second, I thought Leo wouldn't notice. That he

was too busy fishing a card out of the battered leather wallet he'd taken out of his pocket.

But he did notice.

He stiffened next to me. Bent his head down so his hair hung in his face and shifted to turn his left side away from her.

I cleared my throat and her eyes flicked back to me. Putting my good hand on my hip, I leveled her with a glare.

She seemed to get the message. Or maybe she was more shocked by my appearance than his. But at least she didn't gape at Leo again.

I plucked the receipt from her hand and grabbed the bag.

"Have a nice day," she said, her voice trailing off as we walked away.

Neither of us said anything as we went outside and got in my car. I wished Leo would hold my hand again—that had felt nice—but I was carrying the grocery bag. And he didn't reach for me, anyway.

A few minutes later, we were pulling back into the winery. We passed the main building and pulled up in front of Leo's house.

"You did it," I said. "How do you feel?"

"Not as bad as I thought I would. Although it's messed up how badly I want to go inside and close all the blinds. Maybe even hide in bed."

Snuggle under the covers with Leo? Oh my god, that sounded good. Although he hadn't necessarily meant *with me.*

I was really getting ahead of myself here.

"Well, I think you did amazing. Twice in less than twenty-four hours? Most guys can't do that."

That got a laugh out of him. He turned to me and gave me one of those rare smiles. "Thanks, Hannah."

I loved that he'd called me by my real name. My nickname

was fun—and he'd given it to me—but hearing him say *Hannah* did funny things to my insides.

So did seeing him smile.

We went inside, and I felt like today was a win. I was bruised and sore, but I already felt like I'd cast off the old Hannah and left her behind. My injuries would heal.

And so would his.

16

HANNAH

*W*hen Leo had first offered me a place to stay, I knew he hadn't meant *his* place. There were three guest cottages on the winery property: the one that had become Leo's house, plus two others. Cooper lived in one with his girlfriend, Amelia. The other was empty—the perfect place for me to live while I got my life in order.

But Leo didn't suggest I move my things into the other cottage. And I didn't bring it up, either.

Instead, I went right on living with him. He'd insisted on letting me sleep in his room and after a while, I stopped protesting. He claimed he didn't sleep much, anyway, which seemed to be true. We were both night owls, but I wasn't sure when Leo slept. If I got up in the middle of the night, I'd find him awake, sitting at his desk. And he was always up before me in the morning.

At first, I worried that I was intruding on his personal space and that I'd wear out my welcome. But as time went by, I noticed him making space for me.

We didn't talk about that either. But one night he moved things around on his desk so we could game next to each other.

A few days later, I woke up to my work PC all set up beside his array of monitors, with a second office chair right next to his.

I started putting my favorite coffee mug away in his cupboard. Seemingly out of nowhere, a toothbrush holder appeared in the bathroom with room for two brushes, along with more towels in the little cupboard. I stopped repacking my clothes and putting them away in my suitcase, and started hanging things up in his closet.

Little by little, I settled in. My injuries healed. For the first few days, we hunkered down in his house and didn't leave again. It was like we both needed time to recover. But after a while, Leo started showing me around. Taking me on long walks around the property. I met his family. Had dinner with his mom.

None of them asked why I wasn't living in the other cottage. And they seemed to regard me with a sense of awe—or maybe it was disbelief. I got the feeling that they hadn't expected me to be real. Or perhaps they hadn't expected me to stay.

Weeks went by. Then a month. I worked next to Leo. Gamed with him at night. Took care of my clients. I changed my address and sent a brief email to my parents to tell them I'd moved. I didn't hear from Jace, although he wasn't allowed to contact me and, as far as I could tell, he didn't know where I was.

We spent time with Leo's family—I loved how close they were—and took walks around the winery grounds. I coaxed Leo into going into town sometimes. We did things like grocery shopping and even graduated to sitting in a small café for coffee.

I loved it here. The slower pace of life. The quiet. I felt safer and more comfortable than I had in years. Sharing space with Leo felt as natural as breathing.

But we lived like roommates, and I wasn't sure what to make of that.

I sat at the desk—what had become *our* desk—with my morning coffee while Leo worked out on the other side of the room. Cooper and Zoe often came over to lift with him, but today it was just Leo. And god, he was magnificent.

I'd never seen him without pants and long sleeves. But even fully dressed, he was a sight. Broad shoulders, thick arms. And those thighs. He filled out a pair of jeans—or sweats, my god—like no other. He worked out almost every day, and it showed. His body was incredible.

Not for the first time, I fantasized about what he looked like under those clothes as I watched him from the corner of my eye. The downside to our living arrangement? Being in close quarters with this man almost twenty-four/seven. It was a little bit like torture.

I'd been attracted to Leo from the first time I saw him—when I'd had no idea who he was. And I was just as drawn to him now. If anything, the tension between us grew the longer I stayed.

Was he feeling it too? I really didn't know. He seemed to want me here. The little changes he'd made had to mean something. Of course, they might just mean we were friends and he liked having a roommate.

I pretended to be busy on my computer while I watched him do another set of bench presses. His sleeves slipped down a little and I could see the tattoos that covered his left arm. I'd caught a quick glimpse of his legs once, and he had ink down his left leg too, all the way to his ankle. I would have given just about anything for a peek under his clothes. How far did his ink go? Was it just his arm and leg? Or did the design extend onto his chest and torso? What about his left thigh?

As careful as he was to not let skin show, I'd probably never find out.

He got up and grabbed a towel to wipe the sweat from his face. I took advantage of the moment and looked. Not from my peripheral vision. Straight on.

I couldn't understand why he was so self-conscious about his appearance. Granted, his scars were extensive. But the damage hadn't ruined him. If anything, it made him more intriguing. He was scruffy and brooding, with his thick beard and deep, stormy eyes.

He was beautiful.

I looked away so he wouldn't notice me staring and shifted in my chair. Watching Leo work out always made me tingly between the legs. And taking care of business myself had become increasingly unsatisfying.

But I couldn't tell if this attraction was one-sided. It was entirely possible that Leo was just lonely, and liked having me around as a friend and roommate.

He went back to the bathroom to shower and change—he always changed his clothes in the bathroom—and I once again wondered how long this living arrangement was going to last. He couldn't keep sleeping on the couch forever.

Glancing at the bathroom door, I nibbled on my lip. The shower turned on. Was he just showering in there? Or was he taking care of other things?

How long had it been since he'd been with a woman? I had a very strong suspicion that he hadn't had sex since before his injury. Years. That was *years* ago. But I'd be shocked if he had. He was so careful to stay covered. Hiding skin wasn't exactly conducive to sex.

Although, hell, I'd find a way.

I needed to stop thinking about having sex with Leo. We were friends, and I was so grateful for that.

But god, I wanted more. I couldn't deny it any more than the ocean could deny the moon. The tide rose and fell, and I wanted Leo Miles.

He came out about fifteen minutes later—fully dressed, of course—toweling off his damp hair. "Do you feel like going out?

It's cold, but not raining. I should probably go outside. I don't think I did yesterday."

"I don't think I did either," I said with a laugh. I was almost as much of a homebody as he was. Almost. "Sure, let's get some fresh air."

I went back to the bedroom and dressed in a sweatshirt and jeans, then put my hair in a ponytail. Leo had his coat on when I came out, the hood already pulled up. I wondered if he bundled up so much when the weather was hot, or if he just went out less. Or maybe at night.

We went outside and the early November air was indeed chilly. I zipped up my coat and tucked my hands in the pockets.

I followed Leo as he cut around behind his house to a trail that led away from the main grounds. It wasn't lost on me that he avoided the guest areas of the winery. I didn't really mind. I wasn't as reclusive as Leo, but I was an introvert at heart. And there was something about living like this—just the two of us most of the time. I felt like I got him to myself, and I liked it.

He glanced over at me as we walked and gave me one of those heart-melting smiles. "Thanks for coming with me. This is nice."

"Yeah, it is."

Sometimes he held my hand when we walked, but I'd stupidly put my hands in my pockets. He'd done the same. But I was on his right. Maybe if I just took out my hand and slipped it in the crook of his elbow...

I did, holding my breath as I moved closer and tucked my hand in his arm. He glanced at me again, but didn't pull away. My heart did a little happy dance.

"I'm going with my mom to see my father today," he said.

I knew his father was in jail awaiting trial. Leo had told me the basics—his affairs, and his secret family. How he'd tried to take their land in the still-pending divorce, and later planted an illegal opium poppy crop on some unused acreage on the other side of their huge property. In short, his father sounded like a total piece of shit. "Wow. That's a big deal."

"It is. But she told me she's going and I decided I need to go with her. She shouldn't go alone."

I wondered why Roland wasn't taking her. Or even Brynn. I knew it wouldn't be Cooper. The one time I'd seen their father mentioned in front of him, Cooper had gotten so angry, Amelia had needed to take him outside for a solid fifteen minutes to calm him down.

But I didn't ask why he was going instead of someone else. If Leo felt he needed to be the one to go with her, I didn't need to make it harder by questioning his choice.

"Do you want me to come with you?"

"Thanks, but no," he said. "I appreciate the offer, but this is just something I need to handle."

I squeezed his bicep, enjoying how the solid muscle felt beneath my hand. "Sure. I understand."

We came to a clearing with a large fire pit in the center. Surrounding it were a bunch of weathered camping chairs and homemade wooden benches.

"That's a big fire pit," I said.

"Have we not been over here?"

"No. What do you guys burn in there? That circle is huge."

"Just wood, usually. Cooper's a bit of a pyromaniac, especially when there's beer involved. Ben built this, thinking a big fire pit would keep things contained no matter what they decided to burn."

"Did it work?"

"Not really. Cooper just started building bigger fires."

I tilted my head, looking at the charred pieces of wood in the center. There was a rusty coil amid the blackened logs. "Is that a metal spring?"

"Probably," he said. "Must be from someone's mattress."

"A mattress? Why would you burn a mattress?"

"It's... I don't know, it's a thing my family does. Cooper and Chase burned my mom's mattress after she kicked my dad out. They burned Zoe's after she and Roland got married. Then Chase burned his when he was engaged to Brynn. That mattress had seen a lot of action, if you know what I mean."

I laughed. "So it was like a symbol of him leaving his manwhore days behind?"

"Exactly. Then Cooper burned his for Amelia. They always come back out here and clean up the stuff that doesn't burn, but I guess they missed some last time. Anyway, if you haven't figured it out by now, my family's fucking weird."

I laughed again, harder this time. "They're not weird. They're amazing."

"You think so?"

I looked up at him. "Is that a serious question? Yes, your family's awesome."

He raised his eyebrows at me.

"Burning mattresses is pretty extra, I'll give you that. But you're really lucky to have them."

"Yeah, you're right about that. I'm very lucky to have them. Even Cooper and Chase. Hell, sometimes especially Cooper and Chase." He paused for a moment, his gaze on the charred remains of wood and mattress parts. "Have you talked to your parents at all since you've been here?"

"Not really." I nestled closer to him, taking comfort in his warmth. My parents were a sensitive subject. "I emailed them to let them know I'm here. They didn't say much in response. Just *Thanks for letting us know*."

"What happened with them?"

"It's a long story."

"You don't have to talk about it if you don't want to," he said.

"No, it's okay. I don't mind. It started in high school. I got in some trouble and it put a lot of strain on our relationship."

"What kind of trouble?" he asked.

"Well…" I hesitated. "I kind of hacked into my high school's network. We had a web-based portal where everyone had to log in and get messages from teachers and assignments and stuff. I hacked some other students' cell phones and got screenshots of their text conversations and posted a bunch of them there."

"Why?"

"They were classic mean girls. Huge bullies. They ruled that school, and the other girls either worshiped them or were terrified of them. Or both. They targeted this one girl at school, I don't even know why. She was shy and overweight and they were just so mean to her. So I hacked into their phones and took screenshots of their text conversations. They were bashing each other, bashing their boyfriends, talking about getting drugs and who bought them alcohol, all kinds of crazy stuff."

"Holy shit."

"I know. A lot of people got in trouble. Kids got kicked off athletic teams because they were named. Fights broke out in the hallways because the girls were all cheating on their supposed boyfriends. It was chaos."

"And you got caught, I take it," he said.

I groaned. "Yeah. I got sloppy. It turned into a really big deal. I only got probation, but now I have a criminal record. And I got expelled from my high school. I still graduated—I went to an online school for the rest of the year—but I lost my college acceptances. I took a few years off after graduation and worked as a waitress while I taught myself graphic design. I went to college after that, but it kind of put a dent in my life for a while."

"And your parents?"

"My dad was a strict military man," I said. "He didn't care

why I'd done it. I'd broken rules—broken laws—and that was unforgivable."

"He didn't care that you were trying to help someone?"

"Not at the time. He softened up later, but then…" I sighed. "Then I started dating Jace. They came to visit and met him when we'd only been together a few months. I was still under the impression that Jace wasn't an abusive ass. My parents saw right through him. They told me, and I thought they were being judgmental. We got in a big argument about it. They said some hurtful things, but I did too. Worse things, really. Our relationship has been strained ever since."

"What about now?" he asked. "Do they know you're not with him anymore?"

"Yeah, I told them. But it's not like that fixes everything, you know? I pushed them away pretty hard over the last couple of years."

"That sucks."

"It does. I guess it's one of those things I'll have to figure out how to handle."

"Those things aren't easy," he said. "Let me know if I can help."

"Thanks."

He smiled down at me again. I loved it when he did that. His blue-gray eyes crinkled at the corners, sending warm fuzzies tickling through me.

Without really thinking about it, I popped up on my tip-toes and went in for a kiss.

Leo stepped back, pulling his arm from my grasp, and turned before my lips had a chance to land on anything other than air.

Oh god. I covered my mouth and looked away, so embarrassed I thought I might die right there. Why had I done that?

And why had he stopped me?

"Hannah—"

"No." I put my other hand up. "No, it's fine. I'm sorry. I don't know what I was thinking. Can we just pretend that didn't happen?"

"Gigz, I'm sorry."

And there it was. My nickname. My gamer identity. Gigz wasn't anyone's girl—certainly not Leo's. She was Badger's gamer buddy. His friend. And that was fine. I understood Leo's gentle reminder of who we were to each other. And I didn't want to mess that up, regardless of what my traitorous lady parts had to say about it.

"It's fine." I turned to look at him. I didn't want this to get so awkward that we couldn't be friends anymore. I'd do just about anything to avoid that. "I just got a little carried away. It won't happen again. Are we cool?"

There was tension around his eyes and his hands were clenched. "Yeah, of course we are."

"Good."

I didn't slip my hand in his as we walked back to his house—even though he didn't have his hands in his pockets. I walked beside him, keeping a little distance between us. Which I should have been doing all along.

But my heart was more than a little bit bruised.

17

LEO

I was either a man of iron will, or the world's biggest idiot. I wasn't sure which.

Hannah had tried to kiss me, and I'd pulled away. My reaction had been partially instinct. I flinched when people got too close, especially if they were anywhere near my face.

But I couldn't blame this on a knee-jerk reaction. I'd felt her coming—known exactly what she'd been about to do—and I'd made the conscious choice to stop her.

It wasn't that I didn't want to kiss her. I wanted her so badly it drove me crazy. Living with her was practically self-flagellation. I loved it—loved having her near me all the time. But I wanted her in all sorts of ways I shouldn't. Ways that I *couldn't*. And it was killing me to deny myself.

But I was too broken to love her. I was too broken to love anyone.

Selfishly, I'd kept her in my house. Conveniently failed to suggest we move her things into the other cottage. Made room for her on my desk. Put her things away in my cupboards and closets, all the while telling myself I could maintain distance. Enjoy having her close, but allow her to live her own life.

I was a fucking liar.

We got back home and after hanging up her coat, Hannah went to our desk and put on her headphones, saying she had work to do. Which was probably true. But I knew I'd hurt her feelings, and I hated that it had been necessary. I'd have to find a way to explain it to her.

But how? Remind her that I was a mental basket-case?

I'd have to figure it out later. I didn't want my mom deciding to go see Dad without me, so I said goodbye to Hannah. She smiled and wiggled her fingers at me in a little wave. I decided to take that as a good sign. She didn't seem too upset.

I found my mom at her house, putting on her coat.

"Hi, Leo. I was just about to leave."

"And I'm still going with you."

"Honey, are you sure?" She slid her arms into her coat and adjusted the collar.

"Yes." My instinct to protect my mom was very strong—especially when it came to my dad—but that wasn't why I needed to do this. Or at least, it wasn't the only reason. "Look, if you don't want an audience when you talk to him, that's fine. I'll give you privacy. But I don't want you going alone. And I want to talk to him, too."

"That's fair. But are you sure you can handle... all of this?"

"Yes, I'm sure. I've been out since that first time."

"You've been out with Hannah," Mom said. "And this isn't a trip to the grocery store. This is a lot, Leo. You don't have to."

Her insistence that I didn't have to only hardened my resolve. "Yeah, I kind of do."

She looked at me for a long moment before nodding. "Okay. Let's go."

We went outside and got into her car. She didn't watch me as she drove out of the winery and into town, heading toward the highway. I was glad for that. I hated that it was still so hard for me to leave.

But it was. Really fucking hard, if I was being honest. And it was so much worse without Hannah.

That realization hit me like a punch to the gut. I couldn't keep using Hannah as a crutch to make me functional. That wasn't fair to her. But damn it, I would have been much calmer if she'd have been here. Just her presence was enough to keep me stable.

It was on me, today. And Mom was right. This wasn't a quick trip to the store. Or even a meal in a restaurant. Those things were uncomfortable, but Hannah had helped me through them. This was a trip to see my piece of shit father—in prison, no less.

"Does he know you're coming?" I asked.

Mom shook her head. "No."

That was probably for the best.

We drove in silence for a while. It was about an hour to where Dad was being held. I had a feeling Mom wanted to say something. Or maybe she was worried about me. She kept glancing over like she was about to talk, then closing her mouth again.

"Life with your dad wasn't always terrible," she said, finally breaking the silence.

"Yeah, I know. It wasn't for me, either."

She glanced at me. "It's good to hear you say that. I know he wasn't a good father most of the time."

"No, but... he was sometimes. Honestly, I don't know if that's better or worse. Sometimes I think it would be easier to just hate him."

"I know what you mean," she said. "It's hard to reconcile the good memories I have of him, and us, with the things he's done."

"He must have been a lot different when you got married." I

couldn't imagine my mom choosing to be with the man my father was now.

"We were both different. I was young and so naive. He came into my life and swept me off my feet. Looking back, I think that was the part he enjoyed. He liked the chase. When that was over..." She shrugged.

"Then why get married?" I asked. "Why did he commit to you—on paper, at least—if he didn't want it?"

"Probably expectations," she said. "That was just what you did. Date someone, marry them, start a career, raise a family."

"But that life was never enough for him."

"He wasn't happy being put in charge of Salishan," she said. "But my parents' health kept declining and little by little, he took on more responsibility. I think he felt trapped."

"That's no excuse."

"No, it isn't." She paused for a long moment. "I almost left him when you were little. It was when he'd started seeing Naomi, but I had no idea about that at the time. I just knew he was gone more than he was home, leaving me alone to raise our kids mostly on my own."

"Why didn't you?"

"Fear. I don't like admitting that, but it's the truth. I was afraid of being a single mom. Afraid he'd disappear from your lives completely. And afraid of what would happen to Salishan. Fear is what kept me from leaving him a thousand times over the years. I thought it was better to keep our family together."

"I'm sorry, Mom."

"So often life doesn't turn out the way we think it will." She glanced at me from the corner of her eye. "I think we've both learned that lesson."

"Isn't that the truth."

I thought back on the guy I'd been before. I hardly remembered him. I'd been quiet and easygoing. Star athlete. Lots of friends. A far cry from the deformed recluse I'd become.

No, life hadn't turned out the way I'd though it would.

When we got to our destination, we parked outside the prison—a sprawling complex of concrete buildings surrounded by tall fences and barbed wire. It was so strange to think of my dad being here. How had he let things go to shit so badly? Why hadn't his life been enough? Why throw it all away like this?

I wasn't sure if he'd tell me. But I was going to ask.

We checked in and got visitor badges. Even after being patted down, the guards eyed me, as if I looked like I belonged on the other side of the bars. I kept my head down and let my mom do the talking. Focused on staying calm.

Although now that we were here, I *was* calm. Strangely so. A sense of purpose had once again stolen over me. I was here for a reason: to get some answers out of my father.

A guard led us back to the visiting room. I'd wondered if there would be clear Plexiglas walls, with Dad on a phone on the other side. But here, prisoners were led into the room and allowed to sit with their visitors at a table while several guards watched from the perimeter.

We sat at a table and waited. There was one other prisoner here with a visitor—a young man with a shaved head and tattoos down his arms to his knuckles. He sat with a woman who was probably his wife or girlfriend. They held hands and spoke in soft voices while a guard stood nearby, watching.

The door opened and another guard entered, leading my father.

He looked like shit. But it wasn't the blue prison garb or the handcuffs. His hair had gone almost entirely gray and his skin was sallow. His eyes landed on Mom and he stopped in his tracks before reaching our table.

Then he looked at me.

"Leo?" he asked, his voice filled with awe.

I knew why. He'd probably figured I was a lost cause. That I'd never leave Salishan again. He smiled, his eyes filled with pride. And I hated that his approval could still make me feel good.

"Do you want me to wait outside?" I asked my mom, my voice low.

"No. You can stay."

Dad looked between the two of us as he took his seat. "When they told me I had visitors, you two were the last people I expected to see."

Mom pulled a folder out of her bag and set it on the table. "This is the divorce settlement. You're going to sign it."

He looked down at the folder and before he said a word, I knew he wasn't going to argue. His shoulders sagged, his head bowing forward. The man didn't have any fight left in him.

"All right," he said, not lifting his eyes. "I'll sign."

Mom slid a pen across the table. Her back was stick-straight, her eyes never leaving my father. Dad skimmed the pages and signed or initialed where she'd put markers.

He signed the final page and closed the folder, then pushed it across the table. Mom grabbed it and flipped through every page, checking to make sure it was complete, before putting it back in her bag. "Goodbye, Lawrence."

"For what it's worth," he said as she started to stand, "I'm sorry."

Mom slowly lowered herself back into her chair. Her voice was ice cold. "You're *sorry*?"

Dad nodded.

"If I ever find it within myself to forgive you, it won't be because you apologized, and it certainly won't be for you," Mom said. "It will be for me. I won't sit here and try to console you. It's not my job to make you feel better for your mistakes anymore. You put me through hell—betrayed me in every way imaginable. Do you think signing these papers makes things right? It's the absolute *least* you can do after everything you've done to your family."

"I know. Shannon, I—"

"Don't even say my name," she said. "You don't have that privilege anymore. The only reason I don't regret every moment of the last thirty-five years of my life is that you gave me four beautiful children. And honestly? I hate you more for what you did to them than what you did to me. The only consolation I have is that now you have to live with what you've done. You'll have to spend the rest of your miserable life knowing that you had everything and threw it all away. Now you have nothing, and I have everything."

He watched her, speechless, as she stood and gathered her things.

She met my eyes and I nodded. I needed a minute with him. She seemed to understand. The guard let her out and she left without looking back.

Dad's eyes were on the door.

"Did you expect anything else?" I asked, my voice low.

He shook his head and turned his gaze to me. "No. How long have you been leaving the winery?"

"I'm not here to talk about me."

"That's fine, but Leo, I thought you—"

"I said I'm not here to talk about me." I held his eyes, my expression carefully neutral.

"Then why are you here?" he asked. "To tell me how many things I've done wrong? Believe me, I'm well aware of that."

"It's easy to decide to be penitent after you've been caught."

He leaned back in his chair and rubbed his hands up and down his face. "What do you want?"

"I want answers. The rest of the family doesn't care—or maybe they just don't want to have to be in the same room with you long enough to find out—but I do. I want to know."

"Fine. What do you want to know?"

I'd thought about this for a long time—what I'd ask him if I had the chance. There were so many things. His affair with Naomi Harris. His other children, Grace and Elijah. The latest mistress. I could have asked how many there had been. Had there ever been a time when he'd been faithful to Mom? I could have asked why he hadn't been satisfied with his own family. With us. But those weren't the things I needed to know.

"Why did you try to take Salishan away from Mom?" I asked. "Why go after the land?"

"Because I dedicated my life to that place. I sacrificed my dreams—my career—to run Salishan. I didn't ask for that."

"Don't give me that shit. That has nothing to do with it. Mom offered to buy you out—her original deal was fair—and you came back with a counter that would have left her with nothing. Why? After everything else you did, why go after her land? You hated the winery. Are you really that much of a hateful bastard that you couldn't stand it if she got to keep Salishan?"

He took a deep breath. "No. I know there's no way you'll believe me, but I wasn't trying to hurt your mother."

"Then why?"

He cleared his throat and lowered his voice. "I owe a lot of money, and I don't mean credit cards or to a bank."

"Why? What were you doing?"

"Gambling, mostly," he said. "It started out as just a way to blow off steam. I'd take a road trip, hit up a few casinos. Nothing big. I was under a lot of pressure. Salishan was struggling, and I had other expenses—"

"You mean a second family."

He cleared his throat. "So you do know."

"About Naomi Harris? And Grace and Elijah? Yeah, we know."

"Well, I guess it doesn't matter, now."

"It matters, but that's not why I'm here. How did you go from hitting up a few casinos to growing drugs? It obviously wasn't to pay your youngest son's medical bills. Roland had to do that for you."

"Leo, it's complicated."

"Don't patronize me. You could have settled with Mom, but you didn't. You went after her entire life. And then you put us all in danger with your dumbass drug operation. For what? So you could act like a high roller at some poker tables?"

"They were going to kill me," he hissed. "I gave them everything I had, but it wasn't enough."

"Is that why you're still here? No bail money?"

"Yes."

"Your latest girlfriend didn't want to help?"

"Kristen..." He trailed off, looking away. "She left several months ago."

I stared at him for a long moment. He was barely recognizable. There'd been a time when I'd looked up to this man. When I'd sought his approval. But now, I couldn't even drum up any pity. He'd made so many terrible choices. So many mistakes. Sitting here in front of me was a man who'd lost absolutely everything. His family. His home. His career. His freedom. And he deserved everything that had happened to him.

Maybe there was justice in this world.

"I'm glad you signed the divorce papers," I said, my voice cold. "I didn't want to have to make you."

"Leo..."

"What, Dad?"

"It's good to see you."

I stood. I wasn't going to let him indulge in some father-son bullshit. "Whatever. You fucked up and now you can live with the consequences."

Like my mom had done before me, I walked out without looking back.

18

LEO

*H*annah wasn't here when I got home. I had a text saying she'd gone out for dinner and drinks with *the girls*. That meant Zoe, Brynn, and Amelia. I liked that she got along with my sisters. Amelia wasn't a sister yet, technically, but we all knew Cooper was going to marry her someday.

However, I was worried about how we'd left things. She'd shared things with me, then tried to kiss me, and I'd turned away. When I'd left, she'd seemed fine. But I didn't trust that. My gut was telling me she wasn't.

For now, I sat down at my desk and pulled up the security footage archives. I'd spent the drive home turning over the things my dad had said. Gambling debt. That wasn't good, especially if the people he owed money to knew about Salishan. And Mom. They might decide to come after us for their money. Or use us as leverage to get to Dad.

I'd need to warn Grace, too.

I pinched the bridge of my nose. I'd been worried Dad's arrest wouldn't mean the end. Whoever he'd been working with on that drug deal might still be a problem. Goddamn him. His level of selfishness was staggering. And he'd thought we might have some kind of father-son moment because I'd finally left the winery?

Piece of shit.

I spent some time scanning through the footage, particularly in front of the Big House. I didn't watch the security feeds in their entirety, but I sometimes let them run on a separate screen while I was doing other things, just to get a feel for who was coming and going. And a few weeks ago, I'd noticed a guy wandering around the grounds. He hadn't done anything particularly suspicious, but something about him had tickled my instincts.

Guests wandered around the property all the time. It was one of the reasons people came here, especially when the weather was nice. We gave tours, of course, but people often walked through the main grounds and gardens on their own. Usually it was couples or small groups, but it wasn't unusual for someone to be here alone.

But I had a nagging feeling about this guy. I found the section of the security feed I'd seen before. There he was, outside the Big House. He stood near the parking lot wearing a pair of sunglasses, looking at his phone. Pretty normal behavior.

Then something—or someone—off-camera caught his attention. He looked up, tracked their movement, lifted his phone and took several pictures.

Guests taking photos wasn't unusual either. People did that all the time. But what had he been taking a picture of?

I brought up a different feed—a camera that showed another angle. Found the same date and time. I watched for a few seconds and it felt like my heart jumped into my throat. A woman walked across the bottom of the screen, right where the two camera feeds met, at exactly the same moment the man had taken several pictures.

It was my mom.

From this angle, I couldn't quite see her face, but there was no mistaking her. Some guy had been standing around, watching, and then taken photos of my mother.

Why? Was he a random guest? Had he taken other photos? Had he targeted her specifically? I backed up the footage, trying to track what else he'd done.

I saw him walk near the Big House. He wasn't in a vehicle—maybe he'd parked in town. Had he done that on purpose so his license plate couldn't be tracked?

He went into the Big House. Came out several minutes later. Stood near the parking lot, idly watching his surroundings. Then he'd taken several pictures of my mom.

After that, he'd walked back toward town.

Fuck.

This wasn't good. I didn't know who this guy was, or what connection he might have to my dad, if any. But it didn't seem coincidental that my dad had recently been arrested, owed bad people money, and this guy had been here scoping out his wife. Soon-to-be-ex-wife, but maybe they didn't know that. Or maybe they didn't care.

If this guy had been here before, that might tell me more. I had a hacked version of some facial recognition software. It was powerful stuff. I decided to run the last month's worth of security footage through it to see if that guy had been here before. I isolated the image and started the scan.

I needed to talk to Roland. And figure out how to increase security, especially around Mom. She wasn't going to like it. Maybe I'd have Ben talk to her. He had a knack for that sort of thing, especially where she was concerned.

Before the scan was finished, Hannah came home. She looked adorable in a blue cardigan and vintage Wonder Woman t-shirt. She tossed her purse onto the couch and pulled off her shoes.

"Hey, you're back," she said. "How did it go?"

"He signed the divorce papers."

"Oh good. I'm happy for your mom."

"Me too."

"How was it for you, though?" she asked.

"It sucked, actually," I said. "But it was good that I went."

"Good," she said. "Dinner was fun. Zoe is hilarious. Brynn and Amelia are fun to hang out with too. But I'm telling you, Zoe is basically my spirit animal."

I smiled. "She's pretty cool."

"Yeah, she is." Hannah tucked herself onto the couch, in what had become her corner, pulling a blanket into her lap. "I ate too much, though. I'm so full."

I gazed at her, curled up in the corner of the couch. She was a lot smaller than me. I wanted to pull her into my lap and hold her. Tell her I was sorry for not kissing her. I wanted to tell her the truth—confess how much I wanted her. How I fantasized about her constantly. Saw her in my dreams.

But I couldn't. I had to protect her, even if that meant protecting her from me.

Something was bothering her. I could see it. She nibbled on her bottom lip and her eyes darted around. Was it what had happened between us earlier? Or had something happened while I was gone?

"What's on your mind?" I asked.

"What? Nothing. Why?"

"You look pensive."

"Do I? I guess I do, but you've had a long day. We don't need to do this now."

"Do this? Do what? Now you have to tell me."

She glanced away and took a breath. "Okay... I've had some time to think about this, and I think it's time I move into the other cottage."

It felt like the floor dropped out from under me. The sensation of dread that poured through my veins was ridiculous. The Hummingbird Cottage was a short walk from here. It wasn't like she'd just said she wanted to move back to Seattle. But I hated the thought of her leaving so much, I curled my hands into fists.

She was mine, and I wanted her here.

God, Leo, what the fuck. She's not yours.

"Why?"

"Well, you don't really have room for me here. You've been sleeping on the couch for over a month, which is just silly."

"I told you I don't mind."

"I know, but we talked before about the other guest cottage." She gestured toward the door. "I'll pay your mom rent, that's not a problem. And you can have your space back."

What was I supposed to say to that? She was right. Except...

"No."

"Excuse me?" she asked. "What do you mean, no?"

Holy shit, had I said that out loud? "I mean, no, you shouldn't move over to the other cottage."

"Why not?"

Great question. How are you going to answer that one, Leo? "Because I like having you here."

"You like..." She trailed off, then threw her hands up in the air. "Really, Leo? That's nice of you to say, but I'm getting some seriously mixed messages here."

"I know."

"You do? Lovely. Then what's going on? Are we just friends, or roommates, or..."

Here was my chance. A few words, and I'd friend-zone her for good. It was the right thing to do. She deserved so much better than me.

Tell her. Say it. Do the right thing, even if it hurts.

"No. I don't want to be just friends." I stood, turning away, and ran my fingers through my hair. There went that plan. "This whole thing is fucking killing me, Hannah. I like you. You're basically my every fantasy come true, and you're right here, under my roof. Sleeping in my fucking bed. But I'm a goddamn mess. And you just got out of a shitty relationship. I can't ask you to jump into another one."

"Okay, first of all, my shitty relationship ended long before Jace hit me," she said. "I was afraid to actually leave, but it was over with him a long time ago. And second, you're nothing like Jace."

"You don't understand. My life is a disaster and I don't know if I'll ever be able to fix it."

"It's not as bad as you think. You've been doing so well."

"Sure, when we're together. When you're with me, it's not so bad. But I left with my mom today and I felt like I would have chewed my own arm off to get home. What am I supposed to do, keep you like my little sidekick so I can try to live a normal life? How is that fair to you?"

"Maybe I want to be your little sidekick."

"We both know that's not going to work," I said. "You're going to get sick of being my crutch."

"That's the thing about crutches, though. You don't need them forever. Just until you can walk on your own again."

"What if I can't ever walk on my own?"

She hesitated, her lips parted. "Two months ago, did you think you'd ever leave Salishan?"

"I didn't know."

"But a part of you thought you probably wouldn't, right? Part of you had accepted that."

"Yes."

"But you did. You left."

"Only because you needed me," I said.

"That was just the catalyst. If it hadn't been me, maybe it

would have been something else. The important thing is that you did. And every time you do it again, you get a little closer to that being a normal thing you do."

"I don't think it's ever going to be normal, Hannah. That's my point."

"But my point is that this is a process. You're healing. And yeah, maybe it's hard, and maybe it's slower than you want. But my crutches analogy stands. You use them now and soon you won't need them anymore."

"It's not just leaving Salishan. I'm not okay. I have panic attacks and an unhealthy obsession with security. It feels like needles when people touch me and—"

"Wait." She held up a hand. "It feels like needles when someone touches you?"

"Yeah."

"Oh my god, Leo, I'm so sorry. I didn't realize."

"No, not you. It doesn't happen when you touch me."

"Really?"

Fuck, why was I telling her all this? This was the opposite of what I should be doing. I needed to keep her out, not let her in.

But I'd already said it. "Yes, really. People touching me is jarring. It's almost like I'm overly sensitive or something. It hurts, so I avoid it. I can handle brief touches from certain people. But when you touch me..."

"What?" she asked, her voice soft.

I closed my eyes. "It feels good."

A heartbeat later, her arms slid around my waist and she rested her head on my chest. Her body nestled against me, so warm and comforting. I leaned my head down to rest my cheek against the top of her head, and wrapped my arms around her.

Well, shit. This wasn't what I'd meant to do. But god, it felt good.

"I'm a mess, Hannah," I said softly. "You don't even know the half of it."

"I know you are. But I'm kind of a mess, too."

I wasn't ready for this. For a relationship. Hannah deserved a man who was whole. Not a broken shell. But I couldn't resist her. Couldn't resist this. It felt too fucking good.

And would that be so bad? To have something that felt good for once?

I pulled her close again, wrapping my arms around her. Breathed in her scent. "Please stay with me. Don't go."

"I'll stay on one condition."

"What's that?"

"You stop sleeping on the couch."

"I'm not making *you* sleep on the couch."

She laughed, her body vibrating against me. "No, dork. I mean sleep in your room with me. The bed is huge. We can both sleep in there."

She had no idea how tempting that was. Or how terrifying.

"I'm not trying to get in your pants," she said, pulling back to look up at me again. "I just mean if we're both going to live here, we should be comfortable. If we can't be, then it's not going to work."

I was saying yes to a long list of things I should be saying no to. But I didn't think I could deny Hannah anything when she was pressed against me like this. It was almost euphoric. I hadn't felt this good in... I had no idea how long.

"Okay, I'll stop sleeping on the couch. Is that all? You'll stay?"

"Yes. I'll stay."

19

HANNAH

The bed moved slightly, and I blinked my eyes open. Morning light peeked through the blinds, casting a soft glow. The bed moved again, and I held my breath.

Oh my god, was he actually in here?

Ostensibly, Leo had started sleeping in his room with me. But for the past few nights, he'd gone to bed well after I had, and been up before I'd awoken.

I carefully turned over. If he was still asleep, I didn't want to wake him.

There he was, in all his beautiful, bearded glory.

He was dressed in a long-sleeved shirt—as usual—but surprisingly, he wasn't turned away from me. He was on his back, his right arm stretched out, almost as if he were reaching for me.

Of course, he wasn't. He was asleep. But his warm body beckoned to me. I wanted to tuck myself next to him. Curl around him and breathe him in.

Would he let me? I wasn't sure—and wasn't sure if I wanted to deal with the rejection if he pulled away.

I decided to take the chance anyway.

Lifting the covers so I wouldn't get tangled, I scooted closer. The sheets near him were warm. I moved past his arm and snuggled next to his body, gently resting my head where his shoulder met his chest.

He inhaled a sharp breath and his body stiffened. I slipped my arm across his stomach—I'd hugged him around the waist before—and nestled against him, almost afraid to look up.

As he exhaled, his body didn't just relax. It melted. He groaned softly, a low noise in his throat, and wrapped his right arm around me. His muscles clenched and released, and he rested his cheek against the top of my head.

I closed my eyes in bliss. Neither of us said anything, but we didn't need to. I stretched my top leg across his so I could get closer. His arm flexed in response, tightening me against him.

I was fully awake now, my lady parts singing. With a deep breath to inhale that insanely masculine scent, I opened my eyes.

The sheets were down below his waist, and there was a sliver of skin showing between his shirt and pajama pants. It felt almost scandalous to see it. He was always so careful to keep his body covered, seeing a glimpse of skin was exhilarating.

Not just skin. A hint of dark hair, right in the center.

Oh good fucking god. Leo had a happy trail.

I would have given just about anything to trace my fingers through that delicious little patch of body hair. He was so relaxed. So calm. There wasn't an ounce of tension in his body. Maybe I could just try...

With painful slowness, I moved my hand across the waistband of his pants. Nibbled my lip as my fingers found skin. It was the tiniest brush of contact, but Leo shivered.

He *shivered* at my touch.

My heart sped up and heat rushed between my legs. It was all I could do to keep from dry-humping him like an overly excited puppy. Forcing myself to stay calm and move slowly, I spread my fingers across his skin.

Leo growled, his chest vibrating against my cheek. His arm flexed, like hot steel around me, clamping my body against his.

His coarse patch of hair tickled my fingertips. How far did it extend? What would he do if I kept going? Slipped my hand up his shirt?

Or down his pants?

I could slide my hand into those adorable pajama pants and wrap my fingers around his cock. I salivated at the thought of my hand pumping him. My mouth around him. What a rush it would be to make him come. To feel him let go for me. I'd swallow every bit of it and then beg him to fuck me senseless as soon as he was hard again.

But I had a feeling I'd need to coax him into it. Turning my face slightly, I pressed my lips against his neck. His chin lifted, tilting his jaw to the side ever so slightly. Giving me access. Inviting me in.

Oh my god, yes.

I kissed his neck again, his beard prickling my skin. His chest rose and fell with a deep breath and he traced his hand up and down my back, another low groan in his throat.

I glanced down the length of his body, to the bulge in his pants. Licked my lips. Daring to explore a little further, I slipped the tips of my fingers beneath his waistband. It was a tiny movement, almost nothing at all. But his body reacted, his hips lifting.

Noise blared from the bedside table—the obnoxious techno music I used as an alarm—and we both jerked at the sound.

Fuck.

His arm dropped and I rolled over to turn it off, severing contact.

I felt the absence of his warm body as I fumbled for my

stupid phone. It took me three tries to turn off the alarm while the harsh electronic sounds mocked me.

"I'm so sorry." I rolled back over, but I already knew the moment had passed. "I'm meeting your mom for breakfast and I didn't want to be late."

He'd pulled his shirt down—no more tantalizing peek at his happy trail. But he tilted his face—not quite enough that I'd see him straight on—and smiled. "It's okay. I needed to get up anyway."

I was torn between the intense desire to Velcro myself to him —scars be damned—and the need to get up and get ready for breakfast. I wasn't sure why Shannon had asked me to meet her, but the last thing I wanted was to be late.

Reaching over with my foot, I brushed my toes against his leg. "You're nice to snuggle with."

"Am I?"

"Yeah. Who would have thought Mister Broody-Don't-Touch-Me would be so cuddly?"

He let out a soft laugh. "Thanks, I think."

I wiggled my toes against him again. "You're welcome."

"It felt really good..."

My heart lit up like a sparkler, although I could hear his unspoken *but*. It felt really good, *but*... But what, I wasn't sure. But we couldn't take it further? But he wouldn't take his clothes off? But he wasn't ever going to let me close enough to his face to kiss him properly?

I didn't know, but I didn't have time to figure it out right now. I had set the alarm as a just-in-case safety measure, thinking I'd probably be up before it went off. I needed to get moving so I wouldn't be late meeting his mom.

"It felt good to me, too."

～

I HUGGED my coat around me as I walked across the winery grounds to Shannon's house. Clear skies overnight had dropped the temperature below freezing, leaving a coating of frost all over the ground. I wondered if we'd get snow this winter. It had been a long time since I'd lived somewhere that snowed regularly. It sounded nice. A great excuse to stay in bed, cozied up with Leo.

God, that man.

My hand still tingled with the memory of his skin. That delicious patch of body hair. Who knew what would have happened if my stupid alarm hadn't ruined everything. He'd wanted me. I'd felt him responding, felt his walls coming down.

The frustrating interruption simply hardened my determination to try again.

Shannon's house was a short walk from the main area of the winery, set apart just enough to give her privacy from the guests. It loomed over the landscape, looking more like a bed and breakfast than a single person's house.

Of course, she hadn't always lived here alone. She'd raised her family here. And from what Leo had told me, her parents had lived there too, until they'd passed away.

I walked up the steps to the wide porch. What must it have been like to grow up here? From the outside, it looked like paradise. Beautiful surroundings. Acres of vineyards, with the mountains in the background. A town small enough to still feel safe. A big house with plenty of space. Room for children to roam and play.

But I also knew it hadn't been as idyllic as the setting. Shannon had been through a lot in her life, as had her kids. I could sympathize with that to a degree. Not that I could compare my ill-fated relationship with Jace to everything Leo's father had put them through. But I knew what it was like to feel trapped, and I suspected she'd spent many years feeling that way.

I knocked and a few seconds later, Shannon answered, wearing a blue apron over her t-shirt and jeans.

"Hi, Hannah," she said with a smile, stepping aside to let me in. "Thanks for coming over."

"Thanks for having me."

Leo's mom was beautiful, with streaks of silver in her hair that sparkled in the light and tiny lines around her eyes that crinkled with her smile. I liked Shannon, and I desperately wanted her to like me. I'd seen her with Zoe and Amelia, and felt a brush of envy at their closeness. When we'd met, I'd been such a mess—black and blue from the man who'd hit me —and I wondered if she'd ever see me as being good enough for Leo.

I went inside and took off my coat, hanging it up on a hook near the door.

Shannon waved me into the kitchen. "The dining table is so big. It's nice for when everyone comes over, but it's cozier in here."

Her kitchen was bright and cheerful, with dark wood cabinets and light gray countertops. It was dated in a charming way. The appliances weren't new and there were dull spots where bits of wood looked worn from years of use. She had vintage tea towels hanging from a rack and a cupboard with glass doors displayed a collection of tea cups on one side, wine glasses on the other.

She'd set out breakfast on a round table in a nook next to the window. A basket of blueberry muffins, still steaming, sat next to a butter dish. There were scrambled eggs and a plate piled with bacon, plus a stack of toast and a bowl of sliced fruit.

"I always make too much food," she said, gesturing at the table. It was probably enough for at least four, if not more. "But it's fine. At least one of my boys will wind up eating the leftovers. Probably Cooper. Or Chase, if he wanders over here first."

"It looks amazing."

"Thank you. Can I get you tea, or coffee?"

I sat down at the table. "I like both, so whatever you're having is fine."

"Tea it is, then."

She brought over two mismatched tea cups and a teapot. There was already a little basket of tea bags on the table. I chose one and she poured hot water for me.

My tummy tingled with nerves and I nibbled on my lip as she sat down. I'd spent time with Shannon before, but always with Leo. This was just the two of us, and I didn't know why she'd asked to see me. For all I knew, she was about to very sweetly ask me to get out of her son's life forever.

God, I hoped not.

"You're probably wondering why I asked you here," she said.

"Yes, actually."

She smiled. "I was looking at your website the other day. You do beautiful work."

My website? So it wasn't about Leo? "Oh... thank you."

"I've been thinking that Salishan needs a new look. We've been using the same logo for years, and our website needs refreshing. I thought maybe you could help us with that."

This was about work? Relief washed over me. "I can definitely do that. Do you have anything specific in mind?"

"I'm not sure," she said. "Graphics aren't my strength. I'm just thinking something simple and clean. Elegant. Something that signifies that this is a new chapter for us."

"A new chapter. I like that."

She dunked her tea bag a few times, then took it out and set it on the saucer. "The last time we updated our branding was probably... ten years ago? Maybe more. It's definitely time."

I had a feeling it wasn't just the passage of time that had prompted her to pursue this change. Her husband was out of the picture, her divorce about to be finalized. Maybe this was one of the ways she was moving forward.

"So, full disclosure," I said. "I have a packed client list right now, so I can't get to it immediately. But I'd really love to work on this. If you can wait just a little while, I'll come up with a few concepts and get your feedback. Once we hit on something you like, we can take it from there."

"That sounds great. It's not an urgent project. We can certainly wait until your schedule opens up."

"Great, thank you."

She blew on her tea and took a sip. "How's winery life treating you?"

That prickle of anxiety was back. Things with Leo were so tenuous. I wasn't sure what it all meant. But all I could do was be honest. "It's wonderful. I love it here."

Shannon smiled. "That's good to hear."

"Thanks for letting me stay."

"Of course. Although I should be thanking you."

"Why?"

She paused, glancing down at her tea. "I don't suppose it would surprise anyone that of all my children, I worry about Leo the most."

It wasn't surprising at all. "I can understand that."

"I never expected parenting adults to be so challenging." She laughed softly, shaking her head. "In some ways, it's harder than when they were little. And parenting those four when they were small wasn't easy."

"I bet it was exhausting."

"It was. Wonderful, and exhausting. But now... I can't fix things for them anymore. When they're little, everything is simple. If they get hurt, it's mostly skinned elbows and knees.

You clean them up, give them a bandage, and send them on their way."

"And now their hurts need more than bandages."

"Yes, they do," she said. "I haven't really thanked you for everything you've done for Leo."

My cheeks warmed. "I don't know that I've done all that much."

"You have. Since you've been here, I've seen him smile more than I have in years. I can't possibly thank you enough for that."

"He's always been a good friend to me. I'm just trying to do the same."

"That's priceless, Hannah. Thank you."

We talked a little more about ideas for Salishan's branding while we ate breakfast. The food was delicious, and I was stuffed by the time we moved to the other room. She brought us more tea, and we settled onto the couch in her living room.

"Would it be too much of a cliché if I showed you pictures from when Leo was little?" she asked.

I had to stifle a gasp. Photos of a young Leo? Yes, please. "I'd love to see pictures."

Shannon got a leather-bound photo album from a bookcase and brought it to the couch. She set the heavy book in her lap and I scooted closer so I could see.

"He's going to grumble at me for showing you," she said, flipping the pages. "There he is. Baby Leo."

A chubby blue-eyed baby, dressed in nothing but a blue t-shirt and a diaper, smiled from the page.

"That's Leo? He was so cute."

"He really was." She flipped a few more pages. "Here he is with Roland around the time Cooper was born. Leo was two."

"Aw, look at them."

She pointed out more as she went through the book and I

saw Leo go from a baby to a toddler to a boy. He was always smiling, his blue eyes bright.

"What was he like when he was little?" I asked. "Quiet and serious?"

"No." Shannon traced her finger down a page. "He was quieter than his brothers, but that's not hard when one of your brothers is Cooper."

I laughed. "That's true."

"Leo was easy," she said with a small shrug. "He was laid-back and happy most of the time. Almost never got in trouble. Did well in school. Loved sports. Had lots of friends."

She turned to the back of the book and pulled out a loose photo. I immediately recognized teenage Roland and Cooper. Brynn was on the end, with Cooper's arm around her shoulders —just a little girl.

In between Roland and Cooper was Leo.

I stared at the fresh, young face. It looked exactly like him, and nothing like him all at once. Short hair. Smooth, square jaw. Wide smile.

"Leo was about seventeen here. Roland would have been nineteen. Cooper fifteen, and Brynn was around ten." She paused. "This was the boy I sent off to basic training, about a year after this picture. So young and innocent."

Sudden tears pricked my eyes and I swallowed the lump in my throat. He looked so different. But it wasn't the fact that his face was now scarred, or he'd grown out his hair and beard. His eyes weren't the same. The eyes of this Leo were bright blue and clear. The eyes of a young man who had no idea the things he'd soon face.

"It must have been hard when he was injured," I said.

"The worst part was not knowing what was happening," she said. "We heard he'd been hurt. Then we were told he might not make it. But we weren't given any details. It was weeks before I was able to fly out and see him."

"That's so awful."

"It was. It was such a relief when he was finally able to come home. Although I still don't know how it happened."

"You don't know how he was injured?"

"I know there was an explosion, but that's all. He's never talked about it."

"Wow."

"After his accident, I thought I might never see him again," she said. "And then he came home and I started to realize I was still in danger of losing him, just in a different way. But now..."

I hesitated, waiting to see if she would finish.

"Now I have hope for him again," she said, her voice soft. She took a deep breath, and turned to look at me. "I'm sorry, I'm getting all nostalgic on you."

"I don't mind. Thanks for sharing these pictures."

"My pleasure." She gazed at the photo of her smiling children. "It's fun to reminisce sometimes, even if it's bittersweet."

We looked through more photos as we finished our tea. She showed me older pictures—her grandparents, who had founded Salishan. Her parents, who had continued the family business. I soaked it all in, loving every second. My parents had kept some photos from my childhood, but most were on old CDs or USB drives. Being in the military, we'd moved every few years, and my mom had become an expert at minimalism. Shannon's collection of family photo albums seemed like a decadent luxury. An intimate glimpse into this family that I was quickly becoming enamored with.

Eventually we finished our tea and I helped Shannon put the books away. She thanked me for coming and hugged me goodbye. It felt like I'd won the lottery. Had Shannon Miles really accepted me? It seemed that at least for now, she had.

I paused on the front porch outside. Spending the morning with Shannon made me think about my own parents. I hadn't tried to contact them since I'd told them I moved. Maybe I should try to talk to them, instead of just an email. It would be nice to hear their voices again.

Before I could talk myself out of it, I took out my phone and called my mom. She was most likely to answer.

One ring. Two. I waited through two more before her voice-mail picked up.

"Hi, you've reached Josephine Tate. Please leave a message."

Beep.

I hesitated for a second. "Um, hi, Mom. It's Hannah. I just... wanted to call and see how you and Dad are doing. Give me a call when you have time, okay? Thanks, Mom. Bye."

I ended the call, wondering if she was busy, or just didn't want to take my call.

Chase walked up the porch steps as I put my phone back in my pocket. Brynn's husband was dressed in a worn brown jacket, with a dark t-shirt, jeans, and work boots.

He smiled when he noticed me. "Oh hey, Hannah. How's it going?"

"Pretty good." I glanced at his shirt. It read *Married AF* in big block letters. "Nice shirt. Did Brynn get that for you?"

He tugged on the hem and looked down at it. "Nah. Cooper did."

"Cooper bought you that shirt?"

"Yeah," he said, stretching the word out, like he had no idea why I would question it. "He bought himself one, too. You know, for later."

"Oh. Cute."

He grinned. "I know, right? Is Shannon home?"

"Yeah. We just finished breakfast."

His eyes lit up. "Are there leftovers?"

I grinned at him. "Yep. Lots. I think she's expecting you."

He did a fist pump. "Yes. Shannon's such a good cook. I married into the best family. You should really consider marrying Leo. I know he's kind of broody and doesn't like... well, anything. But this family is awesome."

I stared at him, my mouth partially open. "Um..."

He winced. "Sorry. That was probably... forget it. I'll just go inside now."

I moved out of his way and went down the porch steps. Had he really said I should consider marrying Leo? We weren't even dating. Were we? What were we doing?

That was a very good question. Under normal circumstances, I wouldn't have been too concerned with putting a label on things at this point. But these weren't normal circumstances. Leo wasn't a guy I'd started dating a month or two ago. I was living with him and sharing his bed. But interestingly, we weren't in any sort of physical relationship.

Yet. That was going to change. Soon, if I had anything to say about it.

20

LEO

I waited until Hannah left to get in the shower, so amped up I thought I might explode. Did she have any idea what she did to me? Just a little bit of contact—her body cuddled against mine, her hand brushing my skin—and I was ready to fire off like a rocket. I needed to take care of this before she came back. This hard-on was killing me.

Hot water washed over me, streaming through my hair, down my face. I rubbed my beard, wondering if I should trim it. It had gotten thick lately.

I touched my neck, where Hannah had kissed me. The sensation of her lips was still there, branded on my skin. I could practically feel her body pressed against me. Her head on my shoulder. Her leg draped over mine. The way she'd teased the skin across my stomach. Played with the hair that disappeared beneath my pants.

Picturing that—and much more—I grabbed my solid erection. Stroked up and down a few times. I was already primed and ready to go. This wouldn't take long. I imagined Hannah in my bed, her clothes on the floor. Hard, pink nipples wet from my mouth. Smooth skin. Her tattoos painting a picture across her body. Did she have ink on her thighs? In that little dip inside one of her hips?

My cock throbbed in my hand as I stroked faster. Squeezed harder. I closed my eyes and indulged in the fantasies I'd had every day since I'd seen her in person for the first time.

Hannah, her hands playfully bound, stretched above her head, tied to the bed frame. Her legs tipping open, her pussy wet and ready for me. I'd sink my cock inside her. Go as deep as I could. Fuck her while her tits bounced, her cheeks flushed pink, and her eyes rolled back in pleasure.

Then I'd turn her over, lifting her ass into the air. Grab her hips and fuck her from behind. I'd watch my cock as it slid in and out, glistening wet. While her pussy tightened and clenched as she came all over me.

With one hand against the tile to brace myself, I jerked my cock hard. Felt the exquisite pressure build as my balls tightened, on the brink of release. Closing my eyes, I gave in to the fantasy. Stroked my hard length to the image of fucking Hannah until she panted my name.

My dick pulsed as I started to come, the first thick spurts mingling with the water. Groaning, I stroked it out fast. My muscles clenched and released, the intense pressure rolling through my entire body.

I leaned against the tile while I caught my breath, feeling both better and worse. Better because at least I wasn't worried I'd come in my pants the next time Hannah brushed up against me. Worse because this wasn't enough.

But I didn't know if I could ever have what I really wanted.

Hannah disarmed me in ways that were terrifying. She made it so easy to let my guard down—too easy. Although her touch didn't hurt—it felt better than anything I could possibly imagine —I hadn't let her anywhere near my scarred side. And I wasn't sure if I could.

She'd never seen me. Not really. I'd made sure of that. I always did, and not just with her. The only people who'd seen my scarred body were doctors and nurses, and the artist who'd done my tattoos. I'd never shown anyone else.

It wasn't just my appearance, although that was enough to make me question everything I'd done in the last week. Touching her. Holding her. Asking her to stay. Sleeping in bed with her.

The problem was, I was at war with myself. With what my body—and my heart—wanted, and all the things I knew I couldn't give her in return.

AFTER I'D SHOWERED and dressed, I walked across the property to the Big House to see Roland. I needed to talk to him about Dad, and the things I'd found in the security footage.

He was upstairs in his office. Unlike Zoe's office, Roland's was tidy and uncluttered. He had a large desk with dual monitors and several framed photos of Zoe and Hudson.

He looked up when I walked in. "Hey, Leo. How's Hannah?"

Hearing her name made me think of her body next to mine. I cleared my throat. "She's good. Having breakfast with Mom. Do you know anything about that?"

"I do, actually. Mom wants to talk to her about redoing Salishan's logo and branding package. The website, too."

A surge of pride filled me. I might have even puffed out my chest a little. "That's great."

"Yeah, she and Zoe were talking about it the other day. We looked through her website. She's talented. So, what's up?"

I shut the door and took a seat across from him. "I went with Mom to see Dad yesterday."

"She told me. How'd you get her agree to let you go with her?

She didn't even tell me she was going until after you two got back."

"I don't think she meant to tell me, either. Seemed like it kind of slipped out. But I'm glad it did."

"How was it?"

I didn't want to talk about how hard it had been to leave the winery without Hannah. So I focused on Dad. "He looked like shit. I'm sure Mom told you he signed the divorce papers."

"Thank fuck. I swear, I don't think he could have made things worse for her if he'd tried."

"He might have, actually."

"Oh shit. What now?"

"The land grab in his counterproposal to the divorce, and the drugs," I said. "Dad wasn't trying to fund his retirement. He was trying to pay off gambling debt."

"That explains a lot, actually. I couldn't figure out the drugs thing. Why do something so stupid?"

"Desperation. But I'm worried these guys are going to come after us—more specifically, Mom—either to put pressure on Dad, or to try to get their money out of her."

"Jesus."

"I think they're already watching her. There's security footage from about three weeks ago that shows a guy walk onto the property, wander around a little, and then take some pictures. I'm pretty sure he was taking pictures of Mom."

"Do you know who he was?"

"No, but I ran the footage through facial recognition and got a match. He's been here at least three times. Always alone. Always parks somewhere off property."

"To keep us from recording his license plate?"

"That was my thought."

"Fuck," Roland said. "Wait, how do you have facial recognition software?"

I shook my head. "You don't want to know."

He narrowed his eyes, but apparently decided not to push that particular issue. "We need to go to Agent Rawlins with this."

"Right. I'll give him what I have, but I want to see about increasing security. Especially around Mom. I wish I could get her a bodyguard."

"Yeah, but she'd fight you on that. Although..."

"What?"

"What if we get Ben to do it?"

I'd been thinking someone armed, but Ben wasn't a bad idea. I had a feeling Mom wouldn't protest having him around more. "Yeah, good. That's a start."

"I'll give Chase a heads-up so he can watch out for Brynn. I can call Naomi and Grace, too. They need to know. What else?"

"I'll add some cameras to the blind spots. And go through past footage. See if I find anyone, or anything else that looks suspicious."

"Good. I'll call Rawlins, but can you send him what you have so far?"

"I will as soon as I get back to my place."

"Thanks, man." Roland paused, pressing the tips of his fingers together. "Fair warning. Zoe's going to invite you and Hannah over to our place for dinner. I'm not saying you have to come. I know it's still hard for you. But if you say no, I can't be held responsible for what Zoe decides to do."

I laughed, but it was relief, not anxiety, that filled me. I could actually do this. Going to dinner at your brother's house was something normal people did every day. A couple of months ago, I wouldn't have considered it. Hell, they wouldn't have bothered inviting me. But now? It didn't sound half bad, especially if Hannah was with me.

"Thanks, but Zoe won't have to bring out the big guns. I think I can handle dinner."

"Yeah?"

I nodded.

"That's great, man. You seem like you're doing a lot better."

"I'm getting there, I guess."

"Good." He took a deep breath. "Thanks for the heads-up about Dad."

"No problem." I stood. "I'll talk to you later."

I went downstairs and quickly slipped through the lobby and out the front doors. I was planning to go straight home, but I noticed a familiar face coming up the steps. My half-sister, Grace.

"Hey," I said.

"Hey, Leo."

"Here to see Brynn?"

"Yeah, we're meeting for lunch later. But I'm off today, so I came down early."

I wanted to let her know about Dad and warn her to be careful. But standing out here didn't seem like the best place to have this conversation.

And this could be a chance to connect with Grace a little more. She'd become good friends with Brynn, but I hadn't really spent any time with her one-on-one.

Of course, I didn't spend time with many people. I figured I should probably work on that.

"Do you want to grab some coffee?"

"Sure, that would be great." She raised her eyebrows and pointed toward the Big House. "Here? Or..."

I took a deep breath. I needed to be able to do this. "No, I meant at Ridge Coffee."

"Okay. I'd love to."

Ridge Coffee was a short walk from Salishan. My fingers twitched with the impulse to text Hannah to see if she could come, or meet us there. But she was probably still having breakfast with my mom. I didn't want to interrupt. And I needed to get used to venturing out, whether or not Hannah was with me.

I held the door for Grace as we went inside. The décor was cozy, with soft lighting, a few overstuffed chairs, and several round tables. I'd been in here with Hannah before, so it had a certain familiarity. That seemed to help. Plus, it was blessedly empty—just one customer sitting with their laptop.

We ordered coffee and chose a table near the back. I sat facing out, the wall behind me.

"Are you okay?" Grace asked.

I let out a breath and unclenched my fists. "Yeah, sorry. I'm still getting used to this."

"That's okay. It seems like you're doing pretty well."

"I guess. We're a block away and I already can't stop thinking about going back."

"That sucks. Let me know if you need to go."

"Thanks."

She took a sip of her coffee. "I heard you saw Lawrence."

It wasn't surprising to hear her refer to our father by his first name. Dad had been in and out of Grace's life—mostly out, especially in recent years.

"Yeah, I did. It was... interesting."

"Is it bad that I hope he looked terrible?"

I laughed. "No. And he did look terrible."

"He's such an asshole," she said. "I thought he was bad before I knew about you guys. But now? I never in a million years thought I'd wish prison on anyone. But he deserves it."

"He does. Speaking of, I found out more about what he's been into. Gambling—the illegal kind, I think—and he owes a lot of money to some bad people."

"That's not good."

"No, it's not. Have you noticed anyone following you, or your mom? Driving by your house or anything like that? Maybe taking pictures?"

Her brow furrowed. "No, I don't think so."

"Good. I don't want to freak you out or make you worry unnecessarily. Just... be careful. Be on the lookout for people who might be following you."

"I will. And I'll talk to my mom about it, too."

"Thanks."

She lifted her coffee to take a sip and I noticed her ring. She'd said she was engaged, but none of us had ever met her fiancé. In fact, I wasn't sure if I'd ever heard his name. I knew he was out of the picture for some reason. She'd mentioned waiting for him to come home, but I didn't know why. I'd always wondered if he was military.

"Do you mind if I ask about him?" I gestured to her engagement ring. "Is he in the military?"

Glancing down, she stretched out her fingers. "No, he's not in the military. He's in prison."

Whoa. I hadn't expected that answer. "Oh shit. Sorry. I didn't mean to pry."

"It's okay." She closed her fist and drew her hands down into her lap. "It's just hard to talk about Asher."

"Fair enough." I was curious what her fiancé had done to land in prison—and equally curious as to why Grace still wore his ring. But I was smart enough to see that she didn't want to talk about it. I understood the need to keep some things to yourself all too well. "So how's Elijah?"

She smiled, her eyes shining with gratitude at the change of subject. "He's doing great. Growing fast. He misses you guys. I need to bring him out here again soon."

We drank our coffee and chatted about our littlest brother. He wanted to be a firefighter, and he'd taken to wearing black boots and a raincoat everywhere.

After we finished, I walked her back to Salishan. As soon as we passed the entrance, I felt calmer. It was fucking frustrating.

But I had gone, and it had been my idea. Sure, it had been a short walk away, to a place I'd been before. But I figured I could count that as a win, even if I'd been half-distracted by an inexplicable desire to hide the entire time.

Maybe there was a chance I could actually get better.

21

HANNAH

$\mathcal{L}$eo wasn't home when I got back from breakfast with his mom. So I went out to run some errands in town. Afterward, I came back and got to work on my backlog. I was excited to clear my schedule so I could get started on the logo for Salishan.

I was thrilled that Shannon had asked me to work on this. Creating a branding package was one of my favorite things to do. And the idea that she trusted me to take this on gave me a serious case of the warm fuzzies.

When Leo came home a short time later, he gave me a friendly half-smile and pulled up his office chair next to me. And I couldn't get over how right this felt.

You should really consider marrying Leo.

Chase's words echoed in my mind. Thinking about marriage was the dumbest thing. I wasn't sure if we were actually a couple. We hadn't even kissed yet. Marriage was a long way off.

But this? Living and working side-by-side? I could get used to this.

It was comfortable. Easy. I loved sharing space with Leo.

We'd always been good friends, and the transition from an online relationship to the real world had been seamless.

Maybe we weren't a couple, exactly. Not yet. But something was happening. I'd felt it the other day when I'd hugged him. It had been stronger this morning when we'd cuddled in bed. I wanted Leo, there was no doubt about that.

The problem was, he was closed off. He had so many defenses. I didn't think he was shying away from me because he didn't want me. No man growled like a predator just from hugging a woman he only liked platonically.

I glanced at him from the corner of my eye. From this angle, none of his scars were visible. Just the soft glow of his monitors lighting his face. His hair was tucked behind his ear, which was unusual. Typically, it hung down to cover more of his face. His beard was full and thick—and so very, very tempting.

He caught me looking. His eyes flicked toward me, meeting mine, and I didn't look away. I held his gaze for a few more seconds, trying to read him.

What is it you want, Leo?

His brow furrowed, his expression disarmingly sexy. The tension was killing me, knotting me up inside, like a coiled spring. Did he feel it too?

He looked away, clicking a few things with his mouse, and I realized something. He wasn't going to make a move. Not now. Maybe not ever. That defensive wall he kept between himself and the world was too strong. He was so used to hiding behind it, it was as if even he didn't know how to get around it anymore.

Here I was, looking in from the other side. Maybe I needed to be the one to try to find a door—a way in.

Or maybe I'd just make one.

I got up and put my empty mug in the kitchen, then peeked out at him. He was still at his desk, but I had a feeling he wasn't as absorbed in his work as he appeared. He cast glances at my monitor and chair. But when he reached down to adjust himself in his pants, I couldn't take it anymore. I was ready to pounce.

He swiveled his chair around as I walked toward him. "Are you—"

Before he could stop me, I climbed into his lap, straddling him. He leaned away, his arms held up, palms out.

If I was doing this, I was going all in. I pulled my shirt off and dropped it on the floor, leaving me in just my black bra.

"Holy shit," he breathed. "What are you doing?"

"Distracting you with my boobs."

At the word *boobs*, his eyes went to my chest, but he quickly looked away. "What?"

"It's okay, Leo," I said, my voice soothing. I arched my back a little, pressing my boobs closer to his face. "I want you to look."

I traced my finger down the edge of one cup, pulling it closer to my nipple. He made a strangled sound.

"Why are you..." He trailed off, his eyes glued to my chest as I pulled my bra cup lower.

"I told you. I'm distracting you."

"Why?"

"Because I want you to let me kiss you."

He looked up.

"And touch your face."

"But—"

"Eyes down, Leo."

"Gigz—"

Oh I was Gigz, now, was I? He wanted to make this difficult? Fine. I pushed my bra strap down my shoulder, loosening the cup. His gaze shot back to my chest and I went in for the kill, popping my nipple out of the top of the lace.

"Oh my god."

"Do you want to touch me?" I whispered.

He growled, low in his throat. I could feel his cock harden against me through our clothes.

"Go ahead. I want you to."

His hand came up, but he paused, so I rolled my hips, grinding into his dick.

"Oh fuck," he said, his eyes closing. His hand cupped my breast, his palm pressing against my erect nipple.

I wanted to cry out with joy. My nerve endings fired, so sensitive just this simple touch took my breath away. He had so much power over my body. What was I going to do if we ever got naked?

My spontaneous plan was working. He was totally absorbed in my tits—for the moment, at least. I moved in closer, tilting my head, and pressed my wet lips to the right corner of his mouth.

His body tensed, but I squeezed my thighs to press myself against his cock. The feel of his beard scratching my face was better than I'd imagined—rough and masculine. His lips barely moved; he was hardly kissing me back. But he didn't pull away or make me stop, either.

Slowly, I rolled my hips, dry-humping him just a little. He growled again and his mouth finally twitched, pressing lightly against mine. I didn't let up, adding tongue to my attack. I teased his lips while I slid the other bra strap down, baring my other breast.

His left hand—the hand he never used—cupped my ass and squeezed. I smiled against his mouth, still kissing the right corner. Yes. God, yes.

He gently massaged my breast and his tongue darted out to meet mine. I held one hand over his, keeping it firmly on me, and with my other, I reached for the scarred side of his face.

My fingers brushed the rippled skin and he jerked away.

"Shh." I ground into his cock, my hand hesitating just inches from the left side of his face. "This feels so good, Leo. Please let me touch you."

I bit my bottom lip as he met my eyes. My cheeks were warm and the insistent pressure between my legs begged to be sated. If this didn't end with an orgasm, I'd be taking care of business by myself later. But mostly, I desperately wanted him to let me do this. To trust me enough to let me in.

He gave me the smallest of nods. Gently, I laid my palm against the left side of his face.

His skin was puckered and hardened in places, not smooth and soft like the rest of him. There were ridges and ripples from his hairline down his neck. His beard covered some of the damage, but it was patchy where the skin had been burned, and his lips didn't quite close on that side.

He closed his eyes, his body shuddering, as I softly brushed his hair back. I stroked the sides of his face and ran my fingers through his hair. His hands moved down to my hips, his grip on me gentle.

Gigz jumped up onto the desk, meowing, but I ignored her. Leo was putty in my hands. He rubbed my hips and lower back while I pressed my fingertips into his scalp. Ran my hands down his face and neck, caressing him. He groaned, his eyes still closed.

How long had it been since he'd been touched like this?

I leaned in closer and pressed my lips to his, starting on the right. His mouth responded, no hesitation this time. He brushed his tongue against mine while his hands slid down to cup my ass.

Moaning softly into his mouth, I moved my hips, rubbing myself against him. He growled again—fuck, that noise he made was sexy—and pressed me into his cock.

I needed all of this and more. With my fingers threaded through his hair, his beard rubbing against my face, I tilted my head to kiss him from the front. No more corner of the mouth. No more avoiding his left side. I planted my lips fully against his and parted them, inviting him in for more.

In that instant, everything changed.

Leo sat up straighter, one hand gripping my ass cheek while the other grabbed the back of my hair. His tongue dove into my mouth, hard and aggressive, taking what he wanted. He kissed me deep, pulling my body closer, holding me tight.

His hand fisted around my hair and he yanked backward, baring my neck.

Fuck. Yes.

I gasped as he planted his mouth on my neck. Moaned as he licked and sucked and scraped his teeth across my skin. He bit down on the sensitive spot above my collar bone, just hard enough to send a rush of heat down my spine, straight between my legs.

With his hand still fisted tight in my hair, he pulled my head back further, forcing me to arch my back. His tongue lapped its way down my skin until he found my nipple. I thought I might die right here. He licked my hard peak, his rough tongue dragging against my sensitive skin.

"Yes, Leo," I breathed as he took my nipple in his mouth and sucked. "God, yes."

Grinding against him, I lost myself in the feel of his tongue as he lavished my tits with attention. Licking, kissing, sucking. Pressure built in my core, the hot tension radiating through me. I wanted him to unleash on me. To make my body do what he wanted.

My nipple popped out of his mouth. Slowly, he dragged his bearded jaw up my chest, my neck, my cheek, until his lips were right at my ear, his breath hot on my skin.

With his hand wrapped tightly in my hair, he pulled my

head to the side. His whisper was gravelly. "I need to taste you. Right fucking now."

It wasn't a question, but there was only one answer. "Yes."

He stood, picking me up as if I weighed nothing, his muscles tight and flexing. I wrapped my legs around his waist and draped my arms over his shoulders. Effortlessly, he carried me into the bedroom and laid me out on the bed.

Yes. Yes. Oh my god, yes.

I reached behind to unclasp my bra and pulled it off while he yanked my pants down. The light was dim—he didn't turn one on—and he made no move to undress. But I wasn't about to complain. My pussy throbbed with need. I'd take whatever he was ready to give me.

There was nothing gentle about the way he ripped my panties off and tossed them on the floor. He lowered himself onto the bed and pushed my legs open.

"Fuck," he muttered, his voice growly and low. He kissed and nibbled on the insides of my thighs, working his way toward my center.

I trembled, desperate for more. His lips and tongue were a soft contrast to the roughness of his beard on my skin. I let my legs tip open farther and reached down to run my hands through his hair.

His tongue reached my slit and he licked slowly up one side, then the other, a groan rumbling in his throat. My eyes rolled back as he did it again. Licking. Teasing. Tasting me.

The pad of his tongue found my clit and I moaned, my body shuddering. He licked up and down a few times, exploring. A few flicks, then a longer lick. My body responded, my hips moving to match his rhythm.

I moaned and writhed against the sheets, breathless at the feel of Leo's mouth on me.

"Fuck, you taste so good," he said. "This pussy. So fucking perfect."

He slipped a finger inside and my back arched, almost involuntarily. A second finger and I cried out from the exquisite pressure.

Growling into me, he clamped down on my clit and sucked while he worked my pussy with his fingers. They curled against my magic spot, sending jolts of pleasure rolling through me.

Then his tongue brushed across my clit. *Flick. Flick. Flick.* It was perfect, steady and unrelenting. Every brush made my pussy clench around his fingers, my hips roll to his rhythm.

Flick. Flick. Flick. Faster. I moaned, raising my arms above my head, surrendering to him. To his mouth, hot and wet between my legs. To his fingers inside me, his tongue on my clit. *Flick. Flick. Flick.*

With a cry, I came apart, the release of my climax rippling through my body. I gasped and trembled, but Leo was relentless, drawing out every last tremor.

My eyes rolled back and my legs dropped to the bed as Leo got up. My breath came fast and the world spun around me.

When I opened my eyes, Leo stood above me, his gaze hungry. Aggressive.

Predatory.

He watched me catch my breath, unblinking, pure lust in his eyes. Without a word, he moved the waistband of his sweats down. Pulled out his cock, letting it spring free in all its glory.

I stared at it. Long and thick and perfect.

When he finally spoke, his voice was practically a growl. "On your knees."

22

LEO

With the taste of Hannah's pussy on my tongue, I watched her gape at me, nodding slowly. Her skin was flushed pink from coming in my mouth—from her cheeks down to her gorgeous tits. She lay on the bed panting, her beautiful body stretched out. Relaxed. Satisfied.

I licked my lips, high as fuck from eating her pussy. From the feel of her hands all over me—touching my face and neck. I hadn't been touched that much in years. I was starved for it.

And kissing her. Unabashedly kissing her without fear. She'd felt the devastation of my face—the ruin of my skin. But she hadn't recoiled. No, she'd caressed me. Kissed me. Drawn her wet tongue across my damaged mouth, moaning while she did it.

She'd broken me wide open.

Of course, the fact that she'd taken off her shirt and put her tits in my face hadn't hurt. She was good, I had to give her that.

At first, I'd been completely in control, like always. I'd kissed her back. Held her. Touched her.

And then I'd snapped.

There was no going back now. I pushed my sweats down my

hips enough to keep my cock out, and waited while she slowly turned over and got on her knees.

Fuck yes.

She put her ass in the air and looked back at me over her shoulder. Bit her lip. Her eyes traveled down to my dick, so I grabbed it. Gave it a few strokes while she watched me.

"Holy shit," she breathed.

I climbed onto the bed behind her and ran my hands along the curves of her ass. Over the swell of her hips. She arched, leaning back, but I didn't take her yet. I caressed her beautiful body. Used both hands. Up and down her back. Over the roundness of her hips and ass. To her sweet pussy, so wet and ready for me.

Leaning over her, I braced myself with one arm and put my mouth near her ear. I had just enough presence of mind—only just—to consider protection. "Baby, I don't have any condoms."

"I'm clean, and I have an IUD. We're good."

And with that, I let go.

Instinct taking over, I straightened and grabbed her hips. Aligned the tip of my cock with her entrance. And thrust deep inside.

I held there for a moment, just feeling the sweetness of her pussy wrapped around me. The heat. The wetness. She pressed her ass back into my groin and moved her hips in a slow circle.

"Fuck, Hannah," I growled.

She felt so good, I couldn't think. Could hardly breathe. All I could do was feel. I pulled out slowly, letting the sensations sink into me. Thrust back in.

"Oh my god, Leo."

Gripping her hips, I pulled her toward me while I drove into her. Once. Twice. Again. Harder. My muscles flexed and I grunted as I pounded her from behind.

"Yes. Harder."

This woman. Letting me touch her. Taste her. Fuck her. I'd wanted this—been desperate for it—from the first time I saw her. And now, in this moment, she was mine.

Pushing her down so she was flat on her belly, I draped myself over her. Kissed her shoulder and the back of her neck. She arched against my groin and gripped the sheets.

"Leo."

Hearing my name on her lips in that breathy whimper set fire to my blood. I brushed her hair to the side, baring more of her neck, and licked her delicate skin. I wanted to consume her. Taste every inch.

"You like that?" I asked, low in her ear. "You like my cock inside you?"

"Yes," she breathed.

I drove in and out of her wet pussy, licking and kissing her. Nibbling on her neck. Pressure built, deep inside, hot tension coiling like a spring.

"This pussy," I growled. "So fucking good."

She moaned in reply, her eyes closed, cheeks flushed pink.

Thrusting harder, I lost myself in the feel of her. Groaned into her ear as my steel-hard cock pushed in and out, gliding through her wetness. Her pussy clenched around me, her heat building.

I threaded my fingers into her hair and pulled her head back. Slid my other hand to her throat and held her there. Her pulse raced and her breath came fast.

She was entirely in my control. Pinned down beneath me.

Mine.

"This pussy is mine, now," I growled into her ear, still driving my cock in and out.

"Yes," she said.

Hard thrust. "Mine."

"Yours."

With my hand still covering her throat, I bit down on her shoulder. Her body shuddered and she cried out.

I pounded her faster, feeling the satisfaction of her back arching, her breath gasping. Her soft moans turning to frenzied cries of pleasure. My cock pulsed with the need for release, the tension in my groin building to a breaking point.

I was lust incarnate. A hot thrusting beast unleashing my fury on her silky-smooth body. I grunted and growled while I fucked her senseless. While I held her tight, feeling her surrender to me.

Her pussy tightened—hard—and she cried out again. I felt her start to come, her muscles spasming in waves around my dick. And I lost my fucking mind.

My eyes rolled back, my balls drew up hard, and my back stiffened. Pulses rippled through me as my cock unleashed. I slammed into her, as deep as I could go, while my cock throbbed, coating her pussy with my come. I could feel the heat of it. The wetness soaking us both.

I kept coming, so I thrust again. And again. The pleasure was so intense, it almost hurt. Hannah panted beneath me, clutching the sheets, as I groaned with the aching intensity.

When I finally finished, I braced myself on top of her, trying to catch my breath. I let my cock slip out, but Hannah barely moved. She just lay under me, sprawled out on the bedsheets, her eyes closed.

"Holy shit, Leo," she said, finally. She didn't open her eyes. "What did you just do to me?"

I slowly came back to myself—regained the ability to think. Blinking a few times, I put my dick back in my pants and tugged the waistband up. *Holy shit* was right. What had *she* just done to *me*?

Her hair fanned out over the sheet—I had no idea where the pillows had gone—and her cheeks were flushed. I gently touched her face with my fingertips, feeling a heady mix of awe and contentment. It had been so long. So fucking long since I'd felt this. Not just sex. A physical connection.

I rolled onto my side next to her.

She smiled and her eyes fluttered open. "I don't know if I can move yet."

"You don't have to."

"Who was that guy who just fucked the life out of me, and where was Leo that whole time?"

I laughed softly.

She propped herself up and nibbled on her lower lip, her expression worried. But she didn't say anything.

Instead of asking what was wrong, I slid my arm around her waist and hauled her against me. Put my face in her hair and took a deep breath.

She buried her face in my chest and when she spoke, her voice was muffled by my shirt. "Oh thank god."

"What?"

"I was afraid you wouldn't let me cuddle. After that, I really need to cuddle."

I wrapped my arms around her, holding her close. Rested my cheek against the top of her head. "Hannah?"

"Yeah?"

I hesitated, unsure of how to put into words what I needed to say. "I meant what I said."

"About what?"

"I want you to be mine."

She pulled away just enough to look up at me. "What?"

"I want you to be mine," I said again. "But the thing is, I'm probably going to be bad at this. I'm too fucked up, and I know it. It's not fair to you, but..."

"But?"

"I'm a terrible person and I want you anyway."

She laughed, tucking herself against me. "You're not a terrible person."

"Does that mean..." I trailed off and she looked up at me again. I didn't know why I needed to do it this way. To ask her and hear her say yes. It was probably going to sound stupid. But I did. I needed this. "Will you be my girlfriend?"

Her lips parted in a smile. "Oh, Leo. Yes. I want to be your girlfriend so much."

"Yeah?"

"More than anything."

I pulled her in close again, casting aside the voice that tried to remind me how near she was to my scars. That didn't matter right now. All that mattered was her. Us. She was mine.

I just hoped I wouldn't fuck it up.

23

LEO

*H*appiness was such a foreign feeling, I wasn't sure how to handle it at first.

Instead of waking up alone, wondering if it was worth dragging myself out of bed, I woke up every day with Hannah next to me. She sat beside me as we worked. Came to dinner at my mom's. We went out together. Stayed in together. Walked through the vineyards as the weather turned colder, threatening snow.

Was it really that easy?

Granted, it wasn't like it had fixed me. I still had a hard time leaving Salishan. I still obsessively tracked the security footage —although the bullshit with my dad had given me a real reason.

But as the weeks went by, I realized I felt different. I smiled more. Even laughed once in a while. Hell, the fact that I smiled and laughed at all was an improvement. Even my therapist was impressed.

And my family? They were basically ridiculous. It was like they'd never seen me with a girlfriend before.

Which, to be fair, they hadn't. Not since before.

Mom hugged Hannah—a lot. Brynn and Amelia took her shopping. Cooper kept trying to give her nicknames, only to decide none of them worked. Even Ben got in on it, asking me for info on Hannah's ex so he could be on the lookout in case the douchebag decided to cause trouble for her.

The only ones being reasonably chill about my new relationship were Roland and Zoe. And that was partly because they were busy with Hudson, and partly because they tended to keep their crazy to themselves.

But I had to admit, it felt good to see my family accept Hannah. She and Zoe got along particularly well. They'd started having lunch together regularly, and they even went out for a girl's night while Roland and I stayed home with the baby.

What a difference a few months had made. For both of us.

Hannah came out of the bedroom, dressed in an off-the-shoulder sweater that gave a peek at her tattoo, with jeans and ankle boots. With her hair in a loose up-do, it made me want to suck on the skin at the base of her throat.

"How do I look?"

I gazed at her. She was so beautiful. So perfect. I still couldn't believe she was with me.

"Well?" she asked.

"Sorry. You look wonderful."

"Are you sure? Should I wear a dress? I can change."

I stood and took her hands. "You look perfect. Why are you so nervous?"

Cooper had made it his mission in life to take Amelia on a double date with me and Hannah. When Chase had discovered Coop's plan, he'd acted ridiculously jealous—those two were such girls—until Cooper had invited him and Brynn along. Zoe had overheard, and the next thing I knew, we'd been roped into a night out with all six of them.

"I don't know why I'm nervous. Maybe I'll text Zoe and see what she's wearing. I think Brynn and Amelia are wearing dresses."

I held her wrists, tugging her back toward me. "You look absolutely beautiful. Don't worry about what they're wearing. Just be you."

She met my eyes. "Okay. Thanks."

We gathered up our things and left. The restaurant was a short drive away. I wasn't too bothered by leaving the winery tonight. Being with Hannah made a difference. She squeezed my hand and smiled as we drove. And it made me feel good that I could do this for her—take her to a nice dinner.

We parked and went inside. Cooper had chosen a nice restaurant. Soft lighting, white tablecloths. They served Salishan wine, so that was a point in their favor.

Everyone else was already here, so the host took us back to our table.

"Hey, bro," Cooper said and turned to Hannah. "Sup, Inky."

"Inky?" she asked.

"Yeah, you know, because of your tats," he said. "Nope, doesn't work. Why can't I come up with a good nickname for you?"

Amelia leaned close and nudged him with her arm. "Maybe because she already has one. Leo calls her Gigz, right?"

"Holy shit," Cooper said, like Amelia had just told him a secret of the universe. "That's true. She doesn't need me to give her a nickname because Leo already did. I'm so relieved. Thanks, man. I'm glad I don't have to shoulder all the responsibility around here. Although when you say Gigz, I think of the cat, not the girl, so that's a little bit confusing. And honestly, I don't think I can call you Gigz anyway. That's definitely a Leo thing. I guess I'll just have to call you Hannah."

"It is my name, so..." Hannah shrugged.

"Exactly," Cooper said.

We took our seats and I tried to ignore the discomfort of having people sitting behind me. Usually when Hannah and I went out, we got a table near a wall, so I could put my back to it. Our table had people on both sides, as well as across from us.

As if she could sense my unease, Hannah put her hand on my leg and gently rubbed my thigh. I grabbed her hand and squeezed.

I made it through ordering my meal without any problems, and by the time we started eating, I felt better. Good, even. I listened to my siblings chat—about everything from life after a baby, to things at Salishan, to Cooper's excited exclamations at how great it was to be on a group date with everyone.

And he was right. It was.

Before I'd started leaving the winery, I'd seen my family regularly. But I'd also known there were things I was missing. Dinners out and movies at the theater. Drinks at the bar with my brothers and hangover breakfasts at Ray's Diner.

But tonight, I wasn't missing anything. I was out at a nice restaurant, with a beautiful date. The food was amazing, and I realized I didn't just spend time with these people because they were related to me. I liked them. Even when they drove me crazy.

I finished my steak and Hannah picked at the potatoes on my plate. Cooper started contemplating dessert and maybe another bottle of wine, when a woman at the table next to us caught my attention.

She looked at me, then leaned across the table to speak to the man she was having dinner with. "Oh my god. Do you see that guy?"

My back tightened.

"Yeah," the man with her said. "Are those burns or something?"

"Maybe," the woman said, her voice laced with disgust.

Hannah stiffened next to me. Was she listening to them too? Or was it something else?

"Why would they let him in here?" the man asked. "For what we're paying for dinner, you'd think they'd keep the ambiance."

"Should we ask the waiter to move us to a different table? I don't want to have to look at that all through dinner."

They seemed to be trying to keep their voices low, but I could fucking hear every word.

Cooper's eyes widened and he opened his mouth, like he was about to say something. Oh shit, he was hearing this too. I was just about to tell Cooper to keep his mouth shut when Hannah turned in her seat.

"Excuse me," she said.

The couple looked over. "Yes?" the man asked.

"I was wondering if you might be willing to move tables," she said, her voice full of mock sweetness. "For what we're paying for dinner, I don't want to have to sit so close to such garbage human beings."

I put my hand on her arm. "Hannah."

She shrugged me off and stood, all five foot nothing of her, and put her hands on her hips. "No, I'm serious. You're going to complain about having to look at someone who was injured in service to his country?"

The couple gaped at her. In fact, our entire section of the restaurant was gaping at her. Our waiter was hurrying over but apparently Hannah wasn't finished.

"How dare you. He's the most wonderful, loving, kind, loyal man I've ever known, and you have the audacity to sit there and judge him for what he looks like? What's wrong with you?"

"Excuse me, ma'am," the waiter said, trying to cut in.

"No," Hannah said. "I refuse to sit here and take this."

I stared at her. At this feisty ball of fire, so riled up her cheeks were flushed. Watching her stand up for me like this, I couldn't even be upset.

In fact, the whole thing was kind of funny.

But I probably shouldn't let her keep lecturing these people. The other customers wanted to go back to their dinners.

I stood and put my hands on her arms. "Okay, Gigz. Let's go."

The rest of our table stood. Our meals were almost finished anyway.

"They have no right to talk about you that way," she said.

"I know," I said, gently guiding her toward the front. "It's okay."

"I'll take care of the check up front," Roland said.

"Thanks."

Hannah let me lead her out the front door and Zoe handed me her coat.

"I cannot believe the nerve of those people." Hannah stomped her foot. "Pieces of shit. For the record, I was holding back in there."

"That was one of the awesomest things I've ever seen in my life," Cooper said. "Well done, sister."

"Hashtag girl crush," Zoe said, looking at Hannah in awe.

"I don't think you actually *say* hashtag," Brynn said.

Zoe shrugged. "I do. Besides, look at her. I'd totally hit that."

"Huh," Cooper said. "That's so weird."

"What?" Zoe asked.

"That reference to two hot women getting it on did nothing for me."

Amelia laughed and smacked his arm. "Cooper."

He grabbed her around the waist and planted a kiss on her mouth. "I'm so mature now."

"Keep telling yourself that, Coop," Zoe said.

Roland came out and slipped his arm around Zoe. "They didn't charge for the meal. The manager apologized. They're asking the couple to leave."

"Good," Hannah said, her voice still full of fire. "Let's wait until they come out and—"

"Okay, tiger," I said, taking her hand. "Maybe we just call it a night."

"Oh, dude," Cooper said.

"What now?" I asked.

Cooper nodded slowly. "I knew it."

"Knew what?"

He nudged Chase with his elbow. "I had a feeling. I was right. It's time."

Chase looked between me and Hannah, a slow smile spreading across his face. "Oh, yeah. It's totally time."

"Time for what?" I asked. "Seriously, what the fuck are you guys talking about?"

"Um, guys?" Brynn said. She looked worried.

"I'll tell you at home," Cooper said, grinning at me. "Don't worry. We're about to fix this date night."

We drove back to Salishan and everyone parked in front of my place.

"What are you guys doing?" I asked as I got out of the car. Cooper and Chase were heading for my front door.

"Bonfire night," Cooper said, his voice cheerful.

"Wait, bonfire?" Oh shit. "Hold on, Coop. We don't have to do that."

"Do what?" Hannah asked.

"Trust me, bro," Cooper said. "We definitely do."

"He's right," Chase said.

"Oh my god, my first mattress bonfire," Amelia said.

Brynn stood off to the side, an amused smile on her face. No help there. Zoe met my eyes and shrugged. Roland was on the phone with Mom, checking on Hudson. No help there, either.

"Hold on," I said, following Cooper and Chase into my house. "How do you know the key code?"

"I've always known," Cooper said. He went straight back to the bedroom.

"Coop, we don't have to burn my mattress."

"Yeah, we do." He stood in the doorway with his hands on his hips. "This'll be a tight fit, but you got it in here somehow, so I'm sure we can get it out."

"We'll need to angle it right, but it'll come out," Chase said.

"It's a perfectly good mattress," I said. "No one else has ever been on it."

"Doesn't matter," Cooper said.

"I don't understand what's going on here," Hannah said.

"It's tradition," Cooper said, as if that answered everything.

"This is going to be so fun," Amelia said from the doorway. "Do you guys need help?"

"Nah, Cookie, we got it," Cooper said.

This whole scene felt like chaos. Chase was already pulling the sheets off and even Roland came in to help.

Hannah looked concerned, or maybe she was just confused. I grabbed her arm and pulled her aside.

"Sorry. They're just... I don't know. My family's fucking weird."

"Are they really going to burn your mattress?"

I sighed. "Yeah."

"I thought they did that to get rid of the bad vibes from past sexual partners or something."

"Usually, yeah..." I trailed off, not sure how to explain it. Because the truth was, I kind of understood. And as crazy and irrational as it was, a part of me wanted them to do it. "I guess in this case, it means something a little different."

She slipped her hand in mine—in my left, and I didn't pull away. "It's tradition?"

"Yeah," I said.

"Okay, yes, this one is a little weird." She watched as Cooper, Chase, and Roland guided my mattress out of the bedroom and to the front door. "But I guess we should just go with it."

We bundled up against the cold and walked out to the fire pit. Cooper and Chase set to work building the fire and before long, flames danced against the dark sky.

I stood behind Hannah, wrapping my arms around her shoulders, and rested my cheek against her head. Flames licked the edges of the mattress as the fire spread. The heat coming off the blaze was enough to warm us, even in the freezing cold night.

"It's pretty," she said.

"Cooper knows how to build a good fire."

It was cathartic, somehow, seeing it burn. It wasn't that I needed to get rid of the traces—real or imagined—of ex-girlfriends or past sexual partners. I hadn't been with anyone except for Hannah since I'd been injured. But it still felt right to do this. Because I knew one thing with absolute certainty. Hannah was it for me.

And maybe it was time I let her know.

"I love you," I said softly into her ear.

She twisted in my grasp so she could look me in the eyes. "Did you just…"

"Yes." I brushed her hair back from her face and cupped her cheeks. The glow of the fire reflected in her eyes. "I love you, Hannah."

"I love you too, Leo."

She popped up on her tiptoes, much like she'd done the first time I brought her here. But this time, I didn't even think about turning away. She pressed her lips to mine and I wrapped her in my arms.

Cooper whistled. Or maybe it was Chase. But I ignored them. Ignored everything, and kissed my girl in the firelight.

24

HANNAH

*M*y cup of tea sent a little tendril of steam into the air. I sat at Shannon's big dining table with my tea and laptop, waiting for her to come back.

I'd finished a few projects and finally had time to get started on Salishan's new branding package. I was hoping Shannon might have some things from the winery's past that I could use as inspiration. This place had such a beautiful history, having been in Shannon's family for three generations. Maybe stationary, old ads, or wine labels. Something that would spark new ideas.

Shannon came down the stairs carrying an old file box and set it on the table. "I'm not sure exactly what's in here, but you're welcome to go through it. There's more in the attic."

It was marked *Salishan Cellars* in faded marker on the outside. I took off the lid and the scent of old paper wafted out. It looked like a jumble of things. Envelopes, papers, smaller boxes.

I pulled out a card, the paper slightly yellowed with age. It was an invitation to a wine tasting—twenty-five years ago.

"I remember this," Shannon said. "We held it outside and had a great turnout. My mom was watching the boys, but

Cooper got out of the house. Leo found him. He just calmly took Grandma's hand and led her to where Cooper was playing in the dirt."

I loved that her memory of this event was shaped by her children. "I bet it helped to have your parents here when your kids were little."

"It was perfect. I miss them." She took a deep breath and set the invitation down. "Anyway, there should be more things like this, with our old logo on them. Is that what you're looking for?"

"Yeah, this is great. Anything that evokes the history of Salishan."

"I'll bring down one more box and let you have at it," she said. "I have some work to do, but you're welcome to stay here as long as you want."

"Thanks."

I spent the next couple of hours looking through the boxes. I found old fliers, a stack of unused wine labels, more invitations to winery events, and clippings from the local newspaper.

Among the newspaper articles was one showing a photo of a man in a military uniform. It was faded with age, the paper brittle to the touch. The caption read, *war hero Thomas Rousseau honored for his service.* Judging by the date, this must have been Shannon's father, Leo's grandfather.

I wondered if his grandfather's military service had inspired Leo to join the Army. And how different his life would be now if he hadn't. I'd seen those old photos of Leo—wearing a big smile, his face whole. Did he regret his choice?

It was hard to imagine that he didn't have regrets. But I also couldn't imagine him as anyone other than the man he was now.

The front door opened, and Zoe came in. "Hey. What are you up to?"

I looked down at the mess spread out in front of me.

"Messing up Shannon's house, apparently. I've been looking through old Salishan stuff, for inspiration."

"Wow, look at all this," Zoe said. She picked up an old flier. "This is pretty."

"It is. I love the classic look of the old materials."

"I do too. I can't wait to see what you come up with."

"Thanks."

She pulled out the chair and sat down next to me. "Did you guys replace the bed yet?"

"Yes, and after a week on a blow-up mattress, it's basically the most comfortable thing ever."

She laughed. "I'm still surprised Leo let them do it. But sometimes it's best to let the goofball boys do their thing. It's always fun, at least."

"I think Leo secretly liked it."

"Probably. Thank you, by the way," she said.

"For what?"

"Whatever it is you're doing to Leo that has him so happy." She winked. "Between the whole thing with Lawrence finally simmering down and Leo actually smiling once in a while, I think everyone is more relaxed. It's nice."

"It's my pleasure. Literally."

She nudged me with her elbow. "Get it, girl."

Shannon came in and shut the door behind her.

"Oh good, you're still here," she said with a smile. "Hey, Zoe. The event must be over?"

"It is," Zoe said. "I think it went well, considering the client kept trying to make menu changes up until this morning. But they all left happy."

"That's good to hear," Shannon said. "Is Huddy with Roland?"

Zoe opened a photo on her phone and held it up. "Sound asleep on Daddy's chest."

"Aw, so sweet," Shannon said.

It was adorable—a crooked selfie of Roland with their son sound asleep, his face squished against his chest.

"Well, if you're both free, I was thinking we could all have a little girl time," Shannon said. "I have some snacks in the kitchen. And wine, of course. Nothing fancy. Brynn and Amelia are on their way over."

"I'm in," Zoe said. "Let me just text Roland to let him know."

A sudden rush of emotion poured through me. Girl time with Shannon and she wanted me to be a part of it? I tucked my hair behind my ear, trying to act casual. Like I wasn't simmering with excitement at being included. "Yeah, I'd love to."

"Great," Shannon said. "Let's get this stuff put away. No more work today."

I helped Shannon clean up the table and we put the boxes aside, then I texted Leo to let him know where I was. Brynn and Amelia arrived, and we all took to the kitchen to get snacks ready. Shannon's *nothing fancy* included artisan cheeses, a variety of crackers, fig spread, and a mini olive bar. And, of course, wine.

Oh, the wine. It was no surprise that wine was a staple on the table in this family. Even Chase and Cooper—who, on the surface, didn't seem like wine connoisseurs—knew and appreciated good wine. Family meals always included the perfect wine pairing, and it was fascinating to hear Shannon talk about what went into each variety.

We all gathered around the table to snack and drink. Brynn talked about her latest classes and Amelia gave Shannon an update on the improvements at the horse ranch. Zoe had us laughing our asses off with some of her worst bridezilla stories.

Shannon mostly listened, a wine glass perched in her hand and a smile on her face. She seemed to have such an easy companionship with the young women in her life. It made me even more honored to be included.

She finished her wine and stood. "I'll open another bottle. Any preferences?"

"Do you have a bottle of Poetic?" Brynn asked. "It's my favorite."

"I'm sure I do." Shannon went into the kitchen and came back a minute later with an open bottle of red. "Oh, the divorce recorded today."

For a second, the room went silent. Amelia clapped her hand over her mouth and Brynn stared at her mom, wide-eyed.

Shannon started pouring the wine, like she hadn't said anything important. "I have a few bottles of white already chilled if anyone prefers."

"What the eff, Shannon?" Zoe asked. "You just drop that bomb on us and think you can change the subject?"

Shannon set the bottle down and took her seat. "Well, it's not like this is a surprise. We all knew it was coming."

Zoe shook her head slowly. "What am I going to do with you? We need to celebrate."

"I thought that's what we were doing," Shannon said, gesturing to the remnants of our impromptu feast.

"Mom, this is not enough," Brynn said. "You've been waiting for this for ages. You're finally free."

"Preach, sister," Zoe said. "It's about time."

"What else should we do?" Shannon asked. "I don't have any dessert made, but—"

"Slumber party," Brynn said.

"Yes!" Amelia almost jumped out of her seat.

"Mom, you don't need to do a thing," Brynn said. "I'll call Chase and he can bring us ice cream or something."

"And we can do facials and pedicures," Amelia said.

"And watch the sappiest chick flick we can find," Brynn said.

"You should call your husband and ask for movie recom-
mendations," Zoe said, winking at Brynn. "You know he loves
chick flicks."

Brynn shrugged. "It's true. He does."

"What do you think?" Zoe asked, looking at me. "You down
for a little Miles-women slumber party?"

Was I ever. "I love this plan."

Shannon laughed and raised her glass. "You girls are the
best."

"To Shannon," Zoe said, lifting her wine glass. "May she
continue to rediscover her fire in this new chapter of her life."

We all lifted our glasses and clinked, with a resounding
chorus of *cheers*.

Brynn and Amelia went to work gathering blankets and
pillows in the living room, making a veritable nest of softness.
The girls all made phone calls to their significant others, asking
them to bring supplies for the night. I texted Leo again.

Me: so this turned into a slumber party at your mom's...

Leo: well that's adorable

Me: I know, right? Would you mind bringing me some jammies?

Leo: of course, be over in a little bit

One by one, the men arrived. Chase brought more food—
including ice cream—along with a bag of stuff for Brynn.
Cooper burst in, dropped Amelia's bag on the floor, and flopped
on the couch, like he was planning on staying himself. Roland
came later—he had to wait for Hudson to wake up—with an
overnight bag for Zoe.

Leo came quietly into the chaos, pausing by the front door,
his eyes sweeping the room. Our gazes met and he smiled. It felt
like the world stopped every time he did that.

I glanced to the side and noticed Shannon watching Leo.
She touched her fingers to her lips, looking back and forth
between the two of us. Leo didn't seem to notice; his eyes stayed

locked on me. I bit my bottom lip, feeling like my heart might burst.

Leo brought me my bag and set it down. "I wasn't sure what you needed, so I grabbed a bunch of stuff."

"Thanks." I stood and he slipped his hand around my waist. "I'm sure it's fine."

He leaned closer and spoke softly in my ear. "I'm going to miss you tonight."

There was nothing better than the feeling of falling asleep next to Leo. "I'll miss you too."

Shannon got up and went to the front door. There must have been a knock, but I hadn't heard it. I'd been too absorbed in the feel of Leo's beard against my forehead.

"Hi, Benjamin," Shannon said.

She opened the door and Ben walked in, looking a bit bewildered at the crowd.

He held up a paper shopping bag. "I had some extra zucchini. I thought you might want some."

"Thank you," Shannon said, taking the bag from him. "You might as well come in."

Ben smiled at her, his eyes crinkling at the corners.

Leo sat and pulled me into his lap, tucking his arm—his left arm, no less—around me. Ben came in and took a seat—it was clear he was comfortable—and I wondered if our girls' night sleepover was still going to happen, now that everyone was here.

Zoe had Hudson in her arms, and she narrowed her eyes as Shannon came back from the kitchen. Her gaze moved to Ben, then back to Shannon again.

"So, Shannon," she said, her voice pitched in a tone of mock innocence. "Have anything to share with the family?"

"Oh." Shannon smoothed down her shirt, her eyes flicking to Ben, then quickly away. "The divorce recorded today. It's final."

The room erupted with cheers. Cooper sprang up and

grabbed his mom in a hug, twirling her around. Chase smiled and clapped, then hugged Brynn. Roland stood next to Zoe, his hands on her shoulders, a smile on his face. Leo's arm tightened around me.

Ben stared at Shannon, his expression unreadable.

"Okay, boys," Zoe said. "Girls' night. Time to go."

Chase scowled at her. Cooper put his mom down and shot Zoe a glare.

Zoe handed Hudson off to Roland. "I'm serious. We have girl stuff to do."

Roland kissed her, then nodded to Chase. He stuck his lip out in a pout, but kissed Brynn goodbye.

Cooper dove onto the couch and put his head in Amelia's lap.

"You too, Coop," Zoe said. "Let's go, buddy."

"Why can't I stay?" Cooper asked.

"Because you're a boy," Zoe said.

Amelia laughed and ran her fingers through Cooper's hair. "It's just one night."

He buried his face in her lap.

Zoe shook her head. "He's such a baby."

I didn't point out that Leo had made no move to go. He kept his arm threaded around my waist.

Ben hadn't moved either. He looked shell-shocked, his eyes focused on nothing.

Chase patted him on the shoulder. "Let's go, man. We'll go get a beer."

"Right," Ben said, blinking hard a few times.

"Come on, Coop," Chase said. "Guys' night with Ben. Let's go."

Cooper groaned and peeled himself off Amelia's lap. "Fine."

Chase glanced at Leo. "You too, Leo. Come get a beer with us."

I felt the tension in Leo's body at Chase's suggestion. It was still hard for him to leave the winery. I tilted my face so I could whisper in his ear. "You can do this. Just text me if you get anxious."

He took a deep breath, leaning his face into my hair. "I love you."

"I love you, too."

He squeezed me with both arms, then let go. I got up, but he wasn't finished. He pulled me into his arms and held me for a long moment.

It didn't escape my notice that none of the guys said anything as they waited by the front door for Leo. No jabs for him to hurry, like they knew he needed this.

I leaned my face against his chest and squeezed him tight. He kissed the top of my head before finally pulling away.

"Have fun tonight."

"I will."

Cooper hesitated by the front door while the other men left, as if still deciding whether or not he was going to go. He darted back in to kiss Amelia one last time before finally following the rest of them.

With the men gone, we all migrated to the living room pillow-and-blanket nest Brynn and Amelia had built. I settled into a spot on the floor amid soft pillows and pulled a cozy throw blanket into my lap. Shannon came around with more wine for everyone, then took a seat on the floor with us.

"Amelia, I don't know how you do it," Zoe said.

"What?" Amelia asked, situating some pillows around her.

"Cooper."

Amelia looked genuinely puzzled. "What about Cooper?"

I'd gotten the impression that Amelia didn't see Cooper as being anything other than completely normal. Which was probably why they were perfect for each other.

"Never mind," Zoe said with a smile. She swirled her wine a few times. "So, Shannon. How does it feel to be officially single again?"

"It's a relief," Shannon said, brushing a strand of hair away from her face. "I'm so glad we didn't have to go to court."

"Me too," Brynn said. "That would have been awful for everyone."

"Plus now you're free to move on," Amelia said. "Do you think you'll date again?"

Shannon laughed. "Oh honey. My time has passed."

Zoe rolled her eyes. "Well, that's bullshit."

"Zoe!" Shannon said.

"I'm not wrong," Zoe said. "You're divorced, not dead."

"I'm not in my twenties, or thirties, or forties, anymore," Shannon said.

"What does that have to do with anything?" Brynn asked.

"I agree," I said. "It's not like life should end after you turn fifty."

Shannon took a sip of her wine. "I'm busy here. I don't know who I'd even date."

"I can think of someone," Zoe said.

Shannon shot her a glare. "If you're referring to who I believe you are referring to, he and I have a very nice friendship. But nothing more than that."

Zoe snorted.

"It's true," she said. "Besides, he's been here through... everything. It's been well over twenty years. I think Cooper was two when he came to work for us."

"What does that have to do with anything?" Brynn asked.

"Benjamin doesn't see me that way," Shannon said.

Zoe snorted again.

Could she really not see it? To me, it was clear as day that Ben had feelings for her. And anyone could see she returned them. But I knew she'd been through a lot. And with her divorce only just being finalized, maybe it was hard for her to see the possibilities that lay ahead.

"One thing I know," I said, reaching for a cookie that one of the guys had brought. "You don't always know what the hard parts of life are going to teach you. Sometimes the worst experiences shape us into who we are, and we're better for it."

"That's so true," Shannon said.

"God, I have such a girl crush on you," Zoe said. She moved her wine glass toward mine and we clinked them. "Words of wisdom."

"Cheers. And by the way." I paused, feeling suddenly a little self-conscious. "Thanks for inviting me tonight."

"You're stuck with us now," Zoe said.

"I think we can all drink to that," Brynn said, holding up her glass.

So we did.

25

HANNAH

*L*eo was nice enough to let me sleep off the rest of my hangover after I dragged myself home from Shannon's house in the morning. We'd been up half the night drinking, talking, and laughing. Fun, but painful in the morning. After about a gallon of water, a nap, and a shower, I felt like myself again.

He came into the bedroom while I was getting dressed and lay down, putting his hands behind his head. His hair fell away from his face, but he didn't move or shift to hide it. He just watched me.

I finished dressing in a tank top and yoga pants and sat on the edge of the bed.

"Did you have fun last night?" Leo asked.

"Yeah, it was really fun," I said. "A little too much fun, maybe. But I feel fine now."

"That happens when Zoe's involved," he said. "You gotta watch out for that one."

I laughed. "I can see that. Did you go out with the guys?"

"I did. It wasn't bad." His brow furrowed, like that surprised him.

"Good. Your mom showed me a bunch of old Salishan stuff. It was neat. I found an article about your grandfather. He was in the military?"

"Yeah." He sat up, and I could see him closing himself off.

In many ways, Leo had opened up a lot. But there were still things he wouldn't talk about. If I got anywhere near the topic of his time in the Army, he shut down the conversation.

"Were you close to your grandparents?"

"Very," he said. "We all lived together growing up, so yeah."

"Did he have anything to do with why you went into the military?"

He looked away. "I guess."

"Why do you do that?"

"Do what?"

"Shut me out," I said. "I feel like you know almost everything about me and there's still so much I don't know about you."

"I'm sure I don't know everything about you," he said.

"More or less," I said. "I've told you about my parents. I told you everything that happened with Jace. Even before we met, I told you things I've never told anyone."

"What things?"

I took a deep breath, trying to think of something. "Like... oh, I know one. Do you remember that time a couple of years ago when we talked for like two hours about shibari and kinbaku?"

"Japanese bondage?" he asked.

"Yeah. I don't know how we even got on the topic. But I told you all about the shibari display I saw at an art museum in Vancouver. And then we started talking about ropes and bondage and what it would feel like."

His voice was low. "You said you were curious."

I nodded once. "I've never admitted I might be into that to someone else. Just you."

"You mean you've never done it?"

"Bondage? No."

He watched me, and it drove me crazy that I couldn't read his expression.

"What?" I asked.

"I just always thought that was something you'd done before."

"Why?"

"It seemed like you knew a lot about it."

I shrugged. "I don't know. I Googled a little."

"But you haven't tried it."

"No," I said, my voice just above a whisper. "Being tied would leave me so... vulnerable. I've never been with someone I trust enough."

He stared at me again in silence, his intense gaze hypnotic. It reminded me of the first time I saw him, across the room at a wedding. I'd been just as mesmerized then as I was now.

After a long moment, he finally spoke. "Do you trust me enough?"

My breath caught in my throat. The idea of Leo tying me up was desperately arousing. My panties were already wet at the mere thought of it. I couldn't quite get a *yes* out, so I nodded.

With that same serious expression, Leo got up and went to his closet. When he turned back around, he had coils of black rope in his hand.

"Do you just happen to have some rope here, for like, practical reasons?" I asked.

He shook his head.

"That's bondage rope."

He nodded.

"Do you know how to use it?"

He nodded again.

I raised my eyebrows. "I don't remember you telling me you knew how to do this."

"I didn't."

"How long have you had that rope?"

"Two years."

I gaped at him. "So you're telling me we talked about kinbaku and you went out and bought bondage rope?"

He looked at the rope in his hands. "I ordered it online."

"And you learned how to use it?"

"I bought a book."

I took a deep breath. This was so unexpected. "Even though you didn't have someone to use it on?"

With his eyes still on me, he uncoiled some of the rope and wound it around one hand, then stretched it taut. "I always imagined it was you."

Oh my god.

He reached over and flipped the light switch. He always turned the lights off before sex. Not that he took his shirt off—ever. But a dark room obviously made him more comfortable, so I never protested. My body reacted to the sudden darkness, warmth rushing between my legs, like I'd developed a classical conditioning response.

His eyes were like steel and his voice had gone gravelly. "Hannah."

"Yes?" I whispered.

"Take your fucking clothes off."

I hurried to obey, pulling my tank top over my head and letting it drop to the floor. He watched while I stripped naked, coiling the rope around one hand, then the other, stretching it tight between them.

"On your knees, back to me," he said. "But stay upright."

I did what he asked, kneeling on the bed in front of him.

He touched the back of my shoulder with the rope. It was surprisingly soft. I trembled as he traced it down my back.

Wordlessly, he caressed my left arm with the rope, then pulled it behind my back. Did the same with my right. He wound the rope around my wrists, slowly binding them together. After tying a knot, he checked the tension, running his finger between the rope and my skin.

"How does that feel?" he asked.

"Good."

He threaded the rope around my arms, weaving it upward. It didn't hurt, but it did leave my arms immobilized.

Leaning in, he kissed the base of my neck. Sometimes he liked to nibble and bite—and I loved it—but this was so soft. So gentle. He ran his hands up and down my bound arms, brushing his lips against my sensitive skin.

"More?" he asked.

I nodded.

He wrapped a rope around my rib cage, just below my breasts, and pulled it behind me. The feel of it tightening made my heart race. He drew it around, under my arm, and across the top of my breasts. I felt him loop it in back and he kissed my shoulder again.

With agonizing slowness, he slid the rope over the top of my shoulder, crossing it beneath the ropes so it cut between my breasts. His body pressed against me from behind as he reached over to tuck the free end under the rope that wound around my ribs. Then he brought it up again, between my breasts, and pulled it down over the opposite shoulder.

The constriction of the rope was both gentle and tight—not enough to hurt my skin or cut off my circulation, but the pressure was intense, like being held. Embraced.

It felt amazing.

He tied it off in the back and I closed my eyes. I was on my knees, my arms bound behind me, a harness of rope encircling my torso. My nipples were hard peaks even in the warm room, as if the mild constriction around my chest increased their sensitivity.

Leo ran his hands over my shoulders and down my arms. Moved around the bed so he was in front of me, caressing me as he went.

"So beautiful," he murmured.

Letting my eyes flutter open, I gazed up at him. He touched my face. Traced his fingertips down my neck, past the ropes at the top of my chest. When he got to my nipples I gasped. They were unbelievably sensitive to his touch.

He leaned down and kissed me, lapping his tongue against mine. His beard was pleasantly rough against my face and he brushed his fingers over my nipples, making me tremble.

"I want to fuck you like this," he growled, tracing his fingers along the ropes.

I didn't think I was capable of speech, so I just nodded. Every touch, every brush of his hair or fingertips, sent tingles and sparks rushing through me. They exploded between my legs, my pussy throbbing with desire.

I wanted to be fucked, and I wanted to be fucked hard.

He moved off the bed and paused, his eyes moving up and down, taking me in. Slowly, he took off his pants and I felt a little thrill. He didn't usually do that in front of me. Scars marred his left leg, and if he did take his pants off all the way, he was behind me when he did it.

His tongue darted out and he bit his lower lip. Without saying a word, he did something I'd never seen him do before.

He took off his shirt.

My heart felt like it might beat out of my chest and tears sprang to my eyes. Not because I didn't like what I saw. Because he'd done it. He'd broken through a barrier. Let me see.

He had a dusting of chest hair and that delicious patch below his navel, leading down. In the dark room, his scarring was hard to make out. He'd covered almost all of it with ink, the tattoos running up his arm, over his chest, and down his torso. His left thigh was inked as well, the black design covering the burned skin.

He was absolutely beautiful.

As much as I wanted to attach myself to his gorgeous body, feeling every inch of skin against mine, I understood what was happening. I was bound. I couldn't touch him unless he let me. Unless he chose to get close enough.

It was why he'd done it.

If he needed these ropes to feel safe—as a crutch to deeper intimacy—I was all for it.

I started to bend forward at the waist and he moved closer to take the rope in his hands. He pulled the free end taut, engaging the ropes around my chest. The harness easily took my weight and he lowered me slowly until my face was against the mattress, my ass in the air.

"Fuck," he growled.

This position was intense. So vulnerable. He got on the bed behind me and caressed the backs of my thighs, kissing them, moving until his mouth was close to my center.

With a long, slow draw of his tongue, he licked up my slit. My eyes rolled back and a tremor ran down my spine.

"So fucking beautiful," he murmured.

He kissed and licked, his tongue dancing across my sensitive skin. But it wasn't enough—not nearly enough.

"I need you to fuck me, Leo."

He flicked his tongue over my clit. "What do you need, baby?"

"I need you to fuck me."

"Mm," he said, his voice vibrating against me. "You need my

cock, don't you, my sweet girl?"

"Yes."

More flicks of his tongue.

"Please, Leo."

I felt him move behind me. I was breathing hard, my pussy positively aching. He held onto my hips and I cried out as he thrust inside.

Yes.

Oh god, yes.

Pressure.

Friction.

Heat.

He gave me everything I needed. Held my hips tight and drove his cock into me. I was completely at his mercy, my arms bound behind my back, my face in his sheets.

And I fucking loved it.

There was no sense of being powerless. He wasn't trying to subjugate me. He was in command. In control. Making my body respond to his. Enjoying my pleasure as much as he was enjoying his own.

The ropes themselves added new sensations as Leo fucked me. Pressure and tension. I felt the contrast of the soft sheets on my skin, my nipples dragging against the fabric as my body shifted with Leo's thrusts.

He reached around and rubbed my clit while he pounded his cock into me. His grunts and growls were so raw. So primal. He pulled on the rope with his other hand, just enough to jerk me backward.

I moaned as my pussy tightened around his erection. I was so close to coming. The binding pressure around my body, Leo's cock driving into me, his fingers teasing my clit, the sound of his low growls. I closed my eyes, losing myself in the sensations. Letting Leo have me. All of me.

I was entirely his.

My pussy clenched hard around him and he grunted.

"Yes, baby," he said. "Fuck yes."

The first pulse of his cock sent me over the edge. I cried out, lost in the feeling of the most powerful orgasm I'd ever had. It rolled through my body, wave after wave of pleasure as he unloaded inside me.

His movements slowed until finally, he stopped. He pulled out and ran his hands gently over my lower back.

"Are you okay?" he whispered.

"Yes."

My body was spent. He helped me move to my side so I could stretch out my legs, and put a pillow beneath my head.

With a soft touch, he caressed my body, running his hands along my arms and shoulders. Up and down my back. He untied my arms first, kissing down my skin as he unwound the rope. He turned me onto my back and brought my wrists to his lips. Kissed them gently.

He babied my entire body, lavishing me with soft kisses as he untied me. The ropes had left marks—although nothing that hurt—and he took his time, running his lips over every inch.

I didn't complain when he got up and put his shirt and underwear back on. I would have loved the chance to run my hands over his chest, but maybe he wasn't ready for that.

Besides, I was so utterly relaxed, I could barely move.

He lay down beside me, propping his head in his hand, and traced his fingertips over my belly. "Thank you."

I drew in a slow breath, enjoying the scent of him. Of us. Feeling the compressions on my skin. The satisfaction of a delicious orgasm. "For what?"

"For trusting me."

"Thank you," I said.

"For what?"

"For what we just experienced together."

"It was incredible, wasn't it?" he asked.

I nodded. "What was it like for you?"

"Intoxicating. You tied up is the sexiest fucking thing I've ever seen. What did it feel like?"

"Different than I expected," I said. "The ropes felt good, in and of themselves. It was like being hugged. I was afraid it would be scary, but it wasn't. It was almost nurturing."

He smiled, still brushing his fingers up and down my belly. "That makes me feel good. I didn't want it to hurt you."

"No, it didn't."

"It was kind of freeing for me, if that makes any sense."

"It does." I reached up and touched his face. "I couldn't have done that with anyone but you."

He leaned down and brought his lips to mine. Kissed me softly. "I love you."

"I love you, too."

He nestled down beside me and gathered me in his arms. I drifted on a cloud of bliss, cuddled against him. It felt so good to let go. To trust. To know Leo would always take care of me.

I just had to show him I'd always do the same. Then maybe he'd let me all the way in.

26

LEO

$\mathcal{I}$ got out of the shower and dried off, running the towel over my face, down my chest. I felt good this morning. Rested. Healthier. The hot morning sex with Hannah probably had something to do with that. I'd tied her up again—just her arms this time—and it had been unbelievable.

I pulled my hair back into a knot and tied it with one of Hannah's hair ties. She'd convinced me to try it when I worked out, and I had to admit, it was nice to have my hair out of my face. Despite Cooper and Chase mercilessly teasing me about my man bun, I'd started wearing it this way sometimes.

After getting dressed, I hung up my towel and went out to the kitchen to get some coffee. Hannah was already at our desk, her hair up, headphones on. She clicked her mouse and moved things on her screen, bopping her head to whatever music she was listening to.

She threw her arms up and wiggled her butt in her chair, whisper-singing the lyrics. I stood in the entrance to the kitchen, smiling as I watched her chair-dance. She was so damn adorable.

How did this beauty end up here, with me?

She turned around and pulled her headphones back. "I can feel you watching me."

"You're cute when you wiggle your ass like that."

She shrugged. "It's a good song. Gets me every time."

"What are you up to today?"

"You're looking at it." She jerked her thumb at her screen. "What about you?"

"They're having some issues at the front desk over at the Big House. I'm going to go take a look."

"Okay, have fun. Say hi to Zoe for me if you see her."

"Sure." I spun her around to give her a kiss.

After putting on my coat and shoes, I ventured out into the cold. When I got to the Big House and went inside, I rubbed my hands together and blew into my fists.

Lindsey was behind the counter, helping a guest, so I stood aside and waited. We weren't quite as busy in the winter, but we still had a full events schedule bringing people to the winery. There was a brunch in the back room this morning—someone's anniversary, if I remembered correctly—but guests were only just starting to arrive.

A couple walked in with a little boy. He was probably three or four, with blond hair, and dressed in a sweater with a bear on the front. The parents waited behind the other guest, their backs to me, but the boy turned to explore the lobby.

His gaze landed on me and his mouth opened. Eyes widened. Wordlessly, he stumbled backward, reaching up as if seeking the solace of his parents' arms.

Trying to get away from me.

Looking down, I turned so the scarred side of my face wouldn't show. But it was too late. He'd seen, and he was terrified.

"Mommy," he whimpered, pointing at me. "Mommy."

"What's the matter, honey?" she asked, her voice soft as she picked him up and situated him on her hip.

"That man." He pointed at me again.

"What man?" She glanced back at me and surprise flitted across her features. But like most adults, she quickly smoothed her expression, and she turned back to her son. "Shh, buddy. Don't point. It's not polite."

"But Mommy."

The kid was almost crying. Most kids were scared of me, so I avoided them if I could. I certainly didn't let them see me straight on. But this little guy had gotten an eyeful, and it was clear his mother's reassurances weren't going to be enough to calm him down.

I ducked out as quickly as I could, heading upstairs. There were mostly offices on the second floor. I could wait up there until the lobby cleared out a bit.

The small meeting room was empty, so I went inside and closed the door. Sank into a chair and rested my forehead in my hands.

My fucking face. Maybe it shouldn't have mattered to me what some little kid thought, but it stung. Normal people didn't inspire fear in children. This was the price I had to pay.

The encounter left me feeling like crap—and like hiding. The impulse was so strong I almost crawled under the table. Now that was some messed-up shit. I had to consciously stop myself from dropping to the floor and covering my head. What the fuck was wrong with me?

Panic. That was what was wrong with me. I had a goddamn case of chronic PTSD and I always would. Recognizing the feeling for what it was didn't help this time. I couldn't escape the intense sensation of imminent danger. Like my life was being threatened.

Get down.

Take cover.

I fought against the panic threatening to overtake me. Tried to breathe. I hated that my brain and body did this to me. Part of me was convinced I was about to die, and my body reacted accordingly. I fucking hated it. Hated that I had to live like this.

Get down.

Take cover.

"Fuck," I growled. I got up and paced around the room, willing myself to stay in here. Not to run out of the building. At least here no one else was around to see me lose my shit.

I backed against the wall and slid down. Put my head down on my knees. *Breathe, Leo. Just fucking breathe.* Why couldn't I remember how? My brain wouldn't work. I couldn't calm down. There was a way through this, if I could just remember how.

My phone buzzed in my pocket. I almost ignored it, but the thought that it might be Hannah made me check. She'd texted me, but the screen was too blurry. I couldn't read it, so I just called her.

"Oh, hey," she said. "I'm so sorry to bug you when you're working, but do you have a second?"

"Hannah," I choked out.

"Leo, what's wrong?"

I gasped for breath. My chest felt like it was being crushed.

"Where are you?" she asked. "The Big House?"

"Upstairs."

"I'm coming. Hang in there with me, okay? You're going to be fine."

I heard the sound of a door close, then what might have been footsteps. Hannah running.

"Stay with me, Leo," she said. "I'm heading over. Just breathe, okay?"

"Yeah."

She kept talking, getting breathless as she ran.

"I'm here," she said. "Where upstairs?"

I couldn't answer. I had no idea where I was.

Footsteps approached outside and she burst through the door.

"Oh god, Leo."

Seconds later, her arms were around me, my head on her chest. We were lying on the floor, although I didn't remember how I'd gotten there.

The sound of her heartbeat was like magic. *Thump. Thump. Thump.* It pulled at me, coaxing my own heart to match its calm rhythm. I kept my eyes closed and breathed. She smelled so good. I only realized I'd been shaking when my body began to stop, the shivering subsiding.

"Shh," Hannah whispered, stroking my back. "You're okay. I'm here. You're okay."

I focused on her voice, letting it anchor me. The world started to come back and I remembered where I was. Upstairs in the Big House. And I'd just had one of the worst panic attacks I'd had in a long time.

Sitting up, I leaned my back against the wall and pushed my hair out of my face. "Jesus."

Hannah sat in front of me and put her hand on my knee. "Do you need me to get someone? Your mom?"

I shook my head. Mom knew how to help me through these, but Hannah's soothing voice had been better than anything else I'd ever tried.

"I'm sorry," I said. "I don't know what happened."

"Don't apologize."

I took another slow breath. "I used to get panic attacks all the time. Daily. I don't get them nearly as often anymore. That was the worst in a long time."

"Does something usually trigger them?"

"Sometimes." I didn't want to tell her about the kid. That

shouldn't have made me panic like that anyway. "They can hit out of the blue, though."

She just nodded and kept rubbing my leg.

Zoe poked her head in. "Hey. Do you need anything?"

Hannah shook her head. "I don't think so."

"I'll be right over here if you do," Zoe said, her voice soft.

"Do you want to stay here for a while?" Hannah asked. "Or go home?"

"Let's go." I didn't want to sit here on the fucking floor anymore. Felt like an idiot.

My body felt jittery from all the adrenaline. I got up and helped Hannah to her feet. That's when I realized she wasn't wearing shoes.

"Did you run over here in socks?"

She glanced down. "Oh. Yeah, I guess I did."

"Damn it, Hannah. I'm sorry."

She threaded her arms around my waist and looked up at me. "It's fine. Why don't we go home and get in bed. I bet snuggling under warm covers will help calm you down. You still feel really tense."

I was tense. Although I still had Lindsey's issue to deal with at the front desk, it would have to wait. I was in no state of mind to troubleshoot computer problems, especially with guests around.

And Hannah's suggestion did sound good. The thought of her in my bed woke up my dick—which was an odd feeling on the tail end of a panic attack. It made me feel quite a bit better, in fact. Like my body had something to do with all the adrenaline coursing through my veins.

I hugged her back, enjoying the feel of her little body against me. "Yeah. Let's go get in bed."

27

LEO

The panic attack at the Big House left me on edge. Hannah had done wonders to calm me down, but the way it had come on bothered me. It had been so sudden, and so debilitating. I hated to think what I would have done if Hannah hadn't texted. Or if she'd texted a few minutes later. Would I have had the presence of mind to call her? Who would have found me if she hadn't come—and what state would I have been in?

I'd thought I'd been doing so well. Leaving the winery, sometimes even without Hannah. I didn't always like it, but I could do it. That was a far cry from where I'd been before her.

But this felt like a relapse waiting to happen.

I had a Skype call with my therapist and he was reassuring, although I could tell he was concerned. He said to try to take it easy and avoid potential triggers. Give my system a chance to reset.

I just hoped it would.

Instead of going back to the Big House to deal with the front desk issue during business hours, I went the next evening, after we'd closed. It was easier that way. The last thing I needed was to wind up backed into a corner, shaking.

I was such a fucking mess.

It was quiet outside when I left and locked the door behind me. I liked being out at night. Darkness cloaked the world, blanketing it all in shadow. Made it easier to stay hidden. It was cold, though, so I zipped my coat and stuffed my hands in my pockets.

Hannah was singing in the shower when I got home. Shaking my head, I took off my coat. She was many things, but a good singer wasn't one of them. Didn't stop her from belting out eighties pop tunes when she thought no one was listening, though.

Fucking adorable.

I sat down and checked the security footage like I always did. There was something calming about it. My therapist said it gave me the illusion of control, but was otherwise a harmless coping tactic. As long as it didn't cross into compulsion territory—which it had, in the beginning—it was probably okay.

Despite my mom's protests, I'd installed a camera outside her house a few weeks ago. It gave me a view of the area in front of her porch, mostly. I clicked over to check the live feed. Her car wasn't there, but that wasn't unusual. She might have been at the store. Or maybe Roland and Zoe's, or out in Tilikum visiting Grace's mom, Naomi.

I checked a few more things, leaving that feed open on one monitor. The shower turned off and Hannah stopped singing.

Headlights flashed in front of Mom's house, the light on the screen catching my attention. Before she could finish parking, a man stepped out of the darkness, right in front of her car.

What the fuck?

She braked hard to avoid hitting him. He stood with his hands casually in his pockets, wearing sunglasses although it was dark outside.

Don't get out of the car, Mom. Drive away.

"Oh hey, you're back." Hannah stood in the hallway wrapped in a towel, her hair hanging wet around her shoulders.

"I'll be right back," I said.

"What's going on?"

I glanced at the screen. The guy was walking around to the driver's side. Why wasn't she leaving? Damn it, Mom.

"Call my mom and tell her to drive away."

"What?"

"Just do it."

I took off outside, running as fast as my feet would carry me. The scar tissue on my thigh hurt from the sudden burst of movement, but I ignored the pain. If that piece of shit put one finger on my mother, I'd turn him inside out.

It only took me a couple of minutes to cover the distance between my house and hers. By the time I got there, her car was still in the same spot—slightly crooked from the hard stop. And it was empty.

"Fuck." I ran up the porch steps and tried the front door. Locked. I punched in the code and threw the door open. "Mom?"

She was standing in the living room, her phone in her hands like she'd been about to make a call. Her face was shockingly white, her eyes wide with fear.

I grabbed my chest, trying to catch my breath. Thank god she was here.

"Jesus fuck, Mom," I said. "What the hell happened?"

She took quick steps toward me and landed in my arms. I held her tight, smoothing down her hair.

"It's okay," I said. "But you need to tell me what just happened."

She moved back and took a deep breath. "A man stepped in front of my car when I got home just now."

"Yeah, I saw that on the security feed. Why didn't you drive away?"

"He had a gun, Leo."

I ground my teeth together. Motherfucker threatened my mother with a gun. I'd fucking kill him.

"He opened his coat and he had a gun. I locked the door, but I was scared. He came over to the window and motioned for me to roll it down. I opened it a tiny crack and he said he just wanted to talk to me."

"What did he say?"

"He said I needed to go pay my husband a visit. And I said *ex-husband*, and he said that doesn't matter. He said I need to tell Lawrence he needs to cooperate or more than mattresses will be burning here."

"What the hell?"

"After that he walked away, but he put that on the hood of my car." She pointed to something on the table.

I walked over and picked it up. It was a thick piece of grapevine—charred and burned.

"Did he really say more than mattresses will burn?" I asked.

She nodded. "Leo, the fire pit isn't on the public grounds. No one goes back there but us. How did he know about the mattresses?"

"It means he's having us watched," I said.

"Should we call the police?" she asked.

"Yeah," I said. "I don't think they'll be able to do anything, but we should file a report. We should call Agent Rawlins, too. And someone needs to stay here with you tonight."

I eyed her, waiting for her to argue, but this time she didn't. She wrapped her arms around herself and nodded.

"What does he want with Lawrence?"

"I don't know. But if they can't get their money out of him, maybe they want something else in return."

"But he's in jail."

I pulled her in for another hug. "I'll find out. I'm not going to let anything happen to you."

A loud knock on the door made her jump.

"Mom?" Cooper's voice was muffled. The lock beeped as he put in the code. The door burst open and he and Amelia came in. "Mom, what's going on?"

Not two seconds later, tires crunched on the gravel outside and headlights flashed through the front window. We heard a car door slam and Ben rushed inside. His eyes landed on my mom and he let out a breath.

"Oh thank god," Ben said. "Hannah called and said something about you being in trouble."

Hannah. She must have called everyone. God, I loved that girl.

We filled them in on what had happened, then went over it again when Roland, Chase, and Brynn arrived. Roland put in a call to Rawlins and the local police came to take a statement.

After the commotion died down, my poor mom looked exhausted. Roland had to go home to Zoe and Hudson, but Cooper, Amelia, Chase, and Brynn all declared they were staying the night. Ben looked pained when he finally left. He was still sitting in his truck outside her house when I went home, and I wondered if he'd stay there all night.

Hannah and I went to bed, but I couldn't sleep. I got up and went to my desk. Pulled up the footage. Who the hell was this guy? And what did they want with Dad?

There was only one way to find out.

∽

I MET the guard's gaze when he inspected my ID. He checked me in, gave me a visitor's badge. And I waited.

I'd gotten a few hours of sleep with Hannah curled up next to me. Then got up early to drive out here.

The visiting room was empty this time. A guard led me in and nodded to a table. I sat and folded my hands in front of me. A few minutes later, another guard brought Dad in.

He looked about the same as last time. Maybe a little worse. He'd lost weight, but it left him looking gaunt, rather than healthy. The prison blues gave his skin a sallow cast and he had dark circles under his eyes.

"Leo," he said as he sat. "I didn't think I'd see you again."

"Listen," I said, leaning close and lowering my voice. "You're going to answer my questions and you're going to tell me the truth. Are we clear?"

"Did something happen?" he asked.

"Yes, something fucking happened," I hissed. "Some asshole threatened Mom last night."

He let out a breath, closing his eyes. "Damn it."

"You don't seem surprised."

"What happened?"

"He told Mom she needs to pay you a visit and tell you to cooperate." I held his gaze, not shying away. Not trying to hide my face. "Cooperate with what?"

He closed his mouth, his eyes darting toward the guard, and shook his head.

"Dad," I said, lowering my voice again. "He flashed a gun at her and threatened to burn down the winery. Cooperate with what? What do they want from you?"

Dad shifted in his chair, then leaned closer. "I can't pay my debt and they're disappointed in how the poppy crop turned out."

"I can't imagine why drug dealers would be mad that their heroin source was destroyed," I said, my voice laced with sarcasm.

"These people aren't playing around," he said. "They know I'm going to prison. The state's case against me is ironclad. I have no defense. So there's no chance of me paying them back."

"They don't want the land, do they?" I asked.

He shook his head. "No. Too complicated."

"Then what?"

His eyes flicked to the guard again. "They want me to take care of something for them. In here."

I blew out a breath and scrubbed my hands up and down my face. "Jesus. They want you to kill someone?"

"God knows I'm no saint," he said. "I've done a lot of things I'm not proud of. But I'm not a murderer, Leo."

"Who is it?"

He shrugged. "Some political insider. They didn't tell me why they want him dead."

"Why you? Other than you owe them money. You're a white-collar criminal, not violent. Why make you do it?"

"Probably opportunity," he said. "He's being held here while he awaits his trial, same as me. My guess is, he has dirt on them, and they don't want him cutting a deal. And they have me by the balls, so they figure they'll use me to do their dirty work."

"And now they're threatening your family."

"I never meant to get your mom involved," he said. "I told them we're divorced."

"I don't think they give a shit."

"Look, I don't know what you want me to do from in here," he said. "I can't do it, Leo. I thought about it, but... I can't."

"Tell me who they are," I said. "I need something. A contact. A phone number. A location. Anything."

"There's a guy who goes by Joe Smith. Cooper met him once. He was my main contact."

"A fake name? That's all you can give me?"

Dad looked away.

"Dad," I said, my voice still quiet, but hard. "I need more than that if I'm going to help."

He leaned closer, lowering his voice to a whisper. "There's another guy. An accountant. He's the money guy. Name's Edward Mozcinski. I met him once. He's the only other one I know. The rest were just goons and I didn't get names of the higher-ups."

"Wait, Edward Mozcinski?" I asked. "Why does that name sound familiar?"

"He was in the media a few years ago," he said. "Someone wrote a book about the family he works for. All those Godfather parallels."

Oh shit. I had heard of this guy. "He works for the Paine family? That's a mob family, Dad."

"Believe me, I'm well aware of that."

"What else do you know?" I asked. "Come on, Dad. You were working with these guys."

"I doubt I know anything the feds don't," he said. "The poker games moved locations every night. I wasn't buying drugs from them, so I don't know anything about their distribution. I was just going to supply them the opium, that was all. Joe texted me sometimes to make sure things were on schedule, and he provided the workers to tend the crop. But I arranged everything through him, and we never met in the same place twice. Except..."

"Except what?"

Dad's eyes flicked to the guard again. "There was this old lumber mill, north of Echo Creek. We met there a couple of times. It's out in the middle of nowhere, so the first time I figured it was just another out-of-the-way location. But the second time, I saw Mozcinski there. I'd seen him once before, and I knew who he was. I thought it was odd that he was out there. It was just a lumber mill."

"Or a front."

"Right," Dad said. "Could have been. But Leo, listen to me. Don't get involved in this. These people, they'll... they'll kill you."

"I'm not getting involved," I said. "The best way to end this is to help the feds get these guys. Haven't you been interviewed? Told them what you know?"

"Jesus, Leo, they'll kill me in here," he said.

"So you're not cooperating," I said. It wasn't a question.

"I gave them what I could."

I shook my head. "Cheating on your wife just wasn't enough for you."

"I've apologized—"

"Bullshit. You betrayed your wife in every way possible, abandoned your family, and now you put us all in danger."

He glanced down. At least he had the decency to look guilty.

"How do you live with yourself, as a man? It's our job to protect those who are weaker than us. As men, that's our duty."

He kept his eyes on the table. "What are you going to do?"

"I'm going to do what you couldn't," I said, rising from my seat. "I'm going to protect my family."

I walked away, hoping to god I never had to look at his face again.

28

HANNAH

*E*verything at Salishan felt like chaos, and I felt like vomiting.

Local police drove through the grounds every few hours. A DEA agent was at Shannon's house, meeting with her and Roland. Amelia and Cooper were with Zoe and Brynn at the Big House, trying to keep the impact to the guests as minimal as possible. Leo had gone to see his dad this morning, and his siblings were mad that he'd gone alone without telling anyone.

I spent my morning trying to ignore the roiling in my stomach. I hadn't slept well, and everyone around me was so stressed. It was rubbing off on me, leaving me edgy and distracted.

I was worried about Leo. Worried about Shannon. Worried about what it meant that someone had threatened her last night.

Leo got home, but he didn't want to talk. He sat down at the desk, his attention focused. He was so tense, it was making me feel worse, so I decided to get out for a little while.

"Where are you going?" he asked, looking up as if suddenly remembering I was here.

"Just out," I said.

"You shouldn't go anywhere alone."

"Your sisters are at the Big House," I said. "I'll just go there."

He stared at me, unblinking.

"I'll be fine," I said. "It's a short walk and I'll text you when I get there. How about that?"

"Okay. Just be careful."

"I will."

The Big House wasn't much better. Zoe had brought Hudson to work with her. She was upstairs in her office trying to get him to nap. Cooper and Amelia had taken a group of guests out on a winery tour, and Brynn was in the tasting room. Chase sat in the corner, looking a little menacing, as if he expected any one of the customers to suddenly turn on his wife.

Ben wandered in, then back out again, his face set with grim determination. I wondered if he'd slept last night. I'd called him first after Leo left, then Cooper. Ben had just said *on my way* and hung up. Today he reminded me of a guard dog walking a patrol.

I didn't stay long. Everyone was busy, and it didn't feel any calmer here. Maybe I could get Leo to talk—see if I could help. I hated feeling useless. These people were in crisis, and I wished there was something I could do.

As I walked back home, a car pulled up behind me. My back tensed. Leo's house was beyond where guests usually came, so it was rare that a car drove back here. The house was just up ahead. For a split second I debated between looking over my shoulder and simply sprinting for home.

The car stopped, so I glanced back.

Oh no.

A man I'd hoped I'd never have to see again slowly got out of the car. Jace.

He was dressed in civilian clothes. I quickly looked him over to see if he might be hiding a gun. I didn't see anything, but it could have been tucked behind his back.

The sick feeling in my stomach intensified and I tasted bile on the back of my tongue. "You're not supposed to be here."

"I just want to talk."

"What part of *protection order* do you not understand?" I asked. "You're supposed to stay away from me."

He put his hands up, as if to appear non-threatening. "I said I just want to talk."

"No," I said, taking a step backward.

"Hannah, come on. Things got out of control, but this is fucked up."

"No, what's fucked up is you putting me in the hospital."

"Look, I know. That was wrong. I shouldn't have done that."

I sighed. "Jace, why are you here?"

"They put me on leave at work," he said. "And I'm going to counseling."

"Mandatory counseling," I said.

"Yeah, but that's not the point."

"Then what is the point?"

He paused for a beat, his eyes boring into me. "You should come home. I know you can't right now. But when the order expires."

My mouth fell open. "Are you serious?"

"Yes. I miss you."

I gaped at him. "You're unbelievable. How did you even find me?"

"You changed your number and you blocked me on everything," he said. "What was I supposed to do?"

"Stay away from me," I said. "You realize I have to report you."

"No, Hannah, don't do that." He held up a hand and walked toward me. "I just want to talk to you. We can work this out."

I took another step backward. "There's nothing to work out. You beat the shit out of me and you think I'm going to come back to you?"

"I got a little out of control, but I'm doing better now."

My heart thumped hard and fear sizzled in my belly. He had that look in his eyes. I'd seen it before. He always got that feverish glaze when he was about to lose his temper. Get violent.

"Back up, Jace."

"I'm not going to hurt you."

"That's great, but you still need to stop."

He came at me, his arm outstretched.

"Leo!" I shouted over my shoulder.

"This is your fucking fault, Hannah," Jace said through clenched teeth. "I'm going to lose everything because of you. If you just fucking come home, they'll see everything's fine. They'll put me back on duty."

"It's not my fault you hit me, asshole."

Jace grabbed my arms but before I could even scream, he let go. I staggered backward, ready to yell for Leo again, but he was already here.

He'd moved so fast, I'd hardly seen him. Before I knew what was happening, he had Jace pinned down on the ground, his arms wrenched behind his back.

How had he done that?

"Don't fucking touch her," Leo growled.

Jace winced. "What the fuck?"

"I said don't touch her." Leo leaned down, his voice cold steel. His knee pressed into the small of Jace's back. "If you so much as lay a finger on her, I'll break every bone in your body."

As if to drive his point home, Leo pulled on one of Jace's arms. Jace cried out in pain.

"Is that understood?" Leo asked.

"Yeah," Jace said through gritted teeth, his face in the dirt.

Leo still didn't let him up. He was so calm, it was almost scary. I had no doubt he'd do exactly what he'd promised if Jace touched me again.

"Holy shit, Leo."

I heard Cooper's voice behind me, then footsteps running toward us.

"Who the fuck is this guy?" Cooper asked. "The one who threatened Mom?"

"No, that's Jace," I said, still staring at them in awe.

"This is Dickmonkey?" Cooper asked, taking a step forward. "What are we going to do with him?"

Leo looked up, his cold gaze meeting Cooper's.

"Nothing," I said quickly. "I'm going to call the police and let them deal with it."

Cooper growled, but took a step back. "Fine. If Rawlins is still here, I bet he'd be happy to babysit him while you wait for the cops."

"That's a good idea, Coop. Can you ask him to come over here?" I put my hand on his arm and nudged him back. Giving Cooper a job seemed prudent. Leo wasn't doing anything other than holding Jace down, but his expression looked a little unhinged. I wanted to save both of them from assault charges.

Leo adjusted his grip and Jace shouted again.

Cooper scowled as he took out his phone. "Are you sure I can't just kick him a few times?"

"No."

Leo kept Jace in the submission hold while Cooper got Agent Rawlins, and I called the police. Rawlins arrived and handcuffed Jace, and the local police arrived a few minutes later.

I watched Jace get arrested—again—this time for violating the protection order.

Leo stood with his arms crossed, his eyes never leaving Jace. He was like a coiled spring—so tense. Seeing him take Jace down had been as frightening as it had been satisfying. I had no idea how he'd moved so fast.

The police drove away and Cooper offered to wait for the tow truck, on its way to take Jace's car. He seemed to take gleeful satisfaction in the fact that not only had Jace been arrested, his car was being impounded as well.

I went inside, feeling like I was ready to shatter. My nerves were raw, my stomach a churning mess. I couldn't believe Jace had shown up here. What the hell had he been thinking? And with everything else Leo's family had to deal with, my drama was the last thing they needed.

With shaky hands, I got myself a glass of water.

Leo stood in the doorway to the kitchen. "Are you okay?"

"No," I said. "I'm angry and scared and overwhelmed. I didn't think I'd see him again and he found me. And then you took him down like you're some kind of fucking ninja."

"I'm sorry if I scared you."

"It's not that. I'm glad you were there. I'm glad you knew how to do that. I just—"

My stomach churned and I clapped a hand over my mouth. *Oh, no.*

I raced to the bathroom, barely making it before the contents of my stomach hurled out into the toilet. I crouched down, heaving, my muscles spasming as I vomited.

Leo was behind me, his hand on my back, murmuring something.

When it was over, I sat back and brushed my hair out of my face. My forehead was covered in a sheen of sweat, my palms clammy.

"Are you done?" Leo asked.

"I think so."

He helped me clean up, then got me a fresh glass of water and put me to bed. My stomach was better, but I was exhausted. It felt like I'd run a marathon on an empty stomach.

I had no idea what time it was, but I didn't care. I curled up in bed and went to sleep.

29

HANNAH

I threw up again early the next morning. Although I felt better when it was over, Leo insisted I go back to bed and take the day off. Yesterday, I'd figured my stomach issues had been mostly stress-related. Today, I assumed I must have picked up a virus.

When it happened again the next morning, I got a little worried.

Leo didn't know—he was out when it happened. And when he came back, I decided not to tell him. I didn't want him to worry. After all, once I'd thrown up, I felt fine.

I wasn't stupid. I knew what could make a woman throw up in the absence of illness. I hadn't worried about condoms with Leo. I'd been tested for everything under the sun when they'd had me in the hospital after Jace's assault, and I had an IUD. Leo hadn't had sex with anyone in years. We both knew we were clean, and I was on birth control. It wasn't like we'd been throwing caution to the wind.

I tried to put it out of my mind. It was probably just the stress.

That afternoon, I had plans to meet Zoe for coffee. Leo

insisted on walking me there—it wasn't far—but I had to make him promise he'd go home and not stand around outside waiting for me. In exchange, I promised to text him when I was done and either walk back with Zoe, or wait for him to come get me.

I went inside and it was a relief to see Zoe already at a table. I ordered a coffee and sat down with her.

"Hey, you," she said. "How've you been?"

I blew out a long breath. "Okay, I guess? Considering everything."

"What a fucking mess," she said.

"I know. I'll be glad when everything feels normal again."

"It will," she said. "By the way, I noticed Leo escorted you here."

"Yeah, he's just really tense after what happened to Shannon. And my ex showing up the other day did not help."

She waved a hand. "Oh, I know. I was just going to say Roland did the same thing. I wouldn't be surprised if he's still sitting out there, watching every person who comes in here."

"These Miles brothers, huh?"

"Yep. Cooper's been driving Amelia to the ranch and then finding excuses to stay. She put him to work cleaning out stalls this morning. And Chase apparently decided he's Brynn's new bouncer."

I laughed. "Wow."

"It's weird," she said. "After what happened to Shannon, I can't decide if they're overreacting or not. Roland and I keep waffling on whether to have the nanny bring Hudson to Salishan during the day, or stay home."

"Do you think the DEA are going to track these guys down?"

"I hope so. It'll be nice to feel like we can relax again," she said. "On the bright side, the new logo looks amazing."

"Thanks." I'd given them several options, and we'd settled on one with a lovely script font. It was reminiscent of their original logo and evoked the classic feel Shannon had wanted. I had to admit, I was proud of it. "I'm happy with how it turned out, and the new website is coming along."

"That's great."

I picked up my coffee, but my stomach did a little flip. I put it down and pressed my hand against my belly.

"You okay?" she asked.

"Yeah. I just haven't been feeling well for the last few days."

"Do you think it's stress? Or are you coming down with something?"

I felt my forehead. "I don't feel warm or anything. It's probably just stress."

Zoe narrowed her eyes. "Tummy trouble?"

"Yeah."

"How many times have you thrown up?"

"What? How do you know if I've thrown up at all?"

"I work with a lot of brides," she said. "I have good instincts. How many times?"

I glanced down. "A few."

"Have you taken a test yet?"

"I can't be pregnant," I said, lowering my voice. "I have an IUD."

"Well, nothing is foolproof," she said. "How long have you had it?"

"About a year, I think."

"Did you go back for a follow-up and get it checked?" she asked.

I stared at her. "Um..."

"You didn't, did you?" she asked. "I'm telling you, I've had more than one puking bride get a positive pregnancy test after telling me she has an IUD. Turns out, she had it put in, but didn't go back for her follow up. Usually it's fine, but once in a while it's not in correctly and..."

"Oh my god, Zoe."

"It's okay," she said, her voice soothing. "Don't panic. You're probably not pregnant. But I think you should take a test to be sure. I have tons of them in my office."

With shaky hands, I texted Leo to let him know Zoe and I were walking back to Salishan together. Thankfully, he didn't insist on coming to walk us back. I wasn't ready to see him yet. I'd probably blurt out that I was about to go take a pregnancy test, and I didn't want to freak him out. Especially because it was probably just stress. With everything else Leo had going on, the last thing he needed was a false pregnancy scare, even a short-lived one.

It felt like everyone was staring at me when we walked into the Big House. They weren't, of course. But it was hard not to imagine that they were watching. Like everyone—from the staff to the guests—knew.

Zoe led me into her office and pulled out a box of pregnancy tests.

"How many of those do you have?" I asked as she handed me a stick wrapped in plastic packaging.

"I always keep them on hand," she said. "You never know when a bride is going to need one."

There was a bathroom down the hall. I scurried in, although no one else was upstairs. Trembling with nervousness, I checked the directions, unwrapped the stick, and took the test.

My heart raced as I waited the three minutes for the result. *It's going to say not pregnant*, I told myself. *And I'm going to feel silly for getting so worked up.*

When the time was up, I grabbed the stick and almost threw up again.

Pregnant.

THE NEXT HOUR went by in a blur.

I showed Zoe the test and begged her for another. Maybe this one had been faulty. She'd indulged me with a knowing look in her eyes, and hadn't been the least bit surprised when the second one came back the same.

She insisted I go to the doctor immediately. Not just to confirm the pregnancy, but to check on the status of my IUD.

The wait at the local urgent care clinic was blessedly short. I took another pregnancy test, and the doctor came back with the same result. I was definitely pregnant.

She checked for my IUD, and sure enough, at some point it had fallen out. I hadn't even realized. She'd been kind and compassionate, and sent me home with a brochure on pregnancy and the names of a few local obstetricians.

Zoe drove me back to Salishan. I sat in her car, feeling shell-shocked. I was pregnant? How was I going to tell Leo?

"You'll be okay," she said, patting my leg. "Just be honest. He'll be surprised, but so are you. I'm sure you guys are going to be fine."

"Thanks, Zoe."

"Of course."

With my heart in my throat, I went inside.

"Hey," Leo said, spinning around in his chair. He was dressed in his usual long-sleeved shirt and jeans, but today he had his hair pulled back. I loved it when he did that.

"Hi."

"How was coffee?"

"Good."

His brow furrowed. "Is everything okay?"

No, Leo. Everything is most definitely not okay. "I kind of need to talk to you about something."

"Sure."

I sank down onto the couch. How was he going to react? We hadn't been together very long. And he'd trusted me to be on birth control.

"Hannah," he said, his voice concerned. "What's wrong?"

I met his eyes. "I'm pregnant."

He stared at me for a long moment, hardly moving, his eyes unblinking. "You're... what?"

"Do I have to say it again? I'm pregnant."

I needed him to do something—anything other than staring at me wordlessly. But he just sat there.

Finally, he stood and ran a hand over his beard. He had the deep groove between his eyebrows he got when he was stressed. "I don't know what to say."

"Well... I know it's a surprise—"

"Yeah," he said, his voice sharp. "It's definitely that."

"It's not like I did this on purpose."

"You told me you were on birth control."

"I know. I was. Or I thought I was. My IUD came out and I didn't know."

"Holy shit." He wandered into the kitchen, then came back. "How does that happen? How does *this* just happen?"

"I don't know. I'm freaking out, too. Why are you acting like it's all my fault? You were there too."

"That's not what I mean."

"Well, what do you mean? Because you're really confusing me right now."

"This isn't good. I can't..." He trailed off, scrubbing his hands up and down his face. "Jesus."

"I know it's unexpected and it's certainly not what either of us would have planned, but is it that bad?"

"Yes, it's that bad," he snapped.

I gaped at him, so shocked I had no idea what to say. My

lungs felt compressed, like I couldn't get enough air, and a sick feeling spread through my stomach.

Touching my fingers to my lips, I took a shaky breath and stood. "All right. If that's how you feel about it."

I went back to the bedroom and pulled out my bag. I had no idea where I was going. I just knew I couldn't stay here. Not tonight.

"What are you doing?" His voice had a hint of hysteria to it.

"Packing. I think we need some space tonight."

I heard him take a deep breath. "Yeah, maybe we do."

Tears stung my eyes as his footsteps retreated behind me. The door opened and closed. And he was gone.

My lower lip trembled, but I bit it hard to keep from crying. I was going to hold myself together. My stomach threatened to upend itself again, but I took slow breaths through my nose to stay calm while I packed.

Was I overreacting? Did I really need to leave?

I stopped packing and waited a while to see if he'd come back. Maybe we could talk this out. He'd been understandably surprised by my news. He hadn't exactly taken it well, but maybe he just needed a little time.

So I waited. And waited. And waited some more.

I texted him to see if he wanted to talk. No reply.

The longer I waited, the more upset I got. Where the hell was he? I'd told him I was having his baby, and his reaction was to run away?

Well, fuck this.

I called Zoe.

"Hey," she said. "Is everything okay?"

"No. No, everything is very much not okay."

"Oh god. What happened?"

"I don't even want to talk about it," I said. "Can I come crash at your place tonight?"

"Yeah, of course. We're here. Come on over."

"Thanks."

I went back to packing, furiously this time. What had I been thinking, staying here? This wasn't my home. It was Leo's house and I'd basically fallen into living with him. Everything about this had been too fast. Too rushed. We'd been friends for a long time, but what he'd done today made me feel like I didn't know him nearly as well as I'd thought.

With a bag of clothes and my essential toiletries, plus my laptop and purse, I headed to my car. I tossed my stuff in the back and slammed the door shut.

"Careful there," a voice said behind me. "You all right?"

I turned to find Ben standing nearby. He was dressed in a thick coat, jeans, and work boots. A knit hat was pulled down over his head.

"Honestly? No. Not really." I brushed my hair out of my face. "What are you doing out here? It's freezing."

"Making the rounds."

I nodded. Of course he was. Everyone was on high alert lately.

"Going somewhere?" he asked.

My breath misted out in a cloud. "Yeah. Zoe's."

His eyes were so kind. I knew he could tell something was wrong, but thankfully he didn't ask. He just nodded. "All right. Have a good night."

"Thanks. You too."

Zoe hugged me when I got to her house. She didn't press for details. Just got me set up in their guest room. I wasn't in any mood to talk, so I thanked her and Roland again for letting me stay and put myself to bed. I was exhausted and heartsick, and I just needed this day to be over.

30

LEO

*I*t was fucking cold out here, but I didn't care.

Walking away from Hannah had been a stupid thing to do. I knew it. But she'd seen me in the middle of a brutal panic attack just the other day. I didn't want her to see me lose my shit again—especially not because of her. And I'd been right on the brink of losing control.

I sat in front of the cold fire pit, the remnants of our last bonfire a charred heap in the center. The sun had gone down, and the temperature was dropping, the cold biting against my skin.

I wanted it to hurt. I wanted to sit out here until I shivered so hard I couldn't stop. Until my skin turned blue and my fingers and toes went numb.

It was better than burning, at least.

Hannah was pregnant. Her news had knocked the wind out of me, crushed the breath from my lungs. I'd accepted a long time ago that I wasn't going to be a father. Pre-Army, I hadn't given that much thought. I'd been too young to worry about whether I'd get married and have a family. But now? I couldn't be a father. It was something I didn't even question.

She was going to have my baby?

I closed my eyes, leaning my head back. Fuck.

Memories flashed through my mind. Children looking at me in horror. Their eyes welling with tears of fear. Pointing. Hiding behind their parents' legs. Crying.

I could live with that when it was a stranger. I'd even prepared myself for the day when my nephew was old enough to be afraid of me. I could handle it.

My own child? That, I couldn't face.

I touched the ruined side of my mouth. There wasn't enough flesh left to keep my lips closed. Even with my beard, it showed. The skin was thick and rippled as it went down my neck. I'd regained use of my arm and hand, but it would never be as strong as it had been before. I didn't even have a fucking ear on my left side.

I deserved it. Deserved it all. But Hannah and the baby she carried? They didn't deserve any of this. They both deserved a man who was whole.

"There you are." Ben came over and pulled up a chair next to me. "That's a shitty fire. Forget matches?"

I shook my head.

We sat in silence for a long moment.

"She went to Zoe's," he said.

"Good." So she had left. At least Roland could watch out for her.

"Maybe you want to sit out here freezing your balls off, but I don't," he said. "You can be silent and brooding at my place with a beer."

I glanced at him. He had a no-nonsense, don't-argue-with-me expression on his face.

"Sure," I said. "Thanks."

Ben lived a short drive from Salishan, up the slope of the

mountain. It was visible from certain parts of our property, but I'd never been here before.

Over the years, he'd remodeled an old log cabin. It smelled like cedar and pine with a hint of wood smoke. He'd furnished it comfortably, with a big couch in front of the wood-burning stove. The walls were bare timbers, the notches so precise not a bit of cold air could get through. Large windows in the front showed the sweeping view. Even in the dark, you could see most of Salishan from here. Vineyards, the main grounds and gardens. My mom's house was visible, the glow of her windows little spots of light.

Ben stoked the fire in his wood stove, then went to the fridge and brought out two beers. "Have a seat."

I took one and sank onto the brown leather couch. Ben sat in a worn recliner, crossing his ankle over his knee. We drank our beer in silence for a while. My toes slowly thawed, the heat from the fire sinking into my bones.

"Well?" Ben asked.

There wasn't much point in being anything but honest. Not with Ben. "Hannah's pregnant."

He didn't respond right away. Took a deep breath and another swig of beer. "She just told you today?"

"Yeah."

"Well, son. If she's at Zoe's, and you're here, I'd say that's a problem."

I stared at the bottle in my hand. "I know."

"You can't hide from this one, Leo," he said.

"I'm not hiding."

He raised an eyebrow.

I got up to pace. "I walked away because I was about to lose it. I thought I was getting better, but I had a fucking panic attack in the Big House a few days ago. I didn't want her to see me like that again. Especially if the reason was *her*, you know? How would that make her feel?"

"You seem pretty calm now. Why didn't you go home?"

"I don't know."

"You do know, you just don't want to talk about it."

"Yeah, well, this is complicated," I said. "And I don't know how to make her understand."

"Regardless, you have a responsibility now."

I leaned against the end of the thick wood mantle, my beer dangling from my fingers. "I know. I'm not going to abandon her."

"No, I don't think you would. You're a better man than that."

"I'll always take care of her, no matter what."

Ben let out a breath, but didn't say more, although I had a feeling he wanted to. Maybe he could tell I already knew I'd screwed up today. That was obvious. I hoped he'd stay quiet. I appreciated the beer, and the warm fire, but I didn't need a lecture right now.

After a few minutes of silence, Ben stood. "Do you want another drink? I don't know about you, but after the week I've had, I could use something stronger."

"Sure. Thanks, Ben."

I would take care of Hannah, and the baby. That was the best I could do. I was too fucking broken. Too damaged. And damn it, they deserved better than that.

Better than me.

31

HANNAH

*A*pparently, morning sickness was just my life now. I slept in, but woke up to roiling nausea and a need to run to the bathroom. Afterward, I cleaned up and took a shower, but I still didn't feel great.

Of course, that could also just be my life now.

When I came downstairs, Zoe gave me crystallized ginger and a tea blend she said had helped when she'd been pregnant with Hudson.

I curled up on the couch with my tea, hoping my stomach was done with its shenanigans for the day. It still felt raw and a little unstable, but the ginger seemed to be helping.

Roland and Zoe's house was filled with reminders of my current state. They had baby stuff everywhere. Hudson's car seat, a baby swing, a little round seat with a wide tray, a highchair in the kitchen. Brightly colored blocks, teething rings, blankets, bottles. They had newborn photos on the wall and a plaster mold of his tiny footprints.

It was all very cute, and very, very overwhelming.

My phone buzzed with a text from Leo. God, finally.

Leo: Just making sure you're safe.

Really? That was the first thing he texted me after yesterday? I rolled my eyes and replied.

Me: I'm at Zoe's.

I held my phone for a while, waiting. He didn't respond.

Zoe came in with Hudson and set him down on a blanket with a few baby toys. "Is Leo still being... very Leo?"

"He texted to ask if I'm *safe*, but that's it."

"Very Leo." She sat on the other side of the couch.

"What am I going to do? I tell him I'm pregnant, and this is his response?"

"What did he say when you told him?" she asked.

"He was shocked, of course," I said. "And that's fine, I didn't expect him to twirl me around with happiness. But he was so agitated. I asked him if it was *that* bad and he said yes, it was. So I said maybe we need a little space tonight, and he left."

"Ouch," Zoe said. "Yeah, he could have handled that better."

"I know this is so out of the blue. It's freaking me out, too. I didn't know if I'd ever have kids. Maybe. Like, years from now."

She gave me a sympathetic smile and scooted down on the floor to dangle a toy above Hudson. He grabbed at it, kicking his feet with excitement.

My phone buzzed again. I checked, hoping it was Leo. But it wasn't. It was Cooper.

Cooper: Hey sister-girl! Where's Leo?

Me: I don't know.

Cooper: Really? Neither of you are home.

Cooper: I came over to work out.

Me: I'm at Zoe's.

Cooper: Then where's Leo?

Me: I told you, I don't know.

Cooper: What's wrong?

Cooper: Is something wrong?

Cooper: I'm getting the sense that something's wrong.

Cooper: Do you need me to come over?

Cooper: I can probably help.

Me: No, that's okay.

Cooper: Are you sure?

Me: Yeah. I'm fine.

Cooper: Oh shit. That bad? What did he do?

Cooper: If you don't want to tell me, it's cool.

Cooper: But seriously, what did he do?

Cooper: He's my brother and there's brother-loyalty at play here, but if you need me to beat his ass for you, I'll totally do it.

Cooper: Only for you, though.

Cooper: I wouldn't do the same for Zoe or Brynn.

Cooper: Actually, yes I would.

Cooper: But only if they really deserved it.

Cooper: Same with Leo.

Cooper: Although Leo could easily kick my ass. He's like a fucking ninja. But I'd still do it if you needed me to.

Cooper: It wouldn't surprise me if he needed someone to knock some sense into him.

Me: No

Me: It's fine, Cooper

Me: You don't need to do anything.

Cooper: You've said fine twice, but okay.

Cooper: I'll wait to hear from you then.

I shook my head and tossed my phone on the couch next to me.

"Cooper?" Zoe asked.

"How did you guess?"

"The bewildered look on your face speaks volumes. Ever been in a group chat with him and Chase?"

I laughed a little. "No."

"It's both insane and hilarious."

"He was offering to kick Leo's ass for me," I said.

She snorted. "I'd like to see him try. Leo would turn him into a pretzel."

I thought about how quickly he'd taken down Jace. "No kidding."

My phone buzzed again. "Seriously?"

Shannon: Just checking in. Is everything okay?

"It's Shannon this time."

"Welcome to the Miles family," Zoe said.

I spent the next couple of hours fielding texts from... everyone. It didn't appear that Leo had told the whole family that I was pregnant, but it was clear they knew something was wrong. I didn't know where Leo was, or if he'd spent the night away from home, but something had tipped them off.

Shannon wanted to make sure I was okay and asked if I wanted to come over for lunch. The thought of food still made me queasy, and I wasn't ready to face Leo's mom. Not yet. Brynn and Amelia both asked what I was doing today, as if they simply wanted to get together with no ulterior motives.

Chase stopped by with a big bag of M&Ms and a handful of movies. Cooper texted again to tell me he'd spotted Leo going home. I even heard from Ben. He called to check up on me, and by his voice I had a very strong suspicion that he knew at least some of what was going on. I was also pretty sure that Leo had spent the night at his house.

Leo texted one more time, to ask if I was still at Zoe's. I replied with a simple *yes*. And that was that.

I didn't know what this all meant for me and Leo. We needed to talk this out—decide how we were going to handle it. Spending the day at Roland and Zoe's—surrounded by baby things and watching them with their son—was making the reality of being pregnant sink in quickly. I was going to have a baby—be responsible for a tiny human being. Did Leo want to be a part of that? Or was this a deal breaker for him?

Leo had some very real struggles, and I was sympathetic to that. But I had a baby to think about now. It would be months before he or she came into the world, but already, my focus was shifting. Maybe I didn't know what would become of my relationship with Leo, but I needed to make sure I was as ready for this as I could be.

Which meant I needed a place to live. And I didn't think it was going to be with Leo.

I found Zoe in the kitchen, washing bottles, the tea kettle on the stove. Roland had taken Hudson out for daddy-son time after his nap.

"I need to find a new place to live," I said.

She looked at me over her shoulder, a soapy bottle in her hand. "What?"

"I've been thinking about this all day. I'm going to have a baby, and I can't sit around waiting for Leo to decide what he wants."

"True."

"I make enough money to support myself. That's not an issue."

"Okay. That's good."

I leaned against the counter. "You're being very non-committal."

"You don't need my permission." She turned off the water and set the bottle on a drying rack. "Are you thinking of going back to Seattle, or staying around here?"

"I'd say close by. I'm not trying to leave. I just need to feel like I have my feet planted on the ground, you know? Leo doesn't..." I trailed off. It would hurt too much to say it out loud. *Leo doesn't seem to want to have this baby.* "I think this is the right thing to do.

You know the area better than I do. Can you help me find a place?"

The tea kettle whistled.

"More tea?"

I put my hand on my belly. It felt better than it had this morning. But tea did sound nice. "Please."

She poured water into two mugs. "Sure, I can help."

I took the mug, wrapping my hands around it, feeling the warmth seep into my skin. It smelled like lemon and ginger. "Thanks."

"You're sure about this?" she asked.

"Yes. I want to stay close, but I really think this is the best thing for me right now."

She blew on her tea, then took a sip. "Okay. I'll see what I can find."

32

LEO

With Hannah staying at Roland and Zoe's, at least I didn't have to worry about her. She was safe with them—maybe even safer than if she'd been here at Salishan.

But god, I missed her.

It had only been a couple of days, but I was crumbling inside without her. It was my fault, and I knew it. I needed to go see her. Sit with her and talk in person, instead of exchanging brief texts that didn't go anywhere.

The problem was, I didn't know what to say.

Darkness was pulling me under again. I could feel it happening. Feel the seductive pull of solitude.

I spent the first night she was gone at Ben's house—we'd gotten into the whiskey. I'd had enough presence of mind to know that walking home drunk in the freezing cold was a bad idea. But since then, I hadn't left home. Hadn't stepped a foot outside.

If I stayed here, I could control my environment—keep tabs on security. With my cameras, I knew who was coming and going in real time.

The still-rational part of me warned that I was slipping. That my constant vigilance was becoming obsessive, rather than necessary.

But it was all I had.

Danger lurked out there. That wasn't my imagination. A man had threatened my mother with a gun. They were a goddamn organized crime family. I didn't know how long we had before they'd either make good on their threat to Mom, or make an example out of Dad.

Agent Rawlins had assured us the DEA was working on a case against them. But the Paine family were experts at evading the law. There was a reason they were still operating, and it wasn't because the DEA was unaware of their existence.

I hated feeling so helpless. My personal life was a fucking disaster, and I didn't know what I was going to do about it. Protecting my family was all I had left to give. Maybe I was a goddamn mess, but I could do that much. I could make sure they were safe. I just had to figure out how.

My phone rang. I didn't recognize the number, and I usually let calls go to voicemail. But something told me I should answer.

"Hello?"

The voice on the other end sounded robotic. "Will you accept charges from the county corrections facility? Press one for yes."

Oh shit. I pressed one and waited.

"Leo?"

"Dad?"

"I wasn't sure if you'd answer."

Something about his voice sounded strange. "What's going on?"

"There was an incident last night."

Oh god. Please tell me he didn't... "What incident?"

"Seeing as I've failed to comply with a certain request, they decided to give me a little nudge."

"And by that you mean..."

"They had someone beat the shit out of me." He grunted, like he was moving and it hurt.

"Where are you?"

"Still in jail," he said. "They didn't do enough damage that I'd need hospitalization. Probably on purpose. They want me here."

"Fuck," I muttered.

"I know there's nothing you can do about it," he said. "And maybe you don't want to. But I wanted you to know in case they try to threaten your mom again."

"Yeah. Okay."

"How is she?"

"Don't ask about her," I said. "Is there anything else?"

"No. No, that's all."

I ended the call without saying goodbye.

Without really thinking about what I was doing, I brought up Hannah's number and hit send. It rang once. I closed my eyes, silently begging her to answer. I needed to hear her voice, even if it was just a few words.

"Leo?"

I let out a breath, my shoulders relaxing. "Hi."

"Um, hi?"

"How are you feeling?"

"Fine, I guess."

"Good. What are you doing today?"

"Really?" She sighed. "I'm with Zoe."

"Okay, good."

"Is that it?"

"Yeah." Squeezing my eyes shut, I pinched the bridge of my

nose. Why was I such a mess? Why couldn't I have a normal conversation with her right now? "Just wanted to see how you are."

"Well, I'm fine, so…"

"Good."

"Jesus," she muttered. "Bye, Leo."

"Bye."

She ended the call. Fuck.

Rawlins needed to know about Dad, so I forced myself to text him. My ability to communicate with other humans was obviously severely lacking, but I managed to give him the important details. Roland would want to know, so I texted him, too. Then I tossed my phone on my desk.

Fuck. Again.

I stared at the front door. I hated that I wasn't sure if I could go outside right now. Had I really backslid so badly? Was I back to hunkering down in this cottage, refusing to come out? I'd been that way for a while, when I'd first come home, except it had been Mom's house I was stuck in. Still healing physically, and beyond broken mentally. I'd been like a fucking animal.

Closing my eyes, I took a few breaths. I wasn't going to fall that far. I couldn't. If I lost my shit completely, I'd be useless. Protecting my family was too important. I couldn't let it come to that.

It was cold out—probably cold enough for snow. I bundled up, steeled myself for whatever my brain and nervous system tried to do to me, and went outside.

I didn't panic. I didn't feel good, but I stayed in control.

Good.

The sky was clear, but the early winter sun didn't do anything to warm the air. Still, sunlight and movement would be good for me right now.

I walked out to the south vineyard, my hands stuffed in my pockets, my breath misting out in front of me. The desire to go home and check the cameras again was almost overwhelming. What if I missed something? What if they took Mom? If anything happened to her—to any of my family—I'd never forgive myself.

Ben was with her. They wouldn't get through him. Chase was with my sister. Zoe and Hannah both home with Roland. Cooper wasn't letting Amelia out of his sight. They were fine.

And I still wanted to check the cameras.

I kept walking. I wouldn't stay out long. But if I gave in to that fear now, I'd only keep spiraling out of control.

Stretching my legs and breathing fresh air felt good. The solace of my family's land surrounded me. The grapevines had gone dormant for the winter, bare of their leaves. There was a stark sort of beauty to it, the brown vines winding up and around the trellises. It was quiet. Subdued.

Only when I felt calm again—when it seemed like my rational brain was mostly in charge—did I turn around and head for home.

When I got back to the main grounds, I spotted Cooper and Chase. It looked like they were heading for my place.

"Hey, Coop."

"Dude," Cooper said, stopping to put his hands on his hips. "What the fuck is going on?"

"With what? Dad?"

"No, with Hannah. But Dad? What are you talking about?"

"Dad got roughed up last night," I said.

"Shit. The fucker deserves it, obviously. But still."

Chase had his arms crossed, but he didn't say anything. There was no love lost between Chase and our dad. Especially because Dad had almost ruined Chase and Brynn's wedding.

"Yeah," I said. "And I don't know what that means for us here. But probably nothing good."

"This is so fucked up," Cooper said.

"I know. But, wait. What about Hannah?"

"Why is she looking for an apartment?" Cooper asked.

"She's what? Who told you that?"

"Amelia," he said. "She left a little while ago to meet Zoe and Brynn. Said they were apartment hunting with Hannah today. What the hell, dude?"

What the fuck?

"Are you gonna talk, or just do the Leo thing where you bottle all your shit up inside?" Cooper asked. "Because it's fucking cold out here and I'll totally deal with freezing my ass off if you want to talk. Or we could go inside. Whatever. But I need to know what it's going to be. I don't want to stand here waiting for you to talk if you aren't going to."

"I vote inside," Chase said, rubbing his hands together.

"Hannah's pregnant," I said suddenly.

Cooper's eyes widened and Chase clamped his mouth shut.

"Oh shit," Cooper said.

Damn it, why had I just blurted it out like that? "I shouldn't have said that. I don't know if she wants me to tell anyone yet."

"Okay, let's think this through," Cooper said. He stepped closer and put an arm around my shoulders. I flinched at the contact, but he didn't seem to notice. "A pregnant girlfriend would normally be a stage-five emergency, but in this case, I think we're at like a stage two. Three, tops. What do you think, Chase?"

"Sounds about right," Chase said. "Three, maybe, considering she's apartment hunting."

The three of us walked toward my house, but I didn't say anything yet. Just let Cooper talk.

"Let's face it, Hannah isn't an ordinary girlfriend. You know it, I know it, Chase knows it. We might as well be up front about it. She's absolutely wifey material."

"Oh, for sure," Chase said.

"*Wifey* material?"

"Yeah. Like, we all know you should marry her."

I had no idea what to say to that.

"That's why we burned the mattress, bro. Now, you're going to argue that it hasn't been that long or some shit," Cooper continued. "And I get it. People seem to think there's some minimum amount of time that you need to be with someone before you know they're the one. I call bullshit on that. You know when you know."

"Also true," Chase said.

"I never said I knew anything."

We got to my house and went inside. Cooper took his arm off my shoulders, but kept talking. Chase pulled up my office chair and sat.

"Oh trust me, bro, I know you didn't," Cooper said.

"What?"

He rolled his eyes. "You're hard-core denying your feelings right now. That's your thing, fine. But dude, you might want to let those bad boys out into the light of day before you really fuck things up with her."

I glanced at Chase, but he was nodding along, like he actually understood what Cooper was talking about.

"I'm not denying my feelings," I said.

"Then why is she out apartment hunting with the girls, instead of curled up in bed with you looking at baby name books?"

"Jesus, Cooper. It's not like we planned to have a baby."

Cooper held his hands up in a gesture of surrender. "I know, I know. I'd be freaking out, too. Actually, no I wouldn't really.

Amelia's totally having my babies, so if it happened sooner than we planned, it would be fine."

"Yeah, same," Chase said.

"Well, that's great for you guys," I said. "But I'm the one with a pregnant girlfriend who's apparently moving out, not just spending a few days at Zoe's while her fucking disaster of a boyfriend gets his shit together."

"Good summary," Cooper said. "I know what you need."

"What?"

He held his arms out wide. "Emotional jumper cables."

"I don't do hugs, Cooper."

"Come on, man." He widened his arms. "It'll help. Bro hug. Come on."

"I'm good."

He lowered his arms and shrugged. "Suit yourself."

Chase slowly raised his hand.

"You need a jump, buddy?" Cooper asked.

"Yeah, dude, things have been really stressful lately," Chase said.

"Cool, man. Bring it in."

Chase stood and they hugged, slapping each other on the back.

"See?" Cooper said as they stepped back. "It works."

"Totally does," Chase said.

Shaking my head, I rolled my eyes. "You two are so weird."

Cooper pulled his phone out of his pocket. He tilted it and looked, then turned it the other direction, his brow furrowing.

"What?" I asked.

"Cookie's been sending me listings for the rentals they're checking out for Hannah. Jesus, this one sucks."

"What do you mean?"

"It's a shithole," he said.

I grabbed the phone out of his hand and swiped through the photos. It was a shithole.

"Oh, hell no," I said. "She's not living in this place."

"Yeah, apparently Hannah said the same thing," Cooper said. "They're on their way to the next one."

"Do you know where it is?"

"I will in a second." He grabbed the phone out of my hand and typed.

Less than a minute later, Amelia sent him the address.

"Let's go," I said.

"Finally," Cooper said. "See, this is what I was getting at. You need to talk to her."

"I'm not ready to talk to her," I said.

"Then what are we doing?" Chase asked.

"I just want to see where she's looking," I said.

"You want to stalk her while she's apartment hunting," Cooper said, raising an eyebrow.

"I didn't say *stalk* her."

"But that's basically what you're suggesting," Cooper said. "So, I'm all for you working things out with Hannah, because she's a badass and I dig her and you're way more fun when you're with her. But I'm going on record with saying I don't think following her is the right move here, buddy."

"She won't even know I'm there," I said. "I just want to check on her."

"I'm even less convinced than I was a second ago," Cooper said. "But fuck it, I'm in."

"Can we stop for snacks?" Chase asked.

"Really?" I asked as we headed out the door.

"Yeah, I think this place is right behind the gas station," Cooper said. "You can run in when we get over there."

"Which gas station?" Chase asked. "The nice one or the shitty one?"

Cooper looked at his phone again. "The shitty one."

Next to the shitty gas station? I looked at him in horror. This was not okay. "Can we just get over there, please? I don't want to find out she signed a lease to live behind the shitty gas station."

"For sure, bro," Cooper said. "You don't want her living here."

Oh my god. What a fucking mess. I followed them to Cooper's truck, wondering what the hell I was doing with my life.

33

HANNAH

*T*he smell got worse the longer we were here. I stepped through the apartment, feeling like I should tip-toe to minimize the amount of physical contact I experienced with this place. The carpet was a dingy beige, so tamped down it looked like it was several decades old. Yellowed walls. The dirty odor of cigarette smoke was only slightly overpowered by the stench of mildew.

I found a dent in the wall in the living room and I had no idea if the appliances in the kitchen even worked. There were rust spots on the linoleum floor and the bathroom was just plain frightening.

"This one is worse than the first two," I said. "God, Zoe, where did you find these?"

Zoe shrugged, scrunching her nose against the smell. "Craigslist."

"Gross."

"Yeah, this is nasty," Amelia said. "I'm voting no."

"Also no," Brynn said. "Besides, that gas station next door is creepy as hell."

"It looked cute in the photos," Zoe said.

"The photos were lies," I said. My stomach was starting to act up. I needed fresh air. "Okay, I've seen enough."

We left through the open door. The apartment manager was outside waiting, and didn't seem surprised when we left without asking for more details.

"What's next?" Brynn asked, looking over Zoe's shoulder. Amelia was on her other side.

I waited, feeling more like a spectator than a participant in my quest to find new lodging.

"Here," Zoe said.

"Does it look any better than the others?" I asked.

Brynn winced. Amelia fake-smiled. Zoe just shrugged again.

"It's so hard to tell from the pictures," Zoe said. "I guess we just have to check it out."

I groaned, but got back in her car.

Zoe had made a list of potential apartments for us to check out, but I was starting to wonder where she'd found these places. Maybe this was just what I had to deal with in my price range. Echo Creek was a small town, so there weren't a lot of options. And tourism meant many of the smaller homes were used as vacation rentals, not primary residences. But there had to be something better than what we'd seen so far.

The next place was a duplex. It didn't look too bad. The paint was faded, but the front steps were in good repair.

"According to the ad, the owners live next door," Zoe said. She knocked on the other door. "It says to come by and they'll let us in."

I stood by Zoe, with Brynn and Amelia on the steps behind us.

A woman in a mint-green bathrobe with a cigarette hanging from her lips answered. "Yeah?"

Zoe cleared her throat. "We're here about the rental?"

"It's only a two-bedroom," she said, her voice hoarse.

"Oh, it's not for all of us," Zoe said. "Just her."

The woman looked me up and down, then shuffled out, fishing a set of keys from her bathrobe pocket. "All right. Go ahead. Just let me know when you're done so I can lock up. If you want the place, it's first and last plus deposit."

"Great, thanks," I said.

She let us in and we walked back through a narrow entryway. It opened up to a small living area. A doorway led to the kitchen and there were stairs leading up to the bedrooms.

"This isn't terrible," Brynn said.

It didn't smell great, but it wasn't awful, either. Probably nothing some scrubbing and air freshener couldn't fix. The carpet looked newish, at least. There was a small stain near the entrance to the kitchen, but otherwise it wasn't too bad.

"No, it's not terrible," Zoe said. She had her arms crossed and she tapped a finger against her elbow.

Did she seem disappointed?

"It's cute," Amelia said. "Although the landlady is a little bit scary."

"True," Zoe said.

I checked out the kitchen—it wasn't great, but it was clean— then headed for the stairs. "Let's check the bedrooms."

The staircase was narrow and creaky, but that wasn't a deal breaker. Upstairs were two small bedrooms and a bathroom in between. The bedrooms were basic. Same carpeting as downstairs. Small closets, but that was okay.

I stopped in the bathroom doorway. It didn't have a window, and with the light off, it was impossible to see anything. I flicked on the light.

Bugs scattered everywhere, little brown and black creepy-crawlies skittering in all directions.

I screamed. Amelia screamed. Brynn raced downstairs with me and Amelia right on her heels.

Zoe came down more slowly, but she was shuddering, clutching her arms around herself. "Oh god."

"It feels like they're crawling on me," Brynn said. "Seriously, Amelia, are there bugs on my back?"

"No. Are there bugs on me?"

"Can we just go?" I asked.

We hurried out the front door. I hugged myself, rubbing my hands over my arms, then stopped to twist around, trying to get a view of my back.

"You're fine," Zoe said. "There's nothing on you."

I shuddered. "It feels like it. Holy crap, that was gross."

"Should we tell scary lady we're leaving?" Amelia asked, pointing to the landlady's side of the duplex.

I looked at Zoe. "This was your find."

"Fine." She went back up the porch and knocked on the other door again.

The woman opened it, the cigarette still hanging out of her mouth. Or maybe it was another one. It was hard to tell. "Application?"

"No thanks," Zoe said. "And you have a bug problem over there."

"Shit," the woman muttered. She turned and started closing the door. "Hank, we got bugs in the rental again."

"Well, that was a bust," Zoe said as she walked down the porch steps.

"Are there no decent places to rent in this town?" I asked. "Brynn and Chase have a perfectly decent apartment. Why aren't there any like that?"

"I wish one was available in our building," Brynn said.

Zoe shrugged. "We can keep looking if you're up for it. Or…"

I was exhausted. I didn't know if it was the parade of shitty apartments or being pregnant, but I felt like I'd been run over by a truck. "Or what?"

"Or there's always the other guest cottage at Salishan."

"Mm hmm," Brynn said, nodding.

"Yeah, that's what I said earlier," Amelia said. "But then Zoe said—"

"Anyway," Zoe said, cutting Amelia off. "I haven't talked to Shannon about it or anything, but obviously she'd be happy to have you stay there."

I put my hands on my hips. "You did this on purpose, didn't you?"

"Did what?" she asked.

"You found the crappiest places in town so I wouldn't leave Salishan."

"Well..."

"Zoe!"

She sighed. "Okay, yes, I did."

"You ass," I said.

"I'm sorry," she said. "I just don't think you should make a huge decision like this yet. I know Leo's being ridiculous, but give him a little time. He'll calm the fuck down and then you guys will figure this out."

"He won't talk to me," I said.

"Leo isn't speaking to you at all?" Brynn asked. "I'm calling him."

"No," I said, putting a hand up. "I don't need you to call him. We've spoken, just not very much. And not about the things we really need to talk about."

"Then I kind of agree with Zoe," Amelia said. "Are you sure moving out is the right thing?"

"Yeah, you know how Leo is," Brynn said.

"Oh my god," I said, frustration bubbling up inside. "Stop making excuses for him. Maybe the rest of you think it's fine for him to go hermit when things get hard, but I don't. That's not helping him. It's like you're all so afraid to push his buttons. I know he's hurt. Believe me, I've seen it. But right now, I'm the one who's unexpectedly pregnant, and he's being a total shit about it."

"What?" Amelia shrieked.

"Oh my god," Brynn said.

Zoe raised her eyebrows. "Okay, you just said it."

I raked my fingers through my hair. "Damn it, this is not how I wanted any of this to go. I was going to wait to tell everyone, but fuck. Yes, I'm pregnant, okay? That's what happened. I told Leo and he said it was a bad thing and we've barely spoken since. So yes, I do think I need to move out. And not to the guest cottage."

"Oh, honey," Amelia said.

Brynn pulled out her phone. "Oh hell no, Leo. I'm calling him."

"Brynn..." I threw my hands up in the air.

"Damn it, Leo," Brynn said into her phone. "Of course you're not answering. I'm coming over when we're done here, and you're going to listen to me, you ass. I can't believe you."

"Okay," Zoe said, her voice soothing. She put a hand on Brynn's arm and gently lowered the phone. "I think he gets it."

"I left a message," Brynn said, crossing her arms.

"Look, Hannah, we're just trying to help you both," Zoe said. "I'm sorry."

Frustration and exhaustion warred for my attention, but tiredness was definitely winning. "Look, we can talk about this later. I'm hungry and tired and just want to be done."

"Fair enough," Zoe said.

We walked over to her car and I noticed a truck up the street. It looked an awful lot like—

"Oh my god."

"What?" Zoe asked.

"Amelia, is that Cooper's truck?" I asked.

She peered at it. "It looks like it."

"And am I seeing things, or are there three men in that truck?"

"Oh shit," Zoe muttered.

"Is that Leo?" I asked, my exhaustion forgotten. "Is he following me? Did you know about this?"

"No," Zoe said. "That's not me."

"Is this just how you all do things?" I asked. "Meddle in each other's lives and drive each other crazy?"

Brynn winced and Amelia shrugged. Zoe opened her mouth as if to explain, but I held up a hand to cut her off.

"Never mind." I glanced at Cooper's truck. It was definitely Leo in there. He wouldn't do more than ask me how my day was, but he'd follow me around? They'd parked up the street, obviously thinking we wouldn't notice them.

I rolled up my sleeves and started stalking toward the truck.

"And there she goes," Zoe said.

"Uh-oh."

"Should we follow her?"

"I think we just need to let her do what she needs to do," Zoe said.

She was right about that. And right now, I needed to give Leo a piece of my mind.

here was no way Hannah was renting this place.
We caught up with the girls at a shithole of a
building next to the gas station—Cooper and Chase had been
right, it was shitty—in time to see them come out. Cooper
parked down the street where they couldn't see us, and we
waited while Zoe looked at something on her phone. Then they
all piled in Zoe's car and left.

Amelia was texting Cooper each listing, so we waited a few
minutes so they wouldn't see us follow.

Cooper's truck had an extended cab with two jump seats in
back. Chase sat crammed in behind me, his knees almost hitting
his chest. We drove to the next address and parked a couple of
blocks down. Watched as the girls went to the front door. A
woman in what looked like a bathrobe came out and let them in
the other side.

"I don't want her living here," I said.

"This is a shitty street," Chase said. "You should definitely do
something about this."

"Okay, this is going to surprise you both, but I'm going to be the mature one in the truck," Cooper said. "You don't get to make that call, bro. It's not up to you to pick where she lives."

"Cooper, look at that place," I said. "It should probably be condemned."

Cooper rested his arm on the steering wheel and gave a little shrug. "Eh. It's not that bad."

"Not that bad? I bet that building down the street is a crack house."

"Is that really a thing?" Chase asked.

"Yes, it's a thing."

"Crack is pretty outdated, though," Chase said. "If anything, it's probably a meth lab."

"Chase," Cooper said. "No."

"I'm just saying."

I pressed the heels of my hands into my eyes. "Jesus, you guys. She's pregnant. She can't live here."

Cooper held up a finger. "Once again, I'd like to point out—"

"I get it," I snapped. "I don't get to tell her what to do. I know."

"I'm just making sure," Cooper said. "Because let's be honest, you've been out of the world for a long time."

"I don't know what that has to do with it." I peered through the windshield, but the girls were still inside. "What are they doing in there? Why is it taking so long?"

"It's not, you're just really fucking agitated right now," Cooper said. "Oh shit. I can't believe I forgot."

"Forgot what?" I asked.

Cooper reached behind his seat and grabbed a shoe box. "I made this for you. I'm going to be honest, I hoped I wouldn't need it. But Ben taught me to be prepared, and when Hannah started staying with you, I figured I'd put some shit together in case things went a little south and you needed it."

"What things? What is this?"

He handed the box to me. "It's a sad-Leo box. We made Zoe a breakup box once and it worked out so well, I figured I'd recycle the idea and do it again."

I stared at the shoe box in my lap. "This is weird."

"If by *weird*, you mean awesome," Cooper said. "Just open it."

I took off the lid. Inside was a random assortment of stuff. "What is all this?"

"Stuff to help you feel better," Cooper said, grinning like he was exceedingly proud of himself.

There were packets of beef jerky—original, peppered, and teriyaki-flavored—potato chips, a deck of cards, and a big bag of M&Ms.

"Those were my contribution," Chase said, pointing to the candy.

I pulled out a DVD copy of *Terminator* and looked at Cooper, raising my eyebrows. "To make me feel better?"

"That's a good flick, dude," he said. "When you're at home being all broody and Leo-ish, you can at least watch a sweet movie."

At the bottom of the box I found a few condoms. "Seriously? What did you think I'd need these for?"

Cooper shrugged. "Always good to be prepared, that's all. Plus I have like a million of those things I don't need anymore. One of the many benefits of being with my forever girl."

"Amen to that," Chase said.

We both glared at him.

"What?" he asked. "Just because I'm married to Brynn, I don't get to agree with you about the sexual awesomeness of being with one amazing woman?"

"No," Cooper and I both said.

He crossed his arms and sat back—as much as he could in the small space. "Fine."

I put the stuff back in the box. In a weird way, it was a nice thing for Cooper to do. "Thanks, man. I appreciate it."

"You got it, bro," Cooper said.

"Should we open the M&Ms?" Chase asked.

"I vote yes," Cooper said. "We still need stakeout snacks."

"Sure." I handed the box to Cooper. "Knock yourself out."

While Cooper and Chase tore into the M&Ms—and the beef jerky—I pondered what he'd said about being prepared, and how I didn't get to pick where Hannah lived. Maybe that was true, but I couldn't sit by and let her move to some dump that was probably up the street from a meth lab.

I pulled out my phone and searched for rentals in Echo Creek.

Ideally, I'd find her someplace close to Salishan. That side of town was much nicer. The rentals probably cost more, especially near downtown. But I'd help make up the difference. I didn't want her to move out at all, but if she was going to, the least I could do was help her find a place.

Besides, maybe it was best if she did. I wasn't going to abandon her. I'd do everything I could to help take care of her, and the baby. But it would be easier on everyone if I kept my distance. My child wasn't going to want for anything, but being raised by a guy like me? There were so many things wrong with that, I didn't know where to begin.

Trying to ignore the sick feeling in the pit of my stomach at the thought of her moving out for good, I saved a few rental options. I'd go see her tonight and we could go look together tomorrow. This was how I could help her.

And if I made sure she was nearby, living on a decent street, all the better.

Brynn and Amelia burst out of the duplex and ran down the front steps. They were followed closely by Hannah, then Zoe.

"What are they doing?" Cooper asked with a laugh.

"Something freaked them out," Chase said.

I let out a breath, my shoulders relaxing a little. Good. If something was wrong, maybe I wouldn't have to worry about Hannah deciding she wanted to live here.

The girls stood out in front of the duplex for a while. We were too far away to really tell what was going on. I glanced up every so often, but kept looking for better rentals. I found a great little house only half a mile from Salishan—not far from Roland and Zoe's. Why hadn't Zoe brought her to this one? It was perfect.

"Uh-oh," Cooper said. "Incoming."

"What?" I glanced up from my phone to find Hannah walking toward the truck.

No, she wasn't *walking*. Her arms swung with her quick stride and I could practically hear her feet pounding against the pavement.

Oh, shit.

I got out of the truck to intercept her. "Hannah."

"Don't even start with me," she snapped, pointing a finger at my face. "Why are you following me?"

"Cooper said you were looking for a place to live and it was by the shitty gas station and I just..." Fuck. What was I supposed to say? "I wanted to make sure you didn't make a mistake."

"A mistake? What the hell are you talking about?"

"You can't live there," I said, gesturing to the building behind her.

"I know I can't live there, but I don't need you sitting outside with these two, watching me like a creeper, to tell me that."

"I'm sorry. I was just worried about you."

She ran her fingers through her hair. "I'm so frustrated with you right now."

"I know. I'm sorry." I glanced back at the truck, but it was empty. Cooper and Chase had wandered over to Amelia and Brynn. Perfect. "Can we talk?"

"Yes," she said. "Finally."

I let her in the passenger side door, then got in on the driver's side, tossing the empty M&M wrapper on the floor.

She folded her hands in her lap and looked over at me expectantly.

"Okay." I took a deep breath. "I know I reacted badly when you told me you were pregnant. It felt like it came out of nowhere and yeah, it freaked me out. But I should have handled it better."

"Thank you."

"But I can't deal with you living over here in some shitty building like that." I brought out my phone and swiped to the rental. "I found this. It's a house, not an apartment, so you'd have more privacy. It's closer to Salishan, and to Zoe. I don't know why she didn't show you this one in the first place."

She blinked at me, her lips parted, but didn't say anything.

"If you're worried about the cost, don't be. I'll help with that. If you have to get your own place, I'd much rather you be close."

"Are you serious?"

"Yeah," I said. "I just want to help."

She took a shaky breath. Alarm raced through me. Something was wrong. Very, very wrong.

"So, Zoe takes me around to all the shittiest places in town so I'll think my best option is to stay at Salishan," she said. "Meanwhile, you're looking for a place to set me up."

"Yeah, I'm—"

"Trying to *help*," she said, enunciating the last word. "Unfucking-believable. This is your solution? I tell you I'm pregnant, you barely speak to me for days, and now you think this is helping?"

"I found out from Cooper that you were apartment hunting," I said. "What am I supposed to do with that information?"

"Not follow me around like a stalker."

I looked away. I was dying inside—breaking apart—and I had no idea how to explain why. How to make her understand. "I don't know how to handle this, Hannah. I don't know what I'm supposed to do."

"You stupid motherfu—"

She stopped, mid-insult—not that it was any less than I deserved—and closed her mouth. She was silent for a long moment, as if contemplating something. I opened and closed my fists, the tension killing me.

"You know what?" she said, finally. "I need a break."

"A break? I thought that's what you were doing at Zoe's."

"No, I need a break from all of you. Otherwise I'm going to say something I can't take back."

I could hear the frustration in her voice, feel the tension coming off her. It beat at me in waves.

"We'll figure out my living arrangements later," she said. "For now, I'm going on vacation."

"A vacation? Now?"

"Yes," she said with conviction. "I think I deserve it at this point."

Before I could say anything else, she got out of the truck and slammed the door behind her.

"Hannah."

I followed her out, but she walked straight for Zoe's car and got in the back seat.

"Damn it."

"I should take her home," Zoe said, her voice sympathetic. "She'll be okay, Leo. Don't worry."

The girls got back into Zoe's car. I watched it pull away from the curb and drive off, feeling like my life had just ended.

35

HANNAH

I woke to the sound of the ocean, the soothing rhythm of waves rousing me from sleep. That, and morning sickness. As much as I would have loved to spend a leisurely morning in the soft sheets, listening to the waves crash, I had to rush to the bathroom.

Lovely way to start my first day on vacation.

Vacation. Right. I was at the beach—a little town on the coast called Jetty Beach, to be exact—but this wasn't really a vacation, no matter what I'd told Leo.

It was a break, though. A much-needed one.

After cleaning up, I went into the kitchen to make some tea. It was the off-season, so I'd had no trouble finding a little beach cabin to rent, even with no notice. I had it for the next three nights, but I'd asked about the possibility of staying longer. The owner had said they'd let me know if they got any other inquiries, but they didn't think they would. It often sat vacant this time of year.

I'd put five hours between me and Leo. Between me and his whole family. A part of me felt relieved. Maybe they'd been trying to help, but I was pissed at most of them. At Zoe, for sabotaging my search for an apartment to get me to stay at the winery. At Cooper and Chase for helping Leo stalk me.

And Leo? I was fucking furious with him.

I sat at the kitchen table with my tea and gazed out at the water. The cabin was on the beach, past the grass-filled dunes, set up on stilts to preserve the ocean view. The sand looked windswept and barren, littered with pieces of seaweed and bits of driftwood left by the retreating tide. The sky was gray with clouds, the water reflecting the dull hue.

The view matched my mood. Gray and stormy.

Leo had made it abundantly clear that this baby was an instant deal-breaker. Although he hadn't explicitly said it, he'd essentially dumped me the moment I told him. And even after I'd had several days to digest that reality, it still surprised me.

I hadn't expected him to be excited, or drop to one knee and propose marriage. Shock was a completely understandable response. I was shocked. I didn't expect him to take the news without at least some level of surprise. Even distress.

But that was it? It was over, just like that? Because I was having his baby?

I hadn't thought Leo would be that guy. Apparently, I was wrong.

Tears fell for the first time since Leo had walked away from me. I'd held them in, biting my lip, hiding behind anger and frustration. But now, in the silence of this little beach cabin, hours from where my life had gone haywire, I broke down.

I put my head down and sobbed. Cried until my shirt was wet, my stomach hurt, and my tea was cold.

Damn you, Leo.

After I'd cried myself out, I made a fresh cup of tea. Then I showered, dressed, and went into town in search of breakfast.

Just as it started to rain, I found a place called Old Town Café with a little sign in the window declaring they had coffee, donuts, and wifi. I went inside, ordered coffee and a homemade donut, and found a table by the window.

Shortly after I sat down, my phone buzzed with a text. I'd told Zoe I was leaving for a few days. Texted Shannon to let her know, too. I'd told Leo I was leaving in person, so I hadn't felt the need to say anything else to him. Since I'd left Echo Creek, I'd had texts from Brynn and Amelia, both apologizing for their part in the shitty apartment hunt. One from Shannon, asking me to let her know when I arrived at my destination—which I had. Even Roland had texted me, late last night, saying he was up with the baby and wanted to make sure I'd made it to where I was going. I'd also gotten a series of heart gifs from Cooper and a text from Chase asking if I needed ice cream.

This time, it was Leo.

Leo: Where are you?

Me: On vacation.

Leo: But where did you go?

Me: I'm fine.

Leo: That's not what I asked. Where are you?

Me: Leo, I'm safe. I need some space.

Leo: How do I know you're really okay?

I groaned and turned the phone around. Snapped a selfie of me flipping off the camera and sent it to him.

Leo: I can't tell where that is.

Me: But you can see I'm fine.

I didn't want to trigger Leo to have a panic attack, but he knew I was fine, he'd seen my face. He didn't need to know where I was. And I was done talking to his ass. I put my phone on the table, face down.

What did he want, anyway? If he didn't want me anymore, why freak out over where I was? Was it some caveman thing about me having his baby? Was this his attempt to *do the right thing*? I didn't want him to grudgingly pay child support for the next eighteen years while he hid in his cave.

I wanted him to *want* me enough. I wanted to *be* enough for him to take a chance.

It was so strange. I'd always felt like Leo and I understood each other. We'd been friends entirely through conversation and banter for so long, but this felt like we were talking right past each other. Like he wasn't hearing a word I was saying. And maybe he was trying to say something to me other than what I was hearing. But if he was, I didn't get it.

With a sigh, I opened my laptop, connected to wifi, and checked my emails. Nothing urgent. But my attention caught on one particular name, the already-opened email still in my inbox. Josephine Tate. My mother.

I'd emailed her a few times since leaving Jace. I hadn't told her that he'd hit me. I didn't want her to tell me she'd known he would. But I had told her that I'd moved, and tried to pick up the thread of conversation after that. Asked how she and Dad were doing, that sort of thing. She'd replied, but her emails were always short.

I didn't blame her. Our relationship had been tense since my teens. It got worse when I was with Jace. Worse still when I'd moved in with him. I'd said things I'd come to regret. That was part of why I'd stopped myself from yelling at Leo yesterday. I knew the pain of words you couldn't take back. And now, it was like we didn't know how to talk to each other.

Maybe it was time I tried to change that.

I finished my donut and went back to the cottage. Instead of emailing, I sent her a text, asking if we could Skype call. I wanted to see her face, especially with what I had to tell her. She texted back to say sure, so I called.

The call chimed a few times, then connected. The screen

opened up on a sunny patio, their succulent garden in the background. But no person.

"Mom? Are you there?"

"Hannah?"

"I think you need to turn the camera around."

"Oh." There was some shuffling, then my mother's face appeared on the screen.

My mom's dark hair had more gray than I remembered. Living in Arizona had given her a perpetual tan and the lines around her eyes had deepened.

"There you are," I said. "Hi."

"Hi," she said. "How have you been?"

I took a deep breath. She had no idea how big that question was. "I don't even know where to begin with that. Is Dad home?"

"He's here." She looked off to the side. "Calvin? Can you come here, please?"

I heard Dad's voice in the background. "Coming."

He sat down beside her and she adjusted her phone so I could see both of them. My dad still looked every bit the military man. His gray hair buzzed short, face smooth. Clothes neat, even though he was wearing a casual shirt—no longer a uniform.

"Hannah," he said, sounding surprised.

"Hi, Dad."

We all sat in an awkward silence for a moment.

I figured I needed to be the one to begin. "I'm just going to jump in and say I owe you both an apology. I said some things to you that I really regret, and I'm sorry. And you were right about Jace. He put me in the hospital when I tried to leave him."

"Oh my god," Mom said. Her phone fell with a bang and all I could see was bright blue sky.

It righted and Dad appeared to be holding it. Mom had a hand over her mouth.

"I'm okay now," I said. "He was awful, and I know you could see it in the beginning when I couldn't. And not only did I not listen to you, I threw it back in your face and told you I didn't need you in my life. That was a really awful thing to do, and I'm so sorry."

"Hannah," Mom murmured, her eyes shining with tears.

"Where is he now?" Dad asked, his voice hard.

"Jail. He violated the protection order."

Dad grunted.

"We owe you an apology, too," Mom said. "We were so worried about you being with Jace, but that doesn't excuse the way we pushed you. I know I said things I regret, too. Honey, I'm sorry."

"I'm sorry too, kiddo," Dad said.

"Thank you," I said.

It felt like a weight had been lifted—a weight I hadn't even realized I'd been carrying. But there was still a lot more to tell.

"A lot has happened since I left Jace. I went to stay with a friend. His name is Leo Miles and he lives at his family's winery in central Washington. That's where I've been living."

"Is that where you are now?" Mom asked.

"No, I'm out at the beach for a few days." I paused, gathering the courage to tell them the truth. "Leo and I went from being friends to... more."

Dad grunted again. "Are you sure that's a good idea? After the last one?"

"I can promise you, Leo is nothing like Jace. And we'd been friends for years before anything happened between us. It wasn't like he was a stranger."

Dad still looked skeptical, but I continued anyway.

"Leo was in the military. He was injured. Severely, actually. I don't know the full story, but he was burned."

"That's terrible," Mom said.

Dad shook his head. "Damn shame."

"I know. But he's…" I paused, thinking about all the things Leo was. I was hurt and angry, but that didn't change the fact that I loved him. "He's a good man. I'm furious with him at the moment, but he is."

"What happened?" Mom asked.

The concern in her voice almost broke me. I hadn't realized until this moment how much I needed my mom right now. I swallowed hard to keep from crying.

"I'm pregnant. And please don't tell me I'm irresponsible or reprimand me for letting this happen. Or even badmouth Leo for being shitty about it. Please. That's not what I need right now." Despite my best efforts, tears leaked from the corners of my eyes. "I just needed you to know what was happening in my life."

"Oh Hannah," Mom said. "We're not going to reprimand you. I'm so glad you called to tell us."

Dad glowered. "Just tell me something. Do I need to come up there and deal with this guy?"

"No, Dad." It was hard not to laugh a little. "No, Leo and I will figure out how to deal with everything."

"Do you want to come here?" Mom asked. "We could make room for you and the baby."

Her offer meant so much to me, I almost couldn't reply. I swallowed back more tears, sniffing hard. "Thank you. I appreciate that so much. I'll think about it. I'm trying not to make any rash decisions right now. That's why I'm out here. I needed to get away where I could think and figure out what I need to do."

"All right," Mom said. "Just let us know."

"I will. It's so good to talk to you both."

"You, too," Mom said. "And even if you decide to stay there, we'd love to see you. Maybe we can come up for a visit. Or you can come here. Whatever's easier."

"I'd love that."

I talked to them for a while longer. They caught me up on their latest adventures in desert gardening. They loved Arizona and planned to stay there for the foreseeable future—a big change for a military couple who'd spent most of their adult lives moving every few years. I told them more about Leo and his family. About Salishan. They thought it sounded magical.

And in so many ways, it was.

By the time we ended the call, I felt better than I had in days. That was a conversation I should have had with them a long time ago. Looking back, I didn't know why I'd waited. Guilt for the things I'd said to them. Fear that they'd still be harsh toward me.

But they hadn't. I'd been honest, and apologized. They had, too. No more misunderstandings. No more talking past each other.

I traced the outside of my phone with my fingertip, thinking about Leo. Had we been talking past each other these last few days? It wasn't like we'd had a single calm conversation since I'd told him I was pregnant.

I did need to look ahead—to focus on how I was going to transition into life as a mother. I couldn't wait for Leo to catch up —not for very long, at least. But maybe we weren't really hearing each other.

And maybe there was something I could do about that, too.

36

LEO

*W*hy the fuck couldn't I find her?

I stared at the photo Hannah had sent me. I'd brought it up on my computer screen to make it larger. Looked at the background for details to see if I could figure out where she was. But it was too close to her face. And her middle finger.

Looked like a restaurant, but that could be anywhere. Rain on the window behind her obscured the view outside. In other words, she'd given me nothing.

Gigz jumped up onto the desk and walked across my keyboard.

"Damn it, cat," I said, but I petted her, scratching her head and running my hand down her back. "Where did she go?"

Gigz just purred.

My family wasn't helping, either. None of them knew where she'd gone. Or if they did, they weren't telling me.

The odd thing was, I wasn't panicking. I was agitated as fuck, but it was out of worry for her, not because my fight or flight response was running on overdrive. I was thinking clearly. My heart rate normal. Breathing fine. I wasn't being choked by an impending sense of doom.

I just hated that she'd left. Hated that I'd driven her away.

I'd borrowed Cooper's truck and driven around town this morning, in case she hadn't gone far. I'd checked the Lodge, the big hotel next door, but hadn't seen her car. Checked restaurants, coffee shops. Stores. No sign of her.

I'd come back and texted her. I hadn't really expected her to reply. But she hadn't told me where she was, so I was still at square one. Except...

Rain. There was rain on the window in the photo she'd sent.

I got up and went to the window. Pushed open the blinds so I could see outside. Dry. Low clouds hung in the air, but it looked like it was about to snow, not rain. And there certainly wasn't rain falling now—hadn't been all day.

That probably meant she'd gone west. Maybe Seattle? I went back to my desk and brought up a weather map. The entire western side of the state showed rain.

Great. That really narrowed it down.

It was better than nothing. She could have gone somewhere familiar. Maybe near her old apartment. A place she'd frequented before she moved here? I brought up her old address on a map and searched for restaurants within a one-mile radius.

Jesus. Were there really that many restaurants near her old apartment?

I printed out the map and went out to find Cooper. I needed to borrow his truck again.

But Cooper wasn't home, and neither was Amelia. Damn it. I walked down toward the Big House. Ben's truck was parked outside, but I didn't find him in the lobby, or upstairs. I did a quick circuit of the other rooms until I found him in a large storeroom near the kitchen.

"Leo," he said, nodding.

"Can I borrow your truck?" I asked.

He crossed his arms. "Does this have anything to do with Hannah?"

"Yeah, of course. She said she needed a break and she was going on vacation. Then she fucking disappeared. I don't know where she is, but I have an idea."

"Leo. Slow down, son."

"I'm calm," I said, putting up my hands. "I mean it, I'm not out of control right now. I'm not panicking. I just need to know where they are."

"They," Ben said quietly, more to himself than to me. "Listen, if she needs a break, it's best that you give her what she asked for."

"There are fucking drug dealers threatening my mom. Threatening to burn this place down. What if they're targeting everyone? What if they know about Hannah? I just want to know where she is so I can be prepared. I don't want to be blindsided by something I could have prevented."

"And what happened last time you followed her?"

"How do you even know about that?"

He shrugged. "I saw Cooper earlier."

I rolled my eyes. "Of course."

"Leo—"

"This hurts, Ben," I said, putting my hand on my chest. "Physically. She's gone and I can't help her if something happens. It's fucking painful."

"So you want her to come back here?" He sat down on a barrel. "Live with you?"

I rubbed the back of my neck and looked away. "Yes. But, no. I can't."

"Why not?"

"Look at me," I roared.

"I am looking at you," he said, his voice completely calm.

"I can't," I said, enunciating the words.

Ben didn't answer. Just scratched his beard.

"It would just be easier if she stayed close," I said. "At least then I could still see her every day."

"You might want to rethink that," he said. "Trust me, it's not easier."

I hesitated for a second. "You know, her divorce is final. You could—"

"We're not talking about me," Ben said, his voice sharp. "We're talking about you, and your girlfriend, who is pregnant with *your* child. And it appears your solution is to set up your little mistake in a house somewhere. Help her financially. Maybe pop in to see her from time to time."

"I never said mista—" *Oh my fucking god*. The realization of what I'd done—of what she must have thought I was doing—hit me like a blow to the chest. That was what my dad had done when Naomi had gotten pregnant with Grace. Fuck, had I become my father? "Oh, shit."

"*Oh shit* is right," Ben said.

"I thought I was helping. She was looking for another place to live, and I thought..." I trailed off, sinking down onto another barrel. "She's not a mistake. She could never be a mistake."

"Does she know you feel that way?"

"No, she probably doesn't."

"Well, that is a problem, now, isn't it?"

I rubbed my hands down my face. "Yeah, it is a problem."

"I agree that you need to be looking out for her, especially now," he said. "But Leo, you need to get out of your own way. Stop trying to have her in your life without actually letting her in."

I stared at the concrete floor for a long moment, letting that sink in. I'd let her get closer to me than anyone. But I'd still held back. I hadn't given her everything—hadn't told her everything. Ben was right.

I had a choice to make—one I should have made already. Let her in, or let her go. There wasn't room for anything in between. Not anymore.

I stood and Ben followed.

"Thanks," I said, not looking at him. It was hard to look people in the eye in general, and I was feeling a hell of a lot of shame at the moment.

Ben stepped toward me, arms slightly lifted. I hesitated, but only for a second. I took a step closer. And for the first time since I was a kid, I hugged him.

He patted me on the back once, then moved back. "Now if you'll excuse me, there are drug dealers threatening your mother. I'm going to keep making sure none of them get anywhere near her."

"Thanks, Ben."

He gave me a casual salute as he walked away.

I didn't feel any better about Hannah being gone. But I wasn't going to chase her. Not yet, at least. If she needed space to think, I'd give it to her.

But I wasn't giving up, either.

As soon as I got home, I plugged in my phone so I'd be ready in case she called. I did my security checks. Grabbed some food. Then I sat down at my desk and logged into our game.

She wasn't on—and I hadn't expected her to be. But I needed to blow off some steam. That and kill time. Pacing around like a caged animal wasn't going to do me any good. I wanted to be calm when we spoke. I had a lot to say, and I didn't want to keep screwing things up.

I played for a while. Mindless stuff. Ran some quests. In the back of my mind, I wondered where she was. Whether she was okay.

Then Gigz popped up on my screen.

She sent me a join request, so I slipped on my headset.

"Hey, Badger," she said. "How's it going?"

I closed my eyes, sinking into the solace of her voice. "Hey, Gigz. I've been better."

"Yeah, me too."

"Are you okay?"

"I'm safe, if that's what you mean," she said. "Still pregnant, though."

I laughed softly, some of the tension melting away. "Yeah. I'd imagine so."

"So we gonna run this thing or not?" she asked.

"Wait, you really want to play?"

"Uh, yeah, that's why I got on. I'm bored. Let's do a dungeon or two."

I leaned back in my chair. "All right. Let's do this."

We played for a while, not talking about anything in the real world. Just the game. A lot like we used to.

Only nothing was the same. She wasn't Gigz anymore. She was my Hannah. And if I hadn't been such a broken mess, she'd still have been here, with me.

"Hannah—"

"It's Gigz in here, Badge."

I sighed. "Okay, Gigz. I screwed this up in pretty much every way imaginable."

"Yeah, you did."

"I'm so, so sorry."

"Thank you for saying sorry," she said, then paused for a moment. "I'm at a cabin in Jetty Beach."

Relief washed over me. At least now I knew where they were. Although, damn it, that was hours away. "Okay. Thank you."

"But Leo, I need to know what you're really apologizing for. Are you sorry that you freaked out when I told you I was pregnant? Or are you sorry that I got pregnant?"

She had no idea how difficult that question was. "Both, but hear me out. I'm sorry for the way I acted. I should have kept it together and I didn't. But yes, I'm sorry I got you pregnant. Not because I think you're a mistake. Because you both deserve so much better than I can give you."

"What is that supposed to mean?"

"You know what a fucking mess I am. I'm more scarred and broken on the inside than on the outside. But the outside is bad enough. Kids are scared of me, Hannah. Even babies. They take one look at me and they cry. When it's a stranger, I can let it go." I closed my eyes and willed myself to say it. To keep talking. Tell her the truth. "How am I supposed to live with that if it's my own child?"

"Leo," she said, her voice filled with sympathy. "Your child isn't going to be afraid of you."

"I've seen it happen over and over."

"But this is your baby," she said. "He or she isn't going to see your scars. This baby is going to see their daddy. That's all."

I didn't know what to say to that. I wanted to believe her. Wanted it more than I knew how to say.

"Why didn't you tell me this before?" she asked. "We could have talked about it."

"I didn't know how."

She sighed. "Yeah, I guess it's easier to talk like this."

"What do you mean?"

"Online. Apart. It was always easy for us. Maybe this is the only way we really work."

"No," I said, sitting up. "No, this is not the only way we work. I know I've been an absolute asshole the last few days. And I am so fucking sorry."

"Then what do you want?"

"I want you."

"Well, at this point, there are some pretty important conditions attached to that."

"I know. Believe me, I know. Listen, I understand what I have to do now. But not like this. Not online. This isn't about Badger and Gigz. It's Leo and Hannah. I need to see you. I need to talk to you in person."

"Leo, I don't know."

"Please," I said. "Please, baby. Come home."

Holding my breath, I waited for her answer. Waited with my heart in her hands.

"Okay," she said. "I'll come back."

She hadn't said *come home*, but that was okay. For now. I'd work up to that part later—in person. I was going to be honest with her. Let her in—completely. I was done holding back. Done being the hidden Miles. I'd let her see me in the bright light of day. Be honest about my flaws, my past, my mistakes. Every last one of them. And if she still wanted me after all that? I'd be hers, body and soul, for the rest of my life.

37

LEO

*T*he security system woke me. I sat up, awake in an instant, and went out to my desk to check the cameras. It was the fire alarm in the Big House.

Oh, fuck. No.

Quickly, I checked the camera feed at my mom's house, but I didn't see anything. I jammed my feet into my shoes while I called 911 to make sure they'd been alerted. Then I threw on my coat, ran outside, and called Ben.

"Yeah?" Ben's voice was husky with sleep.

"There's a fire at the Big House."

"I'll be right there," he said.

"Go to Mom's first."

"Done."

I ran the rest of the way. The front of the Big House looked fine. Praying that it was a false alarm, I went around to the back. Pressed my hand against the side door to the kitchen. It was warm.

Fuck.

I called Roland.

"Leo, what's wrong?" he asked. He sounded surprisingly awake.

"Fire at the Big House. Maybe in the kitchen."

"Don't go inside," he said. "Wait for first responders, Leo. Don't go in there."

I stood outside, itching to do just that while smoke started to leak out of the building. If the fire was small, maybe I could get to a fire extinguisher. Put it out before it spread.

But it was fire. It would burn.

"Leo, say something. Where are you?"

"Outside."

"Fucking stay there, man. Don't do anything stupid. Where's Mom?"

"Home. Ben's on his way over there."

"I'll be there in five minutes. Wait outside for the fire department."

"Yeah." I hung up.

A high-pitched siren trilled in the distance, growing louder. Seconds later, red lights flashed. A fire truck pulled onto the property, an ambulance right behind.

The next hour went by in a chaotic blur. Firefighters rushing inside. Smoke billowing out into the night. Someone asking me to stay back.

I stood outside in the cold and watched as they worked to put out the fire. People came and went around me. My mom, with Ben always close by. Roland, dutifully talking to the fire department and the police who arrived on the scene. Cooper with Amelia in his arms, watching helplessly from the sidelines. Chase and Brynn, next to them, holding each other while we all waited to hear how bad it was. How much damage. How it had started.

Not that I needed them to tell me. I knew exactly how it had started. They'd threatened Mom with a burned grapevine. This was them making good on that promise.

I'd never hated my father as much as I did in that moment.

Finally, we were given the all-clear to go inside. Structurally, the building was still sound. The sprinkler system had activated, but it hadn't been enough. Fortunately for us, the fire hadn't spread far.

While the rest of my family went inside to take stock of the damage, I went home.

I checked the security cameras, poring over the footage from the hours leading up to the fire. Whoever had done this had done an excellent job of avoiding the cameras. There weren't many blind spots, but they'd taken advantage of them.

They hadn't remained totally unseen. I saw him—whoever he was—sneaking around the back of the building. Unfortunately, he was covered, wearing a hood pulled down over his face. I'd give this to the police—at least it would show the fire hadn't been an accident—but I didn't think they'd get anywhere with this.

I sat back in my chair, staring at a still frame of the hooded figure on my monitor. These fuckers weren't going to leave us alone until they got what they wanted.

This was what Hannah was coming back to. The fucking mob threatening my family. Setting fires in the night. Who knew what was next? These people had been evading the authorities for years. Rawlins kept saying the DEA didn't have enough evidence to move in on them.

Fuck this. If they needed evidence, I'd get them evidence.

Hannah was pregnant with my baby. There was no way I was bringing them home to this. I was going to keep them safe, no matter what.

∾

I RACED down the highway in my mom's sedan while the sun rose. She'd probably notice her car was missing before I got back, but I'd apologize for that later. Hers had been the easiest to get off the grounds without anyone seeing.

I was taking a chance with the information Dad had given me, heading to the old lumber mill. I'd done some digging and found it—or what I hoped was the right place. It was about an hour north of Salishan, just outside a half-abandoned little town. The mill was still operating when most of the others in this region had closed decades ago. It was remote, without many people around to ask questions. Not a bad front for a criminal organization.

The DEA probably knew. But as Rawlins had said, it wasn't enough. They needed hard evidence—at least enough for a warrant. And these guys were good. They knew exactly how to cover their tracks. How to stay one step ahead of the law.

But I'd been trained for this.

Working in military intelligence, I'd done this very thing. I'd been good at my job. The guy they sent in when they needed more than what remote hackers could access. There were limits to what a remote hack could do. But a physical hack? With physical control of a device, your target was fucked.

These assholes were about to be fucked.

I drove through a sleepy little town, then turned off the highway. Parked on an old logging road—out of sight of cars driving by—and got out. I checked the map coordinates one last time, then turned off my phone so no one could track my location. I slipped the straps of my backpack over my shoulders and set out on foot.

A few flakes of snow fluttered down as I made my way silently through the trees. The air was cold, but I ignored the discomfort, my mind focused on my objective. If I was going to take this big a risk—if I got caught I was dead—I had to make sure it counted. I could hack a cell phone, if I could get my hands on one. That would track calls and GPS locations. Good, but maybe not good enough.

The lifeblood of any organization—criminal or otherwise—was money. Tracking the money would tell you everything you needed to know.

Which meant I needed to find Edward Mozcinski—specifically, his computer. Dad had said he was the money guy. Their so-called accountant. Hack his machine, and I'd have them all by the balls.

The trees opened up and the old lumber mill came into view. I stopped well clear of the chain-link fence that surrounded the perimeter. Inside was a large weather-beaten building. It looked like a giant warehouse. Fresh tire tracks led in and out but there weren't any cars parked where I could see.

I pulled my hood over my head and drew my face mask up to my nose, then scanned the area, assessing their security. Cameras, likely with motion detectors. Two visible armed guards, and no doubt more that I couldn't see from this vantage point. I wasn't armed, and the phrase *don't bring a knife to gun fight* came to mind. But I didn't own a firearm.

Even if I did, I wouldn't have stood a chance against multiple armed guards. And I absolutely did not want to kill anyone—even these guys. If I got caught, I was dead. There wasn't any way around that.

The armed guards were a good sign, though. A regular lumber mill didn't need to be protected by a tall fence and guys with guns. I was in the right place.

Based on the camera angles, I didn't think they had a good view out to the fence. But just in case, I chose a spot that would be hardest to see.

I dug wire cutters out of my backpack and clipped a section of fence at the bottom—just enough for me to crawl through.

Shoved my backpack through first, then army-crawled under, dragging my body through the freezing dirt.

Keeping my eyes on the closest guard, I crawled until he turned his back on me. Got up and ran, still staying low.

Once I got to the building, I had to move fast. The cameras panned back and forth. I eyed the two closest to me, waiting for my chance. Willing the guard to keep looking in the opposite direction.

Now.

I moved to the door. I had lock-picking tools in my pocket, but I tried the handle first. Unlocked.

These were some cocky motherfuckers. I guessed they figured armed guards were enough.

Not when Leo Miles wanted in.

I slipped inside and dropped low, quickly scanning the surroundings. The cavernous interior was filled with heavy machinery and stacks of lumber. Wood chips and sawdust were everywhere, and it was eerily silent. It was early, but I couldn't count on these people to keep normal business hours. I had no idea when, or if, more people would show up. I had to act fast.

On the far end of the building, a staircase led to an upper section with what were probably offices. Cables ran up the bare walls. I followed the network cables. Most of them went to three of the offices. Those were my best bet.

My footsteps seemed to echo, although it was mostly my heightened senses. Moving quickly, I padded up the stairs. The door to the first office was wide open. I ignored it. The second was locked, but had a flimsy wooden door, and didn't have any network cabling leading to it. I checked the third office's door. Closed, but unlocked. I moved on.

The fourth had blackout curtains in the windows. I touched the door and tried the handle. It was a fireproof steel door with a heavy-duty lock.

This was definitely it.

I pulled out a lock-picking tool and inserted it. Felt for the right pressure and tension. It released with a click. I ducked inside, shutting and locking the door behind me.

The desk was tidy—almost empty. A monitor, keyboard, and mouse. A few files in a neat stack. A leather cup with two expensive looking pens. There were file cabinets behind the desk—probably locked—but I ignored those.

I dropped my backpack and changed my leather gloves for a pair of blue latex—easier for a delicate job. The PC was on the floor, so I sat, pulled a few tools out of my backpack, and got to work.

A noise came from outside, muffled by the solid door. I turned my good ear toward the inner wall. People. It might be the same guards I'd already seen. Or more people might be arriving.

Putting that out of my mind—I had a mission to complete—I opened the computer and carefully installed a PCI card. It wasn't exactly legal, and I definitely wasn't supposed to have it. But once it was in, I'd have access to everything on the PC. Not only that, but I'd programmed it with a keylogger. As soon as I turned the computer on, it would start recording every keystroke.

Emails. Web searches. Bank accounts. Passwords. I'd have it all. And it operated on a cell signal, not on the computer's network. Unless they opened up the box and found it, there was no way to know it was there.

They might, of course. If they had any reason to believe someone had tampered with it. But by then, it would be too late.

I attached the cover and moved the PC carefully back into place. Turned it on, then went to the window and moved the curtain aside just enough to see out.

It wasn't guards. Shit.

CLAIRE KINGSLEY

Two men stood outside the first office, talking. One was dressed in business attire—button-down shirt and slacks. The other looked more like a construction foreman—plaid shirt, faded jeans, and boots. I couldn't hear what they were saying from here.

The computer had powered on, so I let the curtain drop and went back to the desk. The PCI card gave me admin access, so I bypassed the user account—and the need for a password—and logged in.

I heard footsteps outside and my eyes darted to the doorknob. Nothing. Back to the screen. I copied the entire drive—everything on the computer—and started an upload to an encrypted cloud location.

The door handle didn't move. The footsteps passed. Staying calm and controlled, I clicked opened email. It was definitely Edward Mozcinski's computer. Now all I had to do was make sure the copy finished uploading.

That, and get my ass out of here.

My heart thumped uncomfortably hard, but I ignored it. Put everything else out of my mind. Complete the mission. That was all.

More footsteps and voices outside. I went to the window and risked a peek. Different men this time. Plus a woman. This place was filling up. Pressing my good ear to the door, I listened. My eye twitched at the sound of voices. Tools. Machinery. An engine, deep and throaty. A truck, maybe even a large delivery vehicle.

Fuck.

The files finished uploading and I blew out a relieved breath. That was done, at least. I powered off the PC—it had been off when I'd found it—then packed up my tools, changed back into my leather gloves, zipped my backpack, and sat with my back against the door.

I took a few slow breaths, but I was calm. Almost numb to the fear I should have been feeling. I was stuck in here, and if Edward Mozcinski—or anyone else who had access—decided to come in, I was really and truly fucked. I had no weapons. No backup. Special Forces wasn't on standby for an extraction. I had no way out.

I'd faced death once before. Faced it and accepted its inevitability. This time hurt more. A lot more. I didn't want to leave Hannah. I didn't want to leave the baby that now I might never meet.

But I had what I'd come for. This would be more than enough for the DEA to move in on this operation. Take them all down. A lot of people were going to prison because of what I'd just done.

All that was left was making sure someone I trusted had access to those files. Leaning my head back against the door and closing my eyes against the sudden sting of tears, I pulled out my phone. Powered it back on. And called Hannah.

38

HANNAH

*I*t felt like I'd been in the car for twelve hours, not five. Luck had been on my side and traffic had been light, even with snow falling in the pass. But I was exhausted and hungry, and I couldn't wait to get back to Salishan.

After I'd logged off the game last night, I'd tried to sleep. But all I'd been able to do was toss and turn. Eventually, I'd given up. Packed my things and left. I'd been planning to leave in the morning anyway. This way, I'd get back early. As predicted, I was tired. But it was nothing a nap couldn't cure.

That and maybe a snack. Yep, a snack would be good.

But when I pulled into Salishan, all thoughts of naps, and food, went right out the window.

The front entrance to the Big House was blocked off with yellow tape, and the grounds looked deserted. What had happened?

I didn't see anyone as I drove back to Leo's place. The blinds were closed, but that wasn't unusual. I parked and got out, then stopped at the front door. A few days ago, I would have walked right in. I lived here. But did I, still?

Feeling suddenly awkward, I knocked.

No answer.

He was probably still asleep after being up late gaming last night.

I knocked again, harder this time. "Leo?"

Still nothing.

I punched in the code to unlock the door and went inside.

"Hey, Leo? Are you home?"

His monitors were dark, his chair turned around at an odd angle. I took slow steps into the house, a sense of alarm growing in my belly.

"Leo?"

The bathroom door was ajar, the light off. And the bedroom was empty.

He wasn't here.

I pulled out my phone and sent him a text to let him know I was here and ask where he was. Something felt wrong. I waited a few minutes to see if he'd reply, but my text didn't even show as read.

Nausea swirled in my tummy as I ran back out to my car. This wasn't right. Something bad had happened at the Big House—why else would there be yellow tape all over?—and Leo wasn't home. He'd been fine just hours ago. What had I missed?

I went to Shannon's. Her car wasn't outside, but I hoped to god someone was here. I dashed up the porch steps and knocked on the door.

Chase answered, his eyebrows lifting in surprise. "Hey, Hannah."

Not only was Shannon home, the rest of Leo's family was, too. But I didn't see Leo.

"Hey." I hurried in, worry filling me. "What happened? Is everyone okay? Where's Leo? Is he here?"

They all looked at me in silence for a beat. Zoe, Brynn, and Shannon sat at the long dining table with mugs in hand. Roland stood nearby with Hudson in his arms. Amelia sat with Cooper on the couch, rubbing his earlobe. Ben stood with his back to a window, his arms crossed.

"Isn't he at home?" Zoe asked.

"No, I was just there."

Shannon stared at me, her expression stricken, her face pale.

"What happened?" I asked.

"There was a fire in the Big House last night," Zoe said.

"Oh no, is everyone okay?" I asked.

Zoe nodded. "No one was there."

"Oh my god, I'm so sorry. But... you guys don't know where Leo is? I talked to him last night and said I was coming back. He wasn't expecting me this early, but... where else would he be?"

The way they all looked at me, I could tell we were all thinking the same thing. That was an excellent question. Where else would Leo be?

"Maybe he's taking a walk in the vineyards," Chase said.

"He wouldn't have gone to the Big House to look around, would he?" Brynn asked.

I shrugged. "I don't know. I saw all the yellow tape, but I didn't stop to look."

"What are the chances he decided to go get everyone breakfast?" Zoe asked.

"I'm calling him," Cooper said, but put down his phone only a few seconds later. "Straight to voicemail."

The tension in the room made my heart race. I would have loved to believe that Leo was out picking up donuts or bringing espresso, but I knew the chances of that were very slim. And my instincts were screaming at me. Something was wrong.

I checked my phone again. "I texted him when I got here, but he hasn't replied."

"Why would he go somewhere and turn his phone off?" Zoe asked. "Especially if he knows you're coming home."

"I don't know."

"My car isn't here, is it?" Shannon asked, her voice quiet. She stared at the wall, as if she were looking through it.

"No, it isn't," I said.

Roland went over to the front window. Hudson grabbed for the curtain as he looked outside. "It's not there."

"With everything going on, it didn't even register," Shannon said. "We walked right by, but I didn't think about it."

"Why would Leo take your car?" Brynn asked.

"Was the fire arson?" I asked.

Shannon met my eyes. "They don't know for sure."

I tilted my head to the side. "But do you think it was arson?"

She nodded.

I touched my fingers to my lips. I knew where Leo had gone. Or at least, why. "Leo, what are you doing?"

"So Leo thinks he's a one-man army now?" Zoe asked. She glanced at Shannon, who had her hand covering her mouth. "I'm sorry, Shannon. But honestly, what the hell is he thinking?"

My mind raced, searching for a way to find him. Tracking his phone wasn't likely. My text hadn't been read, and Cooper's call had gone directly to voicemail. That probably meant it was turned off. Even if it had been on, it wasn't easy to track a phone if you didn't already have the right app installed.

I might be able to hack into traffic cameras. I'd never done it before, but if you knew where to look, you could learn how to do anything on the Internet. But those were largely in urban areas, and I didn't know where to even start.

"I'm going to see if I can find him, but I can't do anything from here," I said, already halfway to the door.

"I'll go with her," Zoe said. "You okay with the baby?"

"Yeah, I've got him," Roland said.

Zoe followed me out, along with Cooper, Amelia, Brynn, and Chase. My heart raced as we walked to Leo's house. There had to be a way for me to find him. He needed help. I felt it deep in my bones. His dad had been entangled with an organized crime family and I was terrified of what Leo might have gotten himself into.

When we got to the house, I spun Leo's chair around and moved it in front of my workstation. I had my own chair, but sitting in his felt better, somehow. I fired up my machine and wracked my brain for a way to help him.

His family stayed quiet behind me while I searched for ideas. After getting in trouble in high school for hacking, I'd mostly stopped—emphasis on *mostly*. I certainly wasn't an active hacker, but I still had some skills. But getting into someone's firewall when I was already connected to their network—like I'd done when I traced Leo here—was nothing compared to this.

I scanned posts and articles about finding people via their cell phones, but none of it helped if Leo had turned his off. Frustration and fear knotted my belly, although the silent presence of his family behind me kept me steady.

My phone's ring tone blared in the quiet, startling me. I grabbed it, desperately hoping...

"It's him." I swiped to answer. "Leo?"

"Hi baby," he whispered. "Where are you? On your way?"

I lowered my voice. "No, I'm here. I'm home."

"Good. Perfect," he said. "Hannah, listen. I need you to do something for me."

"Okay, but where—"

"Log in to my computer. My main machine."

I scooted over to his side of the desk. He gave me the credentials and I logged in. "Okay. I'm in."

"Now go to my cloud drive. It's password protected. The password is..." He paused. "It's Hannah Miles two five seven, no spaces, no capitals, numbers in digits."

Oh, Leo. "Got it."

"There's a folder there—it's encrypted, but I want you to download it. It should say drive copy."

"Yeah, I see it."

"Are you downloading it?" he asked, still whispering.

"Yes, but please tell me what's going on. You're scaring me."

"The encryption key is in another file. Listen to me carefully, baby. You control that. Understand? Make sure Rawlins understands what he's getting before you give that to him. It's leverage for anything you or my family needs."

"Leverage?" I asked. "What are you—"

"Baby, it's okay. It's everything on the Paine family. Bank accounts, emails, passwords. There's a keylogger that will update in real time to that same directory."

"Oh my god, Leo," I said, my voice shaking. "What did you do?"

"I'm so sorry. I'm sorry I drove you away. And I'm sorry I can't be there now. Hannah, I love you. I love you more than anything."

"Where are you?"

"The Paine's base of operations. It's an old lumber mill, about an hour north of you."

"Well, get the fuck out of there," I said.

He was silent for a few heartbeats. "I can't."

I squeezed my eyes closed. No one else said a word. They didn't need to. I could feel their shock and pain, saturating the room.

"What do you mean, you can't?"

"I got in, but I don't think I'm getting out," he said. "But it's okay. You'll be safe now. You both will."

"Leo, what did you do?"

"I broke in and put a PCI card in their money guy's computer. I got all their data. Everything, Hannah. You give this to the DEA, and these guys are all going down."

"Good, awesome. Then get the hell out."

"There's people everywhere," he said. "Only one way out. I'm stuck."

"No. God, Leo, why?"

"I told you I'd keep you safe."

"I know, but..." I took a deep breath, swallowing back my tears. "No. No, this is not how this is going to end. You said you're where?"

"It's an old lumber mill, just outside a town called Kennett Falls."

I opened Google maps, and searched for Kennett Falls.

"What are you doing?" Zoe asked.

"I'm getting him out."

"Hannah, you can't," he said. "This place is crawling with people. Armed guards. Who knows what else. I can barely see anything from where I am."

"And where are you, exactly?"

"The accountant's office. Door's locked, but only until someone decides to come in."

"How many people?"

"I don't know," he whispered. "I had eyes on two guards when I came in. But people started showing up after I got inside. There's no way I'm walking out of here."

"You will if we create a distraction," I said. "Sit tight. I'm getting you out of there."

I zoomed in on the map and found the lumber mill. The satellite image showed the building. A fence surrounded it. It wasn't far from the town, but there wasn't anything else nearby. Just trees. It was isolated. Easy to defend. Perfect for a criminal operation.

"Is there a sprinkler system?" I asked.

"No," Leo whispered.

"Damn it." If he could trigger the sprinklers, it might be

enough to make everyone evacuate. But fire gave me an idea. Maybe we didn't need sprinklers. Or actual fire. "Is the money guy's PC on?"

"No."

"Power it on for me."

There was a moment of quiet. "Done. It's coming up. What are you doing?"

"I'm going to place a 911 call to report a fire."

"What?" Leo asked.

"Trust me." I explained what I was doing as I worked, as much for everyone here as for Leo. "I'm going to connect to the computer there, but I'm routing through a proxy in Russia. My signal will be untraceable."

"Holy shit, baby," he said. "And connecting to this machine through the card I installed."

"Exactly." It took a few more seconds to connect. "Now time for a voice-over-IP phone call. I'll keep you on speaker, Leo, but stay quiet." I dialed 911 through the computer Leo had hacked. To the 911 operator, it would look like the call was coming directly from the lumber mill.

An operator answered. "Nine one one, please state your emergency."

"Oh my god, there's a fire."

"What's your location?"

"I'm at the lumber mill outside Kennett Falls," I said. "My dad works here, and I don't know where he is. I'm stuck in his office and the door's hot."

"Okay, stay right where you are," she said. "I'm sending emergency responders now."

"Please hurry."

"Miss, is there another way out?" she asked.

"No, just one door."

"Okay, just stay where you are," she said. "They're already on their way."

"Thank you so much."

She was probably about to instruct me to stay on the line, but I ended the call.

"Fuck," Leo whispered.

My heart leapt into my throat. "What happened?"

"Someone just tried the door."

"Don't hang up," I said.

"I'm just turning off the PC," he said. "If I actually get out of here, I don't want them to know it's been touched."

"You *are* getting out of there," I said. "The fire department should be minutes away."

"Hannah, I love you," he said.

"I love you too, but please stop trying to say goodbye."

I bit my lower lip, my entire body rigid with tension. *Please get there before they find him. Please.*

Minutes went by. Leo didn't say anything, but I could hear him breathing on the other end. Everyone behind me was silent. I couldn't even look at his family. I squeezed my eyes shut, hoping for a fucking miracle.

"Something's happening," Leo whispered.

I almost flew out of the chair. "Wait for it. Don't go too soon."

"I know."

My heart raced and my palms were clammy with sweat. "Is it the fire department?"

"I think so," he said. "I hear sirens. Lots of voices out there. Baby, I'm going to hang up now. I'll call you when I'm out."

"I love you."

"I love you too," he said. "So much."

He ended the call.

I'd never been so scared in my life—or so helpless. The man

I loved was sneaking out of a criminal organization's stronghold and there was nothing more I could do to help him.

Please get out, Leo. Please.

We sat in tense silence while the minutes ticked by. My eyes stayed locked on my phone. I tried to imagine Leo. Where was he now? Still in the office? Creeping down a hallway? Was he staying hidden, or trying to blend in and look like he belonged? What would happen if someone caught him?

I stopped myself from pondering that last question. I knew the answer and it wasn't something I could let myself think.

Cooper got up and started to pace in silence while Amelia stood to the side, her arms hugged around herself. Zoe stood nearby, chewing on her thumbnail, tears shining in her eyes. Brynn and Chase sat on the couch together, their hands clasped.

Six minutes since he hung up.

"When do we panic?" Zoe asked.

"Not yet," I said. "He'll get out."

We kept waiting. Another minute ticked by. I stared at my phone, as if I could will him to call. As if the power of my hope and love would change anything.

Eight minutes.

Cooper sat down again, but shook his leg, like he couldn't be still. Amelia sat next to him and rubbed his back, her face drawn with worry.

Nine minutes.

Come on, Leo. Get out of there.

It rang, Leo's number flashing on the screen.

"Oh my god." I swiped to answer so fast I almost dropped it. "Leo?"

"I'm out."

Clutching my chest, I choked out a sob.

"Holy fuck, baby," he said. It sounded like he was running. "Fire trucks, paramedics. They sent everything. The entire place is chaos right now. I can hear more sirens. Maybe cops, I don't know."

"But you're out?"

"Yeah, I crawled back under the fence where I got in," he said. "I'm almost to the car."

Tears ran down my cheeks. I could barely speak. "Leo."

"I'm coming, baby. I'm coming home."

39

LEO

*W*hen I drove through the gates to Salishan Cellars, I was hit with a deep sense of relief. But it was different from the other times I'd returned home. Usually I was jittery with PTSD-induced anxiety. Coming home to my family's land eased my body's tendency to panic.

This time, it was simpler. I'd gone out, knowing I might not return. But I had. I was coming home, and it wasn't my fight against agoraphobia that brought the sense of calm and peace I felt as I drove toward my mom's house. It was knowing I'd made it. I was alive, and Hannah was here waiting for me.

That seemed like a healthy reaction to what I'd been through today.

I'd stayed on the phone with Hannah most of the drive back. We hadn't even talked much. A few words here and there. She'd walked over to my mom's house and sat on the porch, and we'd simply existed in the silence together. Taking comfort in knowing the other was just a word away.

She was still on the porch when I pulled up in front of Mom's house. As soon as I got out of the car, she stood and raced down the steps, launching herself into my arms.

I held her tight, crushing her against me. Finally let the reality of what I'd done sink in. I hadn't thought I'd get this chance again. To hold her. Touch her. Kiss her.

"You crazy asshole," she said, her words muffled by my coat. "Don't you ever do something like that again."

"It's okay," I murmured into her hair. "I love you, Hannah. It's okay."

She trembled with sobs, so I didn't let go. Held her tight and stroked her hair. God, I loved this woman. I wasn't ever letting go of her again. I'd do whatever it took.

Mom's front door opened. I heard shouts of *he's home*, and my family started pouring out.

I kissed the top of Hannah's head and she pulled away. She had tears in her eyes, but she stepped back as my mom approached.

"Come here," Mom said, her eyes glistening. She held out her arms and I stepped into her hug. Then she grabbed Hannah and pulled her in too. "Thank you. Thank you for bringing my son back to me."

And I knew she didn't just mean today.

After my mom finally let go, I hugged everyone. It still didn't feel great to be touched by anyone other than Hannah. But today, I welcomed the embraces of my crazy family. My brothers. My sisters. My mom. Ben. All these people who had loved me through the worst times of my life. Who'd never given up on me. Who would have taken care of Hannah and our baby if I hadn't made it home today.

I loved them all so much.

We went inside and I filled them in on what had happened. They already knew most of it. I told them about the chaos that had ensued after Hannah's fake 911 call. How I'd been able to sneak out while the building was being evacuated. How I'd crept away to the spot in the fence I'd cut to get in. And then ran my ass off into the woods, back to Mom's car.

By the time Hannah and I left and went home, we were both exhausted. We needed to talk—there was so much to say—but we both needed sleep. I curled up beneath the covers with her in my arms and relaxed, feeling good for the first time in days.

HANNAH STIRRED, her warm body shifting against me. Her back was to my front, my arm around her belly. She arched, pressing her ass into my groin and I groaned. She felt so good. I slid my hand up to cup her breast and squeezed gently.

"Mmm," she murmured, nuzzling back against me.

I didn't know what time it was, but it was dark outside. We must have slept for several hours. I kissed her neck and shoulder, gratitude filling me. Nothing had ever felt as good as Hannah in my arms.

But as much as I wanted to keep going—get her naked so I could kiss her all over—I knew we needed to talk first. There was too much to say.

"Are you ready to wake up?" I asked.

She glanced at me over her shoulder. "Yeah, I'm awake."

"How are you feeling?"

"Better."

"Good." I kissed her shoulder again. "We need to talk."

"Yeah, we do." She turned over.

I lay on my side facing her, my head resting on the pillow. Even in the darkness, I felt exposed and vulnerable being this close to her. But that was what we needed. Truth. Vulnerability. No more barriers.

"I need to tell you some things. But... this is going to be hard for me. I need you to know what happened. How I got this." I gestured to my face.

"Are you sure you want to talk about it now?" she asked.

"Yes. The thing is, I never talk about it. My family doesn't even know the whole story. But I really need you to know the truth."

She nodded, tucking her hands beneath her cheek. "Okay."

I took a deep breath. "I can't tell you where I was or exactly what I was doing. It's all classified. But I worked in military intelligence and let's say there are reasons I knew how to do what I did today."

"Yeah, I kind of figured."

"We were overseas, and we were deep in the shit. Every move we made was dangerous. And I fucked up. I trusted an asset too far and compromised our location. It was a bad judgment call and it was all on me." I took another breath. "That breach put a lot of people in danger. Lives were at stake, not to mention the intel we'd collected. There was no way we could let them find what we knew. So I did everything I could to make sure my men got out. And I stayed behind to take care of the rest."

"What do you mean, *take care of the rest*?"

"Destroy the evidence," I said. "I waited as long as I could to give my men time to get clear. Let the enemy get close. And then I blew that shit to kingdom come."

Her lips parted and her eyes shone with sudden tears. "Leo."

"I'd made my peace with it. I knew I wasn't walking away. And that was how it should have been. It was my responsibility. *They* were my responsibility." I rolled to my back and looked at the ceiling. "None of my men made it out. They were ambushed before they could get to safety."

"Oh no," she breathed.

"A few hours later, an extraction team pulled my body out of the wreckage. Except somehow, I was still alive."

"Oh god."

"It wasn't supposed to happen like that. I was the one who fucked up. My men were supposed to get out. Instead, they all got riddled with bullets. And I wasn't dead."

"You set off the explosion that burned you?" she asked, her voice quiet.

I nodded. "I knew I was going to die that day. And it would have been okay. I was ready. But I woke up in a fucking hospital in so much pain I thought I was in hell."

"How long was it before you came home?"

"Months," I said. "I was in a field hospital for a while, then airlifted to another facility for more treatment. They sent me stateside for surgery, then home to recover."

"And then you didn't leave."

"Nope. At first I was just in too much pain to do anything. I was staying at my mom's house and I'd lie in bed most of the day because it fucking hurt to even move. Then I started having panic attacks. Mostly at night. I'd wake up and think the house was on fire or that I'd been shot. One night I ran out into the vineyard. I was so out of it, I thought my dad was trying to kill me. It took him four hours to coax me back inside."

"Oh my god."

"There was talk of admitting me to a mental hospital, but Mom wouldn't let them. I begged her not to. Begged her to let me stay. By then, I was terrified of leaving."

She reached over and gently stroked my arm.

"My sanity started to come back, though. I still had problems with panic attacks, obviously. But I was coherent. My body starting to heal helped. Being in that much pain all the time can make you crazy. Literally. As my burns got better, I started thinking clearly again."

"Is that when you started gaming?" she asked.

"Yeah. It was a good escape. Too good, sometimes. But it helped. And I met you."

"I always knew there was something wrong," she said. "I could hear it in your voice. But I was afraid to ask. I felt like you didn't want me to."

"At the time, I didn't. When I was gaming, especially with you, I could forget for a while. It felt good."

"You realize, you didn't deserve this," she said, reaching up to touch my face.

I didn't shy away. Let her run her fingers across my scarred skin. "Yes, I did. I got people killed. I have to carry that around with me for the rest of my life."

"But you were willing to sacrifice your life for theirs," she said. "Not many people would do that, no matter the circumstances. And you did it again today. You went out there and risked your life to protect your family. To protect me... and our baby."

I turned toward her and slid my hand through her hair. "Of course I did. I'd do anything for you."

"Even raise this baby with me?"

"Yes," I said, not breaking eye contact. "Especially raise our baby with you. I'll be completely honest, I'm terrified. But I won't let fear hold me back anymore. Not when it comes to you."

"This baby is going to love you because you're his or her daddy, Leo. Nothing else is going to matter. Not your face or your scars or anything in your past."

"It's still hard for me to believe that, but I'm going to trust you," I said. "I can't tell you how sorry I am for how I've behaved the last few days. When you told me you were pregnant, I should have taken you in my arms and held you."

"When you left, I thought that meant the baby was a deal breaker for you," she said, her voice trembling. "I thought you'd broken up with me because I was pregnant."

I closed my eyes, feeling awful for how I'd treated her. "God, no. I was surprised. And the fact that I'm kinda fucked up is no excuse. Although maybe if I wasn't, I wouldn't have been such a dick to you. I didn't know how to react, but that doesn't make it okay."

"You've been through a lot lately," she said. "Everything with your dad, and the threats to your family."

"I still should have put you first. I shouldn't have done the things I did, and I'm so sorry."

"I forgive you," she said, tracing her fingers down my beard.

"Thank you. I know I'm a mess, but I'm going to keep trying. I'm going to keep getting better. I promise you."

"I know you will."

"And I don't want you to move out," I said. "I want you to live here, with me. I want you to stay, and marry me, and have my baby and be a family."

Her eyes filled with tears and she smiled. "Leo, did you just propose?"

"Yeah, but I'll do it again and do it right. I just want you to know, I want everything with you. I want you forever, no matter what."

"I want you forever, too," she said through her tears.

"Does that mean you will?"

"Marry you?" she asked. "Yes, I'll marry you. And not because I'm pregnant, either. I think I knew I wanted to marry you about five minutes after we met. I love you, Leo Miles."

"I love you, too, baby."

Hooking my arm around her waist, I hauled her against me. Found her lips with mine and kissed her. Soft at first. But as her hands started to roam, my body responded, my dick hardening between us.

Growling into her mouth, I pushed her onto her back. Delved into her mouth with my tongue as I climbed on top. She welcomed me in, opening her legs and hooking her feet around my thighs. With her hands in my hair, she kissed me back, hungry for more.

I loved this woman with every piece of myself. I'd bared my soul to her—showed her every wound and scar—and she still loved me.

I wanted her to know how much that meant to me. Show her that I trusted her completely. That I was willing to let her in— hide nothing. That I wasn't holding back anymore.

"Wait," I said, and kissed her nose.

She watched me with curiosity in her eyes as I got up and flicked on the light. I stood next to the bed with no way to hide. No darkness. No ropes binding her, controlling her touch. And I took off my clothes.

As many times as we'd been together, I'd never done this. Never with the lights on and without Hannah bound. I stood in front of her, letting her see me. My whole body—scars, tattoos and all.

She dragged her teeth across her bottom lip as her eyes roved up and down my body. "Oh my god, you're so sexy. Get over here and fuck me."

I crawled on the bed and helped her tear her clothes off. For the first time, we were both completely naked and unhindered. She could see me. Touch me. All of me.

Her hands moved across my body, like she wanted to touch everything. Across smooth skin. Over my chest hair. Down my abs. She stroked my injured arm, leaning in to kiss the scarred skin. Her lips blazed a hot trail over my chest. Up my neck. To the ruined side of my face.

She caressed and kissed every inch, taking her time, moving from my cheek, back down my neck to my shoulder and chest. Down my torso to my thigh. It felt so good, I couldn't speak. All I could do was lie there while she loved all my scars and broken parts.

Her perfect skin was like silk against mine. She worked her way back up my body, then slid one leg across my hips, climbing on top of me.

"You've never let me do this before," she said. "You only get naked when I'm tied up."

The heat between her legs was tantalizing against my erection. She sat on top of me, and the sight of her—so beautiful and perfect—rendered me almost speechless. Sitting upright, her legs on either side of my hips. Her round tits and hard, pink nipples. Those sexy as fuck tattoos down her arm.

I ran my hands up her thighs. "I can tie you up, if you want."

"I do love that. Maybe next time." She traced her fingertips over my chest, down my abs. "This is... incredible."

"How did I get so lucky?" I asked, meeting her eyes.

"You deserve this." She leaned down, holding herself up with her hands next to my face, her tits pressing against my chest. "You deserve to be loved, Leo."

I slid my fingers into her hair. "I love you so much. You deserve everything. And I'm going to spend the rest of my life giving it to you."

She moaned against my mouth as I kissed her. Rubbed her wet pussy against my hard length. Grabbing her hips, I pushed my cock inside, groaning at the feel of her.

So fucking good.

Her body slid against mine, skin on skin, my nerve endings firing. I thrust into her as she tilted her hips to drag her clit against me. Our kisses became ragged and messy—lips, tongue, and teeth.

I growled as she slid up and down my cock. Turned my head to bare my neck to her as she nibbled and kissed down my scarred side.

She lifted, sitting up again. Her legs still straddled my hips—my cock buried deep. Her eyes were half-closed, her hair wild, her cheeks pink. I watched in awe as she rode me, taking her pleasure. I gave it to her, enthusiastically. Held her hips and thrust inside her.

Bracing herself against my chest, she slid along my hard length. In, then out. She found her rhythm. Rode me faster.

"Leo," she whimpered. "This feels so good."

Moving my hands up her ribcage, I grabbed her tits. Held them in my hands and squeezed, feeling her hard nipples against my palms.

"That's it, baby," I said.

Her pussy tightened, her heat rising. I could feel the tremors and pulses of her orgasm building. Tension spread from my groin, the exquisite pressure almost overwhelming.

Rolling her hips, she moved faster. Her eyes drifted closed and I felt her fingernails drag across my chest. I was close, but I didn't want to interrupt. Watching her on the brink of coming was one of the most beautiful things I'd ever seen.

A delicious moan left her lips as she started to come. She dropped down, letting her tits hit my chest, still rolling her hips in a steady rhythm. I growled in her ear as her pussy pulsed around my cock.

Holding her tight against me, I waited while she caught her breath. Kissed her neck and shoulder. She lifted up enough to find my lips with hers. I ran my hands through her hair and kissed her, deep and slow.

"Thank you," she said softly.

"Did that feel good?"

"Oh my god," she said. "So good."

"You're so beautiful."

I was still hard, aching for release. I flipped her onto her back and held her legs open. Stayed on my knees so I could watch my cock slide inside her.

Burying my cock deep with every thrust, I drove into her. Felt the heat of her wet pussy surrounding me.

Our eyes locked. I pounded her harder, the pressure building fast. She bit her lip as she watched me fuck her.

No barriers. No darkness. Only us.

I leaned down, chest to chest, bracing myself on top of her. She ran her hands down my back, over my ass. So much skin. So much silky softness against all my hard edges.

With my face in her neck, breathing her in, I drove harder. Growled against her as I thrust. Deeper. Faster. I was immersed in her. Drowning in the feel of her body against mine.

With a groan, low in my throat, I unleashed inside her. My cock throbbed, and I drove in deep. She clutched my back, holding me tight while I came—while my cock pulsed inside her.

So good. So fucking good.

We lay in each other's arms for a long moment before I rolled off her. She wasn't finished touching me. Much like I did when I untied her, she caressed the scarred side of my body, feathering me with kisses. The backs of my fingers. My hand, up my arm. Over my chest and shoulder. She kissed my neck and stroked my beard, finally landing with her lips on mine.

"I love you," she murmured, her mouth still against mine.

"I love you too," I said. "So fucking much."

She nestled against me and my hand trailed down to her stomach. I traced gentle circles below her belly button, enjoying her smooth skin. Caressing my baby, who was having my baby.

Before Hannah, I'd been starved. Withering away to nothing. I'd allowed myself to become a victim of my past, succumbing to loneliness and despair.

But she'd saved me. Over and over, Hannah had saved me.

From the darkness and pain. From the demons that had haunted me for so long. She'd showed me that I could come out into the light. That I could live again.

That's exactly what I was going to do. Live, with her. I was going to love this woman forever. She was having my baby and we were going to be a family. It was still scary, but I was done hiding.

And maybe Hannah was right. Maybe I did deserve to be loved. I knew one thing for sure. I was going to love her, and our child, with every piece of me—broken and whole.

EPILOGUE
LEO

My heart raced and my hands felt clammy. I'd known this day was going to be difficult. That it would push me. But I embraced it. Felt the anxiety knotting my stomach and made the choice to flip the script. This wasn't fear. It was excitement.

I mostly believed that.

Slow breaths helped. As did the feel of Hannah's arm resting against mine. I was so much better. A year ago? I wouldn't have dreamed of getting on a plane. And now, here we were.

"You okay?" she asked, glancing at me.

"Yeah," I said. "Mostly."

"I'm really proud of you," she said. "I know this is hard."

"Thanks."

Our six-month-old daughter sat in her lap, happily chewing on her fist. After a healthy pregnancy, she'd been born on a Tuesday. Watching my baby girl come into the world had been one of the most intense—and incredible—experiences of my life.

We'd named her Madeline Joy. Madeline after my great-grandmother—and because it was the only name we'd both agreed on. And Joy because she and her mommy had brought me out of the darkness and taught me how to be happy again.

Our little Maddy Joy.

I hadn't thought I could love anyone as much as I loved Hannah. But the moment I saw my daughter for the first time, I realized how wrong I'd been. I loved her so much, I thought I might burst with the fullness of it. And if anything, having a baby made me love Hannah even more.

If Hannah was right, and I really did deserve love in my life, I was saturated with it. Surrounded. Drowning in it. And I'd never been happier.

After Hannah had helped me escape the Paine family's stronghold, Roland and I had fed the information to the DEA and FBI. We'd given them everything they needed and more. Only days later, the lumber mill—along with a dozen other locations—had been raided. Everyone connected with their operation had been arrested.

The story had made national news. The media speculated there had been someone on the inside. No one had any idea that it had been me. That a wounded former soldier with a wicked case of agoraphobia and PTSD had broken into their operation and hacked their system.

Most importantly of all, my family was safe.

My dad had pleaded guilty to drug trafficking by possession and been sentenced to twenty years in prison. I honestly wondered if he'd live to see the end of it. He'd be well into his seventies when he got out, and as unhealthy as he'd seemed the last I'd seen him, I wasn't sure he'd live that long.

I'd made peace with that—and with the things my father had done. It would have been easy to hold onto hatred. Resent him for his selfishness. How he'd put my family in such danger. But it was over, now, and I didn't want to live in the past. I was ready to move forward. Dad had lost everything—his career, his wife, his children, his home, and his freedom. He had grandchildren he'd never meet. A family he'd never be a part of. As far as I was concerned, he'd gotten everything he deserved.

People continued to board the plane. Hannah gave Madeline a set of chunky plastic keys. She shook them, then stuffed one in her mouth. She could barely sit up on her own, but she put everything in her mouth.

Silly girl.

A woman about my mom's age stopped in the aisle next to us and glanced down at Madeline. Her eyes swept over the three of us, pausing briefly on my face. My beard was trimmed neater than I used to keep it, and my hair shorter—still long, but no longer obscuring my scars. I met her eyes and smiled.

She smiled back, looking again at my daughter. "She's so cute. What a lovely little family."

"Thank you," Hannah said.

The way I looked still surprised people. It would always be that way. But I'd stopped punishing myself. Started seeing my scars as a sign of survival, instead of forced penance.

Besides, the only person who mattered loved me the way I was.

"Oh, I forgot to tell you," Hannah said. "My parents are picking us up at the airport."

"I thought we were renting a car."

"Well, we were. But my dad went out and bought a new car —one with room for all of us."

"Really? He didn't have to do that."

She shrugged. "I know. But that's my dad for you."

I had a feeling I knew exactly why Calvin and Josephine had bought a new car. The same reason they'd cleaned out not one, but two bedrooms in their home in Arizona, and bought a crib and high chair. They wanted their daughter—and granddaughter—to come visit more than this once.

Hannah's parents had come to Washington to see us three times already. Once shortly after we'd found out Hannah was pregnant. They'd stayed at the Lodge—the hotel next door to our property—but spent most of their time at Salishan.

They'd come again when Hannah and I had gotten married. We'd had a small ceremony—at Salishan, of course. Zoe and my mom had managed to make it magical—everything Hannah had wanted. And they'd visited again just after Madeline had been born.

This time, it was our turn to visit them. We'd have gone sooner, but it was a challenge with a new baby. They'd offered to come to us again, but I'd insisted. I'd known it would be hard for me, but it meant so much to all of them, I was more than willing to do it.

"Your parents are great," I said. "I'm looking forward to this."

"Are you?" she asked.

"Yeah, of course. I love your family."

"No, I know, that's not what I mean." She licked her lips and adjusted Madeline in her lap. "I just want to make sure you're okay. The doctor said this could bring up a lot of stuff for you."

I reached out and brushed her hair back from her face. "I'm okay. And if I'm not, I'll let you know."

She nodded, smiling at me, and turned a squirmy Madeline around to face her. "Good."

Madeline hiccupped and spit-up spewed out of her mouth, all over Hannah's chest.

"Oh, lovely," Hannah said. "Can you take her?"

I was already reaching for her. "Come here, beautiful."

So far, Madeline was built like Hannah—petite with tiny fingers and toes. But her features were all Miles. She looked a lot like me.

I stood her up in my lap, holding around her middle and let her chubby baby legs take her weight. Hannah wiped Madeline's mouth with a burp rag, then did her best to mop up the mess on her shirt.

"What did you do to Mommy, silly?" I asked.

Madeline took her fist out of her mouth and grinned at me.

"That's my girl."

She reached her slobbery hands out and touched my face. Her blue eyes were bright as her fingers moved over my beard. She touched my mouth, my cheek. Her hand moved across the scarred side of my face.

And she smiled.

"Aw, look at Daddy's big girl," Hannah cooed.

I watched my daughter in wonder. This little miracle. Twice, I'd escaped death. And for so long, I'd tried to figure out why. Why me? Why had I lived?

Maybe I was looking at the reason.

Emotion blossomed in my chest. I loved my girls so much.

Hannah had saved me, in every way. She'd pulled me out of darkness. Helped heal the broken pieces inside of me. She'd given me this beautiful daughter, and she didn't know it yet, but I hoped we'd have more. We were a family. Scarred, and a little messy, but a family filled with love that would last a lifetime.

Want more Leo and Hannah? Turn the page for a bonus epilogue.

BONUS EPILOGUE: LEO

I eyed my phone with suspicion as it buzzed. Again. It was the third time in the last few minutes.

"Are you going to check that?" Hannah sat cross-legged in her office chair at our shared desk, one hand on her belly. She had the cutest little baby tummy. I loved how she rubbed it all the time.

"I think it's Cooper."

She lifted her eyebrows. "Is that bad? Maybe he's giving you details about tonight."

Tonight. I suppressed a groan. "That's what I'm afraid of. I think I need to cancel."

"What? You can't cancel."

"I told him I don't want a bachelor party," I said. "It's not my fault he didn't listen."

"He's been planning this for weeks," she said. "Just humor him."

"You don't understand." I picked up my phone and opened his latest texts. "He's been texting me crazy shit for the last two days."

"Like what?"

I held up my phone and scrolled through the texts. "Mostly stripper gifs and alcohol memes. Hannah, I'm not going to a strip club. There's no way."

She giggled. "I don't really think Cooper would take you to a strip club."

"The shit he's been sending me suggests otherwise. Like this." I scrolled to the image. "A guy tossing dollar bills. And this one, a flashing neon sign that says *girls, girls, girls*. Oh, and here." I scrolled again. "A ten-second video of a stripper. She has tassels on her nipples, Hannah."

She put a hand over her mouth and her shoulders shook with laughter.

"This isn't funny. You can't be okay with this. A strip club?"

"It's your bachelor party. I know you're not going to do anything."

"Wait a second." I narrowed my eyes at her. "The girls aren't taking *you* to a strip club, are they?"

"Why would the girls take me to a strip club? I don't need to see boobs when I have these." Winking at me, she grabbed her chest and squeezed.

Seeing her touch herself, I was torn between wanting to clarify—I hadn't meant a female strip club—and wanting to drag her to the bedroom, tie her up, and play *naughty girl*.

I cleared my throat. "I meant a male strip club."

She giggled again. "Oh. No, we're not going to a strip club, male or female. We're going to dinner at the Lodge and then to your mom's for manicures and cheesecake. It's a good old-fashioned pregnant-bride bachelorette party."

"Well, you can have fun tonight, but I should've stopped Cooper from planning this weeks ago. Did you know he threw Brynn a bachelorette party? He baked a penis cake."

Hands on her belly, she nearly doubled over laughing. "Of course he did. But Leo, I'm pretty sure he's not going to bake you a penis cake. If anything, he'll bake a boobs cake or something. You should be reasonably safe."

I got another text—a picture of a stripper on a pole. "Nope. Not safe."

She reached over and patted my leg. "Cooper's just excited. You know how he is. He means well, he just doesn't always know where to draw the line."

"There's no way Amelia's okay with this. I'm texting her."

Hannah just shook her head and laughed, the little traitor.

Me: Can you use your magic on Cooper and get him to chill out?

Amelia: Why, what's wrong? He's in a great mood.

Me: Do you know what he has planned tonight?

Amelia: Yeah

Me: And you're fine with it?

Amelia: Sure. You guys are going to have a blast!

"Well, she's no help," I said, tossing my phone back on my desk.

"Did you expect her to be?" she asked. "You know she's always his co-conspirator."

"True." I took a deep breath and leaned back in my chair.

Hannah came over and climbed in my lap, straddling me. Her belly pressed against my stomach and she slid her fingers through my hair. "You're going to be fine. Your brothers are fun. They just want you to have a good time tonight."

I closed my eyes, enjoying the way she massaged my scalp. Her hands on me felt so good.

"Okay, fine. I'll go."

"That easy? I didn't even have to take my shirt off."

I opened my eyes and looked down at her boobs. "I mean, I refuse. You should try to convince me."

She placed her hands on either side of my face and leaned in to kiss me. I slid my arms around her, tasting her sweet lips.

"I do have to go soon," she said between kisses.

"I know." I kissed her again. "If tonight sucks, will you make it up to me?"

Smiling, she bit her bottom lip. "Yes, I'll make it up to you. If tonight sucks, you can come home and tie me to the bed."

"Maybe I should just stay here and tie you to the bed." I brushed her hair back from her face.

She groaned. "That's not fair. You know my hormones are going crazy right now."

One corner of my mouth turned up in a hint of a smile. I did know that. Now that she was feeling better, pregnant Hannah was fun.

"Later." She tapped my nose. "I'm meeting the girls in fifteen minutes. That's not nearly enough time."

"No, it's definitely not."

I let her up, but before she could walk away, I wrapped an arm around her waist and placed my hand on her belly. She laid her hand over mine and leaned her cheek against my head.

"Don't let Mommy get too crazy tonight," I said.

Hannah just laughed.

I watched her hips sway as she walked back to the bedroom. It looked like I was stuck going to the bachelor party Cooper had planned. Our wedding was this weekend, and despite the fact that I'd told him *no* approximately eight hundred times, my brother had insisted we needed to celebrate. I'd have been happy with having a few beers with my brothers and calling it a night. But of course, Cooper didn't do anything small. It was go big or go home for that guy. And in this case, *go big* apparently meant boobs, judging by the texts he'd been sending me.

This was going to be interesting.

"YOU READY FOR THIS, BRO?" Cooper asked. His grin was about a mile wide. Even though I had a feeling he was about to make me miserable, it was hard to be mad at him. His cheerfulness was infectious.

I shut my front door behind me and hit the lock button. "I guess."

"Whoa, Leo, temper the enthusiasm," Cooper said. "The night hasn't even begun yet. I don't want you to use up all your excitement before we leave home."

Roland stood next to his car, grinning at me. Clearly he was in on this. Chase was next to him, doing something on his phone—probably texting Brynn. Cooper took the blame for most of their stunts, but I knew Chase was responsible at least half the time.

Yeah, I was stuck.

Chase looked up from his phone and put it in his back pocket. "Hey, Coop, don't forget the shirts."

"Good call." Cooper went around to the back of Roland's car and brought out a shopping bag. He pulled out a shirt and tossed it to me.

I caught it, then held it up. It was gray and had my name on the front. On the back it said, *Sorry ladies, I'm getting married* in navy block letters.

"You got shirts?" I asked.

"Of course I did," Cooper said, his brow furrowing like I'd asked a stupid question. He tossed shirts to Chase and Roland, then pulled one out of the bag for himself.

"What do yours say?" I asked.

Chase grinned and held his up. "Name on the front." He turned it around. "*Team Leo* on the back."

Cooper was already changing into his *Team Leo* shirt. Sure enough, it said *Cooper* on the front.

I eyed Roland. Was he really going to go along with this?

"Cool," Roland said. He pulled his shirt off and tugged on his new one.

I froze for a moment, my back clenching, and stared at the shirt. It had short sleeves. And if they were going to change out here in the open, what was I going to do? Duck back inside and put it on? Find a shirt to layer underneath it so I had sleeves?

Fuck it.

I pulled off my shirt, letting it drop to the ground, and quickly put the new t-shirt on.

My brothers didn't make a thing out of it—thank god—but I did catch Cooper mouthing *Awesome*. And yeah, okay, I was kind of proud. I'd just done that.

Wasn't sure how I felt about short sleeves, so I did go back into my house to grab a hoodie. When I came back out, Cooper just patted me on the back.

Ben walked over, dressed in a plaid flannel shirt and jeans. "Hey, boys. You weren't leaving without me, were you?"

"Hell no," Cooper said. He dug into the bag and got out another shirt. Tossed it to Ben.

Relief swept over me. There was no way Ben would come to a strip club with us. Cooper must have been fucking with me.

Ben looked at the shirt, then glanced at the others. He took off his flannel, replacing it with the t-shirt. Naturally, his said *Ben* on the front, *Team Leo* on the back.

"We ready?" Roland asked.

"The plan still the same?" Ben asked.

"Hell yes," Cooper said, his eyes flicking to me. "We're gonna get crazy tonight."

"Good." Ben pulled a wad of dollar bills out of his back pocket. "I'm prepared."

"Fuck yes," Cooper said, laughing and pointing at Ben's cash.

I stared at him. He had to be kidding me. Ben had dollar bills for strippers?

"Dude, Ben's the man," Chase said.

Roland opened the driver's side door. "Okay, let's go, I guess."

I could not believe what was happening. My brothers—and Ben—were actually taking me to a strip club for my bachelor party?

Too bewildered to argue, I got in the car. Roland drove out of Salishan and across town. I hadn't even realized there was a strip club in Echo Creek. But sure enough, over near the industrial area, Roland pulled into a half-empty parking lot. A sad-looking sign proclaimed *The Boobie Trap* with a cartoonish silhouette of a woman with huge tits.

"This is going to be so awesome," Cooper said.

I shook my head. Hannah knew where I was. She couldn't get mad at me for this. I'd told her I didn't want to go. I'd just have to suffer through while my brothers had their fun. They were probably just taking me here to see what I'd do.

Everyone piled out of the car, so I followed. I glanced at the faded sign, the pink paint chipping. This was going to be a shit show.

"You guys, I can't," Roland said.

I whipped my gaze over to him. Was he laughing?

Chase started in and pretty soon Cooper was laughing so hard he had to lean against the car to stay upright. Even Ben was chuckling.

"Dude, you're fucking amazing," Cooper said. "I can't believe you let us get this far. Seriously, you're a badass. I didn't mean for us to get all the way over here. I figured you'd tackle me in front of your house and I'd tell you the truth so you wouldn't break my arm. But then you got in the fucking car and Roland actually drove over here. Holy shit. I can't breathe."

Roland put his hands up. "I was just improvising."

"This was a joke?" I asked.

"Obviously," Chase said. "We weren't going to take you to a strip club."

Ben grinned at me. "We were just having a little fun with you."

"Dollar bills?" I asked.

"That was a really nice touch," Chase said.

I shook my head, but I wasn't mad—not even a little. The fact that they'd known they could pull a prank on me was kind of awesome. No tiptoeing around me, worrying about what was going to freak me out. Just my family, fucking with me like guys did.

"Okay, you guys got me," I said. "I really thought this was what we were doing."

"Fuck no," Cooper said. "We are having a bachelor party tonight, but there's no way I'd plan something so lame and predictable. You should know me better than that, Leo."

"Fair enough. So what are we doing?"

"Follow me," Cooper said, and got in the car.

We drove back to Salishan and parked in front of the Big House. I didn't bother asking more questions, just followed them inside. They led me to the main event room and for a terrifying second, I thought they might be about to spring some kind of awful surprise party on me.

But that wasn't it, either. Cooper flipped on the lights, revealing three tables in a U-shape in the center of the room. Five computer stations were spread out around the tables, each fronted by a chair.

"What's this?" I asked.

"Game night," Cooper said.

"Holy shit, are you serious?" I walked to the tables, my eyes traveling over the cables. "Are these networked?"

"They should be," Cooper said. "I mean, it's totally not my area, but between Roland and Chase, they said they got it working. These aren't the best computers or anything, and don't even get me started on how hard it was to sneak all this shit around without you finding it. But we've got internet, and a bunch of games loaded and ready to go. We even have headsets so we can, like, talk to each other and shit. Not that we really need those, but they looked awesome, so I bought five."

"We'll get the supplies," Chase said.

Ben and Roland followed Chase out. They came back a minute later with two coolers and several grocery bags. It took another trip with all four of them to bring the rest of the stuff.

They unloaded a shit ton of snacks—every junk food imaginable—onto the tables. Chips, donuts, candy bars, a huge bag of M&Ms, beef jerky, and pepperoni sticks. Roland opened one of the coolers and pulled out a beer.

"Well, what do you think?" Cooper asked. "I'm shit at video games, but we have beer and grub. And we figured this would be your jam."

"Holy shit," I said.

Cooper stepped closer and lowered his voice. "Be honest. Did I do good?"

"Yeah, Coop. You did great. This is awesome."

He smiled and lifted his eyebrows. His arms twitched.

I knew what he wanted. I lifted my arms and stepped in for a hug.

He hugged me, patting me on the back a few times, then moved back. "Congratulations, bro. I'm really happy for you."

"Thanks, man."

"Dudes, I got a Leo hug," he whisper-yelled, his eyes wide.

I just laughed.

We spread out the food, grabbed beers, and picked stations. Everything seemed to be working fine, so I picked a relatively simple game and helped them all get set up. We put on our headsets—even though Coop was right, we didn't really need them—and got started.

We'd only just gotten through the first level when a familiar name popped up on my screen, asking to chat. I clicked accept.

"Hey, Badger."

"Hey, Gigz."

"How's the rowdy bachelor party? Had a lap dance yet?"

"You knew, didn't you?"

"Yeah," she said. "You're not mad, are you?"

"No, I'm not mad. It was pretty funny, actually. We got all the way over there before they told me it was a joke."

She giggled. "Did you really? Cooper swore to me he wouldn't push it if you seemed like you were genuinely uncomfortable or getting freaked out."

"No, that's the crazy thing—I wasn't."

"Is it weird that I'm proud of you?" she asked.

"Yeah, but I'm kinda proud of myself, too, so I guess we're both weird."

She laughed again—music to my ears. "So, I won't stay on. I just wanted to pop in and see how you were doing."

"I thought you were with the girls tonight," I said. "Pregnant-bride bachelorette party?"

"Nope, we're hanging out tomorrow," she said. "I was just getting out of the way so your brothers could mess with you."

"Do you want to stay on and play? They won't mind."

"Yeah?"

I covered the mic so I wouldn't be too loud in Hannah's ears. "You guys don't mind if Hannah plays with us, right?"

"Hell no," Cooper said. "Bring it on, sister girl."

"Sounds like you're in," I said.

"Awesome. Let's do this."

I glanced at Ben and my brothers, all outfitted with headsets, playing a computer game. For me. Because that was how these guys rolled. They always had my back.

And in a few days, that feisty gamer girl on the other end of the headset—the woman who had once been just a voice in my ear—was going to be my wife.

We were a family. All of us. None of us were perfect, but I wouldn't have traded any of them. Not for anything. And with Hannah in my life—marrying me and having my baby—I really didn't know how things could get any better.

I'd been through hell and come out the other side. And every step had been worth it.

AFTERWORD

Dear reader,

I had Leo Miles in my head for a year before it was time to write him. He was just there, quietly waiting his turn. Probably gaming, honestly.

This book posed a number of challenges for me creatively. How to portray this reclusive, wounded man (that readers had been begging for since Broken Miles). How to create a heroine who is both compassionate and strong enough to love him through his challenges. How to tie up the loose ends and bring Lawrence's story to a satisfying conclusion. And how to give readers the glimpses they love of the rest of the family.

Not to mention the all the anticipation. After all, this is Leo.

It wasn't easy, let me tell you. But I'm so happy with how this book turned out.

As we know from previous books, Leo is wounded, and not just on the outside. He bears visible scars, but the damage you can't see is arguably worse. He struggles with intense anxiety and panic attacks, and has found himself unable to leave his family's property.

In his isolation, he's retreated into online gaming. When he's in that virtual world, he isn't a man with scars. He can forget the weight of his burdens, even if it's only for a little while. And of course, in that world, there's Gigz.

(Apologies to anyone who were confused during the first few pages, thinking he was having a hallucinatory conversation with his cat. I tried to make sure we got to the part where you see the cat and the person aren't the same as quickly as possible.)

(And thanks again to Elizabeth for letting me steal the name Gigz.)

From the start, I loved the idea that Gigz (the woman) is Leo's happy place. His solace. It's a fun twist on the friends-to-lovers trope. They're already good friends, and as many of us know, online friendships can be every bit as real and important to us as the relationships we have in real space.

But Hannah is hurting, too. She's in a tough spot. It can be terribly difficult to break free from an abusive relationship. She doesn't have a support system-even a small one-that she can turn to in her time of need.

Until she meets Leo, of course.

Often in any book, there are certain scenes that define the book for me. They're usually the moments that play over and over in my head long before I'm ready to write the book. Or perhaps pivotal scenes that come to me in a flash while I'm working on the outline.

The scene where Leo asks for someone's keys so he can go to Hannah was one of those. I imagined the moment when Leo finally breaks free of his self-imposed captivity so many times. And when I finally sat down to write it, my fingers flew across the keyboard. The entire scene came to life in vivid detail, from Hannah's tearful phone call to the sound of chairs scraping across the floor as Roland, Chase, and Cooper all head for the door to join him, no questions asked.

In fact, the book is done, and I can still see it.

The other one was the scene where Hannah climbs in Leo's lap and takes her shirt off, coaxing him into letting her touch his face. I knew that scene was going to happen long before I outlined the story, although in my earliest vision, it didn't end the way it does in the book. That scene wasn't intended to lead to the bedroom. But Leo wrestled control of the story right out of my hands and I let him have his way. And quite honestly, it was the right call. Leo knew what he was doing. He was ready.

The weight of reader expectation was never far from my mind as I wrote this book. I spent a year building up this series, and I knew anticipation for Leo's book would be high. I hope Leo's story was everything you hoped it would be.

Thank you so much for reading,

CK

ALSO BY CLAIRE KINGSLEY

For a full and up-to-date listing of Claire Kingsley books visit www. clairekingsleybooks.com/books/

For comprehensive reading order, visit

www.clairekingsleybooks.com/reading-order/

∼

The Haven Brothers

Small-town romantic suspense with CK's signature endearing characters and heartwarming happily ever afters. Can be read as stand-alones.

Obsession Falls (Josiah and Audrey)

Storms and Secrets (Zachary and Marigold)

Temptation Trails (Garrett and Harper)

The rest of the Haven brothers will be getting their own happily ever afters!

∼

How the Grump Saved Christmas (Elias and Isabelle)

A stand-alone, small-town Christmas romance.

∼

The Bailey Brothers

Steamy, small-town family series with a dash of suspense. Five unruly brothers. Epic pranks. A quirky, feuding town. Big HEAs. Best read in order.

Protecting You (Asher and Grace part 1)

Fighting for Us (Asher and Grace part 2)

Unraveling Him (Evan and Fiona)

Rushing In (Gavin and Skylar)

Chasing Her Fire (Logan and Cara)

Rewriting the Stars (Levi and Annika)

∿

The Miles Family

Sexy, sweet, funny, and heartfelt family series with a dash of suspense. Messy family. Epic bromance. Super romantic. Best read in order.

Broken Miles (Roland and Zoe)

Forbidden Miles (Brynn and Chase)

Reckless Miles (Cooper and Amelia)

Hidden Miles (Leo and Hannah)

Gaining Miles: A Miles Family Novella (Ben and Shannon)

∿

Dirty Martini Running Club

Sexy, fun, feel-good romantic comedies with huge... hearts. Can be read as stand-alones.

Everly Dalton's Dating Disasters (Prequel with Everly, Hazel, and Nora)

Faking Ms. Right (Everly and Shepherd)

Falling for My Enemy (Hazel and Corban)

Marrying Mr. Wrong (Sophie and Cox)

Flirting with Forever (Nora and Dex)

Bluewater Billionaires

Hot romantic comedies. Lady billionaire BFFs and the badass heroes who love them. Can be read as stand-alones.

The Mogul and the Muscle (Cameron and Jude)

The Price of Scandal, Wild Open Hearts, and Crazy for Loving You

More Bluewater Billionaire shared-world romantic comedies by Lucy Score, Kathryn Nolan, and Pippa Grant

Bootleg Springs

by Claire Kingsley and Lucy Score

Hot and hilarious small-town romcom series with a dash of mystery and suspense. Best read in order.

Whiskey Chaser (Scarlett and Devlin)

Sidecar Crush (Jameson and Leah Mae)

Moonshine Kiss (Bowie and Cassidy)

Bourbon Bliss (June and George)

Gin Fling (Jonah and Shelby)

Highball Rush (Gibson and I can't tell you)

~

Book Boyfriends

Hot romcoms that will make you laugh and make you swoon. Can be read as stand-alones.

Book Boyfriend (Alex and Mia)

Cocky Roommate (Weston and Kendra)

Hot Single Dad (Caleb and Linnea)

~

Finding Ivy (William and Ivy)

A unique contemporary romance with a hint of mystery. Stand-alone.

~

His Heart (Sebastian and Brooke)

A poignant and emotionally intense story about grief, loss, and the transcendent power of love. Stand-alone.

~

The Always Series

Smoking hot, dirty talking bad boys with some angsty intensity. Can be read as stand-alones.

Always Have (Braxton and Kylie)

Always Will (Selene and Ronan)

Always Ever After (Braxton and Kylie)

~

The Jetty Beach Series

Sexy small-town romance series with swoony heroes, romantic HEAs, and lots of big feels. Can be read as stand-alones.

Behind His Eyes (Ryan and Nicole)

One Crazy Week (Melissa and Jackson)

Messy Perfect Love (Cody and Clover)

Operation Get Her Back (Hunter and Emma)

Weekend Fling (Finn and Juliet)

Good Girl Next Door (Lucas and Becca)

The Path to You (Gabriel and Sadie)

ABOUT THE AUTHOR

Claire Kingsley is a #1 Amazon bestselling author of sexy, heartwarming contemporary romance, romantic comedies, and small-town romantic suspense. She writes sassy, quirky heroines, swoony heroes who love big, romantic happily ever afters, and all the big feels.

She can't imagine life without coffee, great books, and the characters who inhabit her imagination. She lives in the inland Pacific Northwest with her three kids.

www.clairekingsleybooks.com

ACKNOWLEDGMENTS

A million thank yous to everyone who helped make this book a reality.

Thank you to David for late night talks and brainstorming sessions. And for all the coffee and snuggles.

Thank you to Elayne for helping Leo and Hannah shine. And to Cassy for another beautiful cover.

Thank you to Nikki for all your random word vomit. We get some gems in there, don't we? (cough... ropes... cough)

Thank you again to Jodi for taking time out of your busy schedule (#momlife ain't easy) to beta read.

A weird thank you to the Seattle Snowpocalypse of 2019, without which I wouldn't have finished this book on time.

A great big huge I love your faces thank you to all my readers, for loving this series, and this family, right along with me. I've said this before, and I'll go right on saying it - you are why I do what I do. Thank you for coming on this journey with me.

Made in United States
North Haven, CT
12 April 2025

67847957R00231